Thomas B. Wigley

The art of the goldsmith and jeweller

a treatise on the manipulation of gold in the various processes of goldsmith's

work, and the manufacture of personal ornaments, &c., &c. for the use of students

and practical men

Thomas B. Wigley

The art of the goldsmith and jeweller
 a treatise on the manipulation of gold in the various processes of goldsmith's work,
and the manufacture of personal ornaments, &c., &c. for the use of students and
practical men

ISBN/EAN: 9783741172809

Manufactured in Europe, USA, Canada, Australia, Japa

Cover: Foto ©Andreas Hilbeck / pixelio.de

Manufactured and distributed by brebook publishing software
(www.brebook.com)

Thomas B. Wigley

The art of the goldsmith and jeweller

THE ART OF
E GOLDSMITH AND JEWELLER.

GRIFFIN'S METALLURGICAL SERIES

EDITED BY

W. C. ROBERTS-AUSTEN, C.B., D.C.L., F.R.S.,

Chemist and Assayer of the Royal Mint; Professor of Metallurgy in the
Royal College of Science.

In Large 8vo, Handsome Cloth. Fully Illustrated.

INTRODUCTION TO THE STUDY OF METALLURGY. By THE EDITOR. *Fourth Edition.*
With additional Illustrations and Micro-Photographic Plates of Different Varieties
of Steel. 18s.

"No English Text-Book at all approaches this in the COMPLETENESS with which
the most modern views on the subject are dealt with. Professor Austen's volume
will be INVALUABLE."—*Chemical News.*

GOLD (The Metallurgy of). By T. KIRKE ROSE, D.Sc., Assoc.R.S.M., Assistant Assayer
of the Royal Mint. *Third Edition.* 21s.

"Dr. ROSE has secured details of gold-working from ALL PARTS of the world,
. . of GREAT SERVICE to practical men."—*Nature.*

IRON (The Metallurgy of). By THOMAS TURNER, F.I.C., Assoc.R.S.M., Director of
Technical Education for Staffordshire. 16s.

"A THOROUGHLY USEFUL BOOK, which brings the subject UP TO DATE."—
Mining Journal.

STEEL (The Metallurgy of). By F. W. HARBORD, F.I.C., Assoc.R.S.M.

SILVER AND LEAD (The Metallurgy of). By HENRY F. COLLINS, Assoc.R.S.M.,
Assoc.Mem.Inst.C.E. (*At Press.*)

.*.* Other Volumes in Preparation.

METALLURGY (An Elementary Text-Book). By Professor HUMBOLDT SEXTON, F.I.C.,
Professor of Metallurgy in the Glasgow and West of Scotland Technical College.
With numerous Illustrations. 6s.

"Possesses the GREAT ADVANTAGE of giving a course of PRACTICAL WORK."—
Mining Journal.

ELEMENTS OF METALLURGY. A Practical Treatise on the Art of Extracting Metals
from their Ores. By J. ARTHUR PHILLIPS, C.E., F.C.S., F.G.S., and H. BAUERMAN,
F.G.S. CONTENTS—Refractory Materials, Fire-Clays, Fuels, &c., Antimony, Arsenic,
Zinc, Iron, Cobalt, Nickel, Mercury, Bismuth, Lead, Aluminium, Copper, Tin, Gold,
Silver, Platinum, &c. *Third Edition.* Royal 8vo, with numerous Illustrations. 36s.

"The value of this work is almost INESTIMABLE."—*Mining Journal.*

ASSAYING (A Text-Book of). For the use of Mine Managers, Assayers, &c. By J. J.
BERINGER, F.C.S, F.I.C., Principal of the Camborne Mining School, &c., and
C. BERINGER, F.I.C., F.C.S. *Fifth Edition.* 10s. 6d.

"A REALLY MERITORIOUS WORK that may be safely depended upon."—*Nature.*

ELECTRIC SMELTING AND REFINING: A Practical Manual of the Extraction and
Treatment of Metals by Electrical Methods. Being the "Elektro-Metallurgie" of
Dr. W. BORCHERS. Translated from the Second German Edition by WALTER G.
McMILLAN, F.I.C., F.C.S., Secretary to the Institution of Electrical Engineers.
With numerous Illustrations and Three Folding Plates. 21s.

"COMPREHENSIVE and AUTHORITATIVE."—*Electrician.*

CHEMISTRY FOR ENGINEERS AND MANUFACTURERS: A Practical Text-Book. By
BERTRAM BLOUNT, F.I.C., F.C.S., Consulting Chemist to the Crown Agents for the
Colonies, and A. G. BLOXAM, F.I.C., F.C.S., Head of the Chemistry Department,
Goldsmiths' Institute, New Cross. Large 8vo. With Numerous Illustrations.
In Two Vols. Sold separately.

VOL. I. THE CHEMISTRY OF ENGINEERING, BUILDING & METALLURGY.
10s. 6d.

VOL. II. THE CHEMISTRY OF MANUFACTURING PROCESSES. 16s.

"A work which should give FRESH POWER to the Engineer and Manufacturer."—
The Times.

.*.* For full details see the "CATALOGUE OF STANDARD WORKS" at the end of this volume.

LONDON : CHARLES GRIFFIN & CO., LIMITED, EXETER STREET, STRAND.

THE ART OF THE
GOLDSMITH AND JEWELLER:

*A TREATISE ON THE MANIPULATION OF GOLD IN THE
VARIOUS PROCESSES OF GOLDSMITH'S WORK, AND
THE MANUFACTURE OF PERSONAL
ORNAMENTS, &c., &c.*

FOR THE USE OF STUDENTS AND PRACTICAL MEN.

BY

THOMAS B. WIGLEY,

REGISTERED TEACHER IN TECHNOLOGY, AND HONOURS MEDALLIST IN GOLDSMITH'S
WORK OF THE CITY AND GUILDS OF LONDON INSTITUTE, AND HEADMASTER
OF THE JEWELLERS AND SILVERSMITHS' ASSOCIATION
TECHNICAL SCHOOL, BIRMINGHAM.

ASSISTED BY

JOHN H. STANSBIE, B.Sc.(Lond.), F.I.C.,

ASSOCIATE OF MASON UNIVERSITY COLLEGE, AND A LECTURER AT THE BIRMINGHAM
MUNICIPAL TECHNICAL SCHOOL.

With Numerous Illustrations.

LONDON:
CHARLES GRIFFIN AND COMPANY, LIMITED;
EXETER STREET, STRAND.
1898.

PREFACE.

In the preparation of the following pages the Author has had in view the wants both of Technical Students and of those who are already practically engaged in Goldsmith's Work.

He has endeavoured throughout to place before his readers in compact form, not only an account of the many Processes involved in the Goldsmith's Art, but also of the principles underlying these. In this he has been ably assisted by his colleague, Mr. John H. Stansbie, B.Sc., to whom he is indebted for Chapters II., XXII., and XXV., as well as for several important short sections (see Table of Contents), and for valuable help in the revision of the proof-sheets.

The Author's sincere thanks are due also to Councillor J. W. Tonks, of this city, for information on the subject of Civic Insignia, and to Councillor Charles Green, J.P., for the Assay Office Report.

Finally, he has pleasure in expressing his acknowledgment to many leading firms, whose names will be found in the text, for Illustrations of appliances and specialities manufactured by them ; and last, but not least, to his Publishers for the care bestowed upon the book whilst passing through press.

THOMAS B. WIGLEY.

Birmingham, *August*, 1898.

b

CONTENTS.

CHAPTER VII.—FILIGREE WIRE-DRAWING.

CHAPTER VII.—MANUFACTURE OF PERSONAL ORNAMENTS.

CHAPTER VIII.—FINGER RINGS.

CHAPTER IX.—MOUNTING AND SETTING.

CHAPTER X.—MAYORAL CHAINS AND CIVIC INSIGNIA.

CHAPTER XI.—ANTIQUE JEWELLERY AND ITS REVIVAL.

CHAPTER XII.—MANUFACTURE OF GOLD CHAINS.

THE ART OF THE GOLDSMITH
AND JEWELLER.

INTRODUCTION.

SCIENTIFIC discovery has revealed to us new properties and qualities of matter; and mechanical inventors have applied those discoveries for the benefit and improvement of trades in general. These great advances in science and in art, together with the change of fashion, have produced corresponding modifications in the goldsmith's and jewellery trades. The resulting subdivision of labour has been so great that the workman is now looked upon rather as a machine than as an art workman. But it has also compelled him to advance proportionally in skill and in command over the technics of his trade.

It may be asked who and what is a goldsmith or jeweller? For the dealer in jewellery, the pawnbroker. the assistant behind the counter, the draper who sells jewellery, and many others with no claim to the title call themselves "goldsmiths" or "jewellers." What is understood by the craft as the goldsmith or jeweller proper is the man who has studied for a number of years under a master of the craft; has himself mastered not only the technical processes connected with his trade, the general principles of mounting wrought work, the methods of forming and carving ornaments, the art of soldering with the blowpipe, annealing, wiredrawing, polishing, &c.; but has also acquired a knowledge of these higher branches which have raised the trade into an art:—Enamelling, Repoussé, Engraving, Setting, &c., &c.; and last (but by no means least) has made himself so far a scientific chemist and metallurgist as to be thoroughly acquainted with the properties of precious stones, and of the precious metals—the malleability, ductility, and tenacity of gold and silver, &c., &c.

Hence it is only the craftsman possessed of such technical, artistic, and scientific skill as shall enable him to produce and complete a piece of art-work in the precious metals who is entitled to the honourable name of goldsmith or jeweller.

1

This is quite clear enough to anyone who will take the trouble
to think.   If a man calls himself an engineer, it is because he
has studied Applied Mechanics, Mathematics, and Machine
Construction ; if a barrister, he must be familiar with the Law ;
if a physician, with Medicine, &c.   Moreover, if he wishes to
follow any one of the professions, he must pass certain searching
examinations which will prove whether or no he possesses the
knowledge to which he pretends.   Why should it be otherwise
with a craft which requires not mere rule-of-thumb dexterity
alone, but scientific and artistic knowledge on the part of those
who desire to follow the lines of the great masters ?

That a systematic course of study is necessary, is demonstrated
by the present condition of the trade.   Formerly the young goldsmith served an apprenticeship, during which time he was taught
the various branches of the art ; but, now, this system is seldom
adopted, youths being engaged on some one special branch ;
consequently they learn no other—to their own great detriment.
For when fashion changes, or in any way the demand for that
special work ceases, they are thrown upon the labour market
under very disadvantageous circumstances.

The remedy for this has been found in the establishment of
Technical Schools, in which, under the guidance of well qualified
masters, every aspirant is grounded in the first principles of his
trade, is taught the technicalities of every branch of it, and the
different methods of construction, and thereby enabled to become
a good "all round" craftsman in the true old sense of the word—
a strong man in every part of his work.

Freehand and geometrical drawing, modelling, and designing form the essential basis of the goldsmith's art ; and if the
learner is to acquire refinement, he must study the numerous
styles of ornamentation, as the Greek, Etruscan, Renaissance,
Roman, Byzantine, Celtic, &c., &c.   It must, however, be understood, that it is one thing to design a piece of jewellery consisting
solely of gold, or of gold and enamel, and quite another to make
a design for mounting and setting precious stones.   The one
class is quite distinct from the other.   The former belongs to
the goldsmith and the latter to the jeweller.   It is manifest,
then, that a knowledge of *technique* is absolutely necessary in
the study of design.

Designing is a necessary preliminary to all art-work—*e.g.*, if
a casket, mace, badge, bracelet, brooch, tiara, or any article of
jewellery of a special character is required, a drawing of it must
be made in order to ensure that everything is in harmony with
the purpose for which the article is intended.   The beauty of a
design may be quite spoiled by the combination of two or more
styles of ornamentation.   A properly drawn design should show
the details in light and shade, and, if for large work, when a
plan, elevation, and sectional elevation are required, each should

always be drawn to scale. Although a workman can often form a good idea of the intentions of the designer, a detailed working drawing should always be supplied to him, and when the form is intricate, also a model in wax.

Jewellery stands in the foremost rank as art work. Therefore such work should not only manifest good draughtsmanship, but also artistic feeling; it should have the elegant form, the delicately modelled figure, or the natural-looking foliage, such as can only be produced by the skilled and refined worker, the character of the man being reflected in his work.

CHAPTER I.

THE ANCIENT GOLDSMITH'S ART.

No fixed date can be given for the first manufacture of articles in gold and silver, but the earliest records are those mentioned in the Bible. In the Book of Genesis, chapter ii., we read of a place called Pison: "that is it which compasseth the whole land of Havilah, where is gold ; and the gold of that land is good." We also learn that Abraham when he went out of Egypt was very rich, not only in cattle, but also in silver and gold ; and in chapter xxiv. of the same Book we read that Abraham's servant gave to Rebekah a golden earring of half a shekel weight, also two bracelets for her hands of ten shekels weight of gold. The Jewish shekel is equal to ten English troy pennyweights, and as the highest price for pure gold at the present time is 5s. 3d. per pennyweight, a golden shekel would be worth about 52s. 6d. in our present currency. As the Book of Genesis is attributed to Moses, and the date assigned to it about 1500 years before the Christian era, the evidence shows that gold and its workers were known more than 3397 years ago. Moreover, there is ample evidence that the ancient Hebrews were well acquainted with the art of Metallurgy, since gold is referred to in the Bible more than 300 times. We also learn from Genesis that Pharaoh wore a ring upon his hand, which he took off and put upon Joseph's hand, and he also put a chain about his neck ; that King Solomon had his drinking-vessels made of gold, and that the vessels of the House of Lebanon were of pure gold. "The offerings made by foreign nations to Jewish Kings were of gold, silver, and precious stones. The Queen of Sheba offered Solomon 120 talents of gold, 200 shields containing 600 shekels of gold, 300 shields of silver containing 300 minæ. The shields were kept in the temple as royal ornamental treasures, and in the succeeding reign were carried away as spoil of war by the Egyptians." *

The great antiquity of Egyptian gold ornaments and articles of utility is indicated by numerous specimens in our museums, and also in various important discoveries. John Hungerford Pollen, in his *Gold and Silversmith's Work*, refers to a "remark-

* *Gold and Silversmith's Work*, by John Hungerford Pollen.

able set of gold ornaments which was exhibited during the great Exhibition of 1862 in London. It was found by M. August Mariette, in the case containing the mummy of Queen Aah-Hotop, who lived about 1500 B.C., and belonged to the Khedive of Egypt. These ornaments consisted of a poignard with a gold blade on which was engraved a combat between a lion and a bull, with the cartouche of King Amosis, son of the Queen named, and first King of the eighteenth dynasty ; a diadem, on each side (or extremity) of which is a crouching sphinx ; a hatchet, the symbol of divinity, on the blade of which is a representation of Amosis immolating a barbarian, with the whole legend of the same King inscribed on the handle ; a square pectoral brooch set with coloured stones, but which at first sight looks like an enamel ; a jewel with a representation of King Amosis standing on a bark between two divinities, who are pouring over him the water of purification ; a jewel formed by three bees of massive gold ; a gold chain of woven pattern, 3 feet long, from which is suspended a scarabæus ; a bracelet of massive gold ornamented with repoussé figures on a ground of lapis-lazuli, together with the figure of Amosis ; and a boat of massive gold on four wheels of bronze, which was found with the mummy of the Queen, and was a symbol of the departure of the soul of the deceased ; the towers are of silver, and on the prow is a cartouche with the name of King Rameses, husband of the Queen and father of Amosis."

Such were the works of handicraft by the Egyptians. He also states that " the Egyptians worked mines, exacted annual tributes of the precious metals, vases, and other manufactured objects from the conquered provinces in Asia and Africa ; and made statues, vases, and jewels in gold and silver, and silver inlaid with gold." Indeed, it is stated by Mr. Bennett H. Brough * that a papyrus is in existence depicting the workings of au Egyptian gold mine, drawn in the reign of King Mineptah, 1400 years before the Christian era.

The goldsmith's work and metallurgy of the Hebrews were so closely connected with those of ancient Egypt that a consideration of these arts among the Egyptians naturally leads up to a notice of them as developed by the Hebrews, for the sacred vessels of the Jewish tabernacles spoken of in Scripture were made from jewels and vessels of gold and silver borrowed from the Egyptians, and forced upon the Hebrews in order to induce them to leave the country. During the subsequent wandering of the Jews in the desert of Mount Sinai they made numerous golden articles, such as an ark, a seven-branched candlestick, censers for burning incense during solemn acts of worship, tongs, snuffers, and the other necessary utensils for

* *Treatise on Mine Surveying*, 6th ed., London, 1897, p. 2.

trimming and making lights and fires ; even the wooden chests and symbolic figures were covered with beaten gold.

We also find that the ancient goldsmiths worked under the direction of a designer, for the names of the goldsmiths who made the above-mentioned vessels, Bezaleel and Oholiab, have come down to us ; and Moses directed the "goldsmiths to make vessels according to a pattern revealed to him in a vision : all had special lines, parts, and proportions ; special numbers and combinations of numbers were prescribed in the parts and details of composite objects, such as the twelve oxen that supported the fountain of laver of bronze." From this it would seem that while the artificers were bound by certain rules as regards details which were significant as typical of theological truths, they had greater freedom as regards details of ornamentation. But as Moses and his workmen had been trained in Egypt, the probability is that the metallurgy of the Hebrews was very similar to that of the Egyptians.

The Assyrians were well versed in the manipulation of the precious metal. Mr. Layard informs us, "that though the Assyrians may have used mixed metals for gilding external walls, they had abundance of gold and silver, and also transported artificers from conquered countries to their own—such as craftsmen and engravers from Jerusalem to Babylon in the Babylonish captivity." Dr Birch has also remarked (in his observations on the statistical tablets of Kornak), "that the silver vases of Tahai are a remarkable tribute, as they show an excellence in working metals among these people." Mr. Layard also mentions, "offerings of vases of gold and silver, with handles, feet, and covers, in the shape of animals, such as the bull and gazelle (or wild goat), kneeling Asiatics, the heads of lions, and even the god Baal. The tribute obtained by the Egyptians from Naharaina or Mesopotamia consisted of vases of gold, silver, and copper, as well as precious stones."

The history of the goldsmith's art has been so fully dealt with by many excellent publications that the author does not propose giving a complete historical account, but advises the student to carefully study the works on the subject. At the same time he suggests that a visit be made to the principal museums, more especially the British Museum and that at South Kensington, where the student will learn more of the history of the art in a few hours than he would gain from a study of books only for years. The British Museum has examples showing that in some countries the wearing of jewellery as ornaments has preceded the wearing of personal apparel, such as the necklaces and head-ornaments composed of bones and shells from Asia, from the black races of the Pacific, from Australia, and from Melanesia ; the necklaces, armlets, and head-ornaments, composed of teeth, ivory, and beaten metal, from the Solomon Islands; the personal ornaments composed of feathers, the jade ear pendants and breast ornaments, &c., from New Zealand; the head ornaments, ear-rings, and armlets, composed of teeth, shells, and grasses, from the Western Pacific; and the head ornaments, necklaces, and armlets, composed of bones, beads, teeth, &c., as also armlets fashioned out of metal, from East and West Africa. All these are very crude in design, but are very interesting from an historical point of view.

But excellent specimens of workmanship and design will be found in the collection of Egyptian and Assyrian jewellery, consisting of hairpins, ear-rings, bracelets, armlets, finger-rings, anklets, and vases, all wrought of the precious metal. The Assyrians far excelled all the nations of their time, for they promoted the art of the kingdom by the encouragement of foreign talent as well as of native skill. In the Babylonian Collection there are examples of considerable attainment, wrought in the precious metal in the forms of armlets, bracelets, finger-rings, and golden images for the shrine. While excellent taste is displayed in the works of art manufactured by the Greeks, Persians, Japanese, and natives of India.

The room devoted to gold ornaments and gems shows clearly the defects of the modern goldsmith. The personal ornaments wrought by the ancient Phœnicians, although curious in form, are highly executed. The Roman rings are rare examples of jewellery, as also are many of the gold ornaments and finger-rings of the Greeks, Romans, and mediæval periods of Europe.

The gold ornaments from Assyria are of excellent workmanship, amongst them being a very remarkable "*gold cup*, decorated with translucent enamel on relief, which is considered to be the finest known specimen of its kind. The designs are most artistically executed in very slightly sunk relief, over which variously-coloured enamels are melted, the shadows and details being produced by the work underneath. It is only on gold of high standard that the fine ruby colour seen in this specimen can be produced. It is a standing cup, or hanap, of gold of fine quality, weighing nearly 68 ounces, and in its present condition measures 9 inches high, and 7 inches across the cover. It was probably made in the year 1337."*

The Blacas and Castellani Collections of Greek, Etruscan, and Roman ornaments, consisting of wreaths, necklaces, fibulæ brooches, bracelets, pectoral ornaments, rings, rosettes to be sewn on drapery, ornaments for the head, and other ornaments in gold and vitreous enamels, contain the finest specimens of their kind, mostly wrought in beaten gold, and in filigree work † of fine and most delicate designs. They show a skill in manipulating the precious metal which has never been

* The full history will be found in the *British Museum Guide*, 1896.
† The method of filigree work is fully treated in Chapter vi.

surpassed, and their examination will impress upon the
student the fact that he has much to learn before he can
bring himself equal with the most advanced stage of his art.
There are the cases of engraved gems known as the "Townley,
Hamilton, Blacas, Castellani, and Carlisle Collections," which
"represent most, if not all, of the known stages of the glyptic
art, as practised by the Greeks, Etruscans, and Romans,
from a period not later than the seventh century B.C., down to
about the third century A.D."

CHAPTER II.

METALLURGY OF GOLD.*

Physical Properties of Pure Gold.—Gold is a yellow metal which takes a brilliant lustre when its surface is polished. If, however, it is deposited from its solution by the electric current, as in the process of gilding, it has a "dead" appearance, but this gives place to the characteristic lustre when the deposited surface is burnished. Gold can be rolled into thin sheets, or beaten out into very thin leaves without cracking at the edges. This property of a metal is called its **malleability**, and gold is at the head of the list of malleable metals. The metal can be beaten out so thin that a sheet of it having an area of 56 square inches weighs only one grain, and is computed to have a thickness of $\frac{1}{280000}$ of an inch. The sheets are so thin as to be semitransparent, but the transmitted light is bluish-green in colour, and not yellow as in the case of the reflected light. Another important property which gold possesses in the highest degree is that of **ductility**; it can be drawn into extremely thin wire very readily. This property depends upon two others—(1) **tenacity**, or the power of resisting fracture by a direct pull (tensile stress); (2) **softness**. The tensile strength of pure cast gold is given by Prof. Roberts-Austen as being equal to 15,680 lbs. avoirdupois per square inch. This means that a bar of gold having a cross section of 1 square inch would, if fixed at one end in a vertical position, just support a weight of 7 tons hung from the other end. This is a moderate tenacity, and is about five times greater than that of lead, the least tenacious of the common metals. Pure gold is one of the softest of the common metals, being very little harder than lead; it can be readily cut with a knife. **Toughness** is also another characteristic property of the pure metal; this property may be defined as the power to resist fracture by bending or twisting, or to elongate under a tensile stress before fracture.

Gold melts at a temperature of 1102° C., and is sensibly volatile, especially when raised to the temperature of the electric arc. If a very powerful current of electricity is sent through a

* For further information the reader is referred to *The Metallurgy of Gold*, by T. Kirke Rose, D.Sc., 3rd ed. Charles Griffin & Co., Limited.

thin gold wire the metal is entirely dissipated in vapour. When gold is melted in large quantities and allowed to cool very slowly the metal is found to be distinctly crystalline in character. Gold is a very heavy metal, being more than nineteen times heavier than water, and nearly twice as heavy as silver. (Specific gravity = 19·32.) All these properties are more or less modified by the presence of impurities, or by alloying the metal with other metals.

Chemical Properties.—Oxygen does not combine directly with gold even when the metal is raised to a high temperature ; but oxide of gold in combination with ammonia can be obtained by adding ammonia solution to a concentrated solution of gold trichloride. The reddish-yellow solid which is precipitated is called **fulminating gold,** and is a very unstable body.

Sulphur and gold do not unite directly at any temperature, but when the finely-divided metal is fused with either sodium or potassium sulphide, a double sulphide of gold and the other metal is formed. Also, a black precipitate of gold sulphide, Au_2S_3, is obtained when sulphuretted hydrogen gas is passed into a cold solution of gold trichloride. The chemical indifference of gold towards oxygen and sulphur is really its most valuable property from an ornamental point of view, as articles made of the metal may be exposed to the atmosphere and to sulphur fumes for any length of time without tarnishing.

Chlorine gas and finely-divided gold unite directly, with the formation of gold chloride, $AuCl_3$, which is a red solid readily soluble in water. This substance is, perhaps, the most important compound of gold. None of the common acids attack gold, but a mixture of hydrochloric and nitric acids, known as **aqua regia,** dissolves the metal with the formation of gold chloride, $AuCl_3$. The action is due to the liberation of chlorine in the acid mixture. Gold chloride is completely decomposed into gold and chlorine at a temperature of 230° C. It is also readily reduced to the metallic state when in solution in water by such reducing agents as ferrous sulphate (green vitriol), and a solution of sulphur dioxide.

Cyanide of potassium in solution in water dissolves gold slowly with the formation of gold cyanide, $AuCy$, which remains in the solution in combination with potassium cyanide, as a double cyanide, $AuCy.KCy$. The higher compound, $AuCy_3.KCy$, is formed by the addition of potassium cyanide to a solution of gold chloride. Both compounds can be separated from their solution by crystallisation.

Mercury dissolves gold, especially when it is in a finely-divided state, with the formation of gold **amalgams** which are probably more or less definite compounds of the two metals. The amalgams may be separated from the excess of mercury by squeezing the mass in wash leather, when the excess of the liquid metal is forced through the pores of the leather. The pasty amalgam is left in the leather. This property of mercury is extremely useful in the extraction of gold, as the mercury can be almost completely removed by the aid of heat.

Preparation of Pure Gold.—The ordinary fine gold of commerce, although described as 24 carat fine, always contains small quantities of impurities, of which platinum and silver are the most common. For manufacturing purposes the amount of impurity is too small to affect the ordinary properties of the alloys made from fine gold ; but for assay purposes, when great accuracy is required, gold of exceptional purity must be used to check the results. The following is a brief description of a process for obtaining such metal :—A quantity of fine gold is dissolved in aqua regia, evaporated to dryness on a water bath, re-dissolved in distilled water, and again evaporated to drive off the excess of acid. The gold chloride thus obtained is dissolved in a small quantity of distilled water, alcohol and potassium chloride are then added to precipitate traces of platinum chloride. Any precipitate which settles out is filtered off, and washed with alcohol. The filtered liquid now contains the gold ; it is then diluted with a large bulk of distilled water, and allowed to stand for two or three weeks in order to allow any chloride of silver there may be to settle out. The clear liquid is syphoned off, warmed, and crystals of oxalic acid added from time to time until the solution becomes quite colourless, when the whole of the gold will be precipitated as a brown, spongy powder. The oxalic acid acts as a reducing agent, and reduces the gold chloride to the metallic state. The metal so obtained is washed with hydrochloric acid, ammonia and distilled water, and finally with distilled water, to remove all traces of silver chloride. It is then dried, fused in a clay crucible with bisulphate of potassium and borax, and poured into a stone mould. With care this method furnishes gold containing less than 1 part of impurity in 10,000 parts of the metal.

Occurrence of Gold.

A knowledge of the valuable character of gold is as old as the oldest human records, and it was doubtless in use for purposes of adornment even in prehistoric times. No doubt, gold was one of the earliest, if not the earliest, metal in use, the principal reason for this being that it is almost always found in the metallic state, and often in easily accessible surface deposits. Gold is very widely distributed in the earth's crust, and is also present in very small quantity in sea water ; but it is only in certain localities that the metal occurs in sufficient quantity to pay for its extraction from the rocky matter with which it is associated.

How Metals Occur in the Earth.—The earth's crust, as far as it has been made accessible to man, is composed of rocks of various kinds which geologists are able to classify, and to form some very clear ideas of their mode of formation. Since that period in the earth's history when rain began to fall upon, and rivers to flow over, its surface, and alternations of heat and cold to prevail, a constant wearing down of some parts and a building up of others have been, and are still, taking place. What the earth was like before this period there is no certain evidence, but the constituents of the various rocks must have been present in its crust. Those portions of the rocky structure which have been formed by the agency of running water assisted by atmospheric influences are called **stratified rocks** from the fact that they have been deposited in layers or **strata.** This mode of rock formation may be studied on the small scale in any gutter after a heavy fall of rain; the sediment carried down and deposited in parts of the channel is very suggestive. Every river, ancient or modern, has done, or is still doing, similar work, but on a much larger scale. Solid rock, more or less disintegrated by frost and other atmospheric agencies, is transported from the upper to the lower reaches of the river; the finer portions are carried in suspension, the coarser pieces are dragged over the bottom of the stream, have their sharp edges rounded off, and are converted into pebbles. Such pieces of rock are described as water-worn. They are ground into shape by rubbing against each other, the necessary motion being furnished by the rush of water over them. Such a deposit of pebbles intermixed with sand and clay is called **gravel,** and is found in some part of the bed of every river. The precise character of the bottom depends upon the rate of flow of the river, and the nature of the country through which it flows; but the coarser gravels are always nearer the source of the stream, and the finer ones in the lower reaches. The finest particles which are carried in suspension from the mouth of the river are deposited in lake or sea as a silt or mud, which may in time become hardened by pressure into solid rock. Gravels are, therefore, formed from the rocks of the country through which the river flows. Some beds of gravel are found in positions which indicate that they have not been formed by streams flowing through the country under its present configuration; others are of more recent origin, and the courses of the streams that formed them can be traced from the configuration of the surrounding country; others are in the course of formation.

A very powerful agent in rock formation is the internal heat of the earth, which, by means of earthquakes and volcanic action, has considerably modified the earth's crust ever since air and water commenced their combined action in altering its configuration. Rents and fissures have been formed in stratified rocks, and filled either with molten rock or with solid material deposited from its solution in water. Stratified rocks have been covered with layers of molten matter from deep-seated sources. Rocks formed in this way are called igneous or volcanic rocks. Further, volcanic action has so upheaved and distorted the earth's crust in many parts as to bring some of the oldest stratified rocks to the surface.

The common constituents of rocks are silica, alumina, lime, and magnesia; but many bodies of a similar character, though in very much smaller quantities, are also present in various rocks. Among these are compounds of useful metals, such as iron, copper, lead, tin, zinc, &c. The useful metals are, however, rarely found in the metallic state, but are usually combined with oxygen, sulphur, carbon, &c., in oxides, sulphides and carbonates, which are by far the commonest compounds of those metals. These compounds are always mixed with more or less rocky matter which is generally useless, and is called by the miner gangue or veinstone. When the metal is present in sufficient quantity to make its extraction profitable the material which contains it is called an ore of the metal. Ores are usually found either filling up fissures or interstratified with rocks at various depths in the earth's crust, and have to be mined.

Gold Ores.—Gold is one of the few metals which occur in the earth in the metallic or native state. This is due to the fact that the metal has very weak affinities for the common mineralising agents—oxygen, sulphur, &c. The only compound of gold of any note which occurs in the earth is the telluride, and even this is found in such small quantities as to be of very little metallurgical importance. The minerals petzite, $(AuAg)_2Te$, and sylvanite, $(AuAg)Te_3$, double tellurides of gold and silver may be taken as examples. Practically the whole of the gold extracted from its ores is in the metallic state when the process of extraction is commenced. Gold occurs in veins or lodes in the oldest stratified rocks; and when these are exposed to the disintegrating action of rivers the gravels formed from them contain the metal, which is usually present in the form of small particles, but sometimes in masses of considerable size.

Placers.—This is the miner's term for deposits of gravel containing gold. When these deposits are the results of the action of ancient streams they are called ancient placers, and are often situated at considerable depths from the surface. When they are the results of the action of modern streams— that is, are found on or near the surface, and in such positions as may be judged from the configuration of the surrounding country—they are called modern placers. There is usually very little to indicate the position of ancient placers, except when they crop out on the side of a hill or a ravine. The reason for this is that the surface of the country has undergone considerable change, due to volcanic and other agencies, since the rivers which formed the gravels flowed over it.

Nuggets.—The greater part of the gold present in alluvial deposits is in the form of small rounded grains and fine dust, but masses of considerable size have deen found from time to time. These are called nuggets, and the following is a brief description of the more notable of them. The "Welcome" nugget found in Victoria weighed 2,195 ounces; the "Blanch Barkley" found in South Australia weighed 1,752 ounces; and a nugget found in Russia weighed 1,152 ounces. Many masses of smaller size have been found in various goldfields, and their fortunate discoverers thereby considerably enriched.

Vein Gold.—When the metal occurs *in situ*—that is, in veins and lodes which have not been interfered with by surface actions—it is called **vein gold.** The most common vein stone with which gold is associated is quartz rock, which is composed mainly of silica; but such auriferous quartz often contains in addition metallic compounds, of which the most common are iron and copper pyrites, zinc blende, galena (sulphides of iron, copper, zinc, and lead respectively), and an oxide of iron called magnetite. The metal platinum is also sometimes found in gold ore. If such rocks have been broken down to form placer deposits their contained minerals will be found mixed with the earthy matter in the deposits.

Gold Producing Countries.—For the period 1891 to 1896 Australasia and the United States headed the list of gold producers with 24·14 and 22·47 per cent. respectively of the total annual production; Russia produced 17·16, and Africa 16·80 per cent.; South America produced 6·06 per cent. These countries thus account for 86·63 per cent. of the total production; the remainder is found in such countries as China, Japan, British India, Austria, Hungary, Italy, France, Sweden, Great Britain, &c. The last-named country only produces ·05 per cent., and this is mostly found in Wales. The average annual production of the world is roughly valued at £26,500,000; of this, Great Britain's product may be valued at £13,000, so that the gold-mining industry of this country is of very little importance. Excluding the Russian empire, which is partly Asiatic, Austria-Hungary produces more than six times as much gold as the whole of the remaining European countries together, but even this is somewhat small, £311,000, so that the metal does not occur to any extent in Europe. In fact, European gold is mostly obtained during the operations for the extraction of other metals from ores which contain small quantities of the precious metal. At the present time British Columbia is yielding very rich ores of gold. In 1896 the value of the gold production was, in round figures, £43,000,000, and in 1897, £49,600,000;

and probably the amount will increase during the next few years. In 1897 the order of importance was—Africa (23·25 per cent.), United States (23·02 per cent.), Australasia (21·07 per cent.), and Russia (13·54 per cent.).

METHODS OF GOLD EXTRACTION.*

In the following paragraphs will be found short descriptions of the principal methods adopted for the extraction of gold from its ores. The particular method to be applied to an ore depends upon the nature of the ore, its content of the precious metal, and the resources of the surrounding country. Generally speaking, the amount of gold present in an ore is small, and large quantities of material have to be manipulated during its extraction in quantity, so that the ore must be treated at or very near the place where it is found. The transport of large masses of ore over considerable distances would be very costly, and would in the majority of cases more than absorb the value of the gold obtained. A method which could be adopted with advantage in one district due to its surroundings might prove a complete failure in another. It is not intended, however, to discuss the relative advantages of the various methods described, as such a discussion would be beyond the scope of this book.

The materials to be dealt with are found (1) in alluvial deposits; (2) in veins or lodes. The alluvial deposits are again divided into (a) shallow or modern placers; (b) deep or ancient placers.

PLACER MINING.

Extraction of Gold from Shallow Placers.—The sand, pebbles, clay, &c., in gravel are only loosely adherent, and the mass is readily broken up by the miner's pick, or even by the action of water. If this loosely adherent matter is completely removed to the whole depth of the placer, a much more solid mass is reached which formed part of the original surface over which the depositing stream commenced to flow. This solid mass is called the bed or country rock, and often it is only the layer of gravel near the bed rock which contains sufficient gold to pay for working. In this case the poor surface gravel must be stripped off by pick and shovel, or, if the layer is too deep to allow of this, a shaft must be sunk in order to reach the pay dirt. Sometimes, when the nature of the ground would permit,

* Fuller descriptions of the methods of gold extraction will be found in Le Neve Foster's *Ore and Stone Mining*, Rose's *Metallurgy of Gold*, and Johnson's *Getting Gold*.

tunnelling was also resorted to in order to reach the rich gravel.
but this practice has now almost died out. By one or other
of the methods the pay dirt is brought to the surface ready for
further treatment. The presence of the gold in the metallic
state, and the great density of the metal, very greatly facilitate
its separation from the rubbish with which it is mixed. When
the dirt is mixed with water the lighter portions remain suspended in the water for a time, and in this condition may be
removed by pouring off the liquid. In this way, by repeated
breaking up and washing, the main bulk of the dirt may be got
rid of, and only a few of the heavier particles intermixed with
the particles of gold are left behind. These may be removed by
drying the residue, and subjecting it to a blast of air either from
the mouth or from a pair of hand bellows.

The Vanning Pan.—This piece of apparatus is a shallow
sheet-iron pan about 18 inches in diameter, having its sides
sloping outwards at an angle of 30° with the bottom. In some
pans the iron is stamped inwards so as to form a ridge or riffle
about half way up the side, and running about half way round
the pan. Water is essential in the use of this and other apparatus
based upon similar principles. The operation must, therefore,
be carried on near a water supply. The most convenient way
of carrying on the process is in a wooden tub placed near a
water supply. The operator can then stand over the tub and
readily manipulate the pan. A shovelful of the pay dirt is put
into the pan and the whole completely immersed in the water ;
the mass is thoroughly broken up with the hands, and the larger
stones picked out ; the pan is then raised until the contents are
just covered with water, and a side to side, together with a twisting, motion given to it until the mud is washed away. The
contents of the pan now consist of small pebbles which are
picked out ; of silica sand, which can be largely got rid of by a
dexterous twist of the pan in the water, by which the sand is
driven forwards so as to permit of its being scraped or washed
away ; and of a black heavy sand with which the gold is mixed.
The latter is dried, and the sand separated by a blast of air.
This mode of getting rid of the last particles of sand is very
wasteful, as small particles of gold are also blown away.

The Cradle.—This is a rectangular wooden box about 3 feet
long and 18 inches wide. At the bottom are fixed a pair of
rockers at right angles to the direction of its length, and so
arranged that the bottom slopes from back to front. At the
back, near the top, is fixed a rectangular sieve with half-inch
meshes. A piece of blanketing is fastened to the front of the
sieve, and is stretched at an angle underneath the sieve and
towards the back of the cradle, a space being left between
the end of the blanket and the back of the cradle for the
passage of materials into the bottom. Across the bottom, and

at right angles to the direction of its length, are fixed two wooden bars called riffles. The front of the cradle is open for the passage of materials outwards.

Two men are required to work the apparatus—one to shovel the gravel into the sieve, and break it up if necessary ; the other to keep up a continuous rocking motion similar to that imparted to a baby's cradle, and at the same time to pour water over the gravel in the sieve. The constant motion of the cradle, together with the water, serves to break up the mass, and causes it to pass through the sieve, only the pebbles remaining behind. The rough texture of the blanket arrests fine particles of gold, but the larger particles roll down it with the sand into the bottom, where they lodge with the heavier particles of sand behind the riffle bars. The fine sand is washed forwards, and escapes from the cradle at the front. The constant motion of the cradle prevents the fine sand from collecting behind the riffles, choking them up, and thus causing waste of gold by allowing the particles of metal to be washed over the banks of sand. The blanket is removed from time to time and washed in a tub, and the sand removed from behind the riffle bars. The collected matter is treated as described above for the separation of the gold. Sometimes mercury is placed behind the riffle bars to assist in collecting the gold by forming an amalgam with it. The separation of the amalgam from the heavy sand is more readily effected than the separation of metallic gold.

The Sluice.—This apparatus consists essentially of a long shallow wooden trough, with riffle bars fixed at intervals across the bottom at right angles to its length. For its successful working a good supply of water is needed. Also, the head of the sluice must be raised to get a sufficient slope to cause a current of water to traverse it. This is readily effected if the ground has a natural slope, otherwise the sluice has to be supported on trestles of varying height, so as to give the necessary fall from head to tail. The gravel is shovelled into the head of the sluice, and a stream of water is kept constantly running through it. The water carries the earthy matter down, and at the same time disintegrates it. The heavier particles containing the gold are arrested by the riffles, and the lighter portions, which are practically free from gold, leave the lower end as tailings. It is a very common practice to put mercury behind the riffles to assist in the retention of the gold. The current of water is stopped at intervals for "cleaning up," when the amalgam is removed for further treatment (see p. 23). It will be seen that more capital and labour are required for sluicing operations than for working either the pan or cradle. In fact, these latter may be described as primitive apparatus used by individuals in the first rush to a new goldfield.

Extraction of Gold from Deep Placers.—As already indicated, these placers are usually at a considerable depth. They are seldom very rich in gold, and, as a rule, can only be worked when considerable capital is available. The layer of gravel nearest the bed rock is usually the richest portion, and is reached either by tunnelling through the side of the hill, or sinking shafts until the "pay dirt" is reached. It will be sufficient here to describe briefly the first mode of procedure. The tunnel is made, and two long sluices laid side by side along its floor, which has the necessary slope. The bottom of the sluice is made of blocks of wood and pieces of rock, and projections are left which serve as riffles. A considerable quantity of mercury, sometimes as much as a ton of the metal in a single sluice, is placed behind the riffles, and the operation is commenced. Water from a reservoir at a greater elevation than the bed to be worked, so that it may be delivered under considerable pressure, is conveyed by means of pipes to the scene of operation. It is then projected against the face of the bed by a nozzle fitted with a universal joint, which allows of the stream being sent in any direction. The force of the water is such as to wash down the gravel into the head of the sluice, along which it is carried by the escaping water, disintegrated, and its gold separated by the mercury. The object of the double sluice is to allow of continuous working; the stream of materials can be kept going through one while the other is being cleaned up. In this way enormous masses of material are sent through the sluices, and the gravel washed away down to the bed rock without handling. This method of winning the metal is known as hydraulic mining, and the process is called hydraulicking. Large capital is required for its successful prosecution; hence it is usually carried on by companies.

EXTRACTION OF GOLD FROM QUARTZ.

As already mentioned, gold occurs in more or less compact quartz rock, which usually runs in veins at varying depths from the surface. Such gold ores are mined by sinking a shaft, if necessary, and following up the vein. The ore is brought to the surface, and is then ready for further treatment. The metal usually occurs in such material in the form of angular fragments. In some cases the fragments have a distinct crystalline structure, but well-developed crystals of gold are by no means common. The ore has to be crushed to a fine powder before the metal can be separated from the siliceous matter with which it is mixed. Mercury is very largely used to assist in winning the gold in the majority of modern methods; but it must not be supposed that the knowledge of the action of the liquid metal upon gold is of recent date, for the fact that mercury will dissolve gold was known and utilised at least 2000 years ago. Although the greater part of the gold used in ancient times was probably obtained from alluvial deposits, some was extracted from vein stone by crushing and washing, and by the aid of mercury.

When sulphides of metals (such as iron pyrites, copper pyrites, galena, and zinc blende) occur along with the quartz some of the gold appears to be intimately associated with these sulphides, and more difficulty is experienced in the separation of the metal.

Crushing Apparatus —The most primitive kind of crushing apparatus appears to have taken the form of a hollowed-out stone to serve as a mortar, in which the ore was crushed either by hand labour with stone hammers, or by repeatedly raising a heavy stone with some lever arrangement, and allowing it to fall back again into the mortar, and so crush the material to be pulverised. The final stage of the crushing was effected in hand mills in which a movable stone was made to rotate over a fixed one, and the partly crushed material fed in between the two. The powder was then washed to get rid of the earthy matter and separate the gold ; mercury was probably used to assist the operation.

Various kinds of crushing apparatus were used in South America by the Spaniards in the latter half of the sixteenth century. The one which has been most largely used, and is still in use in some parts of Mexico, is called the arrastra. It consists of a circular stone vat, the bottom of which is constructed of hard stones (such as granite or quartz) well cemented in the joints, so as to make the whole practically water-tight. A vertical wooden spindle with horizontal arms is fitted into bearings, one in the centre of the vat floor, and the other in an overhead beam, thus enabling the spindle to be rotated. One of the horizontal arms is of the same length as the radius of the vat, and has a heavy stone suspended from it by means of chains ; the other is much longer, and a mule can be harnessed to the part outside the vat. By causing the mule to move round the outside the stone suspended from the shorter arm is dragged over the floor of the vat. The front of the stone is an inch or two from the floor, and the back in contact with it. To work the apparatus the roughly crushed ore is fed in with a small quantity of water, the mule set in motion, and the action continued until the mass is ground to a fine mud. When the grinding is nearly finished mercury is squirted over the surface of the pulp, and the grinding continued so as to thoroughly incorporate the metal, and bring it into contact with the gold. When the grinding is finished, water is added, and the mule driven slowly to collect the amalgam ; then the pulp is run out, and the amalgam separated. The amalgam may be separated by running the pulp into a vat, through which a slow stream of water is kept running, and keeping it well agitated by rotating vanes worked by mule power. An arrastra, 10 feet in diameter, will treat 1 ton of ore in twenty-four hours, and extract from 70 to 80 per cent. of the gold present. It has been found to yield a profit with certain ores which could not be profitably treated by more elaborate apparatus.

Rock Breakers.—When the ore is in the form of large lumps a preliminary crushing has to be carried out; this is usually effected by some form of rock breaker. The most effective of such apparatus are those in which the ore is fed into the space between two jaws, where it is crushed by the to and fro motion of one of the jaws, the other being fixed. The crushed ore passes through an opening between the jaws, sufficient for the passage of pieces about the size of a walnut.

The Stamp Battery.—The principle of this apparatus is the same as that of the ordinary pestle and mortar, in which the grinding of materials on the small scale is usually carried out. The following is a short description of a five stamp battery :— The mortar is a massive cast-iron trough about 5 feet long, 1 foot wide, and 4 feet high, and weighs about 3 tons. It is flanged round the bottom, and, by means of this, is bolted firmly to a very solid foundation. Between the foundation and the bottom of the mortar a layer of rubber or blanketing is placed to deaden the vibration, which is very considerable, when the apparatus is at work. Along the bottom of the mortar is placed a series of dies, one for each stamp; the front is partly open and fitted with grooves, into which screens of wire gauze or of perforated sheet iron are put, which regulate the fineness of the crushed material which escapes from the mortar. The back usually bulges outward somewhat at the top to allow of the ore being readily fed in. The stamp consists of an iron rod, to the bottom of which is fixed the foot, an iron cylinder of greater diameter than the rod : to this again a shoe made of the hardest white iron is so fixed that it can be removed when worn out. The stamp rods work up and down in guides fixed to a heavy frame. At about one-third of its length from the top of the rod is placed a projection which is caught by a revolving cam, and the stamp is raised vertically until the cam passes from under it when the stamp falls back upon the die, to be raised again by the next revolution of the cam. The cams, one for each stamp, are fixed to a shaft which revolves in bearings on the stamp frame, and is driven by gearing worked by steam or water power. The cams are so arranged on the shaft that the stamps rise and fall one after the other. The height through which the stamp falls may be as much as 18 inches, and the number of drops about 50 per minute. The rate of rise and fall depends upon the rate of revolution of the cam shaft. The total weight of a stamp varies from about 600 to 1000 lbs.

Modern Stamp Battery Practice.—Amalgamated copper plates are now largely used to collect the gold instead of free mercury. The copper plates are carefully cleaned by pickling in aqua fortis, and then well coated with mercury, which adheres to the copper. If the mercury contains a little gold or silver, it absorbs particles of gold more readily than when quite free from these metals, so that a little silver is usually added to mercury used for amalgamating the plates. It is said that if the cleaned copper plates are electro-plated with silver before amalgamation, their absorbing power for gold is increased. The prepared plates are used both inside and outside the mortar.

The ore, previously crushed by a rock breaker, is fed into the mortar with a slow stream of water, and is crushed to a pulp by the action of the stamps. The only way in which the ore is allowed to leave the mortar is through the screen in front, and the fineness of the escaping particles depends upon the size of the meshes; the usual size is from $\frac{1}{24}$ to $\frac{1}{40}$ of an inch. Directly under the screen is an inclined plane, on the bottom of which are placed the amalgamated plates described above. The stream of muddy water which runs through the screen passes over the plates on its way down the plane, and the fine particles of gold it contains are caught by the amalgam. It is also usual to place an amalgamated plate inside the mortar near the screen, and this is found to pick up a considerable quantity of the precious metal. The plates are removed from time to time, and the rich amalgam scraped off. If it is too hard to be thus readily removed, the plate is heated to soften the amalgam, which can then be scraped off. The plates are re-charged with mercury, and are again ready for use. When the stream leaves the end of the inclined plane or table it contains very little free gold; but in ores containing sulphides some of the gold is more or less intimately associated with the metallic compounds, and mercury does not appear to have much action upon this portion of the gold. It is, therefore, carried away with the sulphides in the mud, and if this were allowed to run to waste a considerable proportion of gold would be lost.

Concentration.—The proportion of sulphides to rubbish in the material which leaves the battery is rather small, so that it is found impossible to treat it with profit as it is. By taking advantage of the fact that the particles of sulphides are much denser than the particles of quartz, a more or less perfect separation of them can be effected. Sulphide of lead is about five times, and the sulphides of copper and iron about three times, heavier than quartz, bulk for bulk, so that theoretically the separation should be comparatively easy; but as the particles of ore vary in size as well as in density the separation is somewhat complicated in practice.

As stated above, the gold associated with sulphides in the ore is practically missed. If the ore under treatment is very refractory—that is, contains a large percentage of its gold associated with sulphides, &c.—concentration is absolutely necessary. Some ores are so refractory that only 25 per cent. of the assay value of the ore is obtained by amalgamation, while 75 per cent. remains in the tailings. Much skill has been employed in devising apparatus for concentration; but it is doubtful if any single machine will effect even a near approach to perfect separation. The methods adopted for concentration vary in different districts, and even in different mills in the same district. Only general principles can be touched upon here.

Sizing.—This process effects the separation of the particles of ore suspended in the slow stream of water escaping from the crushing and amalgamating machinery, and sorts them into two or more sizes. It is carried on in large wooden tanks, the sides of which slope downwards and meet, so that a cross-section through the tank at right angles to the direction of its length would have the appearance of a **V**. The apex of the **V** communicates with a channel which rises some distance up the side of the tank, and opens outwards. The tanks are placed in series, and communicate with each other by channels in the top of the adjoining ends. The muddy water is run into the tank at one end of the series, and flows out at the other end practically free from valuable material. The rate of flow through a given tank depends upon its width as well as upon the supply of water. Thus if the tank is narrow the stream is rapid, and only the coarsest particles have time to subside; in a wide tank the conditions are just the opposite and finer particles are allowed to deposit. The deposited matter does not remain in the tank, but is carried through the side channel mentioned above, and delivered outside. Thus the side channel from each tank furnishes a supply of sized and somewhat concentrated material ready for further treatment.

Vanning.—This is a process for the further concentration of the material obtained as described in the last paragraph. In principle, it consists of agitating the material to be concentrated in a stream of water, and allowing the water to carry away the lighter and useless portions. One of the best known machines for the purpose is the **Frue vanner.** The essential part of this machine is an endless india-rubber band made double or treble the thickness at the edges so as to form a shallow endless trough. This band is fitted in an inclined position upon pulleys, so that when the machine is working the band moves uphill, and the stream of water runs in the opposite direction to that of the band. Besides this direct motion there is also a side shake which causes the band to move rapidly to and fro across the direction of its length. Thus any material delivered on to the band would be thoroughly agitated by the two motions. After passing over the upper pulley the band moves downwards into a tank of water in which the rich material is washed off and allowed to subside. The water containing the material to be concentrated is fed in a slow stream upon the upper part of the band and run down to the lower end, where it escapes; but the upward motion of the band retards the rate of flow, and the heavier particles of ore are prevented by friction from being carried down by the moving water. They are, in fact, carried upwards by the moving band, and deposited in the tank, as described above. The concentrated material is collected and treated for the extraction of its gold. The Frue vanner is often used in direct connection with the stamp battery without the process of sizing; in that case it is thought by some authorities that the waste of gold is greater.

Treatment of Gold Amalgam.—The amalgam is put into an iron retort, heated by its own fire, and the mercury volatilised. The vapour is condensed to the liquid state in the stem of the retort, which is made to pass through a water tank, and collected. The residue of gold is melted down in a crucible, and cast into bars.

CHLORINATION OF GOLD ORES AND CONCENTRATES.

The action of chlorine gas upon metallic gold has been already mentioned, and Plattner, in 1848, utilised this action in his method of assaying gold ores. He afterwards proposed to use it for the treatment of such ores on the large scale.

Ores and concentrates containing sulphides cannot be treated directly by the chlorination method, as the presence of sulphur is fatal to the proper action of the gas; but as, however, such materials are usually subjected to the process, all the sulphur must first be removed.

Roasting.—This is a process in which the material is subjected to the action of heat and air. Sulphur, when heated in air, takes fire and burns with a blue flame, forming sulphur dioxide gas by combination with oxygen of the air. The sulphur in a sulphide will also burn with exactly the same result, if the sulphide is subjected to a sufficiently high temperature in the presence of air. But in the case of the sulphides of such metals as copper and iron, as the sulphur leaves the metal, oxygen takes its place and the *corresponding* oxides are formed. On the other hand, sulphides of silver and gold are reduced to the metals on roasting. The oxides of the base metals do not exert any prejudicial effect upon the action of chlorine gas, so that materials in which the sulphides have been converted into oxides can be economically treated. Any furnace in which the conditions described above can be obtained may be used for roasting, and a number of such furnaces are in use. They all belong to the type called the **Reverberatory Furnace**. The essential parts of the furnace are the grate upon which the fuel is burnt for the generation of the heat; and the bed upon which the material is placed. The bed is placed between the grate and the chimney, so that the flame and products of combustion must pass over it on their way to the chimney and impart their heat to the material placed upon it. This is further facilitated by the low roof, which causes the flame to beat down or reverberate upon the bed. As the temperature requires to be varied for the different stages of the operation, the bed of a roasting furnace is usually long, so that the temperature in different parts varies considerably. Near the fire bridge, which separates the grate from the bed, the temperature is highest, and near the flue lowest, with varying temperatures between these two points.

In the roasting process, the rich concentrates are dried, usually by the waste heat of the furnace, and charged upon the bed at the flue end, where the material is subjected to a moderate heat at first. This is necessary, as sulphides soften if heated too strongly at first and clot together, thus retarding the roasting, which proceeds most rapidly when the sulphides are in a finely-divided state. The material is then gradually raked into hotter and hotter portions of the bed until it reaches the fire bridge, where it will withstand a bright-red heat without clotting. When the whole of the sulphur has been removed, the roasted mass is raked out through doors in the side of the furnace and allowed to cool. As the roasting mass is raked down the bed, fresh material is charged in at the flue end, so that the process is practically a continuous one. The furnaces are usually rectangular in section, and the internal parts are built of fire bricks. Sometimes, instead of one long bed, several beds are placed one above another, and the flame made to circulate over each bed in succession. The ore is started on the top bed, which has the lowest temperature, and is gradually transferred to the bottom one. Several hours intervene between the introduction and withdrawal of a given mass of material.

Chlorination.—There are several ways of conducting the operation, but only the **vat process** will be described here. A wooden vat, 7 feet in diameter and 4 feet high, which will hold about 3 tons of the roasted material is used. It has two bottoms, a false and a real one. The false bottom is perforated and is raised above the real one, so that there is a space about 1 inch deep between them. A filter, about 5 inches thick, is formed on the false bottom by putting in layers of small pieces of hard non-calcareous rock ; the size of the pieces in each layer decreases from bottom to top, the last layer being of fine sand. The roasted material is placed on this filter, and a lead pipe passing from a chlorine still, in which the gas is generated by the action of sulphuric acid on a mixture of common salt and black oxide of manganese, is connected with the space between the two bottoms. The chlorine gas is thus passed into the space and gradually finds its way through the filter among the ore. When the smell of the gas is noticed at the top, the lid is luted on, and the action allowed to proceed for about twenty-four hours. At the end of this time the lid is removed and a spray of water directed upon all parts of the surface of the ore. The water gradually soaks through the mass, dissolves the gold chloride formed, and collects in the space between the two bottoms, from which it is drawn by means of a tap. The practice is to use as small a quantity of water as possible, compatible with the complete solution of the gold compound, and the method of spraying is found most effective.

The solution containing the gold has now to be treated for the separation of the metal. This is effected by means of a solution of ferrous sulphate (green vitriol). The solution is run into the precipitating vat, and the sulphate solution added. The gold is precipitated, and is allowed to settle to the bottom of the vat as a brown mud. The liquid, free from gold, is then syphoned off ; the metallic mud collected ; washed ; dried ; fused in crucibles under borax, and cast into bars ; when it is ready for the bullion dealer.

CYANIDE PROCESS.

The fact that a solution of potassium cyanide will dissolve gold has been known for a long time, but the application of this property to the extraction of the metal from its ore on the large scale is of recent date. A patent was taken out for the process by MacArthur and Forrest in 1887. The cyanide process is now somewhat largely used, especially in South Africa, and it is claimed for it that sulphide ores of gold may be treated thus without previous roasting. That it is applicable to all gold ores with equally good results is open to considerable doubt, but in some districts it is worked with much success.

The ore is first crushed by rock breakers and stamp batteries, or by rolls, and is then transferred to vats similar in construction to the one described for the chlorination process, but usually much larger and varying in size to contain from 10 to 50 tons of crushed ore. Coarse matting, or canvas, is usually stretched over the top of the filter to facilitate the removal of the spent ore without disturbing the filter. After the vat has been charged with ore, a solution of potassium cyanide (containing

1 part of the salt in 100 parts of water) is run in on to the top of the ore, in sufficient quantity to just cover it. The action is allowed to proceed for from twelve to twenty-four hours, when practically the whole of the gold will be dissolved. The progress of the operation can be determined from time to time by drawing off a little of the solution and testing it with a strip of clean zinc, upon which gold is deposited. The solution is then run off and pumped back again to the top of the same vat, or to another vat containing fresh ore, so as to get as strong a solution of gold as possible.

The saturated solution is treated with clean shavings of zinc freshly turned on a lathe. This metal has the property of precipitating gold from its solution in cyanide. The zinc shavings are put into alternate compartments of a long divided wooden trough. The gold solution flows in at the bottom of the first compartment containing zinc, passes upwards through the shavings and over the top into the next compartment, which is empty. It then enters the next full compartment from the bottom and passes upwards as before, and so on to the end of the trough. By this mode of procedure the gold slimes are found to collect on the under side of the shavings and to fall to the bottom of the compartment, thus preventing clogging and consequent slow circulation of the liquid through the trough. The slimes, which contain a considerable quantity of zinc, are dried, and then melted down in graphite crucibles with a flux of sand, borax, and sodium bicarbonate. A slag, consisting principally of zinc silicate, is formed and a considerable quantity of zinc is volatilised. The bullion obtained is about 650 fine. The slag also contains gold, some of which is in the form of shots. These are separated by crushing and panning. The crushed slag is then smelted with lead compounds, and the resulting lead cupelled for its gold.

A purer gold can be obtained from the slimes by first roasting them in a muffle furnace, to volatilise the greater portion of the admixed zinc.

It should be remembered that the gold obtained by the methods described in this chapter is never quite pure. It invariably contains silver in greater or less quantity, and often other metals are present in small quantity. The refining of this metal for the production of fine gold is described below.

REFINING CRUDE BULLION.

Crude bullion is usually sent to refineries and mints in bars, which are there treated for the removal of the impurities, and the preparation of the precious metal for minting and manufacturing purposes. Native gold varies much in composition.

containing from 600 to 997 parts of gold per 1000 parts of the metal. Silver is a constant companion of gold, and the following metals are frequent impurities in the native metal — copper, iron, lead, bismuth, antimony, tin, and zinc. Platinum and allied metals are sometimes present.

Partial Refining.—This operation may be carried out by the judicious use of potassium nitrate (saltpetre). To effect this the bars are melted down in a plumbago or clay crucible in an ordinary wind furnace (see Fig. 1, p. 50). A fire-brick is placed on edge on the grate bars, and the crucible, after careful annealing, is put on the brick and surrounded by hot coke. When it is red hot a little borax is dropped in and the charge of metal introduced. When the metal has melted, a little sodium carbonate and saltpetre is added. The nitrate gives up oxygen to the base metals in the mass and converts them into oxides, which are dissolved by the borax ; the carbonate, together with the borax, acts as a flux for any dirt which may be present and the whole forms a fusible slag.

If a considerable quantity of base metal is present the process is modified, as the slag formed with borax and metallic oxides is very corrosive, and rapidly destroys the pot. If a plumbago crucible is used the saltpetre necessary to oxidise the impurities attacks the carbon in the pot and soon destroys it. To avoid this corrosion, bone ash is sprinkled over the molten metal, the surface cleared a little in the centre, and the flux and nitrate added there. The oxides formed are absorbed by the bone ash and their corrosive action is thus retarded. If, at the conclusion of the refining, the slag is too thick, it is thinned by the addition of more borax ; if too thin, more bone ash is added.

At the end of the refining the slag is run off, and if the surface of the metal shows no sign of oxidation on exposure to the air it is ready for pouring.

Toughening of Gold.—Frequently the metal produced by the above process is still quite brittle. This is usually due to the presence of zinc, bismuth, antimony, &c. It can be toughened by the use of ammonium chloride (sal ammoniac) and mercuric chloride (corrosive sublimate). The metal is melted and the surface covered with sal ammoniac. The sublimate is then added, a little at a time, and the furnace brick quickly replaced after each addition. The impurities are converted into volatile chlorides and escape, together with some of the refining agents which are also volatile. The dense vapours given off should not be allowed to escape by any other exit than the flue, as they are very poisonous. The metal is tested for toughness by removing a little with a dipper, and casting it into a thin bar. If this shows the necessary toughness, the operation is finished ; the metal is then covered with charcoal, well stirred by means of a plumbago rod, and poured.

The action of mercuric chloride is very rapid, and a large quantity of metal may be toughened with a small quantity of the chloride.

Removal of Iron.—Brittleness is often caused by the presence of iron ; this is especially the case with lemel bar. This impurity is most readily removed by sulphur, which combines very rapidly with iron at a high temperature, but has no action on gold. If silver is present, it also combines with sulphur, but the action is slow until nearly the whole of the iron has been removed. The regulus of iron sulphide which collects upon the surface of the metal will contain any silver sulphide formed, and is not thrown away. To conduct the operation the metal is melted in a crucible, and the sulphur, in small lumps, added round the side of the pot. Care must be exercised in adding the sulphur ; for if it is dropped indiscriminately on the molten surface, some of the metal may be projected from the pot. When the toughening is finished, the pot is taken from the furnace and allowed to cool ; it is then broken and the regulus or matte detached from the metal.

The moulds used for pouring the refined metal are thoroughly cleaned, wiped over with an oily rag, or blackened, and heated to a temperature below that sufficient to ignite the oil.

Old crucibles, lids, stirrers, and slags are ground up and sorted over for shots of metal. The fine powder is then smelted with lead, or lead-producing compounds, for the extraction of any metal it may contain.

Parting of Gold and Silver.—The result of the refining processes described above is an alloy containing the whole of the gold and silver present in the original metal, and small quantities of base metals, such as copper, lead, &c. The object of the parting process is to remove the silver and other metals, and obtain the gold in the fine state. The modern methods of separation depend upon the fact that, while gold is not dissolved by nitric and sulphuric acids when used singly, silver and copper are dissolved by nitric acid and by hot concentrated sulphuric acid. But gold seems to confer its own properties upon silver and copper when it is present in sufficient quantity in their alloys, and thus enables the latter to resist the action of the common acids. If then the proportion of gold in the alloy to be parted is considerable, it must be reduced by the addition of silver before the parting can be effected. Formerly it was supposed that the separation could not be effected unless the proportions were 1 part gold to 3 parts silver. The process of melting the necesssary silver with the alloy to make up this amount was called **inquartation**. In recent years the quantity of silver has been somewhat reduced, and an alloy of 1 part gold to $2\frac{1}{2}$ parts silver is found to give satisfactory results. Sulphuric acid is almost exclusively used for parting on the large scale, as it enables the process to be carried out at considerably less cost than when nitric acid is used. For parting on the small scale as in assaying, nitric acid is much more convenient, and is exclusively used.

Parting by Sulphuric Acid.—This process is a comparatively recent one; it was described in the seventeenth century, and introduced into Paris at the beginning, and into London towards the middle, of the present century. It is now in extensive use in Europe and America. The best proportions for the alloy seem to be 1 part of gold to 3 parts of silver, but a smaller proportion of silver is used in America. The amount of copper should not exceed 10 per cent., and of lead 5 per cent., and other metals in much smaller proportions. This is the reason for the partial refining already described. Some silver bars contain small quantities of gold, and are known by the name of *doré* bars on that account. They are always used for making the parting alloy when procurable.

Parting on the large scale may be roughly divided into two sections—(a) treatment of alloys rich in gold; (b) of alloys poor in gold. Silver bars containing 1 part of gold in 2000 parts of silver can be profitably treated. The following is a brief description of the process:—

(1) The rich alloy is melted with the requisite quantity of *doré* silver, and the molten mass poured in a thin stream into cold water. The water tank is fitted with a perforated copper tray; the crucible is held about 3 feet above the surface of the water, and moved round in a circle during the pouring. In this way the metal is formed into thin shells as it solidifies in the water. The granulated metal collects on the tray, which is lifted out at the end of the operation, and is allowed to drain.

(2) The granulated alloy is transferred to an iron pot set in its own fireplace. The pot is made of white, fine-grained phosphoric pig iron which will withstand the action of hot concentrated sulphuric acid for a considerable period. It is usually cylindrical in form, and is fitted with a movable lid which can be bolted on and made air-tight. There are two holes in the lid; one, fitted with a water-jointed cap, is for the introduction of acid; the other is connected with a lead pipe which carries off the gases generated during the action. The quantity of alloy treated in one operation depends upon its richness, for rich alloys it is 200 lbs. and upwards; for poor alloys a much larger quantity; 2 to 2½ lbs. of strong sulphuric acid are added for every pound of alloy. The fire is regulated so that the action is not too violent, and is continued for five or six hours. The acid acts upon the silver and copper, with formation of silver and copper sulphates and the copious evolution of sulphur dioxide gas which passes off by the lead pipe. The sulphates remain in solution in the excess of acid. When the action ceases the contents of the pot are allowed to settle,

and the clear liquid ladled out with iron ladles into lead-lined wooden vats containing hot water. The residue is then boiled again with strong acid added hot, allowed to settle and again ladled out. The treatment is usually repeated a third time. The residue is now dipped out with an iron strainer into a lead-lined filter box, and washed first with dilute sulphuric acid and then with hot water. It is then dried, pressed, and melted; and, as it is almost always brittle from traces of lead, tin, &c., it is toughened either with a blast of air or with nitre (as already described). The gold thus obtained is often 996 parts fine.

(3) The silver sulphate crystallises in part when diluted with water in the vats, but dissolves again when heated with steam. The silver is then precipitated in the metallic state by copper. The precipitate is collected, thoroughly washed to remove all traces of copper sulphate, dried, pressed, and melted down.

(4) The copper in the sulphate solution is either recovered by precipitation with iron and used again for the precipitation of more silver, or the solution is evaporated and crystallised to obtain copper sulphate crystals (blue vitriol).

Parting by Chlorine Gas.—Gold chloride is decomposed at a red heat, giving off chlorine gas, and leaving a residue of gold. It follows from this that if chlorine is passed into molten gold which has a temperature above that at which the chloride is decomposed no chloride is formed. On the other hand, silver chloride will withstand a bright-red heat without decomposition, and is not very volatile at the temperature of molten gold. Also, base metals readily combine with chlorine at a high temperature, and form, for the most part, volatile chlorides which are given off in the form of vapour. These reactions between metals and chlorine have been known for many years, but it was not until 1867 that a practical process for the purification of native gold by chlorine was introduced into the Sydney Mint by Mr. F. B. Miller, the assay master there. Previous to 1867 no attempt was made to part the small quantity of silver occurring in the Australian and New Zealand gold coined in the Sydney Mint. Hence, the sovereigns produced there before that date contain several per cent. of silver, which forms part of the alloy. They are on that account paler in colour than British gold coins, or than those of more recent production in Australia.

Miller's Process.—This process is now largely employed for separating small quantities of silver and base metals from native gold. The content of silver in the metal treated rarely exceeds 10 per cent. and is often considerably less than this. The base metals may amount to 1 per cent.

The operation is carried on in a French clay crucible which is first filled with a strong solution of borax and allowed to stand for ten minutes. It is then emptied, dried, and raised to a red heat to vitrify the absorbed borax and thus effectively glaze the inside. The pot is then placed in a plumbago crucible for safety, and the whole raised to redness in an ordinary wind furnace. The charge of gold (about 600 ozs.) is then introduced and melted down, a little borax being sprinkled over the surface. A lid having two holes, one in the centre and one at the side, is put on the pot, and a clay pipe, $\frac{3}{16}$ in. internal diameter, is made red hot, plunged through the centre hole to the bottom of the metal, and clamped in position. The outer end of the pipe is connected by a lead pipe with a chlorine still, in which the gas is generated by heating a mixture of black oxide of manganese and strong hydrochloric acid. A sufficient pressure is maintained to force the gas to the bottom of the molten metal into which it is delivered. The gas is completely absorbed by the metal and dense white fumes, consisting of chlorides of base metals, are given off. The silver is converted into chloride, which collects as a molten layer on the top of the metal. When the silver is all chloridised, brown vapours, consisting principally of chlorine, escape from the hole, and when a piece of white clay tobacco pipe held over the hole has a brownish-yellow stain imparted to it the operation is finished. It is usually an hour to an hour and half from the commencement when the brown fumes appear, the time depending on the amount of silver to be removed.

The crucible is taken from the fire and allowed to stand for the gold to solidify ; the silver chloride is then still in the molten state and is poured from the top of the solid gold into iron moulds. The crucible is then inverted on an iron table and the conical mass of metal allowed to fall out. When cold, it is scraped, or boiled in a strong solution of common salt to remove traces of silver chloride ; it is then remelted and cast into bars. The purified metal averages 996 fine, equal to that produced by parting with acid.

The silver chloride contains some gold as shots and as gold chloride. This is recovered by melting the chloride in a borax-glazed pot under a layer of borax. Carbonate of soda is sprinkled on the top, a little at a time, until about $\frac{1}{10}$ the weight of the chloride has been introduced. The temperature is then raised for about ten minutes. The gold chloride is reduced slowly by the carbonate of soda and collects in the bottom of the crucible with the shots. The metal is then separated as above. A second treatment with a smaller quantity of the carbonate causes a further separation of gold.

The silver is recovered from the chloride by metallic zinc. A slab of the chloride is suspended with a silver band by the side of a zinc plate in a solution of zinc chloride. When metallic connection is made between the two a voltaic action is set up and the silver chloride is rapidly reduced to metallic silver, zinc chloride being formed at the same time. Any copper present in the gold is also present as chloride in the silver chloride and is reduced along with the silver.   At the end of the operation the spongy silver is taken out of the vat, washed, dried, and melted. The silver bars thus obtained contain copper, but for minting purposes this is not objectionable if the copper does not exceed 75 parts per 1000, which represents the composition of the British silver coinage.

If the zinc is replaced by iron and the slab of chloride enclosed in a coarse flannel bag the greater part of the copper chloride can be dissolved out by heating the bath with steam.   The copper is then in great part precipitated by the iron, and is deposited on the bottom of the vat quite separate from the silver, which is all retained in the flannel bag.

The vat commonly used contains seven zinc plates with a slab of chloride placed between each pair of zincs.

Toughening of brittle gold can also be effected by the aid of chlorine gas and with very little loss of metal.   Antimony, lead, zinc, iron, and tin in small quantities are readily removed in a very few minutes, and the metal rendered quite tough and malleable. *

* For fuller details of the metallurgical extraction of gold the student is referred to Phillip and Bauerman's *Elements of Metallurgy*, third edition ; and Rose's *Metallurgy of Gold*, third edition, 1898.

CHAPTER III.

PRICES—ALLOYS—GOLD ALLOYS—GOLD MELTING.

HAVING given the history of gold and noticed the past and present workers in that metal, we will next practically describe the various methods and processes in the manipulation of the precious metal from a commercial point of view.

PRICES.

Fine Gold, Silver, Platinum, Copper, &c., may be purchased from the refiners and bullion dealers in any quantity from 1 dwt. to 100 ozs.

Fine gold is always sold at a uniform standard price according to the quantity purchased, *e.g.* :—

1 oz. and under 5 ozs.,	.	.	.	86s. 0d. per oz.
5 ,, 10 ,,	.	.	.	85s. 6d. ,,
10 ,, 50 ,,	.	.	.	85s. 3d. ,,

Fine Silver.—The price of silver fluctuates according to the rate in the bullion market : thus, in the year 1886, the price for fine silver was 5s. per oz., while in the year 1896 it could be bought at 3s. 0¾d. per oz. for small quantities, and 2s. 9¼d. per oz. for large quantities, *e.g.* :—

1 oz. and upwards.	.		3s. 0¾d. per oz.
20 ,,	.	.	2s. 11¾d. ,,
50 ,,	.	.	2s. 11½d. ,,
100 ,,	.	.	2s. 11¼d. ,,
200 ,,	.	.	2s. 10¾d. ,,
400 ,,	.	.	2s. 10½d. ,,
1000 ,,	.	.	2s. 9¼d. ,,

Platinum.—The price of platinum also fluctuates. At the commencement of the year 1890, when a syndicate was formed, the price was 64s. per oz. ; in August of the same year it was 75s. per oz. ; it then gradually descended to 37s. 6d. per oz. in 1892, and afterwards it steadily increased to 48s. 6d. in 1896. Its great cost is partly owing to its melting point being so high that its fusion requires the aid of electricity or the oxyhydrogen flame.

Copper.—This metal is largely used for forming alloys; it is sold under different forms—viz., grain or shot copper, 1s. 6d. per lb. ; deposited copper in sheet at 1s. 8d. per lb. ; Swedish copper wire at 1s. 9d. per lb. The copper for alloying with gold must be the purest obtainable. The best, within the author's experience, is electro deposited copper which has been melted, rolled, and drawn into wire.

VARIOUS ALLOYS.

Composition is an alloy much used for making various pale bright gold alloys under 10 carats; it is composed of a mixture of copper and spelter. This alloy can be used with greater safety than the spelter and the copper in separate states, because the spelter is so volatile that the greatest care is required to prevent the volatilisation of most of the spelter before the alloy is formed.

The general price for composition for alloying purposes is 1s. 6d. per lb. for the citron, orange, red, and extra red alloy, and 1s. 4d. per lb. for the yellow alloy.

Pin brass is a very good metal for alloying with silver to make silver solder ; the price is 1s. per lb.

GOLD ALLOYS IN SHEET AND WIRE.

Gold of various qualities is prepared by the refiners and bullion dealers for dentists and jewellers—

18-carat gold for dental plates, &c., .	66s. 6d. per oz.
,, green gold, ...	66s. 6d. ,,
,, red ,, special, . .	60s. 0d. ,,
10-carat gold, ...	39s. 0d. ,,
Gold for gilding solution, . . .	86s. 0d. ,,
,, in sheets, .	90s. 0d. ,,
Gold solder from   .   .   . 30s to 45s. 0d.   ,,
Silver ,,   ,,   .   . 2s. 6d. to 4s. 0d.   ,,

The refiners also offer great facilities to those who cannot conveniently prepare the gold they require, by melting and rolling alloyed gold and silver of every quality and size in sheet and in wire to order, guaranteeing that the metal supplied shall be equal to the standard quoted upon the invoice, and undertaking that, in the event of the work failing to pass the official test, an allowance will be made to the purchaser.

STANDARD GOLD FOR HALL MARKING.

Price in sheets, or in wire strips.

22-carat under 1 ounce,	82s. 6d. ; above, 80s. 0d. per ounce.
18 ,, ,, 1 ,,	67s. 6d. :	,,	66s. 6d.	..
15 ,, ,, 1 ,,	57s. 6d. :	,,	55s. 6d.	.,
12 ,, ,, 1 ,,	48s. 0d. :	,,	48s. 0d.	,,
9 ,, ,, 1 ,,	35s. 0d. :	,,	35s. 0d.	..

1s. per ounce is taken off the above prices for quantities of 20 ounces or more. Wire specially drawn to size, 1s. per ounce extra Special coloured gold alloy, 50s. per ounce. Gold solder, 45s. per ounce.

GENERAL CHARGE FOR MELTING GOLD.

Under 25 ounces,		1s. 0d.
,, 50 ,,		2s. 0d.
,, 75 ,,		3s. 0d.
,, 100 ,,		4s. 0d.

GENERAL CHARGE FOR MELTING SILVER.

Under 50 ounces,		1s. 0d.
,, 100 ,,		1s. 6d.
,, 200 ,,		2s. 6d.
,, 300 ,,		3s. 6d.

STANDARD SILVER FOR HALL MARKING.

Price in sheets, or in wire strips.

1 ounce and upwards,	.	.	.	2s. 10½d. per ounce.
20 ,, ,,	.	.	.	2s. 9½d. ,,
50 ,, ,,	.	.	.	2s. 9d. ,,
100 ,, ,,	.	.	.	2s. 8d. ,,

Wire is drawn to any shape and size at the rate of 4d. per ounce extra ; the above prices vary with the variations of the bullion market.

The foregoing list may be very useful to those manufacturers who have no appliances for melting and preparing the gold and silver. But those who have the apparatus for melting, rolling, and wire-drawing, will find it far cheaper to buy the constituent materials in the largest convenient quantities and to perform the necessary operations themselves, or have them performed under their supervision.

THE DECIMAL SYSTEM.

By the Weights and Measures Act, 1875, the adoption of the decimal system of weights, with the ounce troy and grain as basis, is made compulsory for goldsmiths, jewellers, silversmiths, and others. The following table will enable the operator to convert dwts. and grains into decimals of an ounce :—

Grains.	Ounces.	Grains.	Ounces.	Dwts.	Ounces.	Dwts.	Ounces.
1	·002	13	·027	1	·050	11	·550
2	·004	14	·029	2	·100	12	·600
3	·006	15	·031	3	·150	13	·650
4	·008	16	·033	4	·200	14	·700
5	·010	17	·035	5	·250	15	·750
6	·012	18	·037	6	·300	16	·800
7	·015	19	·040	7	·350	17	·850
8	·017	20	·042	8	·400	18	·900
9	·019	21	·044	9	.450	19	·950
10	·021	22	·046	10	.500	20	1·000
11	·023	23	·048				
12	·025	24	·050				

For Example:—Express 12 dwts. 6 grains in decimals of an ounce.
Opposite 12 dwts. will be found .   .   ·600 ounce.
,,   6 grains   ,,   .   .   ·012 ,,

Therefore 12 dwts. 6 grains is equivalent to   ·612   ,,

N.B.—In adding decimal quantities together, it is important to keep the decimal points under each other, thus—

$$0·175$$
$$0·325$$
$$0·725$$
$$1·200$$
$$4·100$$

Total. .   .   6·525 = 6 ounces 10 dwts. 12 grains.

ALLOYS AND THEIR PREPARATION.

The subject of this section is one of great importance to all who are engaged in the working of metals, and especially to those who are constantly preparing and working up alloys containing gold.   The intrinsic value of this metal makes it incumbent upon those who use it to exercise the greatest care in its preparation in the alloyed form.   The softness of the pure metal, and the consequent readiness with which it wears down, renders it necessary to alloy it with a cheaper metal, so as to reduce its cost, and to make it more capable of resisting ordinary wear.

Historical.—The mixing of metals for the purpose of modi-fying their properties was practised by the ancients, and was probably the immediate consequence of the development of the necessary metallurgical operations for the extraction of the then known metals from their ores.   For example, the early Greeks worked alloys of gold and silver, copper and tin, and silver and lead.   The use of brass also is of very ancient date, but it was not made directly from the metals copper and zinc, as the latter was not known in the metallic state until the thirteenth century. The alloy was probably first prepared from an ore containing both the metals; its composition was unknown. Much of the early knowledge of the character of metals, and the effects of mixing them together, is no doubt due to the old alchemists, who, in their efforts to convert the base metals into gold, made many useful discoveries.

The mixing of metals in definite proportions for the production of definite alloys is of more recent date. The necessity of the alloying metals being comparatively pure for the production of uniform alloys, was hardly recognised until the eighteenth century. In fact, by far the greater part of the useful knowledge of the metals and their alloys has been acquired during the last 150 years, and the work is still in progress.

Liquation of Metals.—All metals can be melted, and, when in the molten condition, can be more or less readily alloyed together. The most important point to the metal worker is whether or not the alloy remains practically perfect after solidification. It would seem, at first sight, that metals can be alloyed in all proportions, and that the alloy remains perfect on solidification. That this is not so in all cases can be easily proved by melting together lead and zinc in equal proportions, pouring the mixture, and allowing it to solidify. The lead almost entirely separates from the mixture, and settles to the bottom of the mould, carrying about 1·25 per cent. of zinc with it; the zinc rises to the top accompanied by about 1·5 per cent. of lead. Perfect alloys of lead and zinc can, therefore, only be obtained by keeping within these narrow limits. Fortunately, however, only a few metals separate in this pronounced way. Many metals may be mixed in various proportions, and the mixture will remain practically *homogeneous*, or the same throughout, on solidification. It may be taken for granted that all well-made alloys in common use are fairly homogeneous; if the alloys do not work well it may be attributed to want of homogeneity caused by imperfect mixing or other causes.

As is seen in the case of lead and zinc some metals do not separate perfectly, mixtures of them giving rise to two or more alloys of the metals in different proportions. The term **liquation** is used to denote this separation.

Nature of Alloys.—There are three principal ways of regarding the condition of the two metals in a bi-metallic alloy :—(1) One metal acts as a solvent and dissolves the other in much the same way that water dissolves salt; (2) the two metals are simply mechanically mixed together; (3) the two metals combine together chemically in definite proportions, and the compound thus formed is dissolved in, or mechanically mixed with, the excess of one of the metals. If there are several metals in the mixture two or more of these conditions may co-exist in the alloy. The effect of chemical combination is to considerably modify, if not entirely change, the properties of the reacting metals, with the production of a new body or bodies having entirely new properties. Thus copper and tin in certain proportions produce alloys in which the properties of the constituent metals are profoundly modified; the same is the case with gold and tin. In each case compounds of the two metals are formed, and it is probable that such compounds play an important part in alloys in which the properties of the constituent metals are considerably modified. But in making alloys for practical purposes the object is, in most cases, to only slightly modify the properties of one or more of the metals in the mixture. In fact, those alloys are most useful in which the constituents remain mechanically mixed together on solidification; and those metals which show the least tendency to form chemical compounds, give rise to alloys most nearly coinciding in properties with their constituents—that is, to alloys of distinctly metallic character which have the useful properties of malleability and ductility in sufficient degree to render them workable. For example, an alloy of copper and tin in which the tin exceeds 25 per cent. of the mixture is practically useless; but copper and gold may be alloyed in any proportions without serious alteration in the useful properties of the alloy. The tendency of copper and gold to unite chemically seems to be very feeble; the same may be said of silver and gold.

Metals possess two sets of properties—(1) chemical; (2) physical or mechanical. The most important changes effected by the alloying of metals are those which influence their physical properties. The physical and mechanical properties which the metal-worker has most to do with are fusibility, malleability, ductility, hardness, density, and colour. As regards chemical properties, he is most concerned with the action of the atmosphere and acids upon alloys during the processes of manufacture (annealing, pickling, &c.), and upon the surface of the finished article on standing. Gold is a soft, very malleable and ductile metal of great density and rich in colour. All these properties are affected by mixing it with another metal, but those metals are most suitable for alloying purposes which produce the smallest change in them. Copper and silver are the most suitable alloying metals: they increase the hardness of gold without seriously affecting its malleability and ductility. Pure gold is unaffected by the atmosphere, either at ordinary temperatures or when the metal is heated. It is also proof against the action of the common acids when used singly. Moreover, it confers its properties more or less upon copper and silver when these metals are alloyed with it. Thus, for example, 12-carat gold will withstand the action of nitric acid and of the atmosphere at ordinary temperatures, but some of the copper is oxidised during annealing.

With regard to the homogeneous character of ordinary gold alloys, Professor Roberts-Austen and others have proved that there is little evidence of liquation in gold of good standard, and it is probable that the same is practically true in the case of the poorer alloys, especially when they are well made.

As gold-platinum alloys are sometimes used it is well to bear in mind the experiments of Mr. Matthey upon such bodies. He cast an alloy containing 900 parts of gold and 100 parts of platinum in a spherical mould, cut a disc through the centre of the sphere, and assayed portions taken along a diameter of the disc. He found that the outside portions contained 900 of gold to 98 of platinum, and the centre 845 of gold to 146 of platinum. The experiments, therefore, prove that gold tends to free itself from platinum on solidification, and that a homogeneous alloy of the two metals cannot be obtained.

Eutectic Alloys.—When the solution of a salt in water is gradually cooled below the freezing point of water portions of the solution solidify, and if these solid masses are removed as fast as they form a solution containing a definite proportion of the salt is obtained. This solution has a definite freezing point depending upon the nature of the salt, and acts like a single chemical compound in always melting and freezing at the same temperature. Dr. Guthrie, who investigated these phenomena, extended his observations to alloys, regarding such bodies as solutions of one metal in another, and, therefore, analogous to salt solutions. He selected lead-tin alloys for his experiments on account of the ease with which they melt, and found that on cooling the molten alloys a separation of solid matter took place just as in the case of a salt solution. By separating the solid portions as they were formed he obtained a liquid mass, which solidified completely at 180° C. This alloy contains 34·7 per cent. of lead and 65·3 per cent. of tin, and has the lowest melting point of any alloy of lead and tin. Guthrie called it the **eutectic** alloy.

The introduction of the Le Chatelier pyrometer for the determination of high temperatures, and of improved automatic registering apparatus devised by Prof. Roberts-Austen,[*] has considerably increased the facilities for investigating the melting points of alloys. Much useful work, which will become of great practical value to the metal worker, is now being done. For example, the copper-zinc alloys have been examined, and it is found that, as a rule, two or more **eutectics** are present in each alloy, and that they exert considerable influence upon the physical and mechanical properties of the alloy. It has already been stated that definite compounds of metals with each other result

---

[*] *Introduction to the Study of Metallurgy*, 4th ed., p. 182.

in considerable modifications of the properties of the combining metals; such bodies are of very little practical use.   Eutectic alloys, however, are not themselves chemical compounds, but probably consist of definite compounds dissolved in an excess of one of the metals.   They exert most influence upon the mass of the alloy when their melting points are considerably below the point at which the main bulk of the alloy commences to solidify.   It has been found that the introduction of a small quantity of another metal may prevent the formation of a hurtful eutectic, and thus considerably improve some properties of the alloy.   Thus an alloy of 61 per cent. copper and 39 per cent. zinc had its tenacity considerably increased by the introduction of 1·5 per cent. of iron, and an eutectic of low-melting point present in the original alloy was found to have entirely disappeared.   Gold alloys have not been experimented with to any extent in this direction, but useful information of a practical character is sure to be forthcoming in the near future.   Why an alloy, carefully made of ordinarily pure metals, is defective ? and how the defect can be remedied ? are questions which will be answered by a further study of the melting points of such bodies.

Annealing Alloys.—During the processes of rolling and wire drawing most alloys are hardened ; this is caused by the straining of the ultimate particles or molecules of the mass.   This strain is released during annealing and the metal returns to its normal condition.   M. Charpy, M. Osmond, and Prof. Roberts-Austen have shown that annealing is effective at lower temperatures than is usually supposed.   Thus an alloy of gold and antimony, which is very crystalline when melted and poured into an ingot, can be annealed at a temperature of 250° C.   Its structure becomes minutely granular.   What is true of this alloy is also true of others.   Serious injury is often done by annealing at too high a temperature.

GOLD ALLOYS.

The properties which make gold so valuable in the arts have been fully described in the early part of this work ; and, taking into consideration the high intrinsic value and utility of gold, it may be considered the most perfect of metals.   But as pure gold is too soft for many manufacturing purposes it requires to be hardened by alloying it with other metals, such as silver and copper, in the proportions given in the following table of alloys. Some metals cannot be thus used, as the malleability and ductility of the gold are so reduced by them as to render it unfit for manufacturing purposes.

QUANTITIES OF ALLOY REQUIRED TO REDUCE STANDARD GOLD TO OTHER QUALITIES.

Qualities.	Standard Gold Contains.	Alloy to be Added.
22 carats.	22 parts fine gold.	None.
21 ,,	21 ,,	1 part.
20 ,,	20 ,,	2 parts.
19 ,,	19 ,,	3 ,,
18 ,,	18 ,,	4 ,,
17 ,,	17 ,,	5 ,,
16 ,,	16 ,,	6 ,,
15 ,,	15 ,,	7 ,,
14 ,,	14 ,,	8 ,,
13 ,,	13 ,,	9 ,,
12 ,,	12 ,,	10 ,,
11 ,,	11 ,,	11 ,,
10 ,,	10 ,,	12 ,,
9 ,,	9 ,,	13 ,,
8 ,,	8 ,,	14 ,,
7 ,,	7 ,,	15 ,,

The proportions of silver and copper will be found in the mixed alloys.

QUANTITIES OF ALLOY REQUIRED TO REDUCE FINE GOLD TO OTHER QUALITIES.

Qualities.	Fine Gold.	Alloy to be Added.	Qualities.	Fine Gold.	Alloy to be Added.
24 carats.	24 parts.	None.	15 carats.	15 parts.	9 parts.
23 ,,	23 ,,	1 part.	14 ,,	14 ,,	10 ,,
22 ,,	22 ,,	2 parts.	13 ,,	13 ,,	11 ,,
21 ,,	21 ,,	3 ,,	12 ,,	12 ,,	12 ,,
20 ,,	20 ,,	4 ,,	11 ,,	11 ,,	13 ,,
19 ,,	19 ,,	5 ,,	10 ,,	10 ,,	14 ,,
18 ,,	18 ,,	6 ,,	9 ,,	9 ,,	15 ,,
17 ,,	17 ,,	7 ,,	8 ,,	8 ,,	16 ,,
16 ,,	16 ,,	8 ,,	7 ,,	7 ,,	17 ,,

The proportions of silver and copper will be found in the mixed alloys.

To Alloy 1 Ounce of Standard Gold.

The following table shows the proportions of alloy to be added for making various qualities :—

Qualities.	Standard Gold.			Alloy to be added.			Total.		
	Oz.	dwt.	gr.	Ozs.	dwts.	grs.	Ozs.	dwts.	grs.
21 carats.	1	0	0	0	0	23	1	0	23
20 ,,	1	0	0	0	2	0	1	2	0
19 ,,	1	0	0	0	3	4	1	3	4
18 ,,	1	0	0	0	4	10	1	4	10
17 ,,	1	0	0	0	5	21	1	5	21
16 ,,	1	0	0	0	7	12	1	7	12
15 ,,	1	0	0	0	9	8	1	9	8
14 ,,	1	0	0	0	11	10	1	11	10
13 ,,	1	0	0	0	13	20	1	13	20
12 ,,	1	0	0	0	16	6	1	16	6
11 ,,	1	0	0	1	0	0	2	0	0
10 ,,	1	0	0	1	4	0	2	4	0
9 ,,	1	0	0	1	8	21	2	8	21
8 ,,	1	0	0	1	15	0	2	15	0
7 ,,	1	0	0	2	2	20	3	2	20

The proportions of silver and copper will be found in the mixed alloys.

To Alloy 1 Ounce of Fine Gold.

The following table shows the proportions of alloy to be added for making various qualities :—

Qualities.	Fine Gold.			Alloy to be added.			Total.		
	Oz.	dwt.	gr.	Ozs.	dwts.	grs.	Ozs.	dwts.	gr.s
23 carats.	1	0	0	0	0	20	1	0	20
22 ,,	1	0	0	0	1	18	1	1	18
21 ,,	1	0	0	0	2	20	1	2	20
20 ,,	1	0	0	0	4	0	1	4	0
19 ,,	1	0	0	0	5	6	1	5	6
18 ,,	1	0	0	0	6	16	1	6	16
17 ,,	1	0	0	0	8	5	1	8	5
16 ,,	1	0	0	0	10	0	1	10	0
15 ,,	1	0	0	0	12	0	1	12	0
14 ,,	1	0	0	0	14	6	1	14	6
13 ,,	1	0	0	0	16	22	1	16	22
12 ,,	1	0	0	1	0	0	2	0	0
11 ,,	1	0	0	1	3	15	2	3	15
10 ,,	1	0	0	1	8	0	2	8	0
9 ,,	1	0	0	1	13	8	2	13	8
8 ,,	1	0	0	2	0	0	3	0	0
7 ,,	1	0	0	2	8	12	3	8	12

The proportions of silver and copper will be found in the mixed alloys.

No. 1.—22-Carat Gold Alloy.

	Oz.	dwts.	grs.	Decimals.
Fine Gold,	0	18	10	0·920
,, Silver,	0	0	19	0·040
,, Copper,	0	0	19	0·040
	1	0	0	1·000

No. 2.—18-Carat Gold Alloy.

	Oz.	dwts.	grs.	Decimals.
Fine Gold,	0	15	0	0·750
,, Silver,	0	2	12	0·125
,, Copper,	0	2	12	0·125
	1	0	0	1·000

No. 3.—16-Carat Gold Alloy.

	Oz.	dwts.	grs.	Decimals.
Fine Gold,	0	13	6	0·6625
,, Silver,	0	1	12	0·0750
,, Copper,	0	5	6	0·2625
	1	0	0	1·0000

No. 4.—15-Carat Gold Alloy.

	Oz.	dwts.	grs.	Decimals.
Fine Gold,	0	12	12	0·625
,, Silver,	0	2	12	0·125
,, Copper,	0	5	0	0·250
	1	0	0	1·000

No. 5.—15-Carat Gold Alloy for Setting.

	Oz.	dwts.	grs.	Decimals.
Fine Gold,	0	12	12	0·625
,, Silver,	0	4	12	0·225
,, Copper,	0	3	0	0·150
	1	0	0	1·000

No. 6.—12-Carat Gold Alloy.

	Oz.	dwts.	grs.	Decimals.
Fine Gold,	0	10	0	0·500
,, Silver,	0	3	2	0·154
,, Copper,	0	6	22	0·346
	1	0	0	1·000

No. 7.—10-Carat Gold Alloy.

	Oz.	dwts.	grs.	Decimals.
Fine Gold, .	0	8	8	0·416
,, Silver, .	0	4	2	0·204
,, Copper,	0	7	14	0·380
	1	0	0	1·000

No. 8.—9-Carat Gold Alloy.

	Oz.	dwts.	grs.	Decimals.
Fine Gold, .	0	7	12	0·375
.. Silver, .	0	7	0	0·350
., Copper, .	0	5	12	0·275
	1	0	0	1·000

No. 9.—15-Carat Red Gold Alloy.

	Oz.	dwts.	grs.	Decimals.
Fine Gold, .	0	12	12	0·625
,, Silver, .	0	0	12	0·025
., Copper, .	0	7	0	0·350
	1	0	0	1·000

No. 10.—15-Carat Red Gold Alloy.

	Oz.	dwts.	grs.	Decimals.
Fine Gold, .	0	12	12	0·625
.. Copper, .	0	7	12	0·375
	1	0	0	1·000

No. 11.—15-Carat Green Gold Alloy.

	Oz.	dwts.	grs.	Decimals.
Fine Gold, .	0	12	12	0·625
,, Silver, .	0	7	12	0·375
	1	0	0	1·000

DRY COLOURING GOLD ALLOYS.

No. 12.—18-Carat Alloy.

	Oz.	dwts.	grs.	Decimals.
Fine Gold, .	0	15	0	0·750
.. Silver, .	0	2	4	0·108
.. Copper, .	0	2	20	0·142
	1	0	0	1·000

No. 13.—Another 18-Carat Alloy.

	Oz.	dwts.	grs.	Decimals.
Fine Gold, .	0	18	0	0·900
,, Silver, .	0	2	18	0·137
,, Copper, .	0	3	18	0·187
	1	4	12	1·224

N.B.—For hall-marking it is always safe to add 2 grains of fine gold per ounce to each of the above alloys (Nos. 1 to 11).

No. 14.—Alloy for Dry Coloured Rings.

	Oz.	dwts.	grs.	Decimals.
Fine Gold, .	1	0	0	1·000
,, Silver, .	0	4	6	0·212
,, Copper,.	0	4	6	0·212
	1	8	12	1·424

No. 15.—Another 18-Carat Alloy.

	Oz.	dwts.	grs.	Decimals.
Fine Gold, .	0	15	0	0·750
,, Silver, .	0	2	14	0·129
,, Copper,.	0	2	10	0·121
	1	0	0	1·000

No. 16.—Coloured Gold Alloy.

	Oz.	dwts.	grs.	Decimals.
Fine Gold, .	0	11	0	0·550
,, Silver, .	0	2	0	0·100
,, Copper, .	0	7	0	0·350
	1	0	0	1·000

No. 17.—Coloured Gold Alloy.

	Oz.	dwts.	grs.	Decimals.
Fine Gold, .	0	11	6	0·5625
,, Silver, .	0	2	12	0·1250
,, Copper,.	0	6	6	0·3125
	1	0	0	1·0000

No. 18.—Coloured Gold Alloy.

	Oz.	dwts.	grs.	Decimals.
Fine Gold, .	0	11	12	0·5750
,, Silver, .	0	2	6	0·1125
,, Copper, .	0	6	6	0·3125
	1	0	0	1·0000

No. 19.—Alloy for Gold Pens.

	Oz.	dwts.	grs.	Decimals.
Fine Gold, .	1	0	0	1·000
,, Silver, .	0	5	0	0·250
,. Copper, .	0	7	18	0·387
,, Spelter,.	0	1	6	0·063
	1	14	0	1·700

No. 20.—Alloy for Common Gold Pens.

	Oz.	dwts.	grs.	Decimals.
Fine Gold, .	1	0	0	1·000
,, Silver, .	1	0	0	1·000
,, Copper, .	1	0	0	1·000
	3	0	0	3·000

For the decoration of articles of jewellery, &c., with leaves, flowers, and ornaments of different colours the following alloys will be found useful :—

No. 21.—Green Gold Alloy.

	Oz.	dwts.	grs.	Decimals.
Fine Gold, .	1	0	0	1·000
,, Silver, .	0	6	16	0·333
	1	6	16	1·333

No. 22.—Green Gold Alloy.

	Oz.	dwts.	grs.	Decimals.
Fine Gold, .	1	0	0	1·000
,, Silver, .	0	4	4	0·208
	1	4	4	1·208

No. 23.—Red Gold Alloy.

	Oz.	dwts.	grs.	Decimals.
Fine Gold, .	1	0	0	1·000
,, Copper, .	0	10	0	0·500
	1	10	0	1·500

No. 24.—Red Gold Alloy.

	Oz.	dwts.	grs.	Decimals.
Fine Gold, .	1	0	0	1·000
,, Copper, .	0	5	0	0·250
	1	5	0	1·250

No. 25.—Blue Gold Alloy.

	Oz.	dwts.	grs.	Decimals.
Fine Gold,	0	18	0	0·900
,, Iron,	0	6	0	0·300
	1	4	0	1·200

No. 26.—White Gold Alloy.

	Oz.	dwts.	grs.	Decimals.
Fine Gold, .	0	12	0	0·600
,, Silver, .	0	12	0	0·600
	1	4	0	1·200

No. 27.—Alloy of Gold for Enamelling.

	Oz.	dwts.	grs.	Decimals.
Fine gold, .	1	0	0	1·000
,, silver, .	0	1	12	0·075
,, copper, .	0	2	12	0·125
	1	4	0	1·200

No. 28.—Another Alloy, Cheaper.

	Oz.	dwts.	grs.	Decimals.
Fine gold, .	1	0	0	1·000
,, silver, .	0	9	0	0·450
,, copper, .	0	3	12	0·175
	1	12	12	1·625

No. 29.—For Transparent Enamelling.

	Ozs.	dwts.	grs.	Decimals.
Fine gold, . .	1	0	0	1·000
,, silver, . .	0	14	0	0·700
,, copper, . .	0	6	0	0·300
	2	0	0	2·000

No. 30.—Solder for Enamelled Work.

	Ozs.	dwts.	grs.	Decimals.
Fine gold, .	1	0	0	1·000
,, silver, .	1	0	0	1·000
,, copper, .	0	10	0	0·500
Silver solder,	0	8	8	0·417
	2	18	8	2·917

No. 31.—Alloy for Chains.

	Oz.	dwts.	grs.	Decimals.
Fine gold, .	0	11	6	0·562
,, silver, .	0	2	5	0·111
,, copper, .	0	6	13	0·327
	1	0	0	1·000

TO REDUCE VARIOUS QUALITIES OF GOLD TO STANDARDS SUITABLE
FOR SEVERAL PROCESSES OF COLOURING MENTIONED.

As some manufacturers prefer using **Coin Gold** instead of
Fine Gold, the following tables will show the proportions for
reducing 22-carat coins to the various standard qualities.

No. 32.—The Composition of an Ounce of Sovereign Gold--22-carats.

	Oz.	dwts.	grs.	Decimals.
Fine Gold, .	0	18	8	0·917
,, Copper, .	0	1	16	0·083
	1	0	0	1·000

No. 33.—To reduce 22-carat to 18-carat suitable for Dry Colouring.

	Oz.	dwts.	grs.	Decimals.
Sovereign Gold,	1	0	12	1·025
Fine Silver, .	0	2	0	0·100
,, Copper, .	0	2	12	0·125
	1	5	0	1·250

No. 34.—To reduce 22-carat to 16-carat suitable for Wet Colouring.

	Oz.	dwts.	grs.	Decimals.
Sovereign Gold, . .	1	0	12	1·0250
Fine Silver, . . .	0	2	6	0·1125
,, Copper, . . .	0	5	6	0·2625
	1	8	0	1·4000

No. 35.—To reduce 22-carat to 15-carat suitable for Wet Colouring.

	Oz.	dwts.	grs.	Decimals.
Sovereign Gold,	1	0	12	1·025
Fine Silver, .	0	3	0	0·150
,, Copper, .	0	6	12	0·325
	1	10	0	1·500

No. 36.—To reduce 22-carat to 14-carat suitable for Wet Colouring.

	Oz.	dwts.	grs.	Decimals.
Sovereign Gold,	1	0	12	1·0250
Fine Silver, .	0	3	18	0·1875
,, Copper, .	0	7	18	0·3875
	1	12	0	1·6000

No. 37.—To reduce 22-Carat to 13-Carat suitable for Wet Colouring.

	Oz. dwts. grs.			Decimals.
Sovereign Gold, . .	1	0	12	1·025
Fine Silver, . . .	0	4	10	0·221
,, Copper, . . .	0	9	14	0·479
	1	14	12	1·725

No. 38.—To reduce 18-Carat to 16-Carat suitable for Wet Colouring.

	Oz. dwts. grs.			Decimals.
18-Carat Scrap, . .	1	0	0	1·0000
Fine Silver, . . .	0	0	6	0·0125
,, Copper, . . .	0	2	6	0·1125
	1	2	12	1·1250

No. 39.—To reduce 18-Carat to 15-Carat suitable for Wet Colouring.

	Oz. dwts. grs.			Decimals.
18-Carat Scrap, .	1	0	0	1·000
Fine Silver, . .	0	1	0	0·050
,, Copper, . .	0	3	0	0·150
	1	4	0	1·200

No. 40.—To reduce 18-Carat to 14-Carat suitable for Wet Colouring.

	Oz. dwts. grs.			Decimals.
18-Carat Scrap, .	1	0	0	1·000
Fine Silver, .	0	1	0	0·050
,, Copper, .	0	4	18	0·236
	1	5	18	1·286

No. 41.—To reduce 18-Carat to 13-Carat suitable for Wet Colouring.

	Oz. dwts. grs			Decimals.
18-Carat Scrap, . .	1	0	0	1·000
Fine Silver, . .	0	1	12	0·075
,, Copper, . .	0	6	6	0·312
	1	7	18	1·387

No. 42.   **Silver Solder Alloy.**

	Oz. dwts. grs.			Decimals.
Fine Silver, .	1	0	0	1·000
,, Copper, .	0	5	0	0·250
Composition, .	0	5	0	0·250
	1	10	0	1·500

4

No. 43.—Best Easy Silver Solder.

	Oz.	dwts.	grs.	Decimals.
Fine Silver, .	1	0	0	1·000
Pin Brass, .	0	10	0	0·500
	1	10	0	1·500

NOTE.—The process of melting the above solder is to place the silver in the crucible first, with a little borax as flux. When the silver is in a molten state, the brass pins (which should be wrapped in paper) are gently dropped in ; as soon as the brass pins have melted give the crucible a slight shake to properly mix the alloy, and then gently pour the mixture into an ingot mould. Brass pins are used because the good quality of the solder depends upon the alloy of which they are composed.

Another alloy for a good white silver solder may be obtained by taking the following proportions :—To every dwt. of coin silver add 8 grains of English brass pins, and melt the mixture in the way described in the preceding paragraph.

THE PROCESS OF MELTING.

A good furnace is required for melting gold or silver satisfactorily. Goldsmiths generally use a wind furnace about 9 inches square and 18 inches deep, lined with fire-brick and cased with

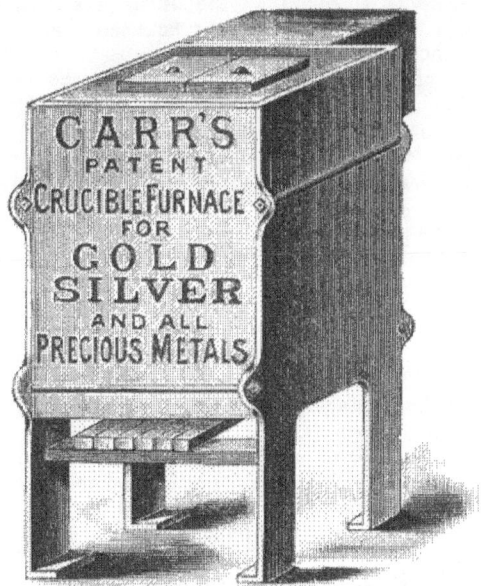

Fig. 1.—Carr's Patent Crucible Casting Furnace.

ordinary bricks. The horizontal draught hole is 6 inches × 3 inches, and the capacity of the ashpit should be at least equal to that of the furnace. The bars, six in number, should be about 1 inch thick and 16 inches long, tapered at each end, so that when the melting is done, the bars can be withdrawn and the fire allowed to fall into the ashpit. The furnace must be connected with a chimney at least 30 or 40 feet high, in order to obtain a strong draught. The mouth of the furnace is usually closed by two fire-bricks, each being strongly clamped with a piece of flat bar iron secured firmly. To regulate the draught a suitable damper is fixed in the flue at a convenient height.

The common form, however, has been greatly improved upon lately. Fig. 1 illustrates one of Carr's patent crucible casting furnaces adapted for the use of goldsmiths, jewellers, and gold and silver refiners. It is composed of a frame of cast iron lined internally with fire-brick, so that there is no need for outside brickwork. It has several advantages over the old-fashioned brick furnace. In the first place, it is easily fixed and need not be taken down for relining; secondly, there is great saving in wear and tear of crucibles, furnace, and in coke; thirdly, more heats of metal can be obtained per day, as well as for each crucible. The fire-brick lining in the front is not built down to the bottom, but a rectangular space is left above the fire bars; this arrangement, which allows the air to pass from the front over the bars, as well as from below between them, constitutes the basis of the patent.

This class of furnace has been supplied to the Birmingham Technical School and gives satisfaction. These furnaces are also made with wrought-iron frames instead of cast iron: the former, being much stronger and lighter, are very convenient for exportation, and have been adopted by several leading manufacturers.

The processes of preparing the sweepings and polishings described in a later chapter likewise require that the furnace be well constructed.

Crucibles for Melting and Refining.—There are several kinds of crucibles used by goldsmiths, silversmiths, and refiners, the most generally used being "Morgan's patent crucibles," represented by Fig. 2. Their quality is uniform; they withstand a great heat without danger, and their average durability for gold and silver alloys, copper, and other metals is forty to fifty pourings; in some cases one hundred melts have been obtained from the same pot. There are other kinds known as the "clay crucibles." Fig. 3 represents the form called the "Battersea round crucible," which is usually sold in nests containing nine crucibles each. Fig. 4 illustrates the kind used by the refiners and goldsmiths of London and Birmingham called the "London round crucible." Fig. 5 represents the kind known as the "skittle pot," which is particularly well suited for most refining purposes ; the constricted form of the top prevents the boiling over of the fluxes.   The author has used the above-mentioned forms and has found them to be most satisfactory.

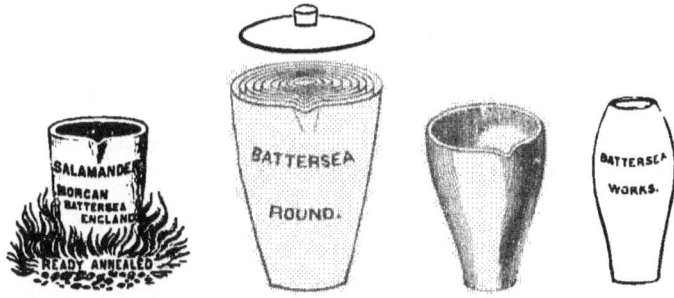

Fig. 2.—Morgan's   Fig. 3.—Battersea   Fig. 4.—London   †Fig. 5.
Patent Crucible.   Round Crucible.   Round Crucible. Skittle Pot.

There are also the " Battersea triangular crucible," the " Hessian clay crucible," and the " blacklead crucible."   A new crucible is now being put upon the market by the Carbon Crucible Syndicate ; it gets hot very rapidly on the fire, and meltings can be made in it with much greater rapidity than in either the clay or the blacklead crucible, but it is not so durable as the latter.   Another advantage is that the carbon forming the material in this crucible largely prevents the oxidation of copper in the making of gold, silver, and copper alloys.

ALLOYING OF GOLD.

The next process to be considered is the preparation of the gold alloys.   When alloying gold, strict care should be observed in mixing the proper portions for the various qualities of gold : each part must be accurately weighed and a note of the weight and quality of each mixture should be put with it, as different qualities require different treatment in the melting (see pp. 53-58).

Scales and Weights.—Fig. 6 represents the form of balance generally used by the bullion dealer and the goldsmith for weighing the precious metal, and Fig. 7 the weights ; the larger sizes are called " cup " weights, and are usually made from 1 oz. to 20 ozs. ; the smaller sizes are circular discs having weights ranging from 0·010 to 0·500 of an oz., and thin square weights from ·001 to ·005 of an oz.—that is, from $\frac{1}{2}$ a grain to 10 dwts. of the old troy weight.

Preparation for Melting Gold Alloys.—Having weighed out the different metals for particular qualities of gold, the next process is that of melting them into bars of alloy. This process is very important, as much depends upon the melting ; for just as a house with a faulty foundation is sure to be ruined, so gold and alloys which have not been properly melted and cast will be useless for making up into articles of any description. A few practical hints may therefore be of service to those who wish to learn the best method of bringing their work to a successful issue.

As a rule, the gold, silver, and copper, as purchased from the bullion dealer, is in each case sufficiently pure for general manu-

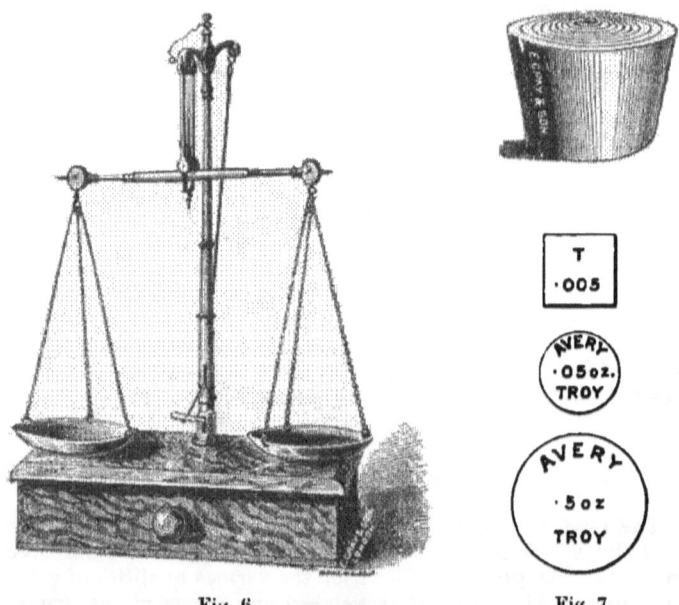

Fig. 6.   Fig. 7.

facture, but great care is required in melting and casting the precious metal into perfect bars for manipulation.

In the first place, gold and its alloys should be melted in the best plumbago crucibles (Fig. 2). These crucibles should be carefully annealed in an inverted position before using, as this will enable them to be used a great many times. New crucibles should be rubbed inside with powdered charcoal, in order to prevent any particles of metal adhering to them. The copper should be placed in the crucible first, then the silver and the gold, and over all a layer of powdered charcoal to prevent the surface oxidising. In making an alloy, of which zinc, composition, or brass forms one of the constituents, such metal must be added after the others have melted owing to the volatility of the zinc.

The zinc alloy should be held by the tongs inside the pot until it is nearly melted before allowing it to fall into the molten metal already in the pot, as this prevents chilling of the alloy. But in every case when melting gold alloys it is absolutely necessary to vigorously stir the liquid mixture with a red-hot iron rod, for the purpose of promoting an intimate union between the constituent parts of the alloy. While the gold is in the process of melting, the mould (or "ingot" as it is called in the trade) should be prepared, and made ready by one of the following methods :—

Before liquid metal of any kind is poured into a mould, the latter should be made warm ; in fact, it must not be either too hot or too cold, as both extremes are dangerous ; if too cold, and, therefore, probably damp, it will cause the gold to spit up in the air, so that some of it will be lost ; if too hot, the metal will stick to the sides. In order to prevent this, as also to assist in producing a clean surface to the bar, the mould should be either smoked or greased, a process which can be readily performed without preventing the operator from simultaneously keeping a sharp eye upon the crucible in the fire. The gold is quite ready for pouring when the liquid has the appearance of the yolk of an egg, is quite tranquil and free from spitting or bubbles, and has a thin layer of powdered charcoal covering its surface. When pouring, great care should be taken not to allow any of the charcoal to enter the mould, as its presence therein causes the surface of the bar of gold to be defective. This may be prevented by carefully clearing off the charcoal from the mouth of the crucible by means of a piece of firewood (preferably poplar wood) held in the left hand, while pouring with the right.

The charcoal to be used in the melting of gold alloys should be exceedingly pure and free from any kind of grit or coke dust. Although the gold ingots thus produced may seem to be perfect castings, they may crack while being rolled, a defect which arises from the brittleness caused by the presence of impurities. As such bars cannot be rolled, the only remedy is to remelt them and add a reagent which will remove the impurities. Several reagents have been used and recommended by goldsmiths for the toughening of gold, such as those containing chlorine—as common salt, bichloride of mercury, and sal ammoniac. The author does not advise the use of common salt, as it produces a liquid slag which is apt to run into the mould along with the gold and thus impart an irregular surface to the bar. Borax will produce a similar effect if used in excess. When a bar has cracked in the rolling process, the fracture should be carefully examined; if it has a close grain and a pale yellow colour, it is an indication that lead or tin is present; but if it has a dull brown colour, iron or some other foreign matter is the cause of the brittleness. The author's remedy is to add to the gold alloy, while in the process of remelting, a small quantity of bichloride of mercury with a little charcoal, vigorously stirring the liquid alloy with a red-hot iron rod, and then adding one spoonful of a mixture consisting of 1 part sal ammoniac and 3 parts charcoal. The last addition should be made just before pouring, while stirring the gold with a wooden stick. When the mixture has become tranquil it is poured carefully into the mould. In nine cases out of ten this experiment has proved successful. Should, however, the impurities be stubborn, all difficulties will be removed by reducing the quality of the gold. The quality of gold generally used for setting precious stones in requires to be soft and of such a fineness that the metal will cut clear and bright in the process of setting. The best reagent to use in such cases is a mixture of one part sal ammoniac and two parts charcoal powder, of which one spoonful must be added to the gold when in a liquid state; this should render the gold soft and ensures a clean and bright ingot.

Bars of Gold require to be cast in forms most suitable for the different classes of work they are intended for. Thus bars intended for " sheet " gold should be broad and thin, while those intended for wire strips should be thick and narrow, so that when rolled to the required size in the wire gauge they may be readily slit into long strips prior to being drawn into wire (see p. 60).

Ingot Moulds.— To produce bars of gold or other metals of various thicknesses and sizes, ingot moulds

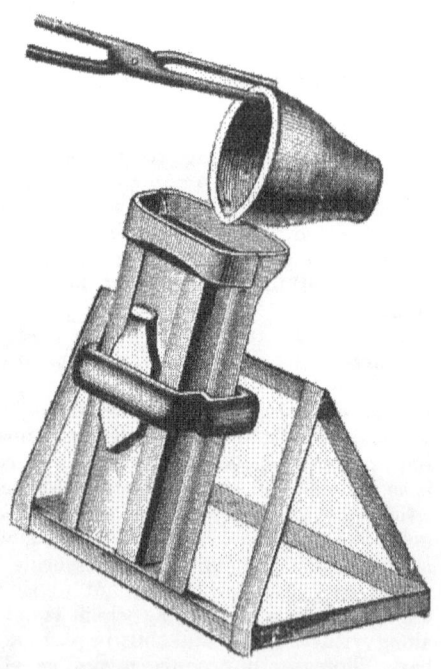

Fig. 8. Improved Ingot Mould.

of different sizes are required. Fig. 8 illustrates one of the improved ingot moulds. Its advantages over the old-shaped mould are considered to be that it has (1) an improved tundish-shaped mouth whereby a free and perfect rest is secured for the crucible while pouring, either on the side or at the end, and (2) that it has an opening sufficiently large to allow of the gold being poured without any risk of it being spilled. The mould is firmly held together by means of steel clamps and a wedge or set pin; the inside is planed perfectly true all over so as to make the edges of the casting even and smooth.

MELTING GOLD AND SILVER.

Very useful and inexpensive gas appliances have been introduced by Messrs. Fletcher & Co., of Warrington, for melting small bars of gold of different qualities, in weights varying from 3 to 20 ozs. The author has used them successfully for severa years.

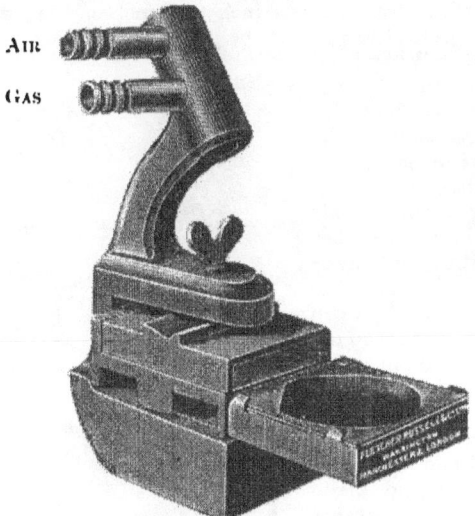

Fig. 9.— Improved Apparatus for Melting Gold.
(Engraving slightly under half-size.)

Fig. 9 represents an improved melting arrangement constructed to melt a bar of 15-carat gold weighing 18 ozs., or a bar of 18-carat gold weighing 20 ozs., in five to six minutes. The process is as follows :—

Melting Gold or Silver rapidly without the use of a Furnace.—The two parts of the ingot mould slide on each other,

Fig. 10.—Foot Blower.

and can be so arranged as to allow of bars of gold or silver being cast to any width from ¼ of an inch to 3 inches. The mould is warmed and greased to prevent the gold from spitting and from sticking to it. When fixed firmly in position by the thumb screw as shown in Fig. 9, the gas tube of the apparatus is connected with the india-rubber tube from the gas supply, and the air tube with the india-rubber tube from the foot blower (Fig. 10). The gold or silver is placed in the open crucible, the gas turned on, and the blower set in action by the foot. The gas jet, aided by a little borax as flux, rapidly melts the metal. When properly melted, the liquid metal should have the appearance of the yolk of an egg; it is then lightly stirred with a piece of wood in order to ensure the thorough mixing of the alloy. When ready

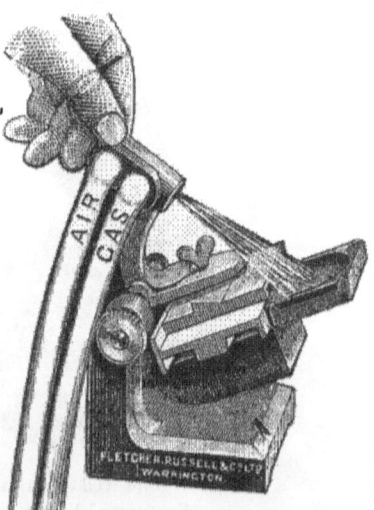

Fig. 11.—Improved Melting Apparatus (small size).

for pouring, the whole apparatus is carefully tilted towards the operator, when the liquid metal runs into the ingot mould. The mould is opened with a pair of gas pliers and the bar turned out quite clear and sound.

Melting Scrap Gold.—If the scrap is bulky, a carbon block is used in order to melt it into a lump before putting it into the open crucible.   The author has, however, found that it is much better and quicker to fill the open crucible with as much as it will hold and to make frequent additions to the mass as it melts, until all is used.

The small sized improved melting arrangement on a swivel stand, shown in Fig. 11, is constructed to melt a bar of gold weighing from 2 to 5 ozs. in about two minutes.   It resembles the larger form in general principle, but differs in the ingot and crucible being movable on a swivel fixed to a heavy cast-iron stand ; its object is to prevent the risk of the apparatus being pulled over by the weight of the rubber tube when disengaged from the hand.   It is only used for small quantities.

CHAPTER IV.

ROLLING AND SLITTING GOLD.

Cost of Rolling Gold.—In order to prevent any loss in rolling the rough bars, the ingots must have all the loose ragged pieces removed by filing. Each bar is then carefully weighed, the weight entered into the mill book, and the bar sent to the mill with instructions to be rolled to the sizes mentioned in the book.

TABLE SHOWING COST OF ROLLING GOLD.

Ozs.	s. F.	Ozs.	s. D.	Ozs.	s. D.
Under, . . . 3	0 6	42	3 1	76	5 5
Above 3 oz. and under:— 9	0 9	43	3 1	77	5 6
10	0 10	44	3 2	78	5 6
11	0 11	45	3 3	79	5 7
12	0 11	46	3 4	80	5 8
13	1 0	47	3 5	81	5 9
14	1 1	48	3 6	82	5 10
15	1 2	49	3 6	83	5 11
16	1 3	50	3 7	84	6 0
17	1 4	51	3 8	85	6 0
18	1 4	52	3 8	86	6 1
19	1 5	53	3 9	87	6 1
20	1 6	54	3 10	88	6 2
21	1 7	55	3 11	89	6 3
22	1 8	56	4 0	90	6 4
23	1 9	57	4 1	91	6 4
24	1 10	58	4 2	92	6 5
25	1 11	59	4 3	93	6 6
26	2 0	60	4 4	94	6 6
27	2 1	61	4 5	95	6 7
28	2 2	62	4 6	96	6 8
29	2 3	63	4 7	97	6 9
30	2 4	64	4 8	98	6 10
31	2 5	65	4 9	99	6 11
32	2 6	66	4 10	100	7 0
33	2 6	67	4 11	101 }	
34	2 7	68	5 0	to }	7 6
35	2 8	69	5 1	120 }	
36	2 9	70	5 1	to }	8 3
37	2 9	71	5 2	130 }	
38	2 10	72	5 3	to }	9 0
39	2 11	73	5 3	140 }	
40	3 0	74	5 4	to }	9 6
41	3 0	75	5 4	150 }	

The gold is generally taken first to the clerk in charge of the office, who weighs it and checks the weight. If correct, the bearer is sent into the mill with a note for the roller responsible for rolling and slitting the gold as required. When finished, the gold is returned to the office and again weighed; if it is short in weight the bearer returns to the mill for all that may be wanting.

The foregoing table shows the charges made for rolling or slitting gold at the Birmingham mills.

Rolling and Slitting.—The process now to be considered is that of rolling the gold after it has been melted and cast into ingots. This is effected by passing the bars through a pair of large steel rolls which are made to revolve in opposite directions by means of powerful spur wheels. After each passage of the bar the rolls are pressed down a little by large screws, thereby flattening out the gold at each pressure. When the bar has passed through a few times it becomes hard; and if passed through too many times it will crack on the edges. Therefore to roll gold successfully, it should be frequently softened by annealing so as to counteract the hardening caused by pressure. This annealing is effected by making the metal red hot in a muffle heated by flame.

The annealer in charge of the muffle has a large movable sheet-iron pan upon which the metal to be annealed is placed. The pan is put into the muffle, allowed to remain there a short time and withdrawn when the metal is red hot; the gold is then taken off by means of a pair of tongs, placed upon the floor to cool, and again passed through the rolling machine. The rolling and annealing are repeated until the size required is obtained. If the bar is to be drawn into wire a somewhat different process is adopted. The bar is first rolled to a given size in the wire gauge (as some manufacturers require a thicker wire than others do), then annealed and afterwards slit. This process is performed by a pair of overlapping circular-cutting rolls, each of which has a number of regularly cut slots, whereby the bar is slit into a number of square wire strips. These strips may also be cut with large lever shears, or by the improved circular shears.

The processes of rolling and slitting of gold and other metals are generally performed at steam rolling mills, where a number of different sized flattening rolls and slitting rolls are kept in motion suitable for every kind of metal, under the charge of rollers, wire-drawers, and annealers, who have a thorough knowledge of the different kinds of metal which come under their charge. Certain qualities of gold, more especially the hard gold alloys used for pin stems and brooch-tong wire, require careful treatment.

LABOUR-SAVING APPLIANCES.

In accordance with the spirit of this age of mechanical labour-saving contrivances, these are as necessary to the goldsmith and jeweller as to other manufacturers. This want has been specially supplied by Mr. Mark Morton, the inventor of the flattening mills, wire-drawing blocks, wire rolls, &c., which are now so largely used in the goldsmiths' workshops. The following is a description of the more important apparatus of this class.

Flattening Mills.—These are among the most important appliances of the practical goldsmith, but more than any other

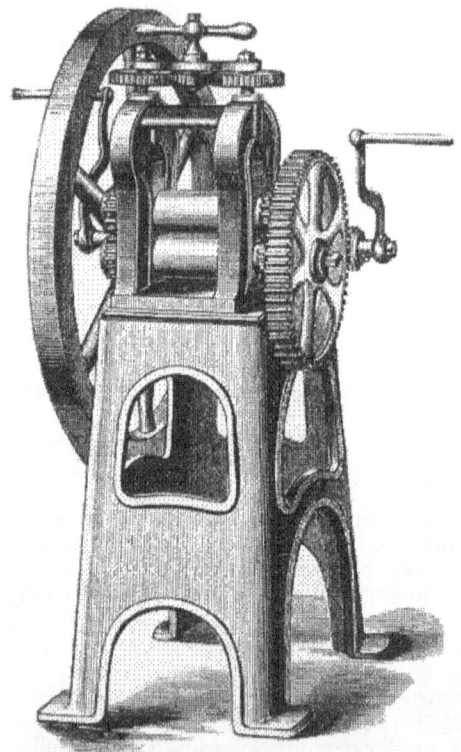

Fig. 12.—Hand-power Roller.

apparatus they require in their construction a special knowledge of the process of hardening, and great skill in the lapping and polishing of an accurate pair of hard, solid, cast-steel rolls, so that they will bear the heavy strain required to reduce gold and silver direct from the ingot, and yet retain the true surface necessary for reducing gold to nearly the thickness of tissue paper.

Fig. 13.—A Motive Power Rolling Mill.

Several types of rolls have been invented both for hand and motive power, ranging from small hand rolls to a complete mill. Fig. 12 will give a very good idea of a most useful mill adapted for hand power.

This particular kind of mill is most useful as it occupies but little space and the rolls can be changed in a few minutes. The mill is fixed on a substantial square stand; it has simultaneous equal roll pressure motion, with gun-metal wheels, steel pressure screws, solid cast-steel rolls (hardened and lapped perfectly true), a pair of malleable-iron double-shrouded pinions, multiplying power gearings, &c.

Fig. 13 illustrates a more powerful mill adapted for easily breaking down ingots of gold or silver from 50 to 100 ozs. in weight; it is worked by steam or by a gas engine of small motive power. This improved rolling mill has the following special features :—The whole mill is fixed on a heavy planed iron bed

Fig. 14.—Engraved Rolls.

and substantial iron stands, which are simply laid on any floor like a common lathe, thus saving the expensive foundation necessary in the old type of mill. It is also fitted with a fly-

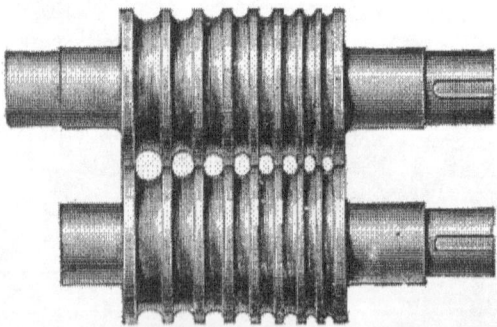

Fig. 15.—Wire Rolls.

wheel driving pulley as shown in the illustration. It has substantial compound spur gearing and double-shrouded malleable-iron pinions which are capable of producing great multiplying power. The rolls are driven by patent hollow-helical, malleable-iron, double-shrouded pinions running in patent solid brackets, and connect both breaking spindles. By this means a smooth worm-like motion is given to the rolls which roll out the metal through the guides perfectly smooth and glossy. A pair of wire rolls can be fitted into the same frame in a few minutes which will emboss various pattern wires like those shown in Fig. 14, and also wire rolls capable of breaking down cast wire strips from 1 inch square to $\frac{3}{16}$ inch round or square as required (Fig 15).

By the introduction of Morton's patent adjustable roll equal pressure indicator, rolling is made exceedingly easy ; this contrivance shows at a glance the exact distance the rolls are apart from each other, and regulates the amount of draft put on each time for any thickness of metal, while the simultaneous motion wheels enable both pressure screws to be instantly turned, thus forming a most complete mill which will break down ingots or wire strips with one set of rolls and will do flattening and finishing with the other set of rolls.

CHAPTER V.

THE WORKSHOP AND TOOLS.

The workshop should be well-fitted with the necessary requirements of the trade, and, in order to produce perfect work, the
tools used must be perfect. In the first place, it is absolutely
necessary that the tools and appliances should be compact and
well arranged, and the method of work well organised, because,
as the tools are usually small and numerous, a great saving of
time is effected if everything is available when and where it is
wanted.

The Work-table or Board.—This is the first requisite, and is
generally constructed of strong oak-board, about 1½ inches thick;
in some cases three, four, or five semi-circular hollows are cut

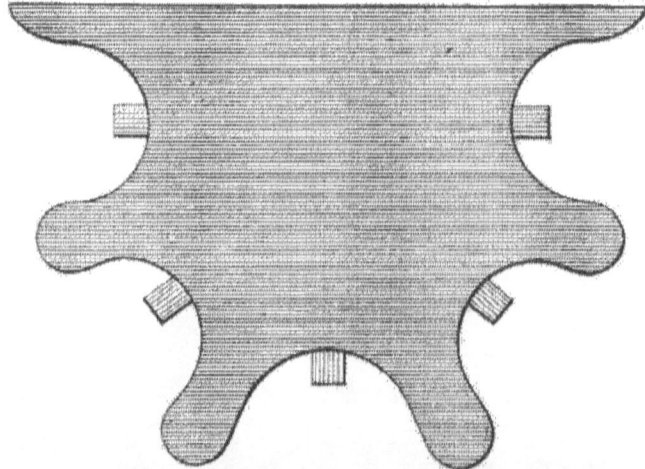

Fig. 16.—Work-table with Semi-circular Hollows.

out of the boards as shown in Fig. 16. This board should be
fixed firmly against a well-lighted window, and be supported by
legs of a sufficient height to enable the workman to sit with com-
fort upon a small stool. By this arrangement, in a well-lighted
workshop, with, say, four boards of five hollows each, twenty
men can work with ease. Fastened firmly underneath each

5

board five "Jeweller skins" are placed, one round each semi-circular portion. This skin is formed of tanned leather of soft finish, and is used for the purpose of catching the filings, termed "Lemel," produced in the process of filing up the work. Some goldsmiths fit a semi-circular tray in the skin; this tray has a sieve in the centre, with a movable box fitted underneath, which forms a receptacle for the lemel; by sweeping them into the box the filings are prevented from getting upon the tools and a waste of gold is avoided. The brush generally used for this purpose is the well-known hare's-foot. In the centre of each place is the indispensable "peg," which is used for the purpose of filing the work against; it is made of box or other hard wood. Fitted underneath the peg is the drawer for keeping some of the many sizes and shapes of tools necessary in the manufacture of wrought goldsmith's work; each place is also fitted with what is termed a "side light," for solder-ing purposes; and in the centre of the board is a gas jet (many are now fitted with the incandescent or electric light), which affords artificially the light required by the five work-men. When a strong, bright light is required, the "glass globe," filled with water, or a lens (Fig. 17), is used to concentrate the light upon the work undergoing manipulation.

Fig. 17.—Lens.

The **Vice Bench** is usually made of strong oak, firmly fixed against the wall, and may be fitted with the new parallel vice (Fig. 18), which can be used for the pur-pose of wire-draw-ing, &c.

The **Draw Bench**, which is used for the purpose of what is called "breaking down" wire, or for drawing tubes, is usually made of strong beech wood; it is about 6 feet long, and fitted with a strong leather strap or chain, fixed at one end round a pivot worked by a hand wheel; at the other end of the strap or chain there is an iron triangular ring in which the draw-pliers work.

Fig. 18.—Patent Movable Parallel Vice.

At the end of the bench is fixed an iron stay with two forks. The draw-plate (Fig. 19) is put on the off-side of the stay, and

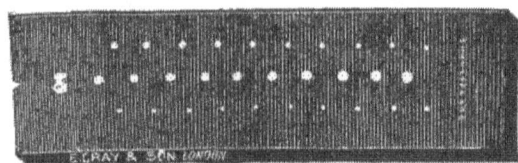

Fig. 19.—Steel Draw-plate.

the point of the wire or tube is put through the hole of the plate as far as it will go ; the point is seized with the pliers, and then, by holding the pliers in the left hand, and pulling the wheel with the right hand, the metal is drawn through the plate (see pp. 80-84, *Wire-drawing*).

The Turning Lathe (Fig. 20) is indispensable in the manu-

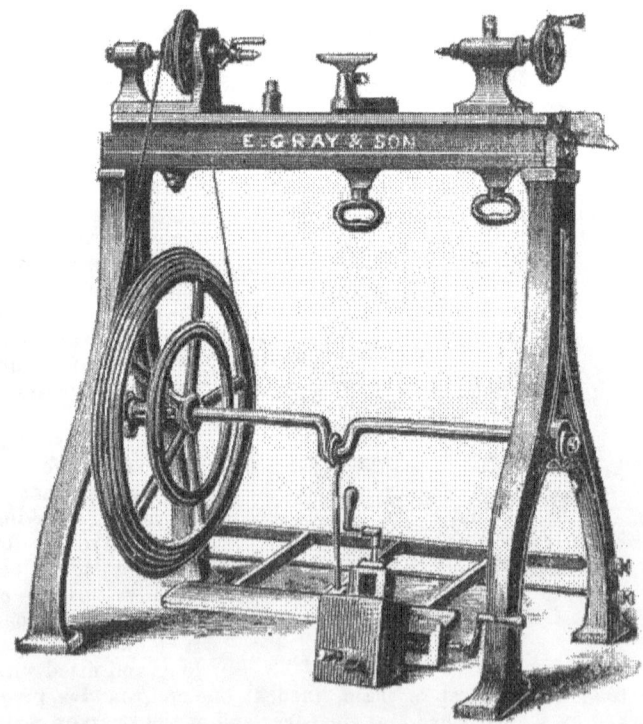

Fig. 20.—Foot Turning Lathe.

facture of goldsmith's work. When fitted as it should be with its various appliances it may be used for the purpose of turning pillars and small fittings, milling bezels, knurling edges of stud backs, sawing off joints, &c., by the aid of the circular saw, and it may be used for many purposes as a time-saver.

The Polishing Lathe.—Fig. 21 is an illustration of a complete arrangement for a polishing and finishing lathe combined. On such a lathe the whole process of polishing and finishing can

Fig. 21.—The Polishing Lathe.

be performed without changing any of the brushes. The oil and pumice or oil and rottenstone brush and felt can be fixed on the right-hand side of the spindle, and the mop and rouge brush on the left side. By this arrangement polishing can be commenced and finished with a minimum of trouble.

This lathe should be fixed to a strong wooden bench, and can be worked with motive power or by treadle.

Lapping and Gold Cutting Lathe.—This lathe (Fig. 22)

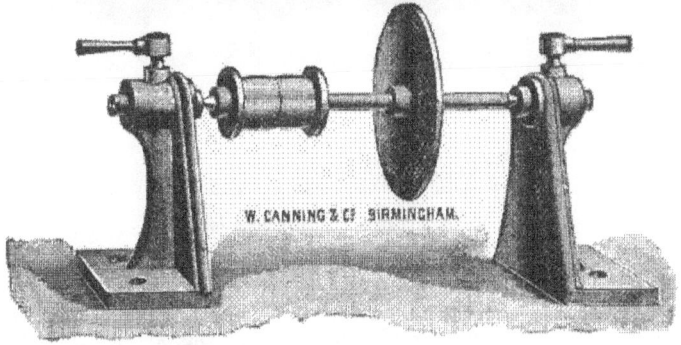

Fig. 22.—Lapping and Gold Cutting Lathe.

is suitable for fixing upon a strong wooden bench, which should be covered with zinc so that it can be cleaned with ease. It may be fixed side by side with the polishing lathe, and can be worked with motive power or with a treadle. This kind of appliance is not only indispensable for chain work, but is also most useful for goldsmith's work in general. The process is termed "gold cutting." The lap is a circular disc about ¼ inch thick and 10 inches in diameter; it is fixed upon the spindle of the lathe so as to revolve perfectly true. It is made ready for use by what is termed "edging in"—a process which is thus conducted. Mix some fine emery powder with a little water into a paste; then, as the lap is revolving, keep it covered with the wet emery by means of a small brush in the left hand. In the right hand hold a well-selected pebble, and press it against the lap as it revolves, being careful to move the pebble all over the surface. A guard should be placed over the lap to prevent the wet emery from sprinkling over the operator while performing this process. When the operation is finished, the lap will have a surface that will cut the gold articles pressed against it; hence the term "gold cutting," which consists in facetting chains and beads, lapping flat surfaces upon chains, seals, rings, bracelets, brooches, &c.

Pair Rolling Mills.—These are indispensable for reducing small pieces of gold or any other kind of metal (see pp. 61-62).

Wire Rolls.—These also are most useful in what is termed the "breaking down" of wire, as also for pointing wire strips, to save filing (see p. 63).

Planishing Tools.—Fig. 23 represents a pair of planishing

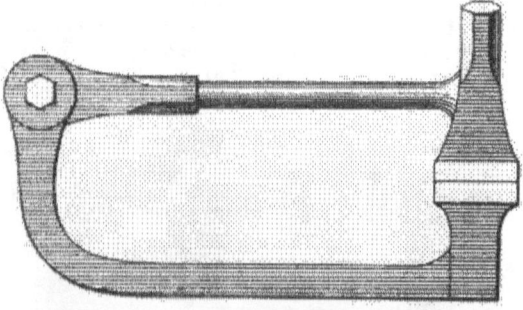

Fig. 23.—A pair of Planishing Tools.

tools made of wrought iron with hardened polished steel faces; they are most useful for flattening edges for lockets and bracelets, or any articles that require to be kept perfectly flat. If the faces are flat and well polished, the article may be flattened out to any size regularly, and much more quickly than with the hammer.

Shears.—There are several kinds of hand shears used for the purpose of cutting sheet metal or thin wire, viz.—left snipe-nose shears, right snipe-nose shears, and bent-nose shears. Two of these are shown in Fig. 24 ; the snipe-nose shears are for cutting

Fig. 24.—(1) Left Snipe-nose Shears.   (2) Bent-nose Shears.

metal in straight strips or for clipping ; the bent-nose shears are for cutting out curved parts.

Sparrow-hawk (Fig. 25).—This tool is most useful when fixed either in the vice or in what is termed a "sparrow-hawk block," for the purpose of flanging bezels, enlarging rings, and also for shaping tapered or conical tubes.

Fig. 25. —Sparrow-hawk.

Hammers.—The hammer is an indispensable tool ; in fact, several kinds are needed in the goldsmith's work ; they are distinguished by the shape of their heads.

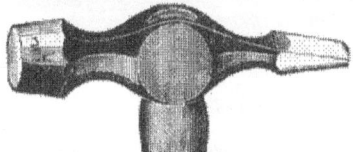 

Fig. 26.—Steel-head Hammer with Flat   Fig. 27. —Hammer with Flat
Face and Pointed Pane.   Face and Ball Pane.

Fig. 26 illustrates a steel-head hammer with a flat face and pointed pane ; it is acknowledged to be most useful for general purposes.

Fig. 27.—This kind of hammer has a flat face and a ball pane which is most useful for raising, as also for repairing holes in drawplates by knocking them up first and then opening the holes with a drift.

Fig. 28.—This kind is mostly used for small work; there are two patterns, one with a flat, the other with a round face.

Fig. 28.—Hammer.

Fig. 29.—Hammer with Double Face.

Fig. 29.—This pattern of hammer is termed a "double face" hammer; it has a flat face and also a slightly rounded face.

Fig. 30.—Hammer.

Fig. 31.—Chaser's Hammer.

Fig. 30.—This pattern of hammer is in very general use; the face, being flat, is used for ordinary flattening purposes, and the pane is rounded to serve for fluting tube in preparation for drawing.

Fig. 31.—This hammer is called a "chaser's" hammer and, generally, is not used for any other purpose. There are several sizes suitable for different kinds of work.

Pliers.—These are the most useful tools employed by goldsmiths and jewellers, as it is with them they fashion and shape the most complicated and delicate parts of their work. There are several kinds of pliers, which are known by the particular shape of the nose; thus these are termed "snipe-nose" (Fig. 32),

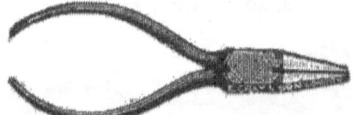

Fig. 32.—Snipe-nose Pliers.

" half-round snipe-nose," " round nose," "flat nose," "large half-round" (for large work), and "belchering" pliers (for belchering bezels, &c.).

Nippers.—There are also several kinds of nippers. Fig. 33

Fig. 33.—Cutting Nippers.

represents the form generally used by the goldsmith for cutting wire. There are also the side nippers, which are used for the purpose of cutting off wire when joined to the article in course of making, when the straight nippers would be inadequate for the purpose.

Piercing Nippers.—Fig. 34 shows a most useful tool for piercing small holes in metal for many purposes, especially in the process of saw-piercing when a hole has to be drilled or

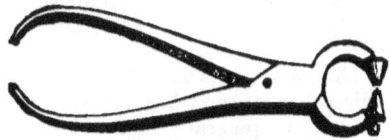

Fig. 34.—Piercing Nippers.

pierced in the metal to give the saw working room; for thin metal these tools will entirely dispense with drilling.

Slide Pliers.—There are two kinds of slide pliers, viz., the dog-nose slide (Fig. 35), and the vice-nose slide. These tools are most useful for many purposes, such as holding small parts that require filing into shape, or holding wire while under the process of filing. The article under consideration is held in

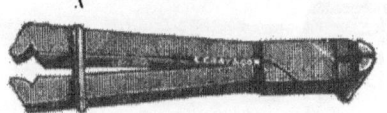

Fig. 35.—Slide Pliers.

the jaws of the pliers, and the slide, A, is pressed down the handle portion until the article becomes as firm as it would be if held in a vice; by this means the process of filing out shapes can be performed with much greater precision than with ordinary pliers.

Hand Vice (Fig 36).—It is generally used for holding large

Fig. 36.—Hand Vice.

Fig. 37.--Dividers.

articles during the process of filing, when the slide pliers are inadequate for the purpose.

Dividers.—This tool (Fig. 37) is used for measuring short distances upon the metal, in place of the well-known compasses. The bow at the top forms a spring, and by means of the thumb screw the distance required is maintained. It is also most useful in marking out circles upon the metal for any purpose required.

Callipers.—This tool resembles the dividers, but the legs are bow-shaped so as to adapt them for measuring the diameter of beads, tubes, &c.

Line Rule.—This tool also is used for measuring the diameter of tubes, wires, discs, beads, &c., when the workman is instructed to work by lines. It is generally made of boxwood or ivory, with a metal slide, the length being 3 inches. As each inch is divided into forty lines, very accurate gaugings can be made.

Joint Tool.—The tool shown in Fig. 38 is useful for making joints. Without it the workman is labouring under disadvantages, since in making joints for bracelets, lockets, or cigarette cases, it is necessary that each knuckle should fit close and also open true. To use this tool, the operator places the end of the piece of drawn joint in the triangular hole, and forces it forward

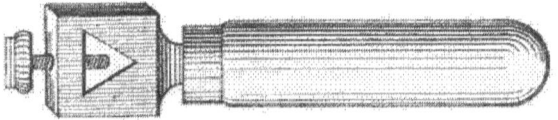

Fig. 38.—Joint Tool.

with the thumb screw. Then a file is passed over the face of the tool and the joint brought perfectly level with it; as this face is made of hardened steel, the joint yields to, but the face resists, the action of the file. Then the length of joint required is cut off, and the other end is passed through the same process; by the use of such a tool much time is saved and joints can be made perfect.

Treblets.—There are several kinds of treblets used in the manufacture of goldsmith's work. The ring treblet (Fig. 39) is used for shaping finger-rings; oval treblets are used for shaping the collars and edges of lockets and bracelets; and odd shape treblets (such as the oblong, square, shield, and heart shapes) are generally used for shaping bezels and settings for seals, &c. All treblets are taper; some are made of solid steel turned perfectly true, others are made of cast iron case-hardened.

The Doming Stake.—Fig. 40 is also called a "brass stamp" because it is generally made of brass or bronze metal, and is

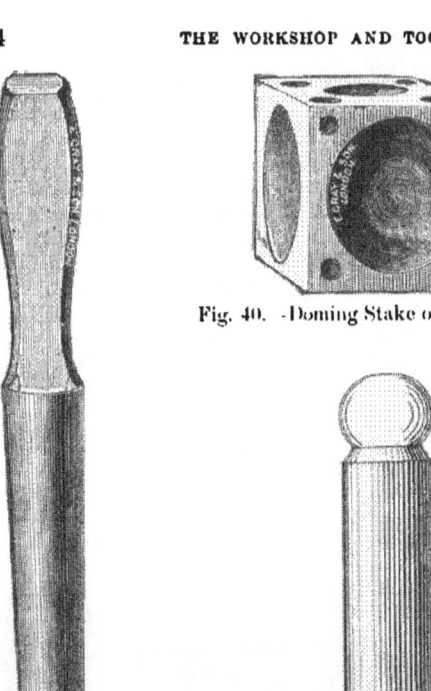

Fig. 40. -Doming Stake or Brass Stamp.

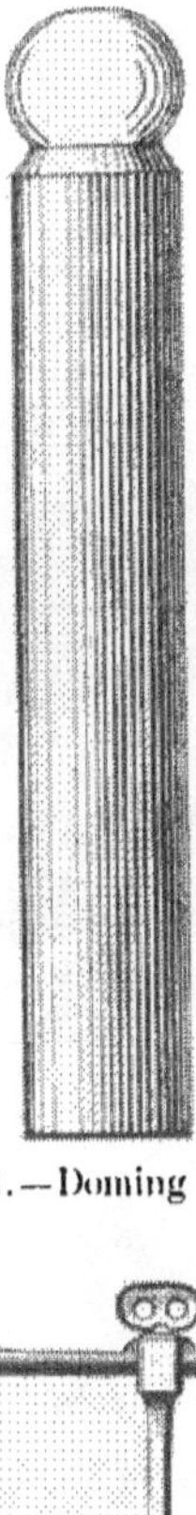

Fig. 41.—Doming Punch.

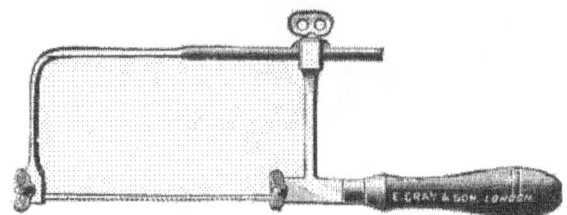

Fig. 39.- -Ring
Treblet.

Fig. 42.—Saw-frame and Saw.

used in conjunction with a set of **doming punches** (Fig. 41) made of steel, each terminating in a ball-shaped end, the size of which is from 15 to 30 millimetres in diameter. These tools are most useful in raising half beads or for doming back, &c.

The Saw-frame (Fig. 42) is used for saw-piercing ornaments out of flat metal, and also for the open work in engraved designs; and for many other purposes. The saws used with it vary in size; some are exceedingly fine, and are used for cutting out the small parts that cannot be removed by small files. The saw is fixed in its place by means of the thumb screws at the top and bottom ends as shown in Fig. 42, the bow part forming a spring to keep the saw tight. The best kind of piercing saws are those with round backs, as they can be made to turn round sharp curves.

The Back-saw is most useful for cutting tube or other articles in gold or silver when the piercing-saw is inadequate. The frame is usually made of a double piece of metal to hold the blade, and the teeth on each blade are cut specially suited to the kind of work it is intended for.

Corn Tongs are indispensable in the jewellery trade. There are many forms, one of which is shown in Fig. 43. They are

Fig. 43.—Corn Tongs.

used for picking up small shots and minute pieces of gold to place upon the article in course of manufacture, as also for picking up gems and arranging them in designs or " matching up," as it is termed.

Gauges or Size Plates.—Several kinds are used in the trade.

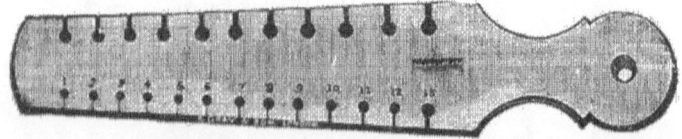

Fig. 44.—Long Metal Gauge.

Fig. 44 shows a long **metal gauge** used for sizing the thickness of gold, silver, or other metals when rolled into sheets.

The improved **micrometer gauge** (Fig. 45) gauges thicknesses of from $\frac{1}{100}$ mm. to 25 mm. It is worked with a set screw, and is used in many manufactories. The **wire gauge**, generally used

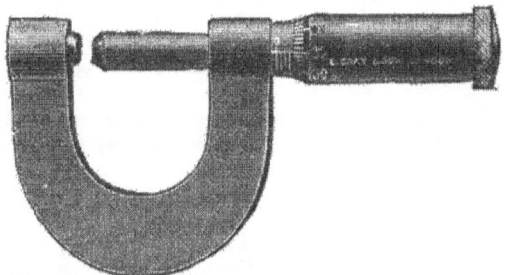

Fig. 45.—Micrometer Gauge.

for sizing the thickness of wire in the process of wire-drawing, is very similar to the metal gauge, but has larger slots.

Side Drill Stock.—This is generally rotated by means of a bow made of cane and a string of cat-gut. The string is wound round the wheel, A (Fig. 46). The spike, B, is pressed against the board, and the drill against the article to be drilled; then by moving the bow backwards and forwards a rotary motion is produced, which causes the drill to penetrate the article.

Fig. 46.—Side Drill Stock.

Another kind, called the **Archimedean drill stock**, dispenses with the bow altogether.

Files constitute a very important class of goldsmith's tools. They are made in a variety of forms, and the articles manufactured have many shapes and forms. For instance, there are flat files, half-round files, three-square files, double half-round, pillar files, knife files, round files, square files, safe-edge files, flat gapper, round-edge gapper, round-joint files, and a variety of odd shape files.

The cut of a file is known by its special name. The **bastard** is a rather rough file, and is generally used for removing surplus metal: the **smooth** is used for smoothing up various parts of the article after the rough parts have been removed; and the **superfine smooth** is generally used for the more delicate parts in the finishing process of manufacture. The length ranges from 3 inches to 12 inches.

Needle files for working the intricate parts of the article are made in all shapes and sizes, and the **riffles** and **circular files** are very various in shape and cut.

In order to save time every workman should have a full kit of tools allotted to him. It should consist of at least **four pairs of pliers, one pair of nippers, two pairs of shears, two hammers, a mallet, a blowpipe, a drill stock,** about one dozen files (assorted), several small **needle files,** saws and saw-frame for piercing, a back saw, dividers, slides, slide-rule burnisher, scorpers for carving, &c.

There should also be kept at hand several shapes of rough cut files for the purpose of pointing wire or making steel punches.

Upright Drill Stock.—This kind of stock (Fig. 47) is useful both to the goldsmith and to the setter, as, when fitted with different sizes of drills, articles can have holes drilled in them of any size required for setting the stones.

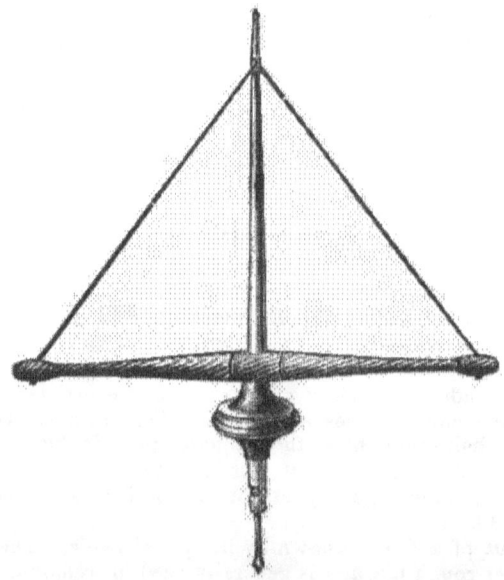

Fig. 47.—Upright Drill Stock.

Scorpers.—These tools are much used for setting stones, both for opening the holes after drilling, so as to adapt them to the special shape of the stones, and for cutting up the parts containing the stones in bright relief. They are named according to their particular shape; thus there are flat scorpers, round scorpers, spit-sticks, bull-sticks, gravers, and knife tools. Prior to being used they are sharpened on a grindstone and afterwards finished on an **oilstone**. One form of the latter is shown in Fig. 48, and is called the **Washita oilstone**. The **Arkansas** and

Fig. 48.—Fine Washita Oilstone.

the **Turkey** oilstones are each favoured by some, but the **Washita** is preferred by most workers.

The Graining Tool (or perloir) is most essential to the setter for forming small grains, and for pressing them over the edge of the stones to keep them secure. It is made of steel tapered towards the point, but terminating in a small bright concavity which the setter presses upon the grain of gold so as to produce a small bright bead or grain; the size of the hollow varies according to the size of the grains required.

Fig. 49.—Fions.

The concavities are brightened by pressing them on polished steel heads like beads, fixed to a plate of metal. The tool is called **Fions** and is shown in Fig. 49.

ENGRAVER'S TOOLS.

The tools generally used are the **lozenge graver** (or Burin), also the **square graver**, the **taper square**, and **lozenge shape graver**, the **tint tool, shaders** and **thread tools**, and **flat scorper** of different sizes.

The Chuck and Bullet.—The chuck is made of boxwood and

Fig. 50. En-graver's Bul-let, Sandbag and Chuck.

is used as the support for small articles while being engraved; the article is secured to the chuck by means of cement (see p. 231). Then the chuck is screwed on to what is called a **bullet**, made of iron, and the bullet is held in position upon a ring-shaped sand-bag, which enables the operator to turn the article in any direction required (see Fig. 50).

Larger articles are held in position either by the hand upon a sandbag, or are fixed upon a **cement block**, which is made of wood to the size required.

CHASER'S TOOLS.

In addition to the hammer (Fig. 31) punches of various shapes, called **chasing tools**, are required ; a few of these are shown in Fig. 51.

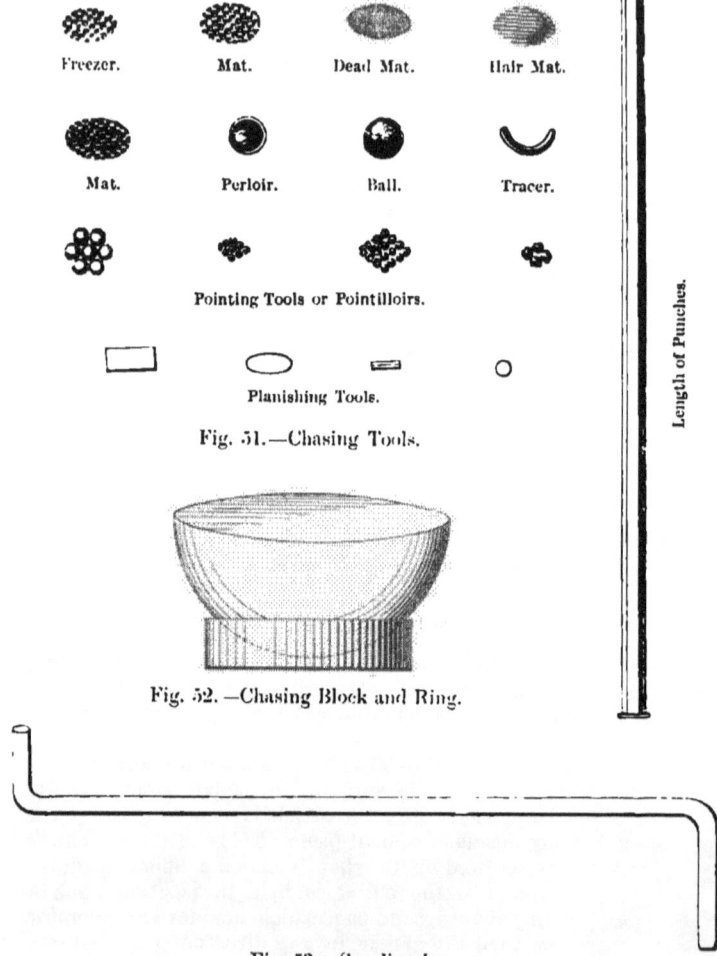

Freezer.   Mat.   Dead Mat.   Hair Mat.

Mat.   Perloir.   Ball.   Tracer.

Pointing Tools or Pointilloirs.

Planishing Tools.

Length of Punches.

Fig. 51.—Chasing Tools.

Fig. 52.—Chasing Block and Ring.

Fig. 53.—Snarling Iron.

Fig. 53 represents a snarling iron, which is used for raising protuberances on the surface of hollow articles for *repoussé* work.

CHAPTER VI.

FILIGREE WIRE-DRAWING.

In treating this subject one may emphatically declare that " there is nothing new under the sun ; " for, to acquire a knowledge of the history of wire-drawing we again turn to Scripture history and we find in the Book of Exodus, Chapter xxxix., verses 2-3, " And he made the ephod of gold, blue, and purple, and scarlet, and fine twined linen. And they did beat the gold into thin plates, and cut into wires, to work it in the blue, and in the purple, and in the scarlet, and in the fine linen, with cunning work."

From the above passages we gather the facts that the ancient goldsmith knew the ductility of the precious metals, and also knew the processes of wire-drawing for the decoration of the garments of the priests of the tabernacles.

But the inventive genius of man has not deteriorated ; it rather appears to be unlimited, for at the present day many thousand ounces of gold and silver, in addition to a large quantity of metal of less value, are drawn into wire of extreme fineness for purposes similar to those above described. In this chapter the important and highly interesting subject of wire-drawing will be dealt with and each succeeding stage of the process described.

It may be mentioned that, although 1 oz. of gold can be drawn into 20,000 yards of wire, the average length obtained from best quality is about 1500 yards.

Fine wire is used not only for the purpose of decorating garments and uniforms for state occasions, but a very large quantity is also made into brushes for scratch-brushing gold and silver work. It is also used for Etruscan work which is composed of fine filigree wires, twisted and arranged in intricate patterns, so that great care and judgment are required in manipulating the metals into wire.

WIRE-DRAWING APPLIANCES.

Wire-drawing forms one of the most important processes in the manufacture of jewellery, including chains, &c. After the metal has been rolled and slit into wire it should be annealed, then the rough edges filed off and the wire pointed. It is better to roll the point on the wire when thick to prevent wasting the gold as much as possible. A powerful draw-bench is fitted with a chain or band; at one end draw-pliers are attached, and at

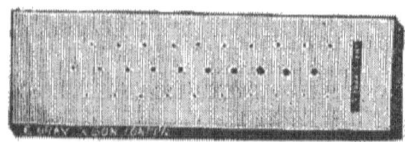

Fig. 54.—Draw-plate with Three Rows with Fine Holes.

the other a large hand-wheel. With this apparatus the wire is drawn through the holes of the steel plate, similar to Fig. 54. As the wire is hardened by this process it requires to be softened from time to time by annealing, to allow of its being easily worked. When the wire is sufficiently thin, the draw-plate is fixed firmly in a vice and the wire is pulled through the holes by means of the draw-tongs (Fig. 55) until the proper size is obtained.

Fig. 55.—Draw-tongs.

Draw-plates are of several kinds; hardened steel plates are generally used for thick wire, and smaller ones for finer wire;

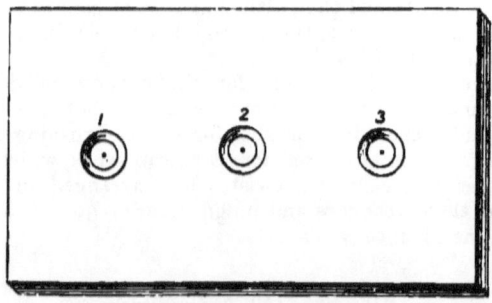

Fig. 56.—Ruby Plate.

but for drawing the wire used in filigree work, which is as fine as hair, ruby plates (Fig. 56) are necessary. A ruby plate consists of a thick plate of brass, in which is securely fitted one

or more rubies, each perforated by a very fine hole. These
plates are very expensive, but with care will last a long time.

Chainmakers use "soft steel plates" (Fig. 57), formed of thick
steel with holes countersunk at the back. In this case the

Fig. 57.--Soft Draw-plate.

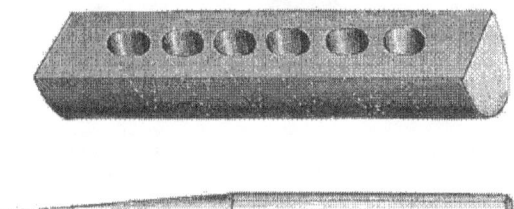

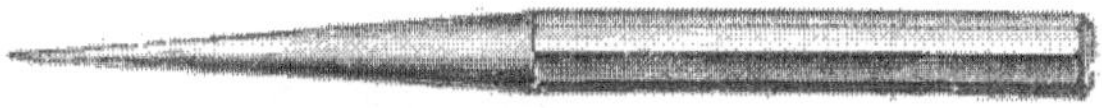

Fig. 58.—Taper Steel Drift.

wire-drawer is not dependent on the holes being already of the
right size, as he can easily regulate the size by knocking up
the holes with a round-faced hammer, and then driving in the
drift (Fig. 58), so as to make a perfect hole, free from any rough
edges, which if left would cut the wire. Great improvements
have been made in the process of wire-drawing. Fig. 59 repre-

Fig. 59.—Two-speed Wire-drawing Jigger Block.

sents a most efficient appliance called the "**two-speed wire-drawing jigger block**," by means of which wire-drawers having only a very small motive power engine and limited room can rapidly and easily break down "wire strips" direct from the "slitters." The draw-bench is attached to an iron table, and is fitted with a multiplying power gearing, so that any amount of "draft" can be pulled through the plate at one pinch by turning the handle.

Another, called the "**hand wire-drawing block**" (Fig. 60), is especially designed for the purpose of saving time and labour.

Fig. 60.—Hand Wire-drawing Block.

In order to reduce a medium sized wire to one of extreme fineness, the wire is first coiled on the cage, H, its end filed or rolled to a point until it will just enter the draw-plate, B; this is seized by the draw-pliers, C; on moving the handle about half a turn, the wire is pulled through a short distance, and the plate, B, is brought against the stop pegs, D; next, the end of the wire is secured in the vice, E; then, by turning the handle aided by the multiplying gear wheels, G, any length of wire can be drawn off the cage, H, on to the revolving drum, F. As the wire becomes finer, the power required lessens, so that the speed can instantly be increased, without taking off the handle, by means of the double-speed gear wheels, until the wire becomes fine enough for the multiplying power to be dispensed with; and then, by putting the handle on the drum spindle, the full speed can be obtained.

Fig. 61 represents a very handy appliance for the purpose of drawing fine wire for filigree work. Its construction is so simple that with it a boy can easily reduce wire to any size,

It is composed of two drums; the wire is put on drum No 1 and one end left long enough to put through the plate drawn up against the stop pegs fixed between the two drums; a short length of wire having been drawn through the plate, the point is fixed in a hole in drum No. 2, the handle turned, and the wire drawn off from one drum on to the other through the plate placed between them; next the handle is reversed and the wire drawn from drum No. 2 through the plate on to drum No. 1; and the process is repeated until the wire requires annealing. The coil of wire is loosened by withdrawing a piece of metal fixed in a slot on the drum, and is taken off and annealed.

Fig. 61.—The Filigree Wire-drawing Machine.

At the Birmingham Jewellers' and Silversmiths' Association Technical School, three machines made by Mr. Morton have been used by the author for educational purposes; experience has shown them to be highly efficient in their action.

ANNEALING.

The process of annealing or of softening gold that has been hardened by manipulation is a very important one and requires great care, as the treatment must be adapted to the quality of the gold. For instance, if a bar of 22-carat gold and a bar of common gold, say, 7 or 9-carat, be put on the annealing pan in the muffle and left there till red hot and then be withdrawn, the common gold will be found to have a scorched appearance, showing that it has been over-heated, and been thereby rendered absolutely unworkable; while the 22-carat gold will be just sufficiently annealed. All gold alloys should be annealed at a red heat only, not at a bright white heat, which is quite destructive of the working properties of gold. The method of annealing gold varies with its form. Flat gold, for example, should be annealed either by placing it upon an iron pan in a muffle, or by heating it upon a "lamp" with a large gas jet, using a blowpipe as in Fig. 62.

In the latter case the gold must be made uniformly red hot throughout, for if there is any irregularity the gold will be harder in some parts than others. When annealed, the gold should be carefully lifted from the pan with iron tongs, and gently placed on iron or on stone to cool; if allowed to fall while red hot it will very likely be broken. If the flat gold is thin, it will occupy less space in annealing if it be coiled and a piece of wire wound round it.

Wire.—Similar care is required for annealing wire, as a continuous wire cannot be drawn if imperfectly annealed, for gold is apt to break at the places which have not been made red hot. The best method for annealing wire for filigree work is as follows :—Coil the wire round a bezel or a chuck loosely; remove

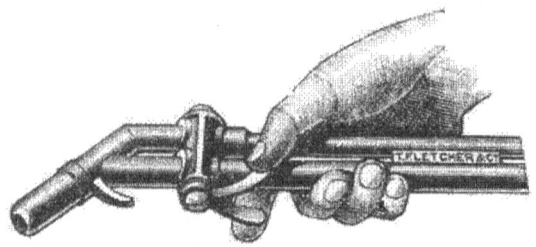

Fig. 62.—Blowpipe.

the coil; bind it with iron wire so as to keep it compact; place it in the centre of an iron pan which has been previously sprinkled with a little sawdust, then cover the wire entirely with a little more sawdust; the pan is then put over a fire, and again withdrawn as soon as the sawdust begins to burn; after this has been allowed to burn quietly for a little time, the ashes and burning dust are blown off and the red-hot wire is allowed to cool, when it will be found properly and evenly annealed.

All gold articles are also annealed after they have been subjected to any process which hardens them, such as the drawing of tubes, the raising of bracelets, raising the backs or fronts of brooches, shaping bezels and rings, and stampings. Pin stems, brooch tongs, &c., which have to be left hard, do not require annealing after the last process. Small articles are generally annealed upon what is called a "boss," which is formed of scrap binding wire flattened and fastened upon a twisted wire handle, the ends of which hold the "boss" in position. "Pumice coal" is also used for annealing flat articles, and lump charcoal for annealing thin light work; the latter is also used for melting small shots, soldering ornaments, and for other purposes.

CHAPTER VII.

THE MANUFACTURE OF PERSONAL ORNAMENTS.

Much has been written about the origin and history of jewellery, and the important part it has played in the adornment of the person by all classes of individuals; but the literature dealing with the actual processes of manufacture is comparatively small. We will now describe the modern methods of manipulating the precious metal into articles of jewellery. It is supposed that, everything being ready, the workman is required to make an article of jewellery, such as a bracelet.

BRACELETS.

Many forms and shapes are worn, but the methods of construction may be reduced to four, and be exemplified by (1) the **Band Bracelet**; (2) the **Tube Bracelet**; (3) the **Wire Bracelet**; and (4) the **Flexible Bracelet.**

(1) BAND BRACELET.

Fig. 63 represents a **Band Bracelet** with an inside lining, and with a diamond star set flush with the front. The first process is to draw the edges in the way about to be described. Cut off

Fig. 63.—Band Bracelet.

a piece of gold (Fig. 63) corresponding to about size No. 6 in the gauge plate, and a little wider than twice the depth of the required edge, say $\frac{1}{4}$ deep; it should, therefore, be about $\frac{5}{16}$ inch wide, and $7\frac{1}{2}$ inches long. This strip is fluted with the pane of the hammer, then annealed, flattened double, and a thin strip of flat brass wire placed between. The next process is to draw it through an oblong-holed draw-plate, until the required depth is obtained; after annealing and cooling, it is turned up into the shape required with a pair of half-round pliers, with the nick inside. The usual inside measurement for a bracelet is 6¾ inches. When flattened and put into a good shape, the outside edge is filed with a three-square file until the brass is seen, thus forming two separate edges of precisely the same size; the brass wire being of no further use is thrown away.

The next process is to cut off a piece of gold for the front, of the required width and length, and to solder the two ends together. It is then boiled out in pickle as described (p. 231); the surface of the front regulated by tapping the gold with a hammer, or mallet, upon a stake shaped for the purpose, until the surface is perfectly smooth; annealed upon an iron bracelet shape; again boiled out in pickle, and the edges fitted inside carefully. If there is any fear of the edges dropping out of place during the process of soldering, it is well to tie them in by means of iron binding wire. The parts to be soldered are charged with pallions (or panels) of solder, which solder is cut into various sizes with the shears (Fig. 24); a fluxing agent is required to allow of the solder flushing properly. This agent is borax paste prepared by rubbing lump borax with a little water on a piece of slate, called a **borax slate**, and applied to the surface to be soldered with a small camel-hair pencil, called a **borax pencil**; the small pallions of solder are then placed on the prepared surface.

The bracelet is now transferred to a boss of iron wire held by a handle, and exposed to a side gas blowpipe flame described in Fig. 62, p. 85. Great care is required in order to decide upon the precise moment when the solder has fused, and when the flame should be removed. When properly soldered the article is again boiled out.

The next process is making the star; this is cut out of 18-carat gold (the size being about No. 16 in the metal gauge), filed up perfectly true, inserted in its place quite flush with the surface, and soldered perfectly sound both inside and out; and a bezel about the size of the stone to be set, and as deep as the edges of the bracelet, is soldered on the back of the star. Lining the bracelet is next performed; the lining, which should have the same thickness of gold as the front, is slightly raised with the tools called "bull and butcher," and fitted inside the bracelet, and then charged and soldered by the method just described. The bracelet is again boiled out in pickle to remove the borax, &c., and the edges roughly filed up to re move the surplus gold.

The **snap-plates** are now made and soldered to the bracelet. Take a piece of gold about No. 8 in size that will, when doubled, suffice for the two snap-plates, one for the snap to be soldered into, and the other for the snap to snap into. A piece of thin card having been placed between the plates, they are flattened between the planishers (Fig. 23) ; filed out, as shown in Fig. 64, A, and a cavity gapped in the bracelet into which the snap-plate will fit tightly ; the snap-plates are then charged and soldered soundly to the bracelet.

Joints.—The making and fixing of the joint is the next process. Take a piece of gold about size No. 3 in the gauge, and draw a piece of tube, called **casing**, the diameter of which should be equal to the depth of the bracelet edge ; cut off a piece of the tube ; halve it ; into one half solder two small pieces of joint drawn to fit the casing tightly, and into the other half solder one piece of joint, which has been previously made to fit the gap on the opposite side (see Fig. 64, B). The joint is now fitted into the bracelet by filing a round hole through each edge of the

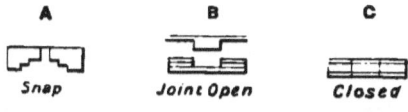

A   B   C

Snap   Joint Open   Closed

Fig. 64.

bracelet, and, by means of the back-saw, cutting through the lining where the joint is to be soldered. The joint is now rouged inside in order to prevent the two surfaces from being soldered together when the joint is being fixed in the bracelet ; the outside is made perfectly clean, and the casing containing the joint put into the bracelet, a strand of binding wire being tied round the front. The casing *only* is carefully charged with two small panels of solder on each side, which are carefully tacked only, not flushed. When cool, file off the surplus gold of the snap which stands up above the surface of the bracelet, and so reveal the cavity made by the burning away of the card which was put between ; into this introduce the back-saw, cut through the lining and thus cause the bracelet to fall into two halves, one being the front, and the other the back half ; after another boiling out the joint can be soldered sound.

The next process is **fitting the snap**. The two plates are first filed perfectly flat with the flat file ; next, the "bottom" plate, as it is called, is fitted and soldered carefully to the back half, and afterwards made to fit closely in the front half ; then the "top" plate is fitted and soldered on to the bottom plate. The process of **snapping** up is now done. It requires great care and experience to make the two halves fit closely and evenly, so that they will file up perfectly. When snapped up, the whole bracelet is filed up all over, smoothed, and polished. Lastly, the thumb bit is fitted and soldered, then finally snapped up ready for preparing it for the colouring process (see p. 152).

(2) TUBE OR HOLLOW BRACELET.

The term "tube or hollow" applies to all shapes and thickness of tubes generally used for drawn bracelets, such as the round tube, oblong tube, knife-shape tube, fluted tube, twisted tube, and many odd shape tube bracelets, as all are called tube or hollow bracelets. But as many of the shapes are produced by the same method, the oblong tube bracelet will be taken as a type, as Fig. 65.

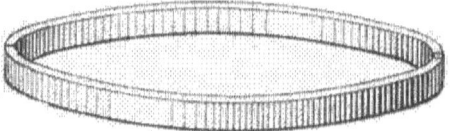

Fig. 65.—Oblong Tube Bracelet.

Oblong Tube Bracelet.—A piece of oblong brass wire is drawn somewhat smaller than the size of the tube required for the bracelet; then a strip of gold is cut off corresponding, say, to size No. 2 in the gauge-plate, 7½ inches long, and in width equal to three sides only of the oblong tube to be drawn; the gold is then fluted so as to fit the brass wire; and, by means of the draw-bench, the two are drawn through the oblong draw-plate to the size required. As the gold covers only three sides of the brass wire it is firmly secured by a binding of strong iron wire and then well annealed; afterwards, the tube is turned up with a strong pair of half-round pliers into the shape of a bracelet, the part without gold being placed inside. The superfluous ends are cut off, the iron wire removed, and the brass wire carefully taken out, the front and edges only of the bracelet being left. The joining is soldered, and the tube regulated ready for the lining, which is made and soldered in the same manner as described in the manufacture of the band bracelet. The joint is also made and put in in precisely the same way, but the snapping is performed differently. In this case the tube is cut through and a small piece of square wire is fitted tightly and soldered into each end near to the front; this serves as the snap-plate. The snap is made of a piece of gold, No. 8 size, doubled up and the inner faces separated by rouge or paper to prevent them uniting when soldering the snap into the bracelet. This is fitted into the front half first, then one end is soldered to the back half, the saw passed carefully through the top plate only, and the top plate properly snapped into the front half. The bracelet is finished by boiling it out in pickle and filing it up in the same way as in the previous example.

The **round tube** and the **knife-shape tube** are produced by a slightly different method. A piece of brass wire is drawn

about 8 inches long and a size smaller than the required size of
the bracelet. A strip of flat gold, No. 2 size in the metal
gauge and wide enough to fit the brass wire accurately, is cut
off, swaged into a semi-tubular form by means of the pane of
the hammer, and then annealed. The gold having been placed
over the brass wire, it is drawn tight by means of the draw-
plate and draw-bench so as to bring the two edges of the gold
quite close together, and strong binding wire is wound tightly
upon the gold to keep the seams close during the subsequent
turning up process. The article is annealed and allowed to cool,
then the gold on the brass is turned up with a pair of large half-
round pliers into the shape of the bracelet, so as to leave the
brass wire projecting about 1 inch more than the gold. The
article is again annealed, but before it is quite cold it is submerged in oil. The brass wire is drawn out by placing the
unprotected end into the draw-plate in the reverse side and in
a hole smaller than the one the gold has passed through ; a
steady, but gentle, pull will extract the wire and leave the gold
tube in a perfect form ; the binding wire is then taken off, the
ends cut so as to fit properly, and the joining in the tube
soldered up ; the jointing and snapping processes are the same
as for the oblong tube bracelet.

(3) WIRE BRACELET.

The **three-wire half-hoop bracelet** (Fig. 66) represents an
" eleven-stone half-hoop bracelet," which is thus made. A set
of stones is selected so arranged in size that, while there is a

Fig. 66.—Three-wire Half-hoop Bracelet.

well-proportioned graduation in size from the centre towards
each end, each pair should have the same shape and thickness. Every stone selected for an article should be weighed
carefully. Fig. 67 shows the scales generally used for the
purpose.

Next, a piece of flat gold is selected, about No. 16 size in the
metal gauge, sufficiently wide to take the stones, and is bent into
the shape of the bracelet. This gold is then fixed on a cement stock
and, by means of a drill fixed in the upright drill stock, eleven
holes are drilled through it; the holes opened to the proper size
to take the stones with scorpers; and the setting filed up into the

required shape. Next, three wires are made, the process being much the same for the knife wire as for the oblong or flat wire bracelet. It will therefore suffice if we describe the method adopted for the construction of the flat wire bracelet, as this is easily filed and converted into one with the knife edge.

After edging the strip of wire, it is drawn through an oblong hole draw-plate to the size required for the two outside wires only. As the centre wire need not be quite so deep as the others, it is drawn through a hole which will give it the same thickness, but only half the depth. When the wires have been properly prepared, annealed, and cut off to the required length (the usual length being 6¾ inches), they are turned up into shape by means of a pair of half-round pliers, and the ends properly closed and soldered (see p. 87). They are finally shaped on the **bracelet iron** and flattened between the planishers. The article is then boiled out in pickle, filed up, and the inside parts smoothed and polished previous to soldering them together. Next, small

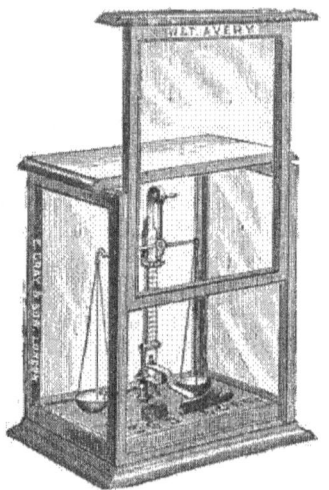

Fig. 67.—Diamond Scales in Glass Case.

shots or wires are soldered, at equal distances, on the centre wire, and the three wires are connected at the back only. Afterwards they are soldered in their proper position.

The fitting of the setting, or "**head**" as it is called, is the next process. A portion of the centre wire corresponding in length with the setting is cut away, then the setting which is soldered upon the two outside edges is closely fitted, while the ends of the centre wire are soldered to the ends of the setting, thereby fixing all wires in their proper position. The processes of jointing and snapping scarcely differ from those described for the bracelets already mentioned. In this, as in every case, the article must be boiled out in the pickle solution and dried in hot sawdust, before proceeding to file up, a process which is thus effected. When the stones are to be transparent, the holes for setting them should be carefully filed out at the back, so as to harmonise with the outline of the setting. This gives a superior finish to the inside of the bracelet, and also adds light to the stones. The wires are also smoothed evenly, and care is taken that the fronts of the wire are properly lapped. In some

instances the sides of the setting are either richly engraved or
carved.   When the whole of the bracelet has been polished
bright, it is ready for setting in one of the various ways noticed
under *Setting.*

(4) FLEXIBLE BRACELET.

Flexible Bracelets are made in many different patterns.
Among others, there are chain bracelets formed of links very
varied in design ; the flexible tablet bracelet, formed of from
six to twenty tablets connected by joints or rings ; and the
diamond flexible bracelet, which is composed of a number of
large brilliants, each of which is set in a square tablet, while
each tablet is pinned through the sides so as to make the whole
flexible.

In order to make a flexible bracelet, say, half an inch wide
with fourteen tablets, each of which is jointed and flexible, the
following is the general method of manufacture :—Two flat wire
edges are made the exact size of the arm (the regular size is
6¾ inches inside measurement) and about three lines deep ; the
ends of each wire are soldered together, the wires shaped as
described in the preceding section, and fitted inside the front.
The front is a piece of flat gold of about No. 3 size in the metal
gauge and a full half inch wide, while the length represents that
of the outside of the edge made.   When the ends have been
soldered together, the article is shaped on a bracelet stake,
either flat or slightly raised as may be required by the design.
The edges are then fitted inside the front, and charged on the
outside, then soldered, special care being taken that the solder
flushes through to the inside.   This is followed by the bracelet
being boiled out in the pickle, after which it is lined.   The
lining is a piece of gold cut to the exact size of the inside of the
edges, and a full half inch wide.   The two edges having been
soldered together, the lining is raised with the "bull and butcher."
These tools consist of a hub or stake made of boxwood or iron,
the centre of which has been filed into a hollow having precisely
the same shape as the lining to be raised, and of a boxwood
punch which exactly fits this hollow.   The lining to be raised
is placed in the hollow, and the hub is fixed firmly in the vice ;
then the lining is moved slowly round the hub with one hand,
at the same time that the punch, held upon it by the other, is
being struck a continuous series of sharp blows with a hammer
by an assistant.   If carefully done the lining will be raised
evenly.   The lining is then annealed into shape, cut through the
soldering place so as to fit inside the bracelet, and soldered in.

The jointing of the tablets is next proceeded with.   The tablets
are marked off into equal proportions by the dividers (Fig. 37),
and cavities filed out with the joint file for the casing which is

to receive the joints, and the casing soldered in. The joints are then put in and each joint is soldered separately. A loose pin having been put through the joints to keep them together, the next tablet is jointed, which process is repeated until all the tablets are complete; when the bracelet has been jointed, the loose pins are taken out. The snap is inserted into one of the tablets (see p. 88) and the bracelet filed up and polished as usual. The tablets are now decorated with wire work, or engraved, according to design, and finally polished ready for finishing by the wet colour process.

The fronts and linings for this class of bracelet are sometimes spun, but this process makes the edges so thin that first-class work cannot be guaranteed.

BROOCHES.

In modern, just as in ancient times, the brooch is used for fastening a garment, but the style of brooch was varied with every change of fashion from the light leaf work enriched with precious stones to the massive wrought article, and, later, to the fine delicately designed **Fichu** or lace brooch. But, however varied may be the style, all brooches are made by the same methods and processes of construction. As an example, we select a wrought brooch having a base like that shown in Fig. 68, which is characterised by having numerous points. If this were made by soldering together as many places as there are points, the jointings would show in the finished brooch, and the brooch would readily lose shape. In order to obviate this defect, the following method is used. The edging is cut off to the required depth, and a length of about $1\frac{1}{2}$ inches cut from the prepared strip. In the centre make a slot with a three-square

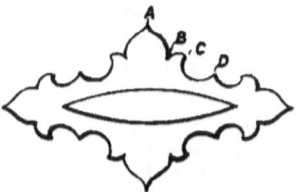

Fig. 68.—Base of Brooch.

file, then bend it; this will form the point A, which must be strengthened with solder; next mark off point B on each side and file on the reverse side relatively to A, bend into form so as to produce the next curve, and solder as before; next the points C are filed on the reverse side to points B, bent into form and soldered; lastly, the curves are bent to produce the points D. The four sections of the brooch are constructed together, which, when complete, are soldered at the four points marked D, thus producing an ornament with 24 sharp bends. This form is filed or rubbed flat, and the front soldered on. In order to do this properly, the front must be made perfectly flat or slightly raised (according to the design), and firmly tied upon the edge with iron binding wire, charged with panels of solder with the aid of a camel-hair pencil and borax, and then soldered as before described.

The article is then boiled out in pickle solution, the surplus gold cut off with the piercing saw (Fig. 42, p. 74), the shape being only partly filed out. The back is next placed upon the form in the same way as the front was put on ; after another boiling out, the shaping with the file is finished so as to leave the edges perfectly sharp, and the curves regular. The parts to be ornamented are then polished and decorated according to the design, and the brooch completed by soldering on the joint and catch. This last process requires great judgment, as the joint and catch should harmonise with the style of brooch, while the pin (known in the trade as the "tong") should be sufficiently strong for the purpose.

Many articles are spoiled by clumsy joints, imperfect catches, or weak pins. After a final polish the article is ready for the finishing-off process, as already described.

EAR-RINGS.

The origin of the ear-ring is thus described in an Eastern legend, which states that "when Hagar ran away to escape the wrath of Abram's wife, Sarai vowed that if her handmaid ever returned she would cause her to be mutilated, thinking thus to destroy her beauty and prevent her causing any further domestic infelicity. Time, however, had the effect of so cooling Sarai's wrath, that when Hagar came back and pleaded with her, she decided to forego her vengeance and restore her ex-handmaid to favour But an oath was not a thing to be trifled with, and as Sarai had solemnly vowed to mutilate Hagar, she was in a quandary to know how to do this without injuring her or marring her fair face. Finally, she hit upon the expedient of piercing a small hole in each of Hagar's ears, and it is said that

Abram, to offset the pretty handmaid's punishment, presented her with two beautiful jewels to suspend from the holes." Therefore, according to this legend, as well as to Bible history, this article of adornment played an important part in human affairs long before the Christian era, and has ever since adorned the queen and peasant alike.

Fig. 69.—Eartops of Modern Form.

Ear-rings have been considered highly becoming to women in general, but especially so to those who have well-shaped ears or pretty faces. Their forms and size have varied from time to time. Formerly the ear-ring was a facsimile of the brooch, forming what is termed a half-set; but now they take the form of eartops, without any drop, and consist of either single stones, as shown in Fig. 69, or a cluster of stones set in a similar way. Sometimes they have the form of a flower, or of a leaf; or, it may be, a bead decorated with wire work, &c.

EAR-STUDS.

Of late years ear-studs have been worn in place of ear-rings. They are constructed similar to the latter, but instead of a hook, there is soldered at the back of the ornament a straight wire about ⅜ in. long; this wire is screwed half-way down, and on the end of it an ornamental nut is screwed. The form generally used is a small disc of gold knurled on the edge, and a hollow bead soldered in the centre; a hole is drilled through both the disc and the bead, and then tapped with a steel tap with the same thread as the wire, thus making it perform the function of a nut.

When this article of jewellery is required to be worn, the nut is removed, and the wire is passed through the hole in the ear from the front, and the nut is then screwed on the wire from the back, thus making the jewel secure.

CHAPTER VIII.

FINGER RINGS.

FINGER rings had become important long before the Christian era. It is stated that in Rome every freeman had the right to use the iron ring; and this use was retained up to the close of the Republic, by those who loved the simplicity of the good old times.

Gold Rings appear to have been first worn by ambassadors to foreign states in their official capacity, while in private they wore their iron ones. Later, it became customary for all the senators, chief magistrates, and **equites** to wear the gold ring. Magistrates and governors of provinces seem to have possessed the privilege of conferring upon inferior officers, or such persons as had distinguished themselves, the right of wearing a gold ring. So generally were gold rings used as ornaments in ancient times, that three bushels of them, it is said, were gathered out of the spoils after Hannibal's victory at Cannæ. This was after the second Punic war.

RINGS

have figured prominently in the legends of the past, as well as in the romance of the present; but those which concern us most as goldsmiths and jewellers are the engagement rings of the nineteenth century, as the designs and prices must be adapted to the tastes and means of all who make engagements to marry. Again, it is now usual for a gentleman to wear an all gold signet ring with his monogram engraved upon the front, to be used generally as a seal, but especially intended for sealing the engagement. Further, the wedding ring is now worn by the bridegroom as well as by the bride, both in this country and on the Continent. In this chapter the more important kinds only will be dealt with, as each of them will exemplify many other patterns.

Signet Rings.—Fig. 70 represents an ordinary form of signet ring; it is one of the many kinds of rings generally worn by gentlemen. Signet rings are mostly cast in solid gold, but some are stamped and lined. In the case of solid rings, a model is first made in some inexpensive metal, such as tin or brass, and perfectly filed up, if it be plain ; or carved, if it is to be decorated.

If a large quantity of rings of the same pattern are to be made several models will be required. The method of casting is described in the chapter on *Casting.* In some cases the rings are cast complete ; but in others the front only is cast, and the "shank" soldered on afterwards. The unfinished rings with shanks straight (as described in the Hall-marking instructions, p. 212), are sent to the Assay Office to be Hall-marked ; when returned from the Assay Office, the shape of the ring is completed and the joining soldered. It is then made perfectly round upon the ring mandril (or treblet, Fig. 39), filed up in order to remove all the marks left by the hammer or by the casting, and finished with finely cut files called "smooths" or "superfine" smooths, so as to be ready for the polishing process. Sand-paper sticks, as also emery sticks, are sometimes used in place of smooths.

Fig. 70.—Ordinary Signet Ring.

If a stone is to be set in the front, the front is cast with a hole in it, sufficient gold being left to produce a bearing for the stone, and a margin for the setting called the "Roman setting" (see *Setting*). The stones generally used for this purpose are the **Bloodstone. Onyx, Sard, Sardonyx, Cat's-eye,** and, sometimes, the **Carbuncle** and the **Lapis-Lazuli.**

Belcher Rings.—The kind generally worn by gentlemen is shown in Fig. 71. These rings are made of various thicknesses, and are sometimes finished perfectly plain, or richly chased all over the front. There are three methods of producing belcher rings—they are (1) either made of thick solid half-round wire ; or (2) they are cast whole; or (3) they are manipulated from the flat metal and left hollow.

Fig. 71.—Belcher Ring.

Method 1.—In this method the wire is drawn through a steel plate to the size required, the requisite length cut off for the size of the ring, and bent into form by a tool specially constructed for that purpose. After the joining has been soldered, the rings are perfectly shaped upon the ring mandril (or treblet) and filed up ready for the polishing process ; when a large quantity is made, the rings are turned in a lathe after soldering, instead of being filed into form. Those which are required to be Hall-marked are sent to the Assay Office in strips.

Method 2.—The cast belcher rings are produced from a model (or pattern) in the same way as the signet rings, and are treated in a like manner.

7

Method 3.—The hollow belcher rings are produced either by spinning, or by means of the "belchering pliers." There is also an improved tool for belchering rings or bracelets, which takes the place of the form known in the trade as a "Bull and Butcher." The front is raised by either of the methods already described, and then the lining is fitted, cleanly soldered at both sides, and filed up in the same way as the cast rings; but care must be exercised to avoid dents or over filing. When this class of rings are Hall-marked the fronts and linings must be sent to the Assay Office separately for the purpose of marking, and if the fronts are to be chased, the chasing should be done before the linings are soldered in; but there is a method by which they may be chased with the linings soldered in, which is by making two small holes inside, boiling the rings in alum, whereby they become solid enough to be chased, and, after chasing, dissolving out the alum with boiling water.

Keeper Rings are generally given as keepsakes or as tokens of friendship; they are mostly worn by ladies. A ring like that shown in Fig. 72 is thus made :—Lengths of flat wire drawn to about size No. 20 or No. 24 in the metal gauge (according to the weight of the ring required) are cut off and sent to the Assay Office to be Hall-marked. On their return from the office they are carefully turned up with a pair of half-round pliers, or by the improved tool for bending rings, the two ends properly joined and soldered, and the rings boiled out in pickle; they are next shaped on the treblet, and filed up into the required form, which process needs great care in setting out, as the outer circumference has to be divided off into a certain number of divisions, to enable a corresponding number of letters to be engraved, chased, enamelled, or soldered on the front. The usual words are the Christian name, or "Mizpah," "In memory of," or the name of the wearer. The finishing is somewhat different from that of other rings, inasmuch as the panels and edges being perfectly flat they are either gilt or coloured and then lapped by the gold-cutter. A cheaper class of keeper rings is manufactured by passing the flat wire through the matting rolls (Fig. 19), and so producing the pattern on the front; afterwards they are made in the manner described in the preceding paragraph.

Fig. 72.—Keeper Ring.

Carved Half-Hoop Rings.—Fig. 73 represents a gem ring, of which there are many forms. But the best class of rings are produced by the following method :—The heads or front halves are cast separately. The gold must be sufficiently thick to allow the stones being let into their places without projecting on the inner side so as to touch the finger. The shank, which is generally made of half-round wire, is soldered on the one side only, and is left quite straight, as they require to be sent in this state to the Assay Office for Hall-marking. When returned, the form of the ring is completed by turning up the shank with pliers so as to form a perfect join, then soldering and shaping on the ring treblet. After boiling the rings out in pickle the stones are let in. For this purpose, the rings are either fixed upon cement sticks, or held in position in tools called "claws," and five holes for the five stones are drilled, quite close together and straight through the solid metal, with the upright drill stock (Fig. 47). The stones are then let into their bearings by "opening out" the cavity or hole to the exact shape of the stone, by cutting the bearing with a scorper, which may be the half-round, the bull-stick, or some other shape of scorper according to the class of work. When the stones have been properly let into their respective places, they are removed and the rings filed into a shape suitable for the process of carving ; the back of the holes should be opened out square, and a partition of gold be left between each stone. The carved designs on the sides vary according to the size of the stone; but,

Fig. 73.—Gem Ring.

in each case, a portion of the scrolls must be carved so as to form claws to hold the stones, which are made secure by the process of setting. The better class of rings have the ornaments cut or pierced through the sides, thus producing open work; this admits light and adds lustre and beauty to the gems. The shoulders also are suitably carved in order to hold the end stones in their position. The rings are then carved, properly smoothed up and polished, and the stones finally set either by the setter or by the mounter himself. Other kinds of rings are produced by a similar method, such as the claw half-hoop rings, and other forms of gem rings. A cheaper class of claw-set rings are produced by stamping the head in two halves and soldering these halves together, but this class of ring is not art-work, as a good carved half-hoop or a claw half-hoop ring can only be made by skilled and experienced workmen.

Gipsy Rings.—A single stone gipsy ring is shown in Fig. 74. These rings are produced by several methods; sometimes the heads or fronts are cast, but inasmuch as cast heads are always porous, and the pores are more pronounced after polishing, this process cannot be recommended for articles which are to be finished perfectly plain. The better method is to produce them out of thick, flat, and well rolled gold, cut into strips or slit, and drawn through a draw-plate having holes of the required width and thickness. This gives a closer grained and much more easily worked metal. The wire is then cut into suitable

Fig. 74.—Gipsy Ring.

lengths for rings. The two ends for the shank (which need not
be so thick as the front) are rolled or swaged into the form of the
shank, and in this state sent to the Assay Office for Hall-marking.
After Hall-marking the shanks are turned up, as before described,
and roughly filed up into the form required to suit the stone.
When the front is being filed a protuberance is left round the
hole for setting the stone. The stone is then let into its place,
and at once properly set by hammering the protuberance over
the stone, which process is thus performed :—First, the hole is
drilled and opened out at the back, so as to suit the stone :
next, the ring is firmly fixed upon a cement stick and the hole
in the ring opened out, so as to produce a bearing for the stone
to rest upon ; then the stone is properly fitted, and then, the
cement stick and disattached ring being fixed either in a vice
or in a block, the protuberance is carefully tapped over the stone
with a small punch and hammer until the surface of the ring is
made level.

The ring is now ready to be smoothed up for the polishing
process. This kind of setting is called "flush setting," or gipsy
setting.

Marquise Rings.—Fig. 75 represents one of the several forms
of marquise rings. Their chief characteristic is the form of the
setting. Some rings have a central elliptical or pippin-shaped
stone surrounded by a border of smaller stones ; others have a
central row of stones. These settings are finished in several
styles ; some are "thread set" ; others have "cut-down" setting ;
but the better class of rings are "claw set." They are thus

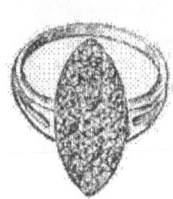

Fig. 75.
Marquise Ring.

made :—A pointed oval, large enough for the
stone, is cut out from a piece of gold about the
size of No. 16 in the metal gauge. Then the
gold is raised by punches into a convex form
for the front, and a bezel made of thick gold
—say No. 10 size in the gauge, and about
$\frac{3}{16}$ inch deep—which is hammered upon the
sparrow-hawk, so as to make the back smaller
than the front ; the setting is then fitted into
the bezel, and soldered soundly. After boiling
out in the ordinary way, the centre is fixed upon
a cement stick, and holes drilled and opened, and each stone let
into its respective place. Then this centre, which is to form the
head of the ring, is removed from the cement stick, and the top
portion only of the bezel is filed into the setting in the form of
a fancy claw or galerie ; next, a ring-shaped piece is cut off the
bottom of the bezel, and the claw is then completed, care being
taken to leave sufficient strength in the claw to hold the stones ;
then the ring-shaped piece is soldered to the bottom of the claw,
and a fine line filed in the middle of it to give a light appearance.
The shanks are made of various forms, but are generally cut off

in strips and sent to the Assay Office with the setting for Hall-marking; when returned, the shoulders are filed or carved into form, and soldered to the setting; afterwards the articles are smoothed up ready for the polishing process. Cluster rings are produced by the same method.

CHAPTER IX.

MOUNTING AND SETTING.

THE goldsmith who can fashion a gold casket, mace, or massive cup, with artistic skill, and ornament it with rich *repoussé* work or enamel devices, without using any jewels, is a master of one important section of the goldsmith's art. But to execute, in excellent form and finish, an ornament composed of many valuable jewels, and to mount the stones in the way best adapted to show up their beauty and lustre require the special art and skill of a jeweller or diamond mounter. The artistic skill needed for mounting precious stones as practised by the goldsmith of the Middle Ages, was far less than that necessary to produce the diamond tiara, spray, bracelet, or pendant of our own time, because the increasing refinement in the artistic tastes of the people has led to a corresponding advance in the diamond mounter's art.

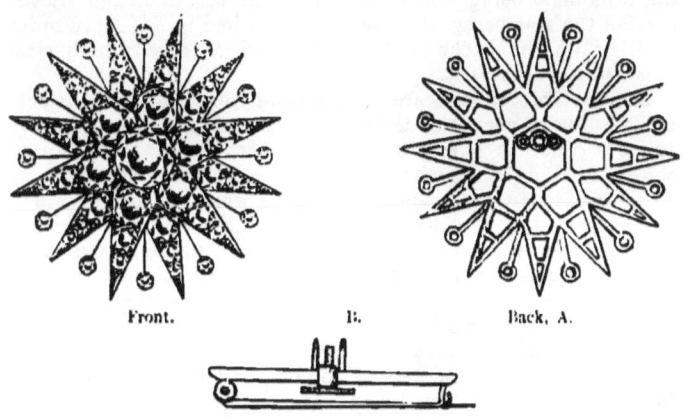

Front.   B.   Back, A.

Fig. 76.—Diamond Star.

The processes used in the production of these articles of adornment will now be described.

The first article to be noticed is the **diamond star**, set in silver, or white gold, shown in Fig. 76. White gold is an alloy composed of 18 parts of fine silver and 2 parts of fine gold, and is an alloy which will keep its colour much longer than pure silver. First, the stones are selected ; next, a star, large enough for the stones to be set in it, is cut out of flat silver or white gold, about No. 24 size in the metal gauge, and then backed by soldering upon it a piece of flat gold about No. 4 size in the same gauge After the article has been boiled out in pickle, it is slightly raised by means of doming punches, or upon a stake, so as to give it a modelled appearance. Next, the article is firmly fixed on a cement stick, holes of the right number and size are made with the drill-stock and drills, and the holes opened out with scorpers, so as to allow the stones to fit on their bearings. When all the stones have been properly fitted, the ornament is removed from the cement stick and filed up until the metal left will just suffice to complete the setting. The collets and the knife-edge wire points are then prepared. The knife-edge wire, which should be made of gold, is drawn through a draw-plate having holes the exact form required, and cut off in equal lengths ready to be soldered against the collets. The collets are made by drawing a strip of silver or white gold through a draw-plate with round holes, so as to form a tube. The joining having been soldered, suitable lengths are cut off, backed with gold, and then soldered against one end of each piece of wire above mentioned. Afterwards, each point is fitted and soldered against the star in its respective place. This is succeeded by the ornament being boiled out in pickle solution, and by the back of the star being filed out, as shown in Fig. 76, A, in order to light up the backs of the stones, and to give a high class finish to the ornament.

Convertible pieces are pieces made for temporary attachment, so as to permit of the same ornament being used for two or more different purposes. For instance, the convertible part, shown in Fig. 76, B, when attached to the diamond star, converts it into an ornament that can be worn as a brooch. The bar is formed of gold knife-edge wire, in the centre of which is an helical screw revolving loosely in a tube, and retained in its place by a ring fixed on the screw. On each side of the tube are soldered two wire pegs, while the top of the screw has soldered to it a small circular disc knurled on the edge, by means of which the screw can be worked by the wearer. The joint and catch are soldered to the bar, and the tong is pinned into the joint in the usual way. On the back of the ornament there is placed a matrix screw, and on each side of it a smaller tube is fixed for the reception of the two wire pegs above described. When the helical screw is turned by the thumb and finger, the two parts are drawn closely together, and the ornament becomes a complete brooch.

If the same ornament should be required to form the centre

of a tiara, a similar arrangement is attached to the wire frame.
If it is to be a pendant, the loop is attached to a suitable piece
and screwed upon the ornament in a similar way.   In fact, it
may be applied to any article, provided the helix and matrix
screws have the same thread.

With similar fittings, other forms of ornaments may be convertible into brooches, pendants, hairpins, bracelets, necklets,
and (in the case of smaller ornaments) eartops.

The interchangeable pin and stud is made convertible by fixing
the helical screw on the back of the front so that it will screw
into a matrix screw soldered at the top of the stem ; it could be
screwed into the stud back, which has a matrix screw of the
same thread.   Gem ornaments of this kind are always highly
polished ; every hole for the setting should be polished by means
of threads, and the other parts must be perfectly polished and
cleanly finished.   The ornament is then ready for setting (see
Setting).

SETTING.

Patience and skill are required for setting gems securely,
tastefully, and satisfactorily.   The styles of settings are so
numerous that a brief description only can be given of the
methods and processes employed.   In order to avoid repetition
it may be stated that, as a rule, the articles are fixed on cement
or on shellac sticks, by means of which they can be held firmly
in any required position.   In order to prevent the cement or
shellac 'rom sticking to the article, the latter is coated with
whiting or wrapped in gold-beater's skin.

Thread Setting is the term applied to the style in which the
ornament is outlined by a thin bright **thread** of gold.   The
stones are securely held in their settings by means of grains
(left during the process of cutting), which are rounded by forcing
them over the stones with a tool called a "graining tool."   Fig.
76 represents a specimen of thread setting ; it also represents
"cut down" setting, in the case of the stones at the end of the
knife-edge wire.

The method of drilling for gems has been already described.
In the case of pearls, corals, and turquoises the article is not
drilled through, but only to a depth sufficient to receive them.
These two principles of drilling are used in every kind of setting.
Therefore they will not need repetition.

Cut-down Setting is produced in quite a different way from
the foregoing.   Fig. 77 represents a diamond crescent in which
the inner circle is thread set, and the outer circle cut down.
The article is mounted in the same way as the star ornament,
with the exception of filing up the outer edge, which is scalloped
to the shape of the stones.   The stones are carefully let into

their places, and the metal forced over their edges by a tool
known as a "grubbing tool"; the surplus metal is then cut
down from the front, leaving small grains,
as shown, which are also pressed against the
stone, so as to fix them more securely and to
add grace to the style of setting.

Claw Setting is exemplified by the claw
set diamond stud (Fig. 78). This style is
called "invisible" setting, because of the
backward tapering of the claw; a front
view shows only the points by which the
stones are held, whereas in the "open claw"
style, in which a small stone is set in, both
the points and the hollows of the claw are
fully exposed to view.

Fig. 77.—Diamond
Crescent with
Thread and
Cut-down Setting.

The method of setting the stones in these
claws is as follows:—A bearing for the stone
is made by cutting a hollow in each point with
a scorper, then the points are bent over the
stones, either by tapping them with a small
hammer, or pressing them over with a blunt
tool; afterwards the points of the claw are
carefully filed, regulated, and burnished over
smoothly.

Fig. 78.—Claw
Setting.

Coronet Setting.—A gem cluster having
a coronet setting is shown in Fig. 79. This
class of setting is mostly produced by the
mounter. A set of stones suitable for a
compact cluster having been selected, a piece
of flat gold (about size No. 20 in the metal
gauge), sufficiently large to receive the stones
is slightly domed, and treated in the same

Fig. 79.—Coronet
Setting.

way as described in making the head of the marquise ring
(Fig. 75). The setting is then fixed on the cement stick, and
the front carefully cut into form, leaving grains between the
central and outer stones wherewith to secure the centre stone,
while the points of the coronet are filed to form grains wherewith to hold the outer side of the stones. In this arrangement
very little gold is visible from the front, while the admittance
of light through the coronet setting adds lustre and beauty to
the stones.

Pavé Setting.—In this style of setting the whole front is
covered or paved with stones as shown in Fig. 80. Great judgment is required in selecting stones of a suitable size. When
properly drilled, the arrangement should be clusters of seven
stones touching each other from every position of the article.
The best metals for this kind of setting are silver or white gold,
as the stones are entirely held in position by the grains

(produced during the drilling process and left standing erect on
their bases) being carefully pressed over the stones with the
graining tool. The stones generally used for this
class of settings are diamonds, pearls, and turquoises; in some designs a rich effect is produced
by setting a ruby, or some other transparent
stone, in the centre of a pearl or turquoise pavé
setting.

Fig. 80.
Pavé Setting.

Star Setting is exemplified in the bracelet
shown in Fig. 63, p. 86. The cutting of the gold
to form the grains, and of the fine points to form
the star, require care and skill; this form is
known in the trade as a "spider star," on account
of the extremely fine tapering of the points from the centre.

Square Setting is done in two styles. In the one, a single
stone is set in a square cut in the gold, which forms the centre
of the ornament, the stones being held by a grain at each of the
four corners; in the other, a number of stones—say, eighteen—
are set in as many squares, each stone being secured by the four
grains at the corners of each square, and separated from each
other by a thin line of gold between each square.

Lozenge Setting.—In this style a single stone is placed
within a lozenge-shaped space cut on the disc or other ornament,
the points of which are sometimes elongated so as to suit the
disc. In some ornaments three or five lozenge-shaped settings
are placed in a row, such as on a bracelet or bar-brooch.

Gipsy Setting has been mentioned in connection with rings
(Chapter viii.), but the style is also used for studs, links,
bracelets, and lockets.

Collet Setting is generally used for the topaz, garnet,
amethyst, aquamarine, chrysolite, and similar stones. A thin
wire to form a bearing is soldered to one side of a strip of thin
flat gold of the depth required; a bezel that will fit the stone is
made of the gold with pliers, and the ends are soldered together.
Then a suitable number of points, like the teeth of a saw, are
formed by filing, and the teeth pressed over the stone, thus
forming teeth or collet setting.

Glass Setting is the term used for setting moonstones, opals,
crystals, and other stones which are cut *en cabochon*. There are
two ways of producing it. In the one, a bezel of thick gold is
made, a bearing cut with a scorper, and the edge burnished
smoothly over the stone. The other is carried out in the same
way, but the bearing is made with wire, as in collet setting,
and the edge is filed and burnished smoothly, as in the first
process.

Floral Setting.—In this style pearls and other stones are set
in the form of flowers and leaves on the discs of brooches, or on
the centre of bracelets, lockets, and other ornaments. The

bright cuts made by the graver or spit stick form the stem of the flowers, &c.

Roman Setting is totally different from any kind above-mentioned. It is used for setting stones in rings, pencil cases, and seals, as shown in Fig. 81. In each case the setter, using a scorper, cuts a bearing to fit the stone in the margin of gold left by the mounter; then in the centre of the margin he cuts a narrow groove. He then fixes the article firmly, either in a vice or in a block, and with a small punch and hammer indents the groove, thereby forcing the gold against the stone, and so securing it; and, finally, he cuts the groove clearly, and polishes it.

Fig. 81. - Roman Setting.

Some Roman setters press the gold against the stone with a grubbing tool; but this method requires skill and unusual strength of the wrist. In the better class of setting, the groove is polished, first with slate points and water, and afterwards with a boxwood stick, using pumice-stone and oil, rotten-stone and oil, and rouge and water, in succession.

This class of setting may also be accomplished in a turning lathe.

CHAPTER X.

MAYORAL CHAINS AND CIVIC INSIGNIA.

IN dealing with this subject the author has pleasure in quoting several passages from the paper read by Mr. J. W. Tonks before the Society for the Encouragement of the Fine Arts on June 13th, 1895, as he is one of the best authorities on it.

He remarked, in the course of his lecture, that there was an increasing interest in this subject—a desire to know how these insignia were adopted, what was their meaning, and what abiding significance they had for art. It was clear that the growing importance of these insignia bore an exact relation to the growing importance and power of English municipal bodies. Investitures by a chain of gold as a symbol of eminent office originated in the earliest recorded times, as shown by the case of Joseph and Daniel in Biblical story, by the passage in an early British poem stating that chiefs wore " chains of regal honour . . . wreathed in many a golden link," and by a later passage in a Saxon poem which describes Athelstan as "the giver of gold chains to his nobles."

In later years the first corporations were poor, and coat armour was not favourable to the wearing of gold chains. Thus, the portrait of the unwarlike Edward II. is the earliest instance known of an individual wearing a chain over his robe; while the Black Prince was afterwards shown wearing a chain and badge over his armour.

Seals of boroughs were the earliest insignia. Towns gathered round castles for defence and trade, and therefore the tower or castle was represented on their seals; others gathered round some famous shrine or sanctuary, and in each case the seal had a representation thereof; while others, which derived their privileges direct from the king, bore his effigy or arms. In old days the seal was important, because, armed with it, the mayor, port reeve, borough reeve, or bailiff, could go before baron or king and defend the charter, or obtain a better one.

The Robe came next. An interesting portrait of a Mayor of Winchester, dated 1184, shows him in a robe richly bordered with fur, much resembling that worn at the present time.

The Mace was the next development. It was originally a weapon of war. It is probably of great antiquity, as some persons consider that the annual public exhibitions of the sceptre of Agamemnon, and the feast held in its honour, were the precursors of the mace associated with the annual mayor's banquet of to-day. In England the skull-cracker, called "the Morning Star of Scandinavia," and the spiked ball of the Danish battle-axe seemed to be prototypes of the mace, which is both a civic symbol and an emblem of justice.

"It may be mentioned that the use of the battle-mace was extended, too, for a reason of a religious kind. The clergymen were not limited in the times of chivalry, as now, to do battle only with their tongues; they turned out manfully in the field of battle to fight like other men. They were not permitted, however, to shed blood; and so the lance and the sword, as also the dagger, were unholy weapons. They were limited to the use of the battle-mace, an instrument which, we have not the least difficulty in understanding, dealt, when wielded by their strong arms, blows of a truly orthodox kind."

The mace gave Royal authority to arrest traitors, the Royal arms upon it being sufficient warrant. Corporate maces, which were at first made of iron or copper, thus represented the Royal authority. Later they were made of silver, and were lavishly adorned with enamel, jewels, and gold, until, in Edward III.'s reign, an Act was passed forbidding a mayor to have carried before him a mace of any metal more costly than copper, except by the special permission of the king. The knocking down of Wat Tyler by the mace showed the use of that weapon in those days.

The Restoration was marked by a burst of civic display, as in every part of England enthusiastic Royalists gave silver maces, on which the motto was, "The freedom of England by God's blessing restored 1660." These maces had the four bars of the Royal crown, with ball and cross. They were graceful in form, about two or three feet in length, and the ornament was symbolic and full of character. The Queen Anne maces were larger and less graceful; a tendency which reached its limit in the huge and corpulent examples of the Georgian period. In the maces of modern boroughs the endeavour has been to avoid either extreme while retaining the central ideas, as may be seen in those belonging to the boroughs of Accrington, Crewe, Worthing, Darwen, Harrogate, and West Bromwich.

Mayoral Chains.—The wearing of mayoral chains is a custom derived from the investiture of the great officers of State. The earliest civic chains consisted of convolutions of gold wire or tube, which sometimes had the S S form seen in the Lancastrian collar; others had York roses, loops, and knots of gold strap or tube, with the portcullis and British lion. The typical badge was a circular or oval plate, on which were engraved, chased, or, sometimes, enamelled the arms of the borough. Then two or three rows of guard chain, held together by clasps at intervals, were adopted. The needs of wear and tear led to a more massive chain being used. Chester marked the period when twisted links, like the tube brooches of the times, gave a bolder effect; Manchester went further and combined enamelled tube ornaments with Lancaster roses. Flat pierced links and opened scroll links with monograms came next in order, and then an escutcheon or shield for a record.

The settlement and adoption of civic and mayoral emblems led up to the modern arrangement of the chain. The fasces, or bundles of sticks carried by the lictors in Roman processions, emblematic of the strength derived from the unity of the municipality in good government and administration, became one of those emblems.

The so-called crown, which in Greek art was originally placed on the head of a female figure and symbolised a city while in Roman times it symbolised the conquest of a city, has been restored to its original meaning. The centre link became a part for heraldic display, the subject of which was the lord of the manor, the donor, the county, or an original seal. The badge itself (which is chiefly the creation of the last thirty years) has developed into a gorgeous heraldic and historic achievement, and has afforded an arduous, but splendid, field for the designer.

At the present time maces, mayoral chains, caskets, and presentation plate have taken a high position in the goldsmith's art, as a large number of corporate bodies now possess them. These modern civic insignia are especially characterised by their enamelled, wrought, and *repoussé* work, which is sometimes equal to the best Italian and French work of the Middle Ages, and by their solid carved work, which has a precision peculiarly its own.

The Methods and Processes used in the Manufacture of Mayoral Chains and Civic Insignia.—As a rule, the manufacture of these articles is entrusted only to the most skilful artists and most experienced goldsmiths, as the former alone can tastefully design an article which shall give a suggestive and heraldic description of the city, or borough, its history and its surroundings; while such a design can only be executed by a goldsmith, who is well acquainted with every branch of the craft, as he has to reproduce a graceful outline, carefully carved ornaments and wreaths, richly enamelled arms, and faithfully modelled crests and emblems.

In the construction of any civic ornament or presentation plate, the separate parts must be joined by means of cores, screws, and nuts, or by joints and pins if practicable; while soldering must be avoided as much as possible.   If many solderings are resorted to, the article will not retain its form, and many difficulties will be experienced.

By studying the various chapters of this work, the student will learn how to prepare the various parts, and will be able to produce a far more satisfactory result, especially when the various parts have to be completed by different workmen.

CHAPTER XI.

ANTIQUE JEWELLERY AND ITS REVIVAL.

ETRUSCAN WORK.

Ancient Etruscan Work.—"Italy was both in ancient times and in the middle ages the greatest centre of European civilisation, also the home of the arts, and jewels have been made in various periods by its Etruscan, Greek, Roman, and other inhabitants.

"Up to the present time the researches of the most learned ethnologists have succeeded in lifting only part of the veil under which the origin of the first inabitants of Italy is concealed.

"But in lapse of time the earlier inhabitants of Italy and their traditions became totally forgotten. Their tombs alone, from time to time discovered and excavated, have retained a faint recollection of them, and offer to the astonished gaze of the modern Italian, vestiges of the genius and customs of his unknown ancestors.

"From these tombs we have been able to ascertain that in the distant ages the arts to which riches gave birth, and which aim at the most delicate fashioning of personal ornaments, were practised with exquisite taste and skill.

"And it has also been revealed to us that these nations possessed the knowledge of some special chemical or mechanical processes quite unknown to us ; and finally, that among all their ancient ornaments that have reached us the most conspicuous for beauty of form and admirable workmanship are those which the Italian soil has yielded." *

The Etruscans, then, are among the most ancient races of the Peninsula, whose origin and early history are very obscure.

About a thousand years after the birth of Christ a revival of the arts set in which rose to its culmination in the fifteenth century, when the new Italian school, headed by Maso Finiguerra, Caradosso, and Benvenuto Cellini, began to create its

---

* *Antique Jewellery and its Revival,* by Signor Alessandro Castellani (of Rome). A paper read before the Institute of France in 1860, the Archæological Institute of London in 1861, and recently at a meeting of the Archæological Branch of the National Science Association at Buffalo, and also before the Pennsylvania Museum and School of Industrial Art.

masterpieces of art. The following anecdote from the *Memoirs of Benvenuto Cellini* will confirm this view :—

He tells us that one day Pope Paul III. showed him a gold Etruscan necklace of exquisite workmanship, which had just been accidentally discovered in the earth. He carefully examined it, and exclaimed, "Ah! it is better not to imitate these Etruscans, for we should be nothing but their humble servants; let us rather strike out a new path which will at least have the merit of originality."

Castellani's Imitations.—But for a more modern revival of antique jewellery we are indebted to Signor Castellani, who, in the year 1814, opened a studio in Rome for the imitation of the jewels of France and England, and it was not long before he succeeded in equalling and surpassing them. Then in the year 1826, the field in which he was engaged appearing too small for him, he sought the aid of chemical science for the means of improving his art; and in the course of the year gave a lecture in the Academy of the Lincei at Rome on the "Chemical Processes of the Colouring of Gold."

As the ancient jewellers were able to separate and reunite pieces of gold almost invisible to the naked eye, and had special methods of melting, soldering, and wire-drawing, it would seem that they used chemical and mechanical agents unknown to jewellers of the present time. Signor Castellani set himself the task of discovering a solder suitable for joining minute specks of gold, such as the Etruscans used. He made numerous experiments, consulted the literature of the subject as given by Pliny, Theophilus, and Benvenuto Cellini; and studied the works of the Indian, Maltese, Genoese, and other artificers. His efforts were, however, not successful until he happily discovered that some of the Etruscan methods were still in use at St. Angelo in Vado in the recesses of the Apennines. He thereupon procured a few workmen from this place and taught them the art of imitating Etruscan jewellery.

After making some very fine works of art, which were circulated all over Italy and other countries, he invented a new process for the production of the granulated gold work, by means of which he achieved inimitable results. The solution of this important problem had engaged his attention for nearly twenty years. He then set to work to discover other methods and processes. In the year 1858 he founded a *fabrique* at Naples, and, after long and assiduous labour, discovered the method of reproducing the granulated work of the Phœnicians and of the Etruscans, some excellent specimens of which reproductions were shown by him at the Vienna Exposition in the year 1873.

Among the most remarkable objects in granulated gold of Greek and Etruscan origin, are the magnificent crown in the Louvre Museum, and the Milo necklace in the British Museum,

8

Fine copies of these excellent works of art, as well as of many others, were made by Signor Castellani, which will perpetuate his fame as a great goldsmith.

And, lastly, quoting his concluding remarks, "as ardent followers of the art, and enemies of all privilege, we do not think that our labour for the cultivation of a purer taste in jewellery by the revival of ancient forms will be lost; and remembering the beautiful adaptation long since made of the philosopher's words: 'they who hold the lamps (of knowledge) will hand them on to others,'* we do not reserve everything for ourselves, being fully satisfied in the thought that others will follow us, and progressing in the road we have chosen, will help to recall the attention and admiration of the modern world towards worthy objects."

Unfortunately, Signor Castellani has not revealed to us the methods and processes he adopted, so that any further attempt to imitate the Etruscan style of jewellery must be preceded by a thorough study of the subject.

Modern Imitations.—The author of this work has for nearly forty years studied and practised the style of jewellery known as modern Etruscan work, and has produced several copies of Signor Castellani's jewellery, as also some faithful imitations of the Indian filigree work, as an employé of several firms.

Fig. 82.—Bracelet Ornaments in the Etruscan style.

A bracelet ornamented in the Etruscan style was designed by him, and now forms part of the collection of modern Birmingham jewellery, which was purchased with a surplus fund from the Art Exhibition held in Bingley Hall in the year 1896.

With a view then to making this beautiful style of ornamentation more generally appreciated, the method of manufacture will be described.

First, the design is drawn, which should be in harmony with the class of article it is intended for. The base or form should not be of strong gold, because the wire decoration would not only make the article heavy, but would also make it more

* Plato, I., *De Rep.*

difficult to solder the parts together. The surfaces to be decorated are well polished, and the wire drawn by the method described in Chapter vi., and prepared into various forms. For instance, two fine round wires are twisted closely together into what is termed **twisted cord**; or two or three strands of wires are first screwed and then twisted together into what is called **screw-twisted cord**; or a single wire is first screwed and then rolled; the last form is generally used for scrolls, or as a frame-work for granulated shots. Although gold is the most ductile of metals, it cannot be properly screwed or twisted unless the annealing has been carefully carried out (see *Annealing*, p. 85).

The decorative ornaments are made of wire coiled on suitably shaped mandrils (or spits) into circles or rings, portions of which may be cut to form other designs. The method for cutting the coil into separate rings, is to procure a piece of flat steel, such as a portion of an old back saw, or a watch spring, and solder it into a slot at one end of a mandril; it is then filed to a knife edge, hardened, and properly tempered. This is the cutter. The coil of rings is slipped on to the mandril, and the end opposite to the cutter is placed in the hole of a drawplate, but on the reverse side to that generally used for drawing wire. On the operator gently pulling the mandril, the cutter cuts the wire into separate rings which are allowed to fall into a small bottle held by an assistant over the cutter and close up to the draw-plate. As soon as the cutter reaches within half an inch of the plate the operation is stopped, in order to avoid any risk of damaging the cutter by bringing it in contact with the drawplate.

This is a quick method of cutting very small rings; large wire rings are better cut with shears. Fine scrolls are made with pliers of suitable shape, but care must be taken not to damage the wire. Fancy wires are made by twisting gold and brass wire together, and removing the brass wire with an aqueous solution of nitric acid. Various plans have been tried for pro-ducing perfectly round fine granulated gold shots. One method is by fusing fine panels of gold between layers of powdered charcoal in a crucible placed in a hot furnace, and then sifting the material through fine sieves; one objection to this method is that it yields an excess of large shots. Another method is to cut a coil of wire into rings, as above described, and to melt them upon a flat piece of charcoal with the gas blowpipe. This yields shots of equal sizes. By a third method, which the author has devised, grains can be obtained as small as those used by the Etruscan workers. The process is to spread gold filings on the surface of a flat piece of charcoal with a camel-hair brush (called a **borax pencil**) saturated with borax paste, and with a gas blowpipe fusing the gold into fine shots. The granules are cleaned by being boiled out in a pickle solution, and then assorted into sizes ready for use. Unsuccessful attempts have been made to fix the filigree wire ornaments and grains by means of a metallic paste, which is conjectured to be the method used by the Etruscans, as also by Signor Castellani.

The method now practised is as follows :—All straight wires are tied upon the article by means of iron binding wire, and then the whole of the surface covered with a borax paste in order to prevent oxidation when exposed to the heat, as such parts show up after the process of wet colouring. The wires, scrolls, ring ornaments, and small grains are carefully placed on the article with the camel-hair brush or the corn-tongs, and temporarily secured by a paste made of borax rubbed up with a little gum-dragon, in order to prevent them from shifting during the process of soldering; sandiver is sometimes used for the same purpose. The several parts are then charged with fine panels of solder, care being taken to use as little solder as possible, and to place it on the wire or grains only, not upon the article. In order to ensure a clean join, and also in order to produce perfect work, the article, the solder, and the borax must be quite clean.

Patience is a most important factor, as undue haste will lead to the exposed parts of the article being covered with solder, which should never be seen in good workmanship. The necessity of both skill and patience is manifest, when it is considered that a single article may consist of a thousand or more pieces, each of which has its separate panel of solder.

CHAPTER XII.

THE MANUFACTURE OF GOLD CHAINS.

This is a highly important branch of the goldsmith's art. It has been stated, upon good authority, that in Birmingham alone there are at least 1200 manufacturing goldsmiths and jewellers, with 20,000 work-people, who every year consume about £1,000,000 worth of gold, and from £400,000 to £500,000 worth of silver, a very large proportion of which is worked up into chains.

The gold alloy used for chains must be exceedingly malleable and ductile, as the tougher it is the better will it stand the various processes it has to undergo.

Solid Curb Chains.—Fig. 83 represents a straight curb chain, which is made either solid or hollow. For the solid chain the wire is drawn to the required size by the usual process (see Chap. vi.), and wound upon a paper-covered oval mandril or spit, which is selected according to the dimensions the rings are

Fig. 83.—Curb Chain.

to be. When the coil of gold rings is annealed, the paper burns away, and the coil is easily removed from the mandril. The coil of rings is then cut into separate links with a back saw, or with a circular saw in the lathe. These are then linked together by the aid of two pairs of pliers, the joinings are soldered soundly and the chain boiled out in pickle to remove the borax, &c. Each link is then formed into the curb by holding one link in one pair of pliers, and giving it a sharp bend with another pair of pliers. When all have been done the whole chain is flattened with a mallet, so as to cause each link to fall into its respective place. The soldered parts are smoothed over, the bar and swivel attached, and the chain polished ready for the finishing process.

Hollow Curb Chains are thus made. A strip of flat gold of a width barely sufficient to envelop a length of round charcoal iron wire is drawn with it through a draw-plate; after it has been annealed, it is wound upon a mandril or spit. This is done by pulling the point of the tube a short distance through the hole it has last been drawn through; then grasping the point and the mandril together with a hand-vice; then winding the tube on the mandril by turning the vice, so as to prevent the gold from puckering. The coil of rings is cut off, soldered and shaped by the process described under *Solid curb chains*, and the iron wire is removed by boiling the chain in diluted sulphuric acid, which is heated in a vessel placed on a sand-bath over a gas jet. The hollow curb links are then boiled out in water to remove all the acid, and then filed up ready for polishing.

Fetter and Knot Chains (Fig. 84) demand much skill for their manufacture, as special care is needed to avoid damaging the wire during the manipulation. They are generally made solid. The wire is drawn to the required size; the fetter links are wound upon flat iron or steel mandrils or spits, wrapped in

Fig. 84.—Fetter and Knot Chain.

paper; then annealed; the paper burnt away; the coil of oblong rings removed from the mandril; and the rings cut off. The other rings are prepared in a similar way. These are then linked in their respective places, the joinings soldered, and the chain filed up ready for polishing.

Cable Link Chains (Fig. 85) are made either with hollow links or with solid links. The solid chain is made of plain oval links formed by drawing round wire, winding it upon an oval mandril, and cutting the coil into rings. The rings are linked together in the form of trace chain, and to each side of every

Fig. 85.—Cable Link Chain.

link is soldered a small connecting bar, which is stamped and clipped to the proper shape and size, and cleanly soldered, thus forming a "cable link." After the chain has been filed up, and the bar and swivel attached, the chain is polished ready for finishing.

Hollow links are made for this class of chain by the process described under *Hollow curb chains*. Extraordinarily large links are produced by stamping and soldering two halves together, and linking them together afterwards.

Prince of Wales Chain, shown in Fig. 86, exemplifies a chain formed entirely of small rings. The wire is drawn by the process described, and the rings are prepared by a person known in the trade as a "preparer"; they are then linked together in a form characteristic of this particular pattern. Then certain parts of the rings are soldered firmly, and, at the same time,

Fig. 86.—Prince of Wales Chain.

flexibly. When finished by the wet colour process this kind of chain has a very rich appearance. Sometimes a lower quality gold is used, which is then gilt by the electro-gilding process, and the gilding polished off the surface in places so as to leave the gilding between the rings, which is very effective.

Half-round Belcher Chains.—One of several kinds of half-round belcher chains is shown in Fig. 87. These chains may have oval, round, or secret links; the last owes its name to a small jack ring being secreted inside each link. The various parts of belcher chains are generally furnished by a "preparer." The rings are prepared by a process different from any described above. The wire is drawn through a round hole in the draw-plate until it is two sizes smaller than is required in the half-round. For instance, if the hollow half-round wire is required

Fig. 87.—Half-round Belcher Chain.

to be No. 20 size, the round wire is drawn through a hole of No. 18 size; after the wire has been annealed it is then passed through a pair of flattening rolls (Fig. 12) until it is reduced to a narrow flat strip, having a thickness equal to about No. 3 size, and a width equal to No. 20 size in the wire gauge.

The gold is then coiled up, annealed, pointed, and the flat wire is drawn through a round hole in the draw-plate in which a small taper steel punch is held, so as to act as a swage, whereby the strip is reduced to a half-round form, and is finished off by drawing it to the right-size through half-round holes.

But the mode of drawing hollow wire is different to that of drawing solid wire. As the surface is liable to be damaged by the pliers, and in this case the pliers are dispensed with for a time, the wire is either wound upon a drum (Fig. 59), or it is first drawn through the plate a short distance with the pliers, then wrapped round the operator's body and gently pulled through the plate; this prevents any plier-marks, and also preserves the shape of the hollow wire.

Matted Link and Lapped Disc Centre Chains—Fig. 88 shows one of many kinds of fancy pattern chains. The initial stages are the same as in chains already described. Ornamental wires, like those shown in the figure, are produced by passing the wire through flattening rolls with matting pattern, as in Fig. 14. The process of drawing is the same; the matted part forming the inside, and the edges the lines for lapping. Each disc is then pierced out with the aid of a press, and, while fixed in another bed, the star is pierced with a separate pair of

Fig. 88.—Matted Link and Lapped Disc Centre Chains.

piercing tools. The discs are next soldered soundly to certain parts, care being taken to keep the chain flexible. When all the various parts have been added, the chain is either coloured by the wet colouring process, or gilt. In either case the discs and the edges of the links are lapped by the gold cutter, so as to leave the rich yellow colour in the matted links, and to make the prominent parts bright and effective.

The methods and processes described in this chapter from a few selected patterns are applicable to many other patterns. It may be repeated that patterns of chains are very numerous, that each has its special name, and that the process of annealing and boiling out must be carried out, when necessary, in every case.

CHAPTER XIII.

PRECIOUS STONES, &c.

THEIR PROPERTIES, FORMS, AND SPECIFIC GRAVITY.

Definition and Properties.—The object of this chapter is to give a brief outline only, not an exhaustive study of the subject, for full details of which the reader is referred to *Precious Stones* (London, 1890), by A. H. Church, F.R.S.; *Diamonds and Precious Stones* (2nd ed., 1867), by Harry Emanuel, F.R.G.S.; *Precious Stones* (4th ed., London, 1884), by E. W. Streeter; and *Gems and Precious Stones of America* (1890), by Kunz. It is not easy to define what a **precious** stone is when so much depends upon adventitious circumstances, such as caprice, time, and place. Then there are hard and beautiful stones, which are rarer than the diamond or the ruby, but which are less costly because there is less demand for them : but which might partly displace those minerals as precious stones if it became the fashion to wear them.

The term "precious" is generally given to substances characterised by beauty, durability, and rarity ; all the true precious stones are minerals, but there are precious minerals, such as native gold and platinum, which are not "stones," and are therefore outside the category of "precious stones," which include such minerals as the diamond, ruby, sapphire, emerald, and the opal, and some animal products, such as the pearl, which is characterised by beauty, rarity, and a fair amount of durability and is therefore associated with precious stones.

The minerals named are highly valued for their brilliancy and colour, but such minerals as spinel, jargoon, and tourmaline generally have small merits as gems. The caprice of fashion largely influences the commercial value of precious stones, as shown by the fluctuation in that of the amethyst, topaz, aquamarine, cat's-eye, and peridot which have all had their day and have been replaced by more modern favourites. Also the emerald has suffered in its time, for, at present, it is only good stones that have great value. In this chapter a brief treatment only is given of "acknowledged gems," and mention is made of the other minerals which are classified as "precious stones."

The order of importance of the properties is—(1) Beauty ; (2) durability ; and (3) rarity, which last rises in importance in proportion as the durability is less.

As the optical properties are the most important they will be first considered. These may be classified under the general heads of "surface" and "substance" as shown in the following table:—

Surface,	Form,	1. Plane.
		2. Curved.
		3. Metallic.
	Lustre,	4. Adamantine.
		5. Resinous.
		6. Vitreous.
		7. Waxy.
		8. Pearly.
		9. Silky.
Substance,	Light,	10. Transparent.
		11. Translucent.
		12. Opalescent.
		13. Chatoyant.
		14. Opaque.
	Colour,	15. Prismatic.
		16. Monochroic.
		17. Pleiochroic.
		18. Fluorescent.

Most of these terms are fully described in the excellent work by A. H. Church, F.R.S., but the physical characteristics on which they depend may be gathered from the following list and descriptions :—

Refraction.	Hardness.
Dispersion.	Specific gravity.
Polarisation.	Form.
Pleiochroism.	Structure.

Refraction of Light.—Light is generally refracted when it passes from one transparent medium into another, as, for instance, from the air into a diamond. It passes through the air in a definite direction, but when it enters the diamond it follows a different path—that is, it is *refracted*.

The diamond, like glass and some crystalline matter, possesses the property of *single* refraction ; but many precious stones have that of *double* refraction. For instance, if the light from a candle flame is viewed through a singly-refracting stone a single image will be seen, but if the same flame is viewed through a doubly-refracting stone, two distinct images will appear, except when the line of vision coincides with the optic axis of the crystal.

All crystals belonging to the cubical system, such as the diamond, spinels, and the garnets, are, like glass and strass, singly refracting ; while the ruby, beryl, topaz, and quartz are all doubly refracting.

Dispersion of Light.—When a ray of light passes from one medium to another it is bent or refracted ; but, as the light is composed of rays having different degrees of refrangibility, the rays are also spread out or *dispersed*. In this way the compound white ray is separated into its component coloured rays, which, in suitably selected minerals, gives rise to prismatic effects. In gems, this play of prismatic hues is known as "fire," which is especially well manifested in the diamond when properly cut—that is, in a diamond in which the facets are cut so as to allow of the greatest dispersion of light.

Polarisation of Light.—Light may be polarised in various ways. If, for example, we assume that a beam of light, freely traversing any medium, has what is called *identical properties on all its sides*, it may be so reflected or refracted by the obstacles it meets with, and will then have *different properties on different sides*—that is, it will be polarised; such light is incapable of being reflected at a certain angle, or of again traversing the crystal in a certain direction. In some doubly refracting crystalline minerals the two oppositely polarised beams are of different colours; while some transparent gem stones are more or less opaque, in one direction at least, to one of the two oppositely polarised beams. These two important facts give rise to the property of pleiochroism, which is seen in many gems.

Pleiochroism.—This property is determined by means of the *dichroiscope*. A precious stone thus examined will, if coloured, show two images of the same hue or of different hues. If the two images of the square opening of the instrument are identical in colour, the specimen is either a garnet, a spinel, or a diamond; but if the colours differ it is a topaz or a beryl.

It may be remarked that the property of polarisation of light and its attendant pleiochroism can only be used by experts, having the necessary apparatus at command. Polarised light cannot be distinguished from ordinary light by the unaided eye.

Hardness.—Gem stones are readily distinguished from each other, and from their imitations, by their degrees of hardness—that is, by their power of resisting abrasion, which is quite distinct from fragility or inability to resist a blow from a very hard stone. For example, diamonds, emeralds, and zircons, though high in the scale of hardness, are readily broken by coming into sudden contact with a hard substance, as in the case of a fall or a slight blow. The following is a table of hardness :—

TABLE OF HARDNESS.*

Diamond,	.	10·0	Iolite, . .	. 7·3
Sapphire,	.	9·0	Cinnamon Stone,	. 7·0
Ruby, .	.	8·8	Jadeite, . .	. 7·0
Chrysoberyl, .	.	8·5	Amethyst, .	. 7·9
Spinel, .	.	8·0	Jade, . .	. 6·5
Topaz, .	.	8·0	Peridot, . .	. 6·3
Aquamarine, .	.	8·0	Moonstone, .	. 6·3
Emerald,	.	7·8	Green Garnet, .	. 6·0
Zircon, .	.	7·8	Turquoise, .	. 6·0
Tourmaline,	.	7·5	Opal, .	. 6·0
Phenakite,	.	7·5	Lapis-Lazuli, .	. 5·2
Almandine,	.	7·3	Catlinite, .	. 4·0

* A. H. Church, F.R.S., in *Precious Stones*, London, 1890.

Form.—The forms of all crystals may be referred to one or other of the six known crystallographic systems :—(1) The cubic, or monometric ; (2) the pyramidal, dimetric, or tetragonal ; (3) the rhombohedral, or hexagonal ; (4) the prismatic, trimetric, or orthorhombic ; (5) the oblique, or monoclinic ; and (6) the triclinic or anorthic. A knowledge of crystalline form is of considerable service to the expert in the examination of crude stones, but natural crystals are generally more or less imperfect, and quite unfit for mounting. A given stone owes much of its value for ornamental purposes to the lapidary's art.

Structure.—A knowledge of the mechanical aggregation or intimate texture of minerals may be obtained by disruption of the mass, or by cleaving or splitting it. Fractured surfaces are not very instructive, as they may be uneven or splintered. A true cleavage surface shows the intimate structure of a body, and in a homogeneous crystalline structure, an examination of the cleavage planes, which are the faces of crystals, may give much useful information. The structure of a stone is often found to be either crystalline, laminar, fibrous, or columnar.

Translucency.—There are five degrees of translucency, or of opacity, which may be arranged in the following order :—

Transparent.—When objects can be seen distinctly through the body.

Semi-transparent.—When objects can be seen dimly through the body.

Translucent.—When light is perceptible, but not objects.

Sub-translucent.—When light is transmitted through their splinters.

Opaque.—When no light is transmitted.

Lustre.—The various kinds of lustre have been classed by mineralogists in the following order :

Metallic.—Having the appearance of the mineral pyrites, or polished metal.

Adamantine.—Possessing the brilliancy of the diamond.

Vitreous.—Resembling the surface of glass, or of the emerald.

Resinous.—Shining, as if rubbed with oil, such as the surface of the garnet.

Pearly.—Having the peculiar lustre of the pearl and the moonstone.

Waxy.—Resembling the surface of the turquoise, or of the coral.

Silky.—Having a fibrous reflection similar to silk, or like that seen in crocidolite.

It must be understood that the above classification is only an approximate representation of the peculiar appearance of the various gems.

Specific Gravity.—The mass of matter which a given body contains determines what is called its *density*, and this property of the body is entirely independent of anything outside itself. The density of a body is usually determined by a process of weighing, and, on this account, density and weight are sometimes used synonymously; but there is really a distinction between them, for the weight of a given body is dependent upon outside bodies, and is caused by the force of gravitation which acts between all bodies and tends to bring them together. The effect decreases with the distance between the centres of the attracting bodies. Thus the weight of a body near the earth's surface is caused by the attraction of the earth, and as the centres of the earth and of the body are nearer at the poles than at the equator, it follows that a given body weighs heavier at the pole than at the equator, when weighed on a spring balance. But the mass of matter does not alter with the weight. What is usually done when two bodies of equal volume are weighed is to measure their relative densities. When one of the bodies is taken as a standard, the ratio between the two weights is called the *specific gravity* of the other body.

The determination of the specific gravity of bodies is of considerable practical importance, and in the case of gem stones may be used for the detection of imitation stones, and for other purposes. The common standard is water, and the process of determining the weights of a stone and of an equal volume of water is a comparatively easy one. If the stone is a large one it is suspended in a loop of silk fibre from a hook underneath the support of the scale pan of a good balance. In this position it is accurately weighed, and then carefully lowered into a glass vessel filled with distilled water, and supported on a small stool placed over the scale pan, but so as not to interfere with its free movement. It is then weighed in the water. The stone is found to be lighter when surrounded by water than when in air, owing to the supporting power of the water, which holds up the stone with the same force it would hold up an equal volume of water. The loss of weight of the stone when weighed in water is, therefore, equal to the weight of a volume of water equal to that of the stone. Since then the weight of the body and the weight of an equal volume of water are known, the specific gravity of the body is at once determined by simple division.

Example.—Determination of the specific gravity of a garnet—

Weight of stone in air $= 21\cdot79$ grains.
  ,,   ,,   water $= 16\cdot36$,,

  ,, equal volume of water $= 5\cdot43$,,

Therefore, $\dfrac{21\cdot79}{5\cdot43} = 4\cdot065 =$ specific gravity of stone.

If the stones are too small to be dealt with in this way, their specific gravity can be found by the use of the specific gravity bottle. The bottle commonly used has the shape shown in Fig.

89. The stopper, A, is ground very accurately into the neck, so as to be quite watertight, and has a fine hole drilled through its centre for the escape of excess liquid. The size of the stones which can be dealt with by this means is only limited by the width of the neck. The stones to be tested are weighed accurately. The bottle is then filled with distilled water, which has been standing near the balance case for some time, and is, therefore, at the same temperature as the case. The stopper is then pressed in, and the surplus water forced out through the centre hole. The bottle is now carefully wiped and weighed. The stopper is then removed, the stones dropped in, and the stopper replaced. It is clear that the stones will replace a volume of

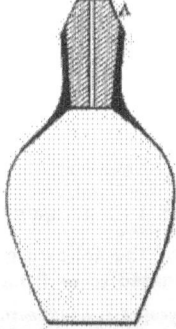

Fig. 89.—Specific Gravity Bottle.

water equal to their own volume. After wiping, the bottle is again weighed. A little consideration will make it clear that the increase in the weight of the bottle when the stones are in, together with the weight of the volume of water displaced by them, is equal to the weight of the stones in air. Therefore, by subtracting the increase in weight from the weight of the stones in air the weight of an equal volume of water is obtained.

Example.—Determination of the specific gravity of small garnets.

Weight of small stones   =   7·58 grains.
 ,,   bottle with stones in = 1055·09 ,,
 ,,   ,,   water alone = 1049·37 ,,
                                ─────────
                                   5·72   ,,

Therefore, Weight of equal volume of water is 7·58 – 5·72 = 1·86 grains.

Then, $\dfrac{7·58}{1·86} = 4·075$ = specific gravity of stones.

The temperature of the water must be taken into consideration if a perfectly accurate result is required. In the examples given above it was 17° C.   From the two results it is seen that the methods compare well together, so that the specific gravity of the stones used may be taken to be 4·07.

SPECIFIC GRAVITY OF STONES.

The following table shows the specific gravity of the stones in general use by the modern jeweller, from which their relative weight may be estimated :—

The Diamond,	.	.	.	.	3·500 to 3·524
,, Ruby,	.	.	.	.	3·900 ,, 4·100
,, Sapphire,	.	.	.	.	3·900 ,, 4·200
,, Chrysoberyl,		.	.	.	3·680 ,, 3·745
,, Spinel Ruby,		.	.	.	3·800
,, Topaz,	.	.	.	.	3·500 ,, 3·600
,, Emerald,	.	.	.	.	2·670 ,, 2·750
,, Garnet,	.	.	.	.	3·500 ,, 4·300
,, Tourmaline,	.	.	.	.	2·990 ,, 3·330
,, Turquoise,	.	.	.	.	2·600
,, Opal,	.	.	.	.	1·900 ,, 2·300
,, Pearl,	.	.	.	.	2·500 ,, 2·600
,, Lapis-Lazuli,		.	.	.	2·380 ,, 2·450
,, Malachite,	.	.	.	.	3·700

QUARTZ AND ROCK-CRYSTALS.

The specific gravity of the following forms of silica, quartz, and rock-crystals is estimated to be from 2·500 to 2·800 :—

Amethyst, cairngorm, chrysoprase, onyx, sardonyx, cornelian, chalcedony, agate, mocha-stone, cat's-eye, jasper, bloodstone, aventurine and rock-crystal.

CHAPTER XIV.

CUTTING DIAMONDS AND OTHER PRECIOUS GEMS.

THE cutting of diamonds and other precious stones is a most important branch of the jewellery trade; and it is only by strict attention to certain scientific laws that the rough stone can be converted into a perfect gem. If the rule of thumb is adopted, the probabilities are that the stone will be ruined by faulty cutting. As before mentioned, gems have different optical properties; therefore it is necessary that each individual stone should be treated differently in order to make the best possible use of its special qualities.

Take, for example, the diamond. Fig. 90 shows a natural crystal of the diamond in the octahedral form. Although the natural surface is not brilliant, yet it has a lustre unsurpassed by any other gem. The lapidary first reduces it to a suitable form by remov-

Fig. 90.
Octahedral Crystal
of Diamond.

ing flakes along the planes of easiest cleavage, which are always parallel to the faces of the octahedron. This is generally performed by a "diamond cleaver." The object of this is (1) to remove the defective parts in the stone, and (2) to form the facets in the rough. In order to do this the operator must have an exact knowledge of the structure and cleavage of the diamond. Splitting a diamond is thus effected. The stone is fastened upon a stick, by means of cement, and the part to be split off is left uncovered; a line is then scratched on the surface with another diamond to mark the exact place. To make the line, three different diamonds are used in succession; the first is a complete crystal, which marks out the direction; the second a sharp splinter, which deepens the impression; and the third a very fine splinter, which makes the mark much deeper. The cement stick is then placed upright in a piece of lead fastened to the cleaver's bench; then a sharp knife is inserted in the mark, made as described, and the stone is split by a smart blow from a hammer. Should, however, the stone be too difficult to split, it is sawn with fine iron wire fitted in a saw-bow, and anointed with diamond powder and olive oil.

Next, the diamonds are faceted, by fixing two diamonds upon

sticks, and then rubbing them together carefully; hence the term "diamond cut diamond." By this process a facet is put upon the stone just where required, the dust resulting from this operation being saved for cutting purposes. Polishing is the next process. For this purpose the stones are soldered into holders, fixed into weighted irons, and placed against steps which are so arranged as to bring the facets of the diamond upon a cast-iron wheel charged with diamond dust and oil, and revolving at a very high speed. When one facet has been polished, the diamond is unsoldered, and fixed in another position for the next facet.

This process was splendidly exhibited at the Industrial Exhibition in Birmingham, in the year 1886, by Mr. William Spencer, who was the first manufacturer to cut diamonds in Birmingham. The author was intimate with him at the time, and learned from him the technical processes which have just been briefly described.

All the different forms into which precious stones are cut may be arranged into two groups—(1) those with plane surfaces; (2) those with curved surfaces; under special circumstances the same stone may have both plane and curved facets. These two groups may be thus subdivided :—

Group 1. Plane Surfaces
{
Brilliant cut,
Rose cut.
Table cut,
Step or trap cut.
}

Group 2. Curved Surfaces
{
Single cabochon.
Double cabochon.
Hollow cabochon.
Tallow top.
}

In describing the different forms into which precious stones are cut, the diamond will be the first noticed.

Group 1.—**Brilliant-cut Diamond.**—There are 58 perfectly arranged facets in a brilliant-cut diamond. The "girdle," or edge forming the widest part of the stone, divides the "crown" from the "pavilion" or base, which is concealed in many instances by the mount or setting. In a perfect stone this girdle must not be too thin, or it is liable to chip in the process of setting. In shallow stones, which are known in the trade as "spread stones," this thin girdle is often met with. A large number of these are in use at the present time, and are mostly cut at Amsterdam, where diamond cutting forms a most important industry, there being thirty-five diamond mills, giving employment to nearly 1,200 people. These spread stones differ in proportions from the well-known double-cut brilliant, which form of cutting is only used for the diamond; hence the word "brilliant" signifies a diamond cut in this fashion. Certain

9

THE DOUBLE-CUT BRILLIANT.

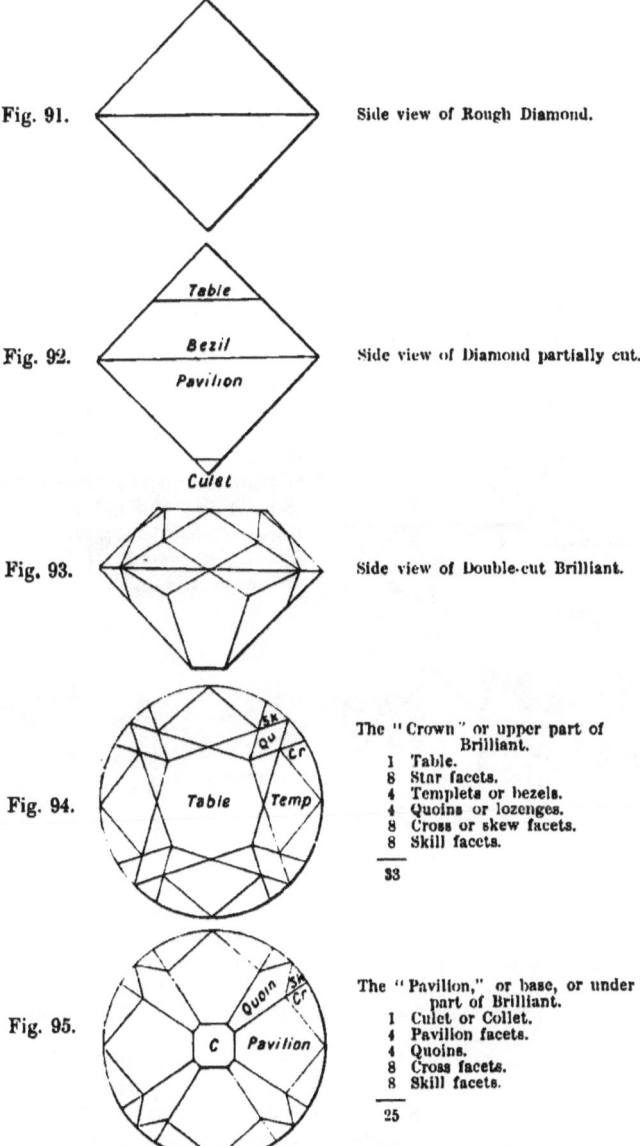

Fig. 91.   Side view of Rough Diamond.

Fig. 92.   Side view of Diamond partially cut.

Fig. 93.   Side view of Double-cut Brilliant.

Fig. 94.

The "Crown" or upper part of Brilliant.

1	Table.
8	Star facets.
4	Templets or bezels.
4	Quoins or lozenges.
8	Cross or skew facets.
8	Skill facets.

33

Fig. 95.

The "Pavilion," or base, or under part of Brilliant.

1	Culet or Collet.
4	Pavilion facets.
4	Quoins.
8	Cross facets.
8	Skill facets.

25

Figs. 91-95.—Showing the forms of a Double-cut Brilliant during the process of cutting.

rules are laid down for the guidance of the lapidary as to the relative proportions, not only of the several classes of facets, but also of the dimensions of the finished stone in every direction. The following are the proportions given by A. H. Church, F.R.S., in his work on precious stones :—

The crown or portion above the girdle should form $\frac{1}{3}$ of the total thickness, while the pavilion or the lower portion forms the remaining $\frac{2}{3}$. The "table" should be $\frac{4}{9}$ of the breadth of the stone, and the culet $\frac{1}{4}$ to $\frac{1}{5}$ of the table.

In many of the brilliants which are used at the present time, the girdle has been made more circular instead of nearly square, and the templet and quoins are nearly of the same size; also there are eight star facets round the culet; thus making a stone of 66 facets in all. To make the matter more clear, the foregoing illustrations (Figs. 94 and 95) show the forms of the brilliant cut with 58 perfectly arranged facets.

The Single-cut Brilliant differs from the double-cut brilliant in the following ways :—(1) The table is square; (2) there are sixteen triangular facets touching the table and the girdle; (3) the under part has twelve triangular facets which touch the girdle; and (4) underneath these are eight long facets; thus making altogether 38 facets. It is shown in Fig. 96.

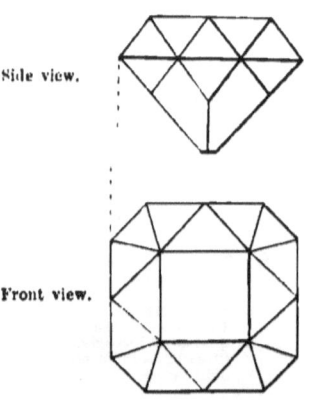

Side view.

Front view.

Fig. 96.—Single-cut Brilliant.

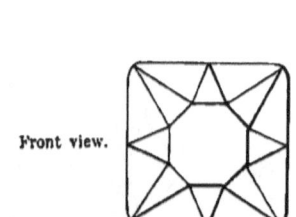

Front view.

Fig. 97.—Star-cut Diamond.

The Old English Star-cut Brilliant.—Fig. 97 shows the style of cutting known as the "star-cut" diamond. The eight facets touching the table form a star and have eight other facets between them, thus forming 16 facets on the front in addition to the table.

The Rose Diamond.—The rose-cut diamond differs from the brilliant cut in several respects. The under part of the rose is perfectly flat, while that of the brilliant is formed of a pointed culet; in the rose, the crown or upper part consists of triangles, whose apices meet at the points and form what are termed "star facets," while their bases touch another row of triangular facets reversed, so that the two sets together form lozenges as shown in Fig. 98.

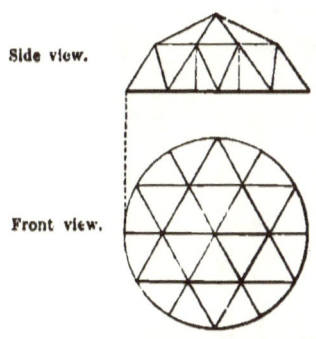

Side view.

Front view.

Fig. 98.—Rose-cut Diamond.

Rose diamonds are frequently cut from rough chips and fashioned to the best advantage, skill being required to waste as little material as possible.

Roses are often cut with fewer facets than are shown in the illustration, especially those called "Antwerp roses," but these are not so brilliant as a full-cut rose.

The Briolet or Briolette is the style applied to the stones which resemble two roses joined together at the base. When the rough stone is perfectly round or pear-shaped, it can be faceted all over with less waste than with any other style. This beautiful form serves well for drops to pendants or necklets, but is very rarely adopted. The pair of eardrops formerly possessed by Marie Antoinette may be taken as an example of this style of cutting.

Gem Cutting.—Other gems are generally cut with a table and facet, but in different forms. The ruby, sapphire, emerald, topaz, garnet, amethyst, aquamarine, tourmaline, &c., are generally cut in this style. "Gem cutting," as it is termed, is much more simple than diamond cutting. Each gem is cut upon a flat lap or disc composed of a special metal; if the metal must be hard, bell metal is used; but in some cases the metal must be nearly as soft as lead.

The grinding agent generally used for gem cutting is emery for soft stones or diamond boart for hard stones.

The polishing is effected on similar laps but made of harder metal, while rotten-stone is generally substituted for the emery. Fig. 99 represents a lapidary's lathe. .

The motion is obtained by working the treadle with the foot (but in large mills the motive power is steam or electricity). The disc is made to revolve in a horizontal position in order that the operator's hands may be free. He holds the gem to be cut (which has been firmly fixed upon a cement stick) against the disc with the one hand, and with the other hand he charges the disc either with emery or with diamond boart, according to the class of stone under manipulation. When one or two facets have been made, the stone is removed and fixed again in another position, and this is repeated until all the facets have been completed. The stone is then polished.

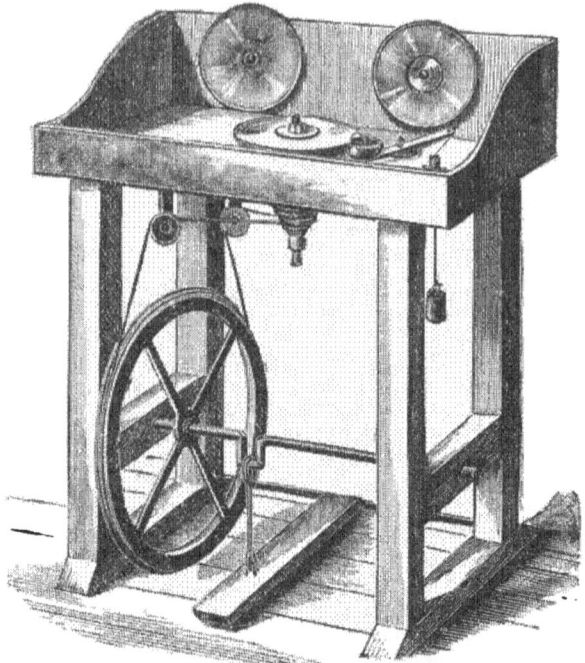

Fig. 99.—Foot Lathe generally used by the Lapidary.

Group 2.—The next class of gems to be considered are those in group 2, such as translucent and opaque stones, which are generally cut *en cabochon*. The opal, turquoise, cat's-eye, moonstone, carbuncle, and the star-sapphire are characteristic examples belonging to this group. The only transparent stone of the present day which is cabochon cut is the garnet, which, when fashioned in this way, is called a "carbuncle."

Figs. 100, 101, 102, and 103 represent the several kinds of cutting in this group.

The Simple Cabochon.—This form is used in cutting turquoise, coral, onyx, and opal.

Fig. 100.—Simple Cabochon.   Fig. 101.—Double Cabochon.

The Double Cabochon.—The cat's-eye and star-sapphire are generally cut in this form.

The Hollow Cabochon.—This is the form used for striped onyx and carbuncles.

Fig. 102.—Hollow Cabochon.　　　　Fig. 103.—Tallow Topped.

The Tallow Topped.—Opals, crystals, and the chrysoprase are cut in this form.

Many stones which are cut *en cabochon* are used for the decoration of articles which have to be handled, such as vases, caskets, maces, and swords, also of those used for ecclesiastical purposes.

Rubies, emeralds, sapphires, and jargoons are often cut in this way, but in such case they lose their characteristic dispersive and reflective powers. As a rule, faceting is essential for developing the beauty and special optical properties of transparent gems.

Another group of stones, which includes blood-stones, sardonyx, jade, cornelian, and lapis-lazuli, extensively used in art jewellery, are cut in a simpler style. The form is simply a flat table surrounded by a perfectly even flange. The base or under part is either flat or slightly rounded ; such stones are usually mounted in rings, seals, pencil cases, &c. The kind of setting is termed " Roman setting " and will be described in another chapter.

Glass Cutting.—As some articles used in jewellery are hair-designs, portraits, &c., such are protected in a "box glass;" the latter is generally cut in the forms called " buff-top glass " or a "bevel-edge glass," and this kind is similar in form to that of the blood-stone. Clear crystals cut to the " tallow topped " form are also employed instead of glass. They wear better and are not so easily scratched.

These glasses or crystals are usually worn in brooches, pendants, lockets, bracelets, seals, and rings.

CHAPTER XV.

POLISHING AND FINISHING.

THESE operations form a very important part of the goldsmith's art, as they require much skill and experience to carry them out, so as to avoid spoiling the more delicate details by converting sharp edges into round ones, and rubbing the thin parts into holes. It is stated that "among the remains of ancient Greek and Etruscan metal work, none show more admirable art than the mirrors, many of which are to be seen in modern collections. The surface of these mirrors is usually an alloy of copper and *stannum* (tin?); according to Beckmann the *stannum* of Pliny is rather an alloy of tin and lead, a sort of (very hard) pewter. Silver came gradually into use for the surface of mirrors, alloyed with other metals, and by degrees it was used almost pure." [*]

This implies that the ancients were able to impart so fine a surface to metal by polishing, that it could be used as a mirror or looking-glass.

Polishing, as understood by the goldsmith, comprises the processes used for removing tool marks, and for giving the last finish to the surface of the article. These vary according to the nature of the ornament, and are described in the present chapter. Certain articles of special design and character require polishing at particular stages during their manufacture. This is done by first rubbing the parts with a "Water of Ayr" stone, which removes the file marks from flat surfaces; and then with a "blue stone," which smoothes them. In fact, discs and other flat surfaces may be coloured by the wet-process after the last process of stoning. Round surfaces are generally polished with circular brushes (Fig. 104) rotated in a lathe, either by means of the foot, or by motive power, as described in Fig. 21, p. 68, and occasionally charged with a polishing mixture consisting of fine powdered pumice-stone (or with crocus, which is preferred by some) mixed with a little oil to the consistency of paste, a little of which is also placed upon the work. As the brush revolves the article is held firmly against it, and the file marks are removed. If a higher polish is required, the article is subjected to the action of another brush charged with a mixture of finely-powdered

---

[*] *Gold- and Silversmiths' Work*, by John Hungerford Pollen, M.A., p. 26.

rotten-stone and oil, which removes the marks produced by the first operation.

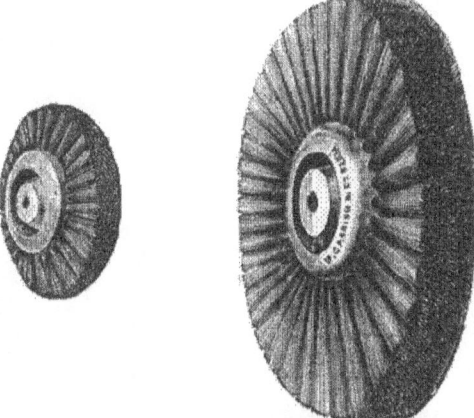

Fig. 104.—Circular Polishing Brushes.

If the article is to be still more highly polished, what is called **bright finished**, it is accomplished by subjecting it either to a circular brush of extra quality white bristles, or a **calico mop** (Fig. 105) charged with a little rouge moistened with water.

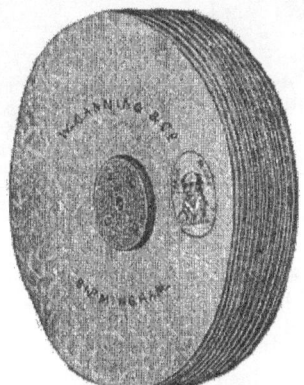

Fig. 105.—Calico Mop.

Felt bobs and **woollen brushes** of various forms are also used in the finishing process (Fig. 106). The insides of rings are finished with a bob similar to A in Fig. 106, while concave articles are finished with a bob like B ; in fact, a variety of differently sized brushes and bobs should be kept in readiness suitable for the various kinds of work manufactured.

But to ensure a good clear finish to bright work the article must be "grease-brushed"—that is, gently brushed all over upon a special circular brush charged with a little tallow from a tallow candle and rouge.

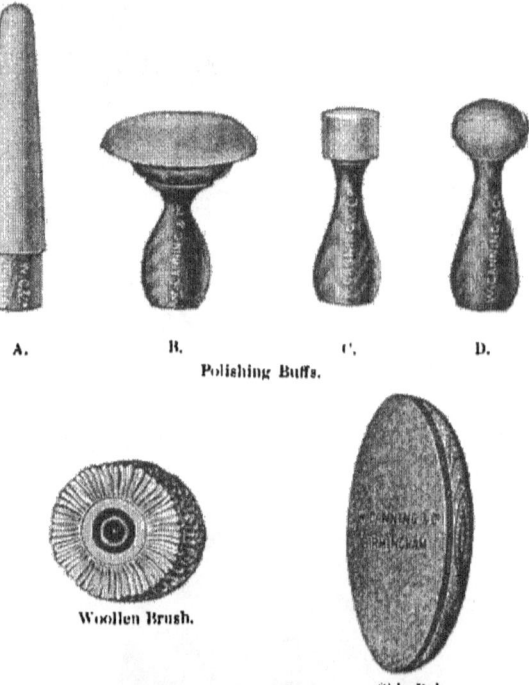

A.   B.   C.   D.

Polishing Buffs.

Woollen Brush.

Side Bob.

Fig. 106.—Polishing Buffs, Side Bob, and Woollen Brush.

It must be borne in mind that the article is always subjected to a special cleaning operation before it undergoes a fresh polishing process. This is done by washing it out in a solution of hot water and washing soda, with a small hand brush (like that shown in Fig. 107, but with ordinary dark bristles), to which

Fig. 107.—Jewellers' Soft White Plate Brush.

a little soap is occasionally applied. It is then dried in warm boxwood sawdust in the drying apparatus (Fig. 108).

After the rougeing process, it is washed out, dried, and then lightly brushed with a soft white plate brush (as Fig. 107), charged with a very small quantity of rouge. Different kinds of goldsmith's work require different treatment, while jeweller's work has to be exceptionally treated on account of the delicate construction of the articles. Take, for example, a tiara, or a spray brooch which has to be set with diamonds and other precious stones. In this class of work, the holes intended to

receive the stones have been skilfully filed out at the back so as to form a suitable design, while the carefully curved knife edge wires are sharp and graceful. This kind of polishing is generally performed by girls, who patiently polish every hole and carefully remove all marks, by means of fine threads (called "polishing threads") charged with suitable polishing materials.

Fig. 108.—Drying Apparatus.

A different process is used for polishing delicately carved half-hoop rings and bracelets. In the first place, every scroll is carefully rubbed over with a hard slate point, then sticked with a sharp pointed boxwood stick occasionally dipped in a paste of pumice-stone and oil, next rubbed with rotten-stone and oil, and, lastly, with rouge and water.

Sometimes a whole day's labour is required to polish a single article, while in other cases a much longer time is necessary; therefore it is quite clear that a perfect knowledge of the many processes of polishing is most essential to ensure success.

Motive Power for Polishing, Scratch Brushing, &c.— Polishing, gold cutting, and scratch brushing performed upon the old principle may answer the purpose very well for some manufacturing goldsmiths, jewellers, or chain makers, &c., but not for those who are compelled by competition to use every modern improvement. For instance, a lathe rotating at a high speed is essential for the production of an excellent finish upon some kinds of goldsmith's work; in such cases the foot lathe is laborious, tedious, and unprofitable. Hence many manufacturers have adopted steam, electric, or other motive power. Fig. 109 shows the Crompton continuous current motor, which is now extensively used for this and other processes in Birmingham.

Gold Cutting is a special mode of finishing certain kinds of work, such as gold chains, flat surfaces, and articles that require faceting. It is done with the lap (Fig. 22), hence the process is called **lapping**; but the proper term is **gold cutting**, as the gold is cut away by means of the lap, producing an even, bright surface on special parts, and giving richness to the design.

Discs and centres of jewellery are improved by being bevelled by the gold cutter; and in many cases the designs of gold chains are entirely finished by this process.

Before the operator commences to lap or facet an electro gilt or a coloured article, a gold chain for example, he must first examine carefully to ascertain that the lap has been properly "headed in" by the process described in Chapter v., p. 69. If it is found to be in proper order, the operator simply cleans the surface with a little cotton waste, and then places the chain in a liquid preparation consisting of four parts of gum arabic and two parts of gamboge; after it is withdrawn, it is dried slowly. This protects the gilding or colour upon the parts which do not require to be lapped, and at the same time gives the operator more freedom in manipulating the article.

Fig. 109.—Crompton's Continuous Current Motor.

A skilful and experienced gold-cutter can so manipulate the links of a chain between the thumb and finger of his right hand, and can place each link in its turn so carefully and precisely against the lap as it revolves, as to produce truly marvellous results. For instance, with a skilful twist of the chain faultless diamond-shaped facets are formed on a belcher link chain.

Square Lapping is produced by a similar process; it adds a sharpness to the links, and produces a high finish unequalled by any other process.

When lapping or faceting is finished, the protective preparation is removed by thoroughly washing in the first instance, and then rinsing the articles in hot water, which is a solvent of the preparation. The article is then dried in warm boxwood-dust. It will then be seen that, while the lapping has added sharpness and lustre to the article, the parts which were protected by the mixture have not been altered. A light rougeing up on the bob or the calico mop completes the finishing process.

The gold taken from the article remains on the lap, but as it is apt to interfere with the lapping, it is occasionally removed by the aid of cotton waste moistened with a little oil, and the cotton waste is treated for the recovery of the gold by the method described in another chapter.

Success in the art of polishing and gold cutting is easily achieved by a strict attention to the methods and processes above described.

Burnishing is used for finally finishing off metallic articles so as to give to the metal a beautiful lustre, which cannot be produced on such articles by any other process, such as, for instance, wedding rings, gem rings which have been dry coloured, certain parts of personal ornaments, gold and silver cups, chalices, croziers, staffs, and other ecclesiastical utensils. Burnishing is generally performed by girls or women, who use tools specially adapted in structure, nature, and form for the different kinds of work.

Steel Burnishers, various in form, are made of the best steel highly polished.

Bloodstone Burnishers have points or heads formed of the finest polished bloodstone mounted in metal, and firmly fixed in suitable handles.

Agate Burnishers are similar, but the points or heads are made of polished agate.

Fig. 110 represents a small, but complete, burnishing outfit, for it must be understood that each operator or "burnisher," as she is called, requires a large and varied stock of burnishing tools; and as many of these are expensive, the possessor generally takes great pride in keeping them in good order. In burnishing, the steel burnisher is the first to be used; it is kept continually moistened with a thick solution of soap-suds. It is held by the handle near to the point or head, and, with a firm downward pressure, it is passed backwards and forwards, with an even rapid motion, all over the parts to be burnished.

This is followed by reburnishing the same parts, either with the bloodstone or the agate burnishing tool, so as to give it a superior finish. Every burnishing tool must be kept highly polished, as well as free from cracks and marks. To keep them in proper order, they should be frequently polished on a leather buff charged with a little putty powder (oxide of tin). **As a** final operation the article is rubbed over with a clean chamois leather and a small quantity of extra fine rouge; special care should be taken that the chamois leather has no grit or dust upon it. In many instances, instead of the chamois leather being used, the article is finished by the "finisher," who submits it to a light rapid process on the calico mop, which removes any marks left by the burnisher.

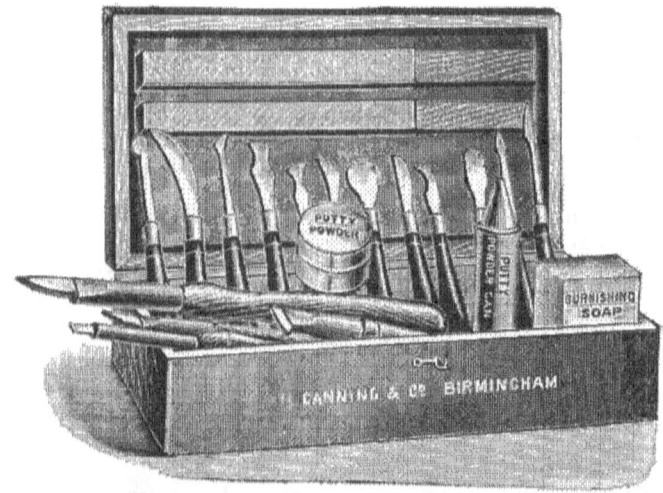

Fig. 110.—Complete Burnishing Outfit.

CHAPTER XVI.

CHASING, EMBOSSING, OR REPOUSSÉ WORK.*

Early History.—The art of chasing has been known from an early date of the world's history. "It has been stated that 'Mentor' and his brother artists were embossers and chasers," † but the method employed by these ancient workers was different from the method practised by the modern artists in this respect. Instead of snarling protuberances upon hollow vessels, "the embossed work was beaten up or executed on bands of metal, and afterwards soldered on the outside of the vessel for which they were intended."† Many examples of this ancient art produced by Egyptians, Assyrians, Greeks, Romans, Byzantines, Celts, Indians, and Chinese, all of more or less artistic value, are to be seen in our national and local museums.

Modern Development.—It was, however, not until the middle of the sixteenth century that Benvenuto Cellini brought the art to the highest point of excellence by the production of many valuable masterpieces of *repoussé* work. Other Italian, as well as French and German, artists have achieved considerable fame in this style of work. Although England cannot boast of many celebrated *repoussé* workers, still some very fine examples have been executed in this country, both by French and English artists, as indicated by several specimens possessed by the South Kensington Museum, members of the Royal family, and various corporate bodies.

There are two *repoussé* artists of the nineteenth century whose works will ever remain examples for the *repoussé* worker to admire and study. Their names are Antoine Vechte and Morel Ladeuil; although both are of French nationality, their finest works were produced in England. The great firms of silversmiths, Messrs. Elkington & Co. of Birmingham, and Messrs. Hunt & Roskell of London, have done much to advance the art industry of this country.

To appreciate the skill of Antoine Vechte, the student need only examine the Amazon shield, which is considered to be his

---

* As this branch of the trade is more applicable to silversmith's work, a fuller consideration of the subject will be reserved for the volume on the art of the silversmith.

† *Gold- and Silversmiths' Work*, by John Hungerford Pollen, M.A., p. 25.

finest production, and displays a feeling, delicacy, and refinement of touch which has never been excelled.

The greatest works in *repoussé* by M. Morel Ladeuil are the Milton shield and the Helicon vase, which, like all his works, are characteristic, full of detail, and clearly expressed ; they prove that he was a great artist and a master craftsman.

But we have a worthy and able successor to Morel Ladeuil in Mr. Thomas Spall of the firm of Messrs. Elkington & Co., Birmingham, whose excellent works will ever claim for him a place of honour. His most important piece of work is the " Virgil shield " executed in silver *repoussé* from the design of Mr. John Watkins of Birmingham and South Kensington. " It has been stated that nothing of the kind so large and striking has ever before emanated from the *atelier* of the silversmith."[*]

The following description will give the student some idea of this excellent piece of work :—" The shield is wrought in the best style of bold *repoussé* ; it measures 3 feet 4 inches diameter ; the subject contains hundreds of well-studied historical figures, which express in high relief vigorous action and accuracy of detail. It took three years patient labour to execute, and is valued at £1,500."

Mr. William Stace, who is also a Birmingham *repoussé* artist, and was formerly with the firm of Messrs. Elkington & Co., has produced several excellent pieces of work for cups, plaques, caskets, and presentation plate. The West Birmingham charity cup shows high qualities which promise much for the future progress of the art. This cup was designed by Mr. Frank Steeley, Art Master of the Branch School of the Municipal School of Art, Vittoria Street, Birmingham, and was entrusted to the well-known firm of Messrs. T. & J. Bragg to execute in silver.

Fig. 111 is an illustration of a belt-clasp in silver *repoussé* work and saw-piercing by Mr. Stace, which not only shows its application, but also the skill of the artist.

Fig. 111.—Belt-clasp.

Repoussé Work * is applied to designs formed by raising protuberances on the surface of sheet metal by hammering from the back or otherwise, and then chasing back again into the exact design required.

Embossing, in connection with metal, has the same meaning.

Chasing has nearly the same significance, but it is restricted to the outer surface only; hence the terms "flat-chasing" and "cast-chasing." The following is a description of the process of *repoussé* work. A piece of metal about one inch larger all round than the proposed design is fixed upon an iron semi-circular block (Fig. 52) filled with cement. When the metal has become cool the design is drawn or traced upon it, and the outline of the design indented by means of a hammer and steel punches called **tracers**, preference being given to those which are slightly blunt, as with sharp ones the metal is more liable to split in later stages of the process. When the outline has been completed the metal is taken off and annealed, and the outline is rendered visible on the reverse side. The metal is then fixed upon a pad of modelling wax with the reverse side uppermost, and the protuberances raised or pushed out by means of the hammer and punches so as to form the rough design. Boxwood punches are used for the bolder details, and steel punches for the smaller parts.

Fig. 112.—Front of Bracelet in Repoussé and Saw-pierced Work.

The metal is again annealed, cleaned, and refixed on the cement block but with the reversed side lowermost, and the background of the design is beaten down into position with planishing and other suitable tools. The planes are next treated, and the most important parts left to be done last; the alternate chasing from back to front is repeated several times until every part has been reduced to its proper position and form.

The surface is next treated in order to produce feeling, expression, and fineness of texture; but excellence in these can only be attained as the result of careful study and long practical experience.

* *Repoussé* work is not generally used for jewellery, but as some designs in jewellery are specially adapted for it, a knowledge of the process is extremely useful.

Repoussé, viz., figure and ornamental, each of which requires a special treatment. There are three degrees of relief, each of which requires study—viz., bas-relief, demi-relievo, and alto-relievo.

Repoussé and Saw-pierced Work is a class of chasing especially applicable to jewellery. Fig. 112 shows the front of a bracelet executed in gold by the author, which will exemplify this mode of applying *repoussé* and saw-pierced work.

A flat band bracelet is wrought by the method described in Fig. 63, but without the star. Then the *repoussé* panel is produced, by the process described above, in demi-relievo. When the *repoussé* and chasing have been completed, the ground work is pierced out with the piercing-saw frame (Fig. 42). The panel is next soldered upon the front of the bracelet, and then the open work is pierced through the bracelet, so as to form the back to the *repoussé* tablet, at the same time that it imparts a light and characteristic effect to the ornament. Other articles of jewellery and goldsmith's work may be wrought by the same method.

Repoussé Work upon Hollow Articles.—When a cup or similar vessel is required to be ornamented with *repoussé* work, another mode of procedure is adopted. If a gold cup is to be treated it is filled solid with cement, and when cool, the design is carefully drawn upon the surface; then the outline is indented in the same way as for flat metal work. The cement is then melted out in an oven or over a gas stove, the cup cleaned by being submerged in hot oil or turpentine, and then dried in box sawdust. The parts to be in relief must now be raised, but, as ordinary punches cannot be applied to the inside, special tools are needed called snarling irons (Fig. 53, p. 79), which are made of different shapes and sizes according to the class of work. Having selected the most suitable tool, it is fixed firmly in a vice. The operator then holds the cup upon the iron with his left hand, and with a hammer in the right hand he taps the snarling iron gently, the vibration of which causes the head of the iron to raise protuberances on the surface where required. When sufficient relief has been obtained, the cup is refilled with cement, and, when cool, the surface is treated in the way already noticed in the description of the flat metal *repoussé* process. The cup is held in position upon a sand-bag in order to protect the surface from damage. When the decoration has been completed, the cement is melted out, and the cup cleaned ready for the finishing process.

Chasing of Cast Figures and Ornaments.—Articles that have been cast have some superfluous metal left from the "get" or "false cores," which is removed by the process called repairing, in which the parts are either chipped, filed, or riffled away, as the case may be. The articles are then chased.

10

The term **chasing** applies to the ornamenting of articles from the front only, but that of "surface chasing" is generally applied to the **feathering** of birds, **hairing** of animals, **scaling** of reptiles and fishes, **texture** of drapery, and the **matting** of foliage, &c. When treating cast representations of the human figure, **riffling, cross-riffling,** and **fleshing** are processes applied in addition to fine-art chasing. The chaser or *repoussé* worker should always follow nature as closely as possible, so far as is consistent with the special purpose of the article he is ornamenting.

CHAPTER XVII.

COLOURING AND FINISHING ARTICLES OF JEWELLERY, &c.

GOLD colouring was first practised in England upwards of seventy years ago. The art was initiated by a Frenchman, and has been extended both by German and by English goldsmiths. Prior to the adoption of gold colouring, articles of jewellery were finished "bright," by the process of polishing and burnishing, which finish could only be obtained with gold alloy containing an excess of copper, and was called red gold or jewellers' gold to distinguish it from the gold used for wedding rings, which was called guinea gold, as the same carat was used for both. The red gold could easily be reduced in standard, so that many articles of jewellery were made of very common gold, in which there was more of the alloying metal than of gold. Coloured gold cannot safely be reduced below a fineness of 12 carats. The author has made an alloy of 9 parts of fine gold and 15 parts of alloy which can be coloured, but the richness of the surface is very inferior to that of 15-carat gold, which is the best quality for wet colouring.

Wet Colouring is the chemical process whereby a gold alloy of low standard has imparted to it the rich yellow colour seen only in fine gold. It is not a process of colouring or gilding as some have supposed, but it is an effect produced by chemical agents which, by removing the superficial alloying metal, changes the surface into one of fine gold.

Colouring Chamber.—The colouring chamber (Fig. 113) may be fitted up in any recess where it can be connected with a flue by which the fumes can be carried away ; the lowermost 3 feet of the chamber is formed of brickwork ; the colour pot, A, rests in a hole, as shown in the figure, and underneath the pot is the gas burner which may be a Fletcher's improved star burner (Fig. 114) ; the gas is supplied by the pipe, C, and the heat is regulated by a cock placed within easy reach of the operator. The boiler, D, which should be made of copper, is fitted with a hot water supply tap ; beneath the boiler there is a gas jet, to the right of which is fixed the cock, E. The vessel, F, is for hot water and should be placed near for the reception of the work when colouring. For convenience the colour pot has an iron handle, G, made by bending strong iron wire round the pot, then wrapping the two ends with string. The string wrapping near

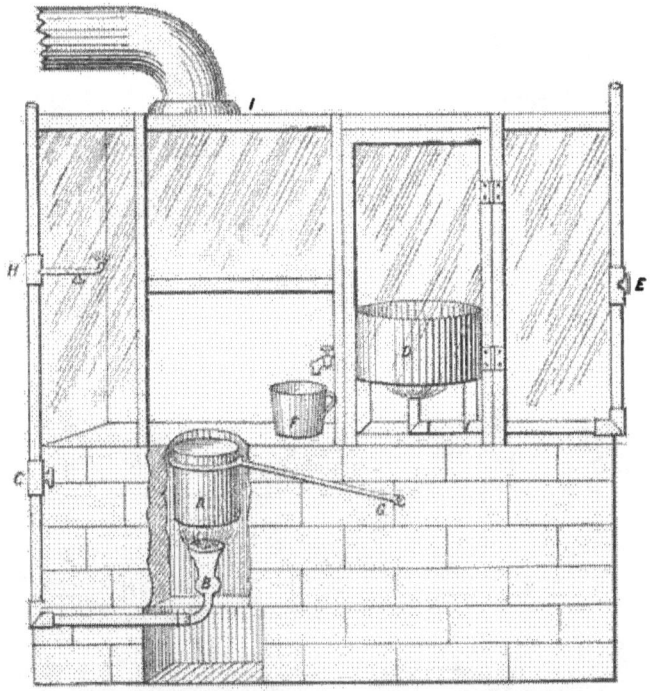

Fig. 113.—Colouring Chamber with glass front; it is partly given in section, so as to show the gas jet fixing and the colour pot.

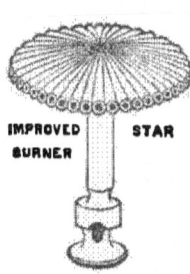

IMPROVED STAR BURNER

Fig. 114.—Fletcher's Improved Star Burner.

the pot is protected from the flame by a covering of iron wire or tin strips. The gas jet, H, inside the chamber permits of the process being watched by the operator. The chamber is closed in by a glass front arranged with a small window that can be raised when the process is being performed. There is also an aperture in front of the boiler, D, which, when opened, allows of the removal of the boiler for the purpose of being cleaned and filled. The cover, I, of the chamber has an aperture through which the fumes can pass into the flue. This chamber is very convenient for all kinds of colouring and chemical operations.

Colouring Apparatus, &c.—In addition to the colouring chamber a complete set comprises a mortar and pestle (Fig. 115); an earthenware jowl (Fig. 116); three earthenware jars (Fig. 117);

Fig. 115.—Mortar and Pestle.

Fig. 116.—Earthenware Jowl.

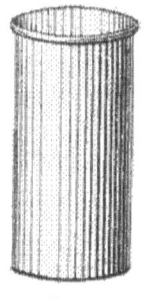

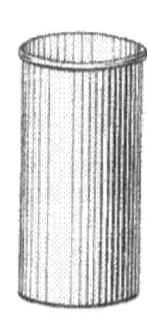

No. 1. No. 2. No. 3.

Fig. 117.—Three Earthenware Jars.

Glass. Bamboo Cane.

Fig 118.—Glass Stirrer.

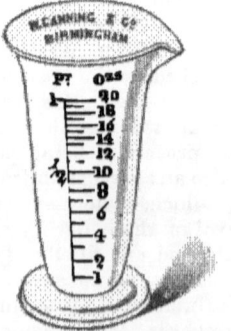

Fig. 119.—Glass Measure.

Fig. 120.—Morgan's Colour Pot.

glass stirrer (Fig. 118); glass measure (Fig. 119); Morgan's colour pot (Fig. 120); also, hydrochloric acid, potassium nitrate, sodium chloride, and a quantity of fine silver or platinum wire for fastening the articles on the colour frame (Fig. 121).

The three earthenware jars (Fig. 117) are placed within easy reach of the operator, and the colour after using (called "old colour") is placed in the first and reserved for use as subsequently described; the water in which the articles have been rinsed is placed in the second; while the third is used for filtering the water into from the other vessels after the sediments have settled.

Preparing the Work for Wet Colouring.—As the chemicals employed in wet colouring are powerful solvents of gold alloys they must be used very cautiously and in strict accordance with the instructions, which are based on the author's long practical experience. All file marks, scratches, and "boil" * are removed by a thorough polishing; the articles are annealed in order to remove the grease and burn off the dirt; boiled out in pickle to produce an even surface; lightly scratch-brushed with a fine brass wire circular brush to remove any stain that may have been produced in boiling out; well rinsed in clean water; dried in hot box sawdust; and wired on the colouring frame shown in Fig. 121.

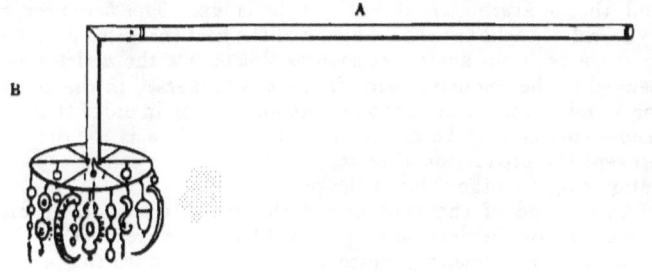

Fig. 121.—Colouring Frame.

A is a stick of wood fitted into the platinum tube or wire, B, supporting a frame of wire of the same metal. The articles are tied on the frame with fine silver or platinum wire, special care being taken that no two come in contact, because a mark is produced wherever they touch each other, which mark has to be removed by polishing. The platinum is the more expensive, but as it is not affected very much by the chemicals it lasts much longer than silver wire.

In preparing the mixture two things have to be considered— (1) The extent of the surface to be coloured; (2) the quantity of each ingredient required. For instance, as the surface of 12

* "Boil" is the term for the green surface produced by repeated boiling in aquafortis pickle.

ounces of solid articles (such as sleeve-links and chains) is the same as that of 4 ounces of hollow articles, the same mixture will do for either, but in order to produce a good colour it is absolutely necessary that the extent of surface shall be quite that required for the given quantity of mixture.

No. 1 Mixture.

Potassium nitrate	(saltpetre), .	. 5 ounces Troy weight.
Sodium chloride	(salt), .	. $2\frac{1}{2}$,, ,,
	(water), .	. $2\frac{1}{2}$,, fluid.
Hydrochloric acid	(muriatic), .	. 5 ,, ,,

The above mixture will colour about 3 ounces of light articles, or 8 ounces of solid articles, such as links and chains.

The saltpetre is well pounded in a mortar with a pestle, (Fig. 115) both of which should be made of Wedgwood ware, and the powder passed through a fine sieve; this quickens the mixing process. The salt is also rubbed through a fine sieve. These two ingredients are poured into a black-lead colour pot about $6\frac{1}{2}$ inches high and $5\frac{1}{4}$ inches in diameter, which is placed over a gas jet as shown in Fig. 113. The ingredients are very carefully dried and mixed by stirring them with a glass rod (Fig. 118) (not a wooden spoon as is sometimes used). When properly mixed and dried the $2\frac{1}{2}$ ounces of hot water are added and the mixture stirred until it boils up. The 5 ounces of hydrochloric acid are then added and the heat increased until the mixture boils up again; as soon as this occurs the articles suspended to the colouring wire frame are immersed in the colour for $3\frac{1}{2}$ minutes, but are kept in constant motion in order that the whole surface may be uniformly coloured. Care is required to prevent the production of scratches or marks as a consequence of rubbing against the sides of the pot.

At the end of the time stated the work is withdrawn and quickly rinsed in clean boiling water placed in a vessel (Fig. 116) close at hand; another $\frac{1}{2}$ ounce of hot water is added to the mixture which causes the colour to sink, but it will soon boil up again. When this takes place the work is re-immersed for 1 minute more, withdrawn, again rinsed in hot water, and soaked in clean hot water until all the acid has been removed from the hollows.

If this process is properly carried out a pure colour will be obtained, while the average loss of weight in articles of higher quality than 14 carats will not exceed 1 dwt. per ounce.

No. 2 Mixture.

Potassium nitrate	(saltpetre), .	. 6 ounces Troy weight.
Sodium chloride	(salt), .	. 3 ,, ,,
	(water), .	. $3\frac{1}{2}$,, fluid.
Hydrochloric acid	(muriatic), .	. 6 ,, ,,

This mixture is suitable for articles having a fineness of 14, 15, and 18 carats, and imparts to them the rich yellow colour of fine gold. It is prepared in the same way as No. 1 mixture, the warming being slowly done, and the stirring effected with a glass rod which, for convenience, may be fixed in a piece of bamboo cane (Fig. 118). The object is to drive off all the moisture from the salts.

When properly dried 3½ ounces of hot water, measured in a 10-ounce glass measure (Fig. 119) are added, and the mixture stirred until complete solution has been effected and boiling commences ; 6 ounces of hydrochloric acid, kept in readiness for the operation, are then added, and a strict watch maintained on the boiling of the mixture. As soon as the mixture rises about half way up the pot the work, ready prepared on the colour wire frame, is immersed therein for 4½ or 5 minutes according to the class of work in hand. The work is quickly withdrawn, and first rinsed and then soaked for about 30 minutes in clean boiling water in order to remove every trace of acid.

No second dip is required by this method as the larger quantity of water added at first compensates for the subsequent drying up of the mixture during the process.

This mixture will colour about 4 ounces of hollow articles and 10 ounces of solid work ; for larger quantities the ingredients must be measured in proportion and a larger colour pot be used, but the time of immersion remains the same—viz., 4½ to 5 minutes as the case may be.

The length of time required for immersion and the amount of colour needed for special kinds of work can be determined by practical experience only.

No. 3 Mixture.

Potassium nitrate (saltpetre),	.	. 6 ounces Troy weight.	
Sodium chloride (salt),	.	. 3 ,, ,,	
(water),	.	. 4 ,, fluid.	
Hydrochloric acid (muriatic),	.	. 5½ ,, ,,	

In selling articles consisting only of gold, such as bracelets, rings, and chains, by what is termed " weight and fashion," the custom is to charge a certain amount per ounce weight, and an additional amount for the workmanship and profit, or fashion. Therefore, as such dealings are very close, and as there is always a waste of gold during the colouring, such loss must be reduced to the lowest possible point. Most of the mixtures for colouring cause a waste of about 1 dwt. per ounce of work.

The above mixture will produce a very good colour on articles having a fineness of 14, 15, and 18 carats, with a loss of about 16 grains to the ounce of work. The ingredients are prepared in the same way as is described in No. 1 mixture, and gently heated, while being stirred with a glass rod, to drive off the water taken up by crystallisation. When properly dried, the 4 ounces of water are added, the heat increased until the mixture boils up, and the 5½ ounces of hydrochloric acid (which must be kept in readiness) added, the stirring being maintained until the mixture boils up again. As soon as this appears, the work (prepared as before described) is immersed and gently moved in the mixture for four minutes, then withdrawn. and rinsed well in boiling water, in order to remove all the acid from the hollow parts; or, if more convenient, the articles can be taken from the colour wire, placed in boiling hot water for half an hour at least, then withdrawn and dried in hot box sawdust, when they are ready for scratch-brushing (see p. 155). This process answers well for gold articles with small surfaces, provided scrupulous cleanliness is observed, the best chemicals are used, and skill combined with care exercised.

Birmingham Wet-colouring Process.—In this process a mixture containing alum is used, but it has been superseded by the more reliable processes devised by the author, and described in the immediately preceding paragraphs. For the sake of comparison a brief account of this method is now given. If carefully carried out it imparts a good colour to articles of jewellery having a fineness of from 14 to 18 carats. The mixture consists of *—

Potassium nitrate	(saltpetre),	. .	14 ounces.
Sodium chloride	(salt),	. . .	7 ,,
	(alum),	. . .	7 ,,
Hydrochloric acid	(muriatic),	. .	2 ,,

The salts are reduced to a fine powder, placed in a large-sized colour pot (about 8 inches high and 7 inches in diameter) which is put over a gas fire and the mixture stirred well with a wooden spoon. As soon as it begins to dissolve and boil up, the muriatic acid is added, whereupon the mixture sinks down, but is stirred well until it again boils up. The moment this happens, the work, ready prepared and fastened on the colour wire, is put into the boiling mixture for four minutes, during which time it is kept slowly moving, all contact with the sides of the pot being carefully avoided. The work is quickly withdrawn, rinsed in hot water, again dipped in the colour mixture for one minute, withdrawn and rinsed; another 2 ounces of hot water must now be added to the mixture, which at once subsides, but will soon boil up again, when the work is placed in it for one minute more, taken out and rinsed. If the colour is not quite right, the work is immersed for another half minute, withdrawn and rinsed in hot water.

This mixture will colour about 10 ounces of solid articles or about 5 ounces of hollow articles, the precise weight depending on the superficial extent of the work to be coloured; the loss should not exceed 1 dwt. for every ounce of work coloured. Success depends upon skilful management and thorough cleanliness. Everything used must be cleaned after each process, and the pot must be free from old colour sticking to the sides.

* *The Practical Gold Worker*, by George E. Gee.

Colouring Repaired Articles.—The old colour reserved, as previously mentioned, is kept for a short time only and is used for "recolouring" repairs from which the colour has been partially removed by polishing, as these will not stand the full colour; but if the repairs have had all the colour polished off, they must pass through the process of full colouring.

Before recolouring, all soft solder must be removed, if possible, as also the parts composed of 9-carat gold (such as the tongs of brooches, and the stems of pins); also stones and pearls, as these will not stand the process. The articles are then entirely covered with a paste of borax, made by rubbing borax with a little water on a slate slab, and annealed red hot. The borax paste prevents the colour surface blistering or chipping off. They are then boiled out in pickle, well rinsed in hot water and dried in hot box sawdust. The broken parts are carefully cleaned, the articles again covered with borax, one or two panels of solder soldered on the broken parts and the articles boiled out again. As the surface has not been interfered with, it will be quite suitable for a recolour. This is done by putting in the colour pot sufficient old colour to cover the articles, then placing the pot over the gas, and adding about half an ounce each of hot water and hydrochloric acid. The boiling mixture is constantly stirred with a glass rod, and when it boils sufficiently the work, which has been fastened on the colour frame, is dipped for two or three minutes, according to the nature of the articles under consideration, then withdrawn, rinsed in boiling hot water, allowed to soak for at least half an hour and then dried in hot box sawdust, after which they are scratch-brushed.*

When examined under the microscope the surface left upon the article by the wet-colour process is seen to consist of fine gold (free from alloy) presenting a rough frosted appearance. This surface can be rendered more beautiful by being scratch-brushed or burnished.

Scratch-brushing and Frosting.—This process is performed by means of a circular brush made of fine brass wire (instead of bristles). Fig. 122 represents a "scratch brush," which is fixed on the spindle of the lathe, as shown in Fig. 125, and made to revolve at a quick speed either by the foot, or by the aid of steam or other applied power.

The box B is a reservoir containing stale beer, which is generally used for scratch-brushing gold articles; the operator stands in front, being protected from the spray by the box A, and holds the article against the brush until every part has assumed a rich bright colour. If the article is to be frosted,

---

* It is most important that hollow articles should have a prolonged soaking, in order to remove every trace of acid; should any of this be left inside the articles, yellow paste soon appears, which, if allowed to remain, will cause the gold to crumble into powder.

the work is held against the brush with the right hand, while with the left a cork is pressed against the brush, which causes the wires to rebound, and brings their points instead of their sides against the article. This produces the frosted appearance called a "rich bloom," which is a speciality for plain articles, such as bracelets, lockets, and brooches.

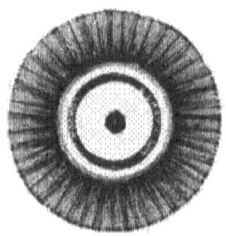

Fig. 123.—Inside Scratch Brush.

Fig. 122.—Circular Scratch Brush.   Fig. 124.—Inside Scratch Brush.

For scratch-brushing or frosting inside work, such as bracelets rings, cups, &c., different brushes of various forms are used, such as are shown in Figs. 123, 124.

Scratch-brushing requires both experience and skill, and, especially, a knowledge of the extent of the colour on the articles. If they are of a lower quality than 14 carats, the colour is very apt to be stripped, but if the quality is 15 carats or 18 carats, a much better frosting can be produced with less risk. It is for this reason that the author recommends that all articles intended for colouring should be made of 15-carat gold, which will stand the process of scratch-brushing several times without any risk whatever.

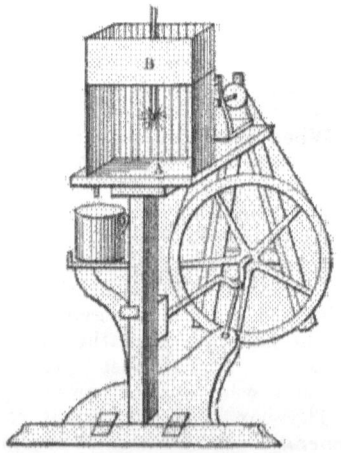

Fig. 125.—Scratch-brushing Lathe.

After it has been scratch-brushed, the work is thoroughly rinsed in clean warm water in order to remove the beer, and then dried in hot box sawdust. The dust must not be allowed to burn, as this would damage the surface of the articles. The articles should be lightly and carefully moved about in the dust, and the final drying quickened by removing the wet dust with a camel-hair brush (Fig. 126).

Fig. 126.—Camel-hair Brush.

The best plan for avoiding all risk of the dust burning is to use the apparatus shown in Fig. 127. This consists of a copper boiler which may be either square or round, about 24 inches in diameter and 18 inches high. The top portion is fitted with a pan, B, for holding the sawdust, and the lower part, A, is filled with water almost up to the level of the bottom of the pan. The water is heated by means of the Bunsen burner, C. This prevents the overheating of the sawdust, and, at the same time, provides a ready and constant supply of hot water for rinsing purposes.

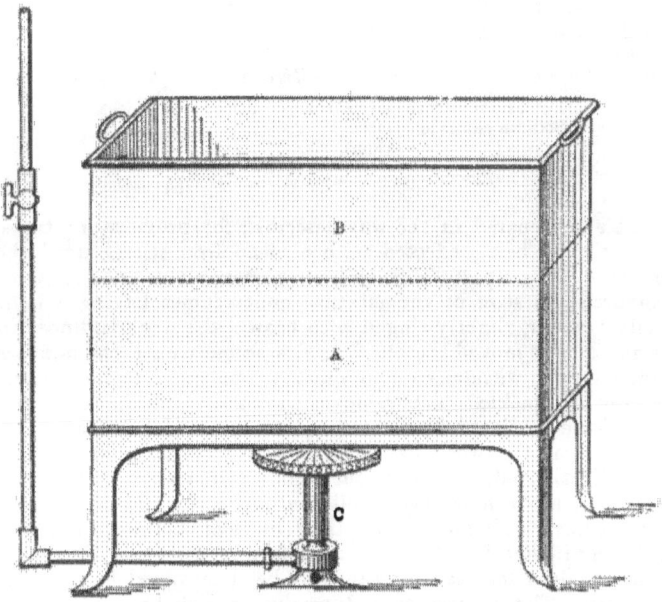

Fig. 127.—Apparatus for Drying-out Work.

DRY COLOURING.

Dry Colouring can only be satisfactorily applied to articles having a fineness of 18 carats or more. After manipulation, they are carefully polished to remove all file marks, scratches, and "boil"; after each process they are washed out with a white bristle brush in hot water to which a little washing soda and soap have been added, in order to remove the grease and dirt, care being taken not to produce any fresh marks; next, they are dried out in the boxdust heater (Fig. 128), which is a copper or galvanised iron boiler holding about 2 gallons of water, and constructed in the same way as the apparatus shown in Fig. 127; when cleaned with the camel-hair brush, they are highly polished by means of rouge, brushes, calico mops and threads, and subjected to a final washing and drying.

Fig. 128.—Boxdust Heater.

The articles are then suspended on the colouring frame (Fig. 121, p. 150) by means of platinum wire, the usual precautions being taken that they do not touch each other. The colour mixture used consists of the following ingredients :—

Dry Colour Mixture.

Potassium nitrate (saltpetre),	.	.	8 ounces.
Sodium chloride (salt),	.	.	4 ,,
(alum),	.	.	4 ,,
			16 ,,

This is prepared in the way described for previous mixtures, the stirring being effected with a clean iron stirrer until the mixture boils up sufficiently high to cover the articles to be coloured; as soon as the mixture emits fumes having a light yellow colour, slightly tinged with brown, the work is dipped in it and gently moved therein for a few seconds until the mixture sinks down, withdrawn and quickly immersed in hot hydrochloric acid pickle. This removes the colour adhering to it, and the nickle is placed in a vessel kept close by for its reception. As soon as the work has been withdrawn, the mixture rises again in the pot, so that if the colour is not what is required, a second dip can be made followed by a rinsing, first in the hydrochloric acid pickle, and then in clean boiling water and a drying in hot box sawdust, as before mentioned. The exact time required for each dip can only be determined by constant practice. The process should produce a rich brilliant colour, which can be greatly improved by burnishing (see p. 140).

Note.—In colouring by either the wet or the dry process, the best chemicals must be used, and the manipulation be quick in order to produce the best results; if the rinsing is done too slowly, the work is liable to be spoiled. Also, as the fumes are highly injurious, their inhalation must be carefully avoided, as

also should their contact with any sores on the hands or elsewhere. If the fumes are inhaled the remedy is to instantly
drink a little milk ; if the hands have sores, cuts, &c., gloves
should be worn.

Chemical Reactions in the Colour Pot —In the preceding
paragraphs the various methods used for " colouring " gold alloys
have been practically treated, and full instructions given for
their application in the workshop. But, in order to render the
information more complete, it is necessary to deal with the
chemical reactions which take place in the " colour " pot more
fully than could be done in describing the technical details of
the process.

Hydrochloric and nitric acids when used singly do not act
upon gold, but a mixture of these acids, known as " aqua regia,"
readily dissolves the metal with the formation of gold chloride.
The dissolution of the metal depends upon a reaction which
takes place between the acids, and causes the liberation of chlorine.
The chemical change is expressed by the equation—

$$HNO_3 + 3\,HCl = NOCl + 2\,H_2O + Cl_2. \quad . \quad . \quad . \quad \text{(i.)}$$

The nitrosyl chloride, $NOCl$, is an orange-yellow coloured gas
which takes little or no part in the dissolution of the metal.
This is effected by the free chlorine which unites directly with
the metal, thus—

$$2\,Au + 3\,Cl_2 = 2\,AuCl_3. \quad . \quad . \quad . \quad . \quad \text{(ii.)}$$

The reactions take place rapidly when the mixture is gently
heated. Other metals, such as copper and silver, are attacked
in a similar manner by aqua regia, with formation of their
respective chlorides ; but silver forms an insoluble chloride
which coats the metal and retards the action by preventing the
ready access of the acid liquid to it. On the other hand, copper
dissolves freely in the solution. What is true of the metals
alone is also true of alloys containing them. Thus, an alloy of
gold and copper in any proportions is freely dissolved by aqua
regia, and the surface of the dissolving metal is kept clean by
the solution of the chlorides in the surrounding liquid ; but if
silver is introduced into the alloy its chloride forms a coating on
the surface which retards the action, and the coating cannot be
removed by simply swilling in hot water. The formation of this
film of silver chloride on the surface of a gold-silver-copper alloy
prevents the inspection of the surface during the partial solution
which takes place in the process of " colouring," and is, therefore,
fatal to the use of a mixture of nitric and hydrochloric acids as a
" colouring " liquid.

The mixture given on p. 151, and recommended as the one
most suitable for general work, contains potassium nitrate, hydrochloric acid, sodium chloride, and water. The reaction which
takes place when this mixture is heated is similar to that ex-

pressed by (i.), but is a little more complicated on account of the substitution of potassium nitrate for nitric acid. The complete change is expressed by the equation—

$$KNO_3 + 4HCl = NOCl + 2H_2O + KCl + Cl_2. \quad . \quad . \quad . \quad \text{(iii.)}$$

The potassium chloride, KCl, has similar properties to sodium chloride and thus assists the latter compound to fulfil its function in the "colouring" process. The free chlorine attacks the metals in the alloy and converts them into chlorides. Silver chloride is, as stated above, insoluble in water and acid, and would cover the surface of the alloy with a dirty white film but for the presence of the sodium chloride, in a concentrated solution of which it is fairly soluble. The function of the common salt is, then, to keep the surface of the work free from silver chloride. But if the "colour" after use is diluted with water the dissolved silver chloride is thrown down as a white precipitate, and may be thus separated from the gold and copper chlorides, which remain in solution, by filtration. This insolubility of silver chloride in dilute salt solution explains the sparing use of water in the "colour" mixture, which should remain perfectly clear during the operation. That is, the relation between the common salt and the water must be such that the silver chloride is completely dissolved as fast as it is formed. The surface of the work can, therefore, be readily examined and the progress of the operation noted. If water is added during the progress of the operation, to make up for loss by evaporation, the quantity added must be carefully regulated so as not to cause a permanent precipitation of silver chloride. The white precipitate formed on the addition of the water should completely dissolve and leave the "colour" quite clear. Should this not be the case the addition of more common salt will usually clear the liquid. It must be borne in mind that the rate of evolution of chlorine depends upon the concentration of the mixture, and this, the quantities of the other ingredients being kept constant, depends upon the quantity of water in the mixture. And since the chlorine is the actual agent in removing the alloyed metals from the surface of the articles the rate of working depends upon this concentration. A slower rate of working is, therefore, brought about by an increase in the quantity of water; but the quantity of salt must be increased to keep the amount per unit volume of the liquid sufficient to completely dissolve the silver chloride as it is formed.

It is usually stated that the colouring process effects the removal of the base metals from the surface of the articles, and leaves pure gold, which gives to the "coloured" surface its pleasing effect. This, however, is only partially true, as the "colour" has a decided action on the gold as well as upon the silver and copper. Further, it is very doubtful if the pale yellow of pure gold would be accepted as a satisfactory colour. The colour most prized has a tinge of red in it; but this varies with the skill of the operator. The peculiar beauty of "coloured" gold is due quite as much to the breaking or "matting" of the surface by the action of the colour as to the alteration in the composition of the alloy on the surface. The alteration in composition is due to the different relative solubilities of the three metals in the mixture, so that the surface alloy is different in composition to the unchanged alloy underneath.

It is a well-known fact that when clean copper is immersed in a solution containing gold or silver some of the copper is taken up by the solution and an equivalent quantity of gold or silver is deposited upon the surface of the copper. While the action is proceeding in the "colour" pot the solution gets richer in gold and silver, but these are probably re-deposited, in part, upon the surface of the alloy and thus exert an influence on the final result. The deposit is, however, loosely adherent, so that most of it is removed by the scratch brush.

CHAPTER XVIII.

ENAMELLING : ITS HISTORY, PROCESSES, AND APPLICABILITY.

History.—The art of enamelling is of great antiquity. Lieut.-Colonel S. S. Jacob, R.E., in his work on the Jeypore enamels, states "that while enamelling on metal is most successfully practised in many parts of India, it is carried to its highest perfection in the enamelling on gold produced at Jeypore in Rajputana. The colours employed rival the tints of the rainbow in purity and brilliancy, and are laid on the gold by the Jeypore artists with such exquisite taste, and in such perfect harmony, that the enamels of Europe and Persia are poor and lustreless in comparison with them."

Labarte, in his *Handbook of Arts of the Middle Ages*, endeavours to prove that the art of enamelling originated in Phœnicia, and thence found its way into Persia, where it was known in the reign of Chosroes (A.D. 531 to 579). It is supposed that the Greeks and Indians in their turn acquired the art from the Persians. He, however, mentions that Mons. Pauthier, in *Histoire de la Chine*, quotes a document, in which it is stated that a merchant of Youëtchi, or Scythia, introduced the art of making glass of different colours into China, in the reign of Thaiwonti (A.D. 422 to 451). We have, therefore, reasons for believing that enamelling, which is only a branch of the art of vitrification, was known at a very early period, if it did not originate, in Scythia, the home of the Turanians.

It is further stated that in the Boulak Museum, at Cairo, may be seen some of the jewels of the Queen Aahhotep (mother of Aahmes I. of the 18th Dynasty), who lived about B.C. 1500, which are ornamented with blue glass, a species of *Cloisonné* enamel. These facts seem to indicate a Turanian origin of the art, which view also seems to be supported by several points connected with its practice in India.

It has been remarked that the best enamellers in Europe have been the Etruscan Florentines, and, in modern India, the Sikhs; both, it has been observed, are of Turanian descent.

The most ancient specimen of Indian enamel now in existence is probably the crutch staff of Maharaja Mān-Singh, of Jeypore,

11

one of the greatest of the chiefs in the Court of Akbar at the close of the sixteenth century.

This staff, upon which the Maharaja leaned when standing before the throne of the Emperor, is 52 inches in length, and is composed of thirty-three cylinders of gold arranged on a strong central core of copper, the whole being surmounted by a crutch of light green jade set with gems. Each of the thirty-two upper cylinders are painted in enamel with figures of animals, landscapes, and flowers, all of which are carefully drawn by one who had evidently studied in the school of nature.

But when we are told that the owner of this magnificent piece of enamel workmanship was one of the pillars of the throne of a true Turanian sovereign—a most munificent patron of the arts, alike of his new home in India and of his ancestral dominions in Central Asia, that he himself governed the kingdom of Cabul, and that he is said to have brought with him from the north several works of art decidedly Turanian in design, it is evident that at this early date Turanian art was in the ascendant.

It is further stated that Maharaja Mān-Singh brought five Sikh enamel workers from Lahore, which statement is supported by the fact that the descendants of these men still procure their colours from that town. The principal enamellers in Jeypore are descended from these Sikhs, and are known as the Singh family; their methods and processes have been handed down from one generation to another, skilled artists being thereby always retained for the instruction of the young.

The Processes of Enamelling.—The various methods and processes carried on at the present time will alone be described, as the object is to make the subject as useful as possible to the craft.

Enamels.—The basis of all enamels is a silicate of tin, the colouring-matters being gold and metallic oxides; gold furnishes red and purple; oxide of iron, red; oxide of antimony or lead with lead and sal ammoniac, yellow; peroxide of copper, green; cobalt oxide, blue; and oxide of manganese, violet. The invention of enamels is, no doubt, due to the discovery that melted glass adheres to metallic surfaces. The beautiful effects of colour so much admired in mosaic designs are produced by enamels.

Enamels are either opaque or transparent, and must have certain special properties. Their fusing point must be lower than that of the article to which they are applied; they must have a glassy appearance after fusion; and they must be unalterable by ordinary acids. Their production forms a special industry in France and Switzerland, so that manufacturers in this country find it cheaper to purchase them than to make them. Even the Jeypore enamellers do not make their own enamels, but obtain them from Lahore.

CLASSIFICATION OF ENAMELS.

Enamels may be thus classified :—

1st.—Enclosed Enamels,	{ Cloisonné. { Champ-levé. { Taille d'epergne.
2nd.—Surface Enamels,	{ Glaze (or earthenware). { Painters' enamel, or On { Email de Limoges. Metal. { Emaux en basse-taille.

Enclosed Enamel.—The most ancient method of enamelling is the **cloisonné** (from the French *cloison*, a partition); it is practised mostly by the Japanese and the Chinese with exquisite taste, both in workmanship and design.

If the article to be enamelled is a **plaque**, the process adopted is as follows :—A carefully finished coloured drawing is made of the design ; then the thin metal, which is to serve as the base for the enamel, is selected, and the design carefully drawn on it or lightly traced with the graver. This done, a fine rectangular shaped wire is made of gold, silver, or other metal, which should not be more than one line deep, and as thin as the design will allow. This wire is then manipulated with pliers into the desired shape, or, for some parts, it is wound on steel spits having the shapes required, and then cut off into single ornaments ; the separate portions are called **cloisons** or cells, the walls of which serve to keep each colour distinct ; hence the term " walled enamel " is sometimes used for this process. The cells are now fixed upon the **plaque** with a special kind of gum, not soldered as some persons have suggested. The Japanese and the Chinese, who are the masters of this class of work, are said to cover the surface with a mucilage (made by letting the tips of the quince simmer in water) which is strong enough to hold the wires in position until the article is ready to receive the enamel paste. This paste is made by pulverising pieces of enamel with water in a porcelain mortar (Fig. 115, p. 149), using a porcelain pestle. When the enamel has been ground sufficiently fine, the water is carefully poured off and the paste left clear and free from dirt ; if there should be any dirt in, it must be removed by adding more water and again pouring off. When quite clear the paste is poured into a small dish and is kept therein ready for the filling process. Each colour enamel must be ground separately, and be kept in a separate dish (which may be obtained in sets of six, each forming a cover for the other). When a small quantity only of an enamel is needed, a small mortar and pestle made of agate is generally used. The cells are filled with the vitreous paste by means of a spatula formed of a piece of metal wire flattened at the ends, and the moisture absorbed by holding a piece of linen against the side of the enamel. The article is then fired in an intensely heated muffle

(Fig. 129), which process requires great care and skilful manipulation, for, should the article be exposed too long in the muffle, the colouring is spoiled, and possibly the original form lost. When the enamel has properly melted, the article is carefully withdrawn from the muffle and allowed to cool. It will then be seen that the enamel has shrunk in passing from the powdery form to the compact state. The cells are again replenished with enamel and fired; and this is repeated until the cells are what is termed "full," which generally requires four or five operations. The back or the inside, as the case may be, of every article must be covered with enamel in order to equalise the expansion and contraction. After firing, the surface is ground to a perfect level with an emery stick and water, polished first on a quickly revolving felt bob supplied with a little powdered pumice-stone and water, and then on a wooden disc supplied with rotten-stone and water, thus making the surface smooth and glassy.

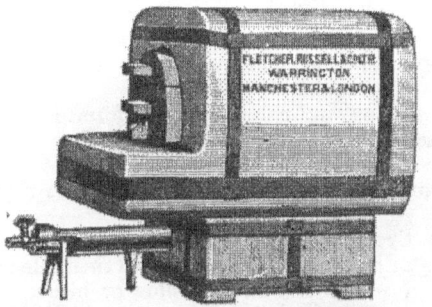

Fig. 129.—Muffle Furnace, arranged for Blast ; External View.

By another method of finishing, **Emaux affleures,** or "levelled enamels" are produced, in which the surface has a soft, dull, but beautiful appearance, something resembling that of stones in mosaic work. Many fine examples of cloisonné enamels may be seen in the South Kensington Museum, London, and in some of our local museums, which manifest great manipulative skill, and a unique arrangement of design, the details of which are, as a rule, minute and intricate.

Champ-levé Enamels.—The processes connected with *champ-levé* enamels are different from those of *cloisonné* in many respects. As before, the design, say for example, the Arms of a city, is carefully drawn and coloured, and a sheet of thick metal is selected. The metal sheet, shaped as required, is cemented to a wooden chuck, which is screwed on a **bullet** resting in a leather **pad,** such as is used by engravers (Fig 50); the design is accurately traced or drawn on the metal, which is then cut away with gravers or scorpers of different sizes, so as to form a sunk surface for the reception of the enamel ; hence the term *champ-levé*, which means "surface raised," or the field "lifted up." The ground work is finished differently for a transparent than for an opaque enamel ; in the former case it is prepared by flinking—that is, by first cutting out the metal to the required design with the flat scorpers, and then cutting a pattern like engine turning or chequering with a narrow half round scorper, which increases the brilliancy of the transparent enamel, and also the finish of the article. Fine silver, or a special gold alloy with an excess of silver, is generally used as the background for transparent enamels ; for red enamel, the best material is either 18- or 22-carat gold. When the cutting has been done, the plate is taken off the chuck, annealed, boiled out in a solution of nitric acid and water, brushed with a little common salt and water to remove stains or grease, and dried in boxdust.

The filling is effected in the same way as described for *cloisonné* enamels, as also the firing, but in this case two or three operations usually suffice. Vigilant care must be taken to exclude every particle of dust or dirt from the surface, as any such will spoil the enamel, and will necessitate its removal and the renewal of the processes.

The grinding off and polishing is performed in a similar way to that described for *cloisonné* enamels. This kind of enamel generally consists largely of metal ornamentation, which is much improved by careful engraving, and adds richness to the design.

Taille de Epergne Enamelling is the reverse of *champ-levé*, as the ornamentation is simply engraved and then filled with enamel, the colour of which is generally blue or black. It is mostly used for mourning rings, band bracelets, charms, and similar jewellery, and also for watch cases. The designs are generally fine scroll ornaments, or interlaced lines, the metal parts being afterwards lightly engraved in order to give a finish to the design. The methods of filling and firing are done in the same way as already described, but as the cavities are small a single operation is generally sufficient.

Surface Enamels are represented by the *Email-des Peintres* of the French, and by similar styles in England. They consist of a thin layer of enamel fused over the surface of metal which is decorated with colours in a style similar to that of porcelain painting. The processes used are less complicated than those employed for the enclosed enamels, but greater artistic skill is required ; the French have named it "Painters' enamel."

This method of enamelling originated with the Italian Renaissance school, Nordon Penicault, of Limoges, who lived in the early part of the fifteenth century, being the first promoter. The Limoges workmen of the sixteenth century painted in their shadowing, or "modelling" of the figure as it is termed, with white enamel paint on a dark enamelled background, and reserved the colouring till the end of the process.

A plate of sheet metal (copper, silver or gold) having been selected, it is raised lightly by hammering until it is concave on one side and convex on the other, in order to prevent the plate from warping when fired. It is then thoroughly cleaned by immersion in a solution of nitric acid and water; after cleaning, the convex part is carefully covered with a dark enamel, and the concave part backed with a coarse enamel in order to protect the metal from the action of the fire. The processes of absorbing the moisture from the enamel and of firing are exactly the same as before described, but great care must be exercised that the enamels cool gradually after the withdrawal from the muffle, as too rapid a change of temperature causes the enamel to chip (or "fly" as it is termed). The design is then carefully drawn on the surface of the enamel, and the entire outline of the design filled with white enamel paint, which is followed by a firing; this causes the white and dark enamel to fuse together, which, in cooling becomes grey; on this the artist paints another layer of white, but avoids touching the parts where the shadows are. After the second firing the repainted parts will be much whiter than the other parts. This process is repeated until the light parts are in sufficient relief, when the somewhat dull effect is brightened up by the addition of colour or gold, either to the drapery or ground work.

This method of working from the shadow to the light, which is quite the reverse of painting upon canvas, gives a softness and effect which cannot be produced in any other way. The name of **Email de Limoges**, or **Email-Limousin**, is generally applied to these enamels, which are sometimes enriched by what is termed "*Email à paillon*," or "**stencil enamel.**" This is done by placing on the parts to be brilliantly coloured a piece of fine gold or silver foil, which is fixed by placing the article in the fire; when cool, the stencil parts are flinked or cut bright with a scorper, then covered with a transparent enamel, and the design enriched by outlining or ornamenting parts of the surface with gold.

Enamel Painting is said to have been discovered by a French goldsmith, Jean Toutin, and is now practised on the Continent, in London, and in Birmingham. Many fine examples have been produced to adorn caskets, civic ornaments, cigarette cases, match boxes, and articles of jewellery.

The mode of application resembles that of water-colour painting on ivory. In this process opaque vitrified colours are fixed on any enamel base. The colours are mixed with a little spirits of tar (not with water), and are fixed by passing the article through the fire, when the tar burns away and leaves the enamel colours on the surface, with a slight change in their tints.

Chinese Enamels are similarly produced. The article is first covered with a white enamel, then fired, afterwards painted with enamel (as in porcelain painting), and fixed by firing.

Russian Enamels are rare and, at the same time, very difficult to produce. They consist of a framework, or network, of gold or other metal wire, with transparent enamel fluxed between the meshes, the wires imitating the settings of stones or stained glass windows. Old examples of this kind are very rare. The museums on the Continent, in London, and in Birmingham have fine examples of enamels made by all the processes described in this chapter. A visit to any of these museums will afford valuable lessons to the student.

In the year 1896 the author paid a special visit to London, Paris, and Switzerland, for the purpose of gathering facts concerning the manipulation of the precious metal. The examples of goldsmith's work and enamels produced on the Continent are admirable. At the Geneva Exposition there were shown, in the section set apart for exhibits of jewellery and watches, some most exquisite examples of transparent enamelling upon watch-backs and watch-brooches. The Limoges style of enamels, and enamel-painted panels on caskets and book covers, were evidently the work of masters of the art of enamelling; while the goldsmith's work and diamond mounting gave proofs of an excellence fully on a level with the advances made in technical education.

CHAPTER XIX.

HERALDIC DISTINCTIONS AND ARMORIAL BEARINGS.

Heraldry is, in its original and more comprehensive sense, the knowledge of all the multifarious duties of a herald; but in the more restricted signification in which the term is used by most modern writers it is a knowledge of the laws that regulate armorial insignia—*i.e.*, the devices that appear on shields, with their attendant crests, supporters, and badges.

In the earliest ages of history we find traces of the use of heraldic distinctions and armorial bearings. Figures of living creatures or symbolical signs were anciently borne as marks of distinction by kingdoms and states, to denote the valour and courage of chiefs or nations, and to render them more terrible to their enemies. By military chiefs and men of note these emblems and devices were adopted in order to insure the identification of their persons by their friends and followers in battle or elsewhere. These devices have been termed "the symbols which distinguished the noble from the ignoble." That heraldic blazonry was well known in early Greece is evident, not only from the Homeric poems but also from the passages in which the author of the *Prometheus*, writing more than 500 years B.C., describes the armour of the kings and chieftains at the renowned siege of Thebes. It is well known that Alexander the Great granted to some of his most eminent captains and soldiers, as a token of high favour and honour and to excite emulation, the right and title to bear emblems and devices on their banners and armour; and the privilege of granting such rights has always been regarded as one peculiarly appertaining to royalty.

Instances occur in remote times of nations, tribes, and individuals who distinguished themselves by particular emblems or ensigns—*e.g.*, the standard of the twelve tribes of Israel, of the Egyptians and Assyrians, and the Roman eagle and cohort ensigns. Figures, symbolical and ornamental, singularly like some of those of heraldry, are found mixed with other emblems in Egypt, China, India, and in Japan, also on Etruscan vases, and on Greek coins; and shields decorated with devices are described by both Homer and Æschylus. Yet there is exhaustive negative evidence that nothing that can be properly called an armorial device was used either on shields or banners before the middle of the twelfth century. The shield of the French knight in the first crusade presented a plain face of solid metal. Nor is there any certain evidence of armorial bearings having been used in the second crusade, 1147 A.D. Coming to more recent times our own history affords an illustration in the case of the famous "Tapestry of Bayeux," where we find an elaborate tableau of the warlike and knightly symbols and devices used by Normans and Saxons respectively at the period of the conquest.

The earliest roll of arms of which we have any notice is in the reign of Henry III. ; and the reign of Edward I. presents us with the earliest heraldic document extant. The famous "Roll of Caerlaverock," a poem in old Norman French, rehearses the names and armorial ensigns of all the barons, knights, &c., who attended Edward at the siege of Caerlaverock Castle, A.D. 1300. Heraldry is therein, for the first time, presented to us as a science, because it had a system, a classification, and a technical language of its own. The principal rules and terms of the art were then in existence, and from about that time the latter are continually found in the fables and romances of France and England.

In the infancy of heraldry every knight seems to have assumed what arms he pleased ; animals, plants, imaginary monsters, things artificial, and objects familiar to pilgrims and crusaders were all fixed upon ; and, whenever it was possible, the object chosen was one whose name bore sufficient resemblance in sound to suggest the name or the title of the bearer of it.

But as coats-of-arms multiplied different knights occasionally fixed upon the same symbols, and the confusion which arose from the similarity of coats-of-arms could only be obviated by a restriction being placed on the bearer's fancy, and regulations being introduced regarding the number, position, and colour of the charges, and the attitudes of the animals represented.

In course of time the right to use a coat-of-arms became, like the *jus imaginum*, the distinctive privilege of the noble, the word being used here in the Continental sense, analogous to the English gentleman ; and the privilege transmitted to all his descendants in the male line.

When a prince made a plebeian a noble, as it was competent for him to do, the patent of nobility defined what arms he was to bear.

In England a proclamation of Henry V. restrained the private assumption of armorial insignia, by prohibiting all who had not borne arms at Agincourt from assuming them, except in virtue of inheritance of a grant from the Crown.

On the establishment of the Heralds' College in 1483, the regulation of matters armorial was to a large extent delegated to the king-of-arms and heralds acting under the earl marshal.

Heraldry is, therefore, in one of its aspects, a faithful chronicler of the history both of royal dynasties and of private families. Every change in the hereditary succession of a kingdom, every union of two houses by marriage, occasions a corresponding change in the coat-of-arms; the position which the members of a house occupy in the family tree is duly indicated, and an armorial shield is thus a record whose nice distinctions indicate to all who understand its language, a number of material facts regarding the owner of it. Heraldry is, in this way, an aid to the study of history, general and local. It has often afforded the key to disputed successions; and seals, baronial and monumental carvings, and shields in church windows, have all been regarded in courts of law as evidence in obscure questions of marriage and descent.

It has been recorded by an eminent writer on Heraldry *:— "In the olden time, in England, the love of heraldry, which was prevalent amongst all classes, was based upon an intelligent appreciation of its worthiness. A part of the feudal system of the Middle Ages, and at once derived from the prevailing form of thought and feeling, and imparting to it a brilliant colouring peculiar to itself, Heraldry exercised a powerful influence upon the manners and habits of the people amongst whom it was in use. By our early ancestors, accordingly, as Mr. Montague has so happily written, 'little given to study of any kind, a knowledge of heraldry was considered indispensable.' And this heraldry grew up spontaneously and naturally, out of the circumstances and requirements of those times. It was invented and introduced, because it was needed for practical use; it was accepted and cherished, because it did much more than fulfil its avowed purpose. At first, simply useful to distinguish particular individuals, especially in war and at the tournament, English heraldry soon became popular; and then, with no less rapidity, it rose to high honour and dignity."

Heraldry has been associated with romance and poetry as well as chivalry. Sir Walter Scott, who was so well versed in antique lore, in *The Lay of the Last Minstrel* depicts the untutored and unlettered William of Deloraine as being so familiar with armorial bearings that the youth could decipher the crane on Baron Cranstoun's crest. The moss-trooping knight of Branksome's Hawthorn Green could read the sculptured scroll on Melrose Abbey, and the meanings of the arms, banners, and knightly and ancient Scottish escutcheons with which the walls and sacred shrines of the venerable fane were emblazoned.

We are further reminded by the sentiment of the poet when he writes, "What! Is it possible? not know the figures of heraldry! of what could your father be thinking?" (*Rob Roy*).

* See *English Heraldry*, by Charles Boutell, M.A.

Although a mere poetic sentiment, it affords an excellent lesson to those living in this age of general technical culture.

And as heraldic ornaments are reproduced by the sculptor, painter, metal-worker, and the goldsmith, it is not the intention of the author to deal fully with the many technicalities connected with the subject, but to notice those points which are of special use to the engraver and to the enameller of goldsmith's work. For, as heraldic ornaments form a most important feature in the goldsmith's art, especially in connection with presentation pieces, such as caskets, mayoral chains, and civic insignia, it is most important that the modern goldsmith should have some knowledge of heraldry ; therefore a brief illustrative description will be given here, the student being strongly recommended to study or consult such a work as *English Heraldry*, by Boutell, for a more complete description of the subject.

Coats-of-Arms.—" From the circumstances that heraldry first found its special use in direct connection with military equipments, knightly exercises, and the *melée* of actual battles mediæval heraldry has also been entitled **armory**. Men wore the ensigns of heraldry about their persons, embroidered upon the garments that partially covered their armour, and so they called them **coats-of-arms** ; they bore these same ensigns on their shields, so they called them **shields-of-arms** ; and in their armorial banners and pennons they again displayed the very same insignia, floating in the wind high above their heads, from the shafts of their lances."*

" **The Shield.**—A coat-of-arms is composed of charges depicted on an escutcheon representing the old knightly shield. The word ' escutcheon ' is derived from the French *écusson*, which signified a shield with arms on it, in contradistinction from the shield generally used.

" The forms of the shields represented in heraldry, as in war, differed at different times, but the points or positions were the same.

" **Marshalling.**—The disposing or arranging of such coats-of-arms as have to be included in one shield."†

" **The Blazoning of Arms.**—To blazon a coat-of-arms is to describe it in the technical language of heraldry ; and, although the works of the fathers of heraldic lore contain much irrelevant matter and some confusion of arrangement, the rules of blazon, by whomsoever devised or perfected, are remarkable for their precision, brevity, and completeness ; great and successful care has been taken to produce clear and simple order, to avoid repetition, and to preserve a certain uniformity of arrangement through much complexity of detail. The technicalities arise in great measure from the use of terms one well knows, and

---

* *English Heraldry*, by Charles Boutell, M.A.
† Chambers's *Encyclopædia*.

language, as was to be expected, shows traces of the French and Franco-Norman channels through which the 'gentle art' reached England."*

To facilitate the description, or, as it is called, blazoning of arms, the different points or positions on the escutcheon have received technical names. English heraldry generally enumerates them as nine, as shown in Fig. 129a. A, the dexter chief point; B, the middle chief; C, the sinister chief; D, the honour or collar point; E, the fesse point; F, nombril or navel point; G, the dexter base; H, the middle base; and I, the sinister base point. To these may be added K, the dexter flank; and L, the sinister flank. This shield or escutcheon, called in blazon the field, and upon which all lines are drawn and charges delineated, represents the shield borne in war upon which the arms of the knight was displayed, and in later times it is still regarded as a suitable form to display heraldic blazonry.

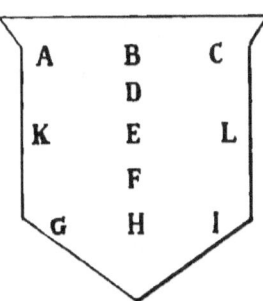

Fig. 129a.—The Parts and Points of a Shield (or Escutcheon).

" In English heraldry the tinctures comprise two metals, five colours, and eight furs. They are symbolised or indicated by dots and lines, which very convenient system is said to have

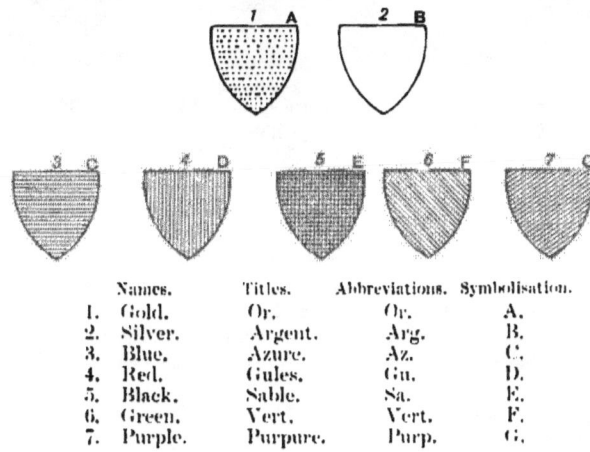

Names.	Titles.	Abbreviations.	Symbolisation.
1. Gold.	Or.	Or.	A.
2. Silver.	Argent.	Arg.	B.
3. Blue.	Azure.	Az.	C.
4. Red.	Gules.	Gu.	D.
5. Black.	Sable.	Sa.	E.
6. Green.	Vert.	Vert.	F.
7. Purple.	Purpure.	Purp.	G.

Fig. 130.—Symbols of Metals and Colours.

* *Encyclopædia Britannica.*

been introduced about the year 1630 by an Italian named Silvestre de Petrasancta.

"But the system which is now in use was not generally adopted till the commencement of the last century." * The names and abbreviations of the metals and colours and their several indications are given in Fig. 130, and the eight furs are shown in Fig. 131.

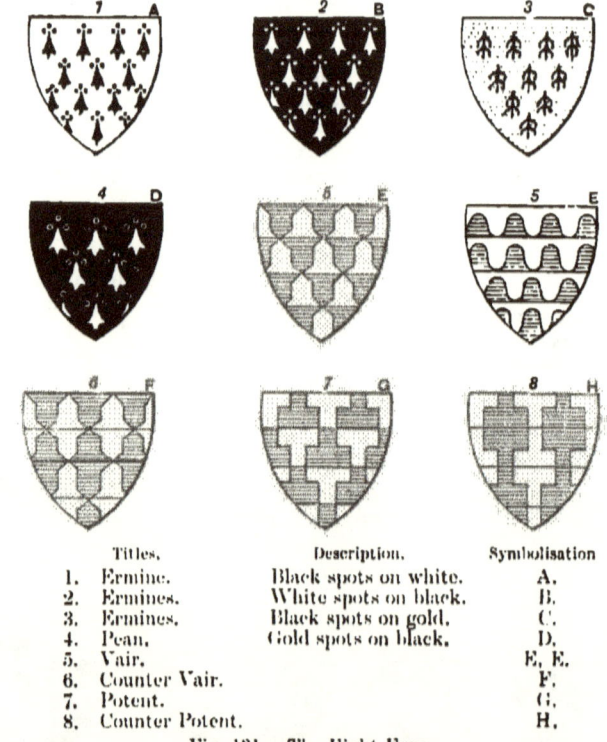

Titles.	Description.	Symbolisation
1. Ermine.	Black spots on white.	A.
2. Ermines.	White spots on black.	B.
3. Erminés.	Black spots on gold.	C.
4. Pean.	Gold spots on black.	D.
5. Vair.		E, E.
6. Counter Vair.		F.
7. Potent.		G.
8. Counter Potent.		H.

Fig. 131.—The Eight Furs.

The true meaning of heraldic engraving may be exemplified by Fig. 132, which illustrates the arms of the City of Birmingham (Warwickshire), a description of which is thus given in the *Book of Public Arms*, edited by A. A. Fox-Davies and M. E. B. Crookes.

Birmingham (Warwickshire). Quarterly first and fourth azure a bend of five lozenges, or second and third per pale indented of the last and gules; over all a fesse ermine, thereon a mural crown of the second; and for the *Crest*, on a wreath of the

* *English Heraldry*, by Charles Boutell, M.A.

colours a mural crown, issuant therefrom a dexter arm embowed, the hand holding a hammer all proper, together with the *Motto* Forward. *Supporters,* on the dexter side a man habited as a smith (representing Industry), holding in the dexter hand a hammer resting on an anvil all proper; and on the sinister side a female figure (representing Art) proper vested argent, wreathed round the temples with laurel vert tied by a riband gules, holding in the dexter hand resting on the shield a book bound, also gules, and in the sinister a painter's pallette or, with two brushes proper.

The arms were granted April 3rd, 1889, and the supporters April 4th, 1889.

Prior to the grant in 1889, arms without crest or supporter were used, and these were as quoted above, but without the fesse. They are really the arms, I believe, of the old family of Bermingham.

CITY OF BIRMINGHAM

Fig 132.—Arms of the City of Birmingham.

CHAPTER XX.

ENGRAVING: ITS ORIGIN, HISTORY, AND PROCESSES.

Early History.—The great antiquity of the art of engraving on metal and stones is shown by the reference made to it in the Bible. In Exodus, chap. xxxv. 30–35, it is stated "that Moses said unto the children of Israel, 'See, the Lord hath called by name Bezaleel, of the tribe of Judah, and he hath filled him with the spirit of God, in wisdom, in understanding, and in knowledge, and in all manner of workmanship;

"'And to devise curious works, to work in gold, and in silver, and in brass, and in the cutting of stones, and to set them, and in carving of wood, to make any manner of cunning work,

"'And he hath put in his heart that he may teach, both he, and Aholiab, of the tribe of Dan. Them hath he filled with wisdom of heart, to work all manner of work, of the engraver, and of the cunning workman.'"

And in chap. xxxii. 2–4, it is written—"and Aaron said unto them, 'Break off the golden ear-rings, which are in the ears of your wives, of your sons, and of your daughters, and bring them unto me. And all the people brake off the golden ear-rings which were in their ears, and brought them unto Aaron. And he received them at their hands, and fashioned it with a graving tool, after he had made it a molten calf.'"

The above passages show that not only was the art of engraving known, but also that teachers were specially appointed to give instruction in various branches connected with the goldsmith's art.

In the British Museum and in the South Kensington Museum, London, may be seen numerous examples of engraving upon metals and stones, wrought by the ancient Egyptians, which are worthy of our notice.

"It has been stated that among the best known artists in gold and silver of ancient times, Mentor is in the front rank. The exact time when he produced his works is not known, but it is said that four pairs of silver vases perished in the burning of the temple of Diana at Ephesus, B.C. 356. Mentor and his brother artists were embossers, chasers, as well as engravers.

"After Mentor, other distinguished artists followed, among whom Pliny mentions Antipater, as the maker of a bowl on which was a sleeping satyr, engraved so wonderfully as to seem laid on in relief." *

Later History.— The style of engraving known as niello-work is said to have been invented by Maso Finiguerra, a native of Florence, and the reported inventor of copper-plate engraving, and also of copper-plate printing. It was practised in the Middle Ages. The processes consisted in cutting incisions in metal with a graver, and filling up the incisions with a special kind of soft black enamel. Maso Finiguerra was followed by other famous artists who did much to bring the art to an important position in Italy. Among them was the wonderful goldsmith Benvenuto Cellini, in whose hands, it is said, the goldsmith's work of the sixteenth century reached its greatest splendour and beauty.

Jean Vauquer (or Vauquier), a native of Blois, who laboured as a designer and copper-plate engraver from about 1670 to 1701, produced some most beautiful designs. His prints were published in Paris as a book of reference under the title of the *Livre-de-Fleurs*, which comprises twelve plates of fifty-one engravings of refined designs suitable for watch-cases, bracelets, lockets, snuff-boxes and other goldsmith and decorative work.

During the eighteenth century England produced some excellent engravers, among others Thomas Bewick, who ranks high as a wood engraver; William Hogarth, the founder of the modern school of gold engravers; the London apprentice, Draper, who did so much to raise the position of the craft, that he became familiarly known as the "father of engravers." He improved the form of the graver (or burin), and did much to advance the art by greatly simplifying the process, and by assisting in the production of more beautiful effects.

Processes.—The tools required are gravers of different shapes, including the lozenge-shaped graver invented by Draper; scorpers, including flat-scorpers, and half-round-scorpers; bull-sticks; shaders; and a scriber. They must be made of the very best steel. When purchased they are unfit for immediate use, and must, therefore, be carefully hardened and tempered, the latter process being performed at a temperature indicated by a colour not deeper than a straw colour. They are then fixed in suitable handles, ground and sharpened ("wetting up" is the trade term) upon an oil-stone (see Fig. 48). If the article to be engraved is small, it is fixed upon a chuck with cement (see *Engraver's Cement*, p. 231); this chuck is screwed on to an iron bullet which fits into a hole in a leather pad (Fig. 50), so as to allow of the article being easily moved round by the left hand while the graver is held in the right. Large articles are cemented to square or oblong wooden blocks, which are held in position upon a circular sand-bag. Extra large work, such as

* John Hungerford Pollen, M.A., *Gold- and Silversmiths' Work.*

trays, cups, tea-services, &c., are not cemented on blocks, but are held by the hand upon large sand-bags. A great amount of skill is required to produce an artistic design, and there must be a combination of technical excellence in the article, with good drawing and artistic beauty in the design.

The design is first drawn accurately on the article with a pencil, and the pencil lines carefully traced with the graver. If the design is to appear in *bas-relief* careful shading is added to the design. If the article is to be finished by the wet-colour process, a suitable ground work is made so as to leave the design in relief; this ground work holds the colour, by which beauty is added to the design.

Arms, crests, monograms, cyphers, inscriptions, devices, and masonic emblems can be faithfully reproduced by the skilled engraver, who applies to each the style of engraving most suitable for it. This important branch of the goldsmith's art has held a high position for many centuries.

CHAPTER XXI.

MOULDING AND CASTING OF ORNAMENTS, &c.

MOULDING and casting were processes well known to the ancient workers, for it is written in the book of Exodus, chap. xxxviii. 5, " and he cast four rings for the four ends of the grate of brass, to be placed for the staves." It is also stated in the Sacred Writings that figures and ornaments were cast in gold, silver, and other metals.

Many metals can be fused at moderate temperatures, and can be cast in the form of any given pattern, in order to form articles which must combine strength and durability, but in which weight is not objectionable. In this chapter we propose dealing with the casting of gold for such articles as rings, charms, animals, figures, and other ornaments used in the goldsmith's art.

Patterns and Models.—The first process is to produce the pattern or model from which the mould or impression is made, for it must be borne in mind that the success of casting depends as much on the skill of the modeller as upon that of the caster. In goldsmith's work the patterns or models are generally made of brass, tin, silver, ivory, modelling wax, or plaster of Paris. As models with rectangular edges will not leave clear impressions without damaging the mould, such parts must be slightly tapered. The inside of rings must be slightly tapered on both sides; carved patterns must not be undercut, but the carving should be such that the pattern will leave the impressions freely. Patterns for casting animals, such as dogs in the position of running, should not have the legs open, but the metal should be cut away afterwards; some models are much lighter and easier to manage if cast in halves; while others should be cast with projecting parts omitted, which are more easily supplied after casting, such as the antlers of the stag, the tail of the greyhound, &c.

Moulding is the term applied to the various operations connected with the preparation of the sand or other materials used for making the moulds. The materials generally used are sand, loam, marl, cuttle-fish bone, bath-brick, blacking and pea-flour. Sand is the most common, and, for general purposes, is the most perfect moulding material. The special qualifications are that the molten metal will not fuse or chemically change it, while better impressions are obtainable from it than from any other material.

Different kinds of castings require different kinds of sand. For some, it must be porous, yet adhesive; for others, it must be very fine and free from grit, but still adhesive enough to retain impressions of the most minute details of the pattern. The best and most suitable sand for casting gold and silver work is that obtained from the redstone quarry at the Birmingham Old Cemetery, which, for more than fifty years, has been used for casting purposes in many cities and towns in England. The value of the quarry has been estimated at £20,000 sterling.*

Core Sand.—The sand generally used for making cores is porous, and, at the same time, very adhesive. For small cores, a mixture of sand (8 parts), clay (1 part), and marl (1 part) if well ground together will easily mould, and will retain its form when baked.

Facing Sand.—As liquid metal is apt to penetrate the pores of raw sand and so produce a rough surface on the casting, the mould sometimes requires to be dusted over with some finely sifted sand or pea-flour, contained in a muslin bag called a **dust-bag**, and faced with carbonaceous matter, generally charcoal powder.

Preparation of the Material for casting Fine Work.—As all goldsmith's work comes under the head of **Fine Casting**, attention will be confined to this branch of the subject. The moulding sand should first be well sifted in order to remove small

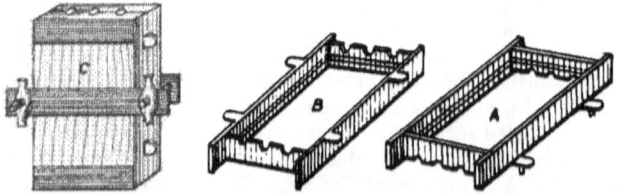

Fig. 133.—Casting Flasks.

stones, grit, or hard lumps of sand, then damped with water and well mixed up in the **moulding tub**, which is an oblong wooden trough made specially for the purpose. The sand is then placed in shallow iron frames, called **flasks**, which hold it in position during the moulding process. These flasks are of various sizes; those generally used for small work are 12 ins. by 8 ins., but larger ones are sometimes required. A flask consists of two parts, as shown in Fig. 133, in which A is the upper or *peg-side*, and B the lower or *eye-side*; sometimes a third frame is used, called the *odd-side*: the sides of each of the frames are about 3 inches deep, and have a slight groove on the inside for the purpose of holding the sand intact.

* *Mixed Metals*, by A. H. Hiorns.

Preparing the Mould.—This process is thus performed : place the eye-side upon a flat board, dust the inside with parting sand, then fill up the frame with the prepared sand, pressing it down with the hands and finishing with the mallet; scrape the surface level with a straight-edge scraper, place one of the outside boards on the top and invert the frame.

The patterns to be cast are laid on the mould in the position most suitable for casting and dusted all over by means of the dust-bag. On carefully removing the patterns a clear outline of each will be left on the sand, which will show what parts must be cut away so as to allow the patterns being let down half way in the mould. The upper or peg-side is now placed upon the lower or eye-side frame, which latter contains the patterns ; the inside is dusted, and the prepared sand is then placed in the frame in the same way as in the former one. Success mainly depends upon the complete manner in which this process is carried out.

The peg-side is then taken off, the patterns carefully removed from the eye-side, and all the loose particles of sand blown away from them by means of small hand bellows. The two surfaces of the mould are next dusted with powdered charcoal, and then faced with soot produced by burning a torch saturated with pitch. The patterns are again placed in position, the mould screwed up tightly, and clear, sharp impressions obtained on the soot-faced mould, from which the patterns are finally removed. After the impressions have been perfectly moulded in each side of the flask, **ingates** or **channels** (the "get" is the term used) are made for the inflow of the molten metal into the impressions made in the mould. This is done by scraping incisions in the sand with a special tool called a **drawer**, an operation which requires much judgment as the flow must be so regulated by them that each impression in the mould shall readily receive just the amount of molten metal that it requires. The loose particles are blown away, and the impressions carefully examined to ascertain if each is perfect ; the two parts of the mould are then carefully dried and tightly screwed together ready for casting.

The metal previously melted in a crucible, either in a furnace or a muffle, is now carefully poured into the channel until the **get** is full. When sufficiently cool, the mould is taken apart, and the castings (which will be attached to the channels in the form of a tree) carefully cut or broken away.

Less labour is required for patterns which are flat and smooth on one side, such as clasps and other ornaments, as impressions can be taken on the one side of the frame only, the other side being formed by perfectly smooth sand.

Core Casting.—This term is applied to the process of casting hollow articles ; such castings are called **cored**. The patterns should, if possible, form their own cores, which is done by making the pattern " leave " half way, and then moulding the core to the shape required, as shown in Fig. 134, where A represents the core.

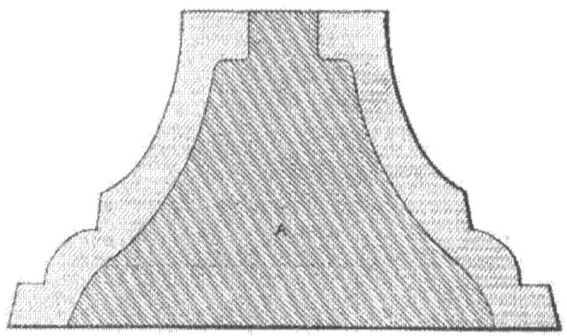

Fig. 134.—Section of Pattern showing Core.

Casting Figures and Other Subjects by the False-coring Process.—This is the most difficult kind of casting, as the patterns are mostly solid. When the pattern is very complicated it is sometimes an advantage to remove a portion of the figure, such as one arm, or part of one leg, to cast these separately and to braze them on afterwards. In other instances, the figure to be cast is pressed so far into the sand as will allow of its easy removal ; the operator then dusts the undercut parts and fits into them pieces of prepared core-sand ; each undercut part is successively laid on until a part is revealed which will leave the sand without breaking any part of the mould. This part is then moulded and removed ; then each separate core is lifted out with two needle points ; and, finally, the pattern is removed. After the mould and cores have been dried, the latter are replaced in their proper relative positions. When the channels or gets have been prepared the molten metal is poured and the casting taken ; the flasks are then unfastened and the figure removed, which will be found to have all the undercut parts quite perfect.

"Cire Perdu" Casting.—This mode of casting, now much used for fine art work, is a revival of the method employed by the celebrated goldsmith, Benvenuto Cellini. It allows of much finer impressions being taken than can be obtained with the ordinary sand mould. The processes are the following :—

Process for the Reproduction of Hollow Figures.—The model is first made. A skeleton iron-wire frame is covered with a clay mixture ; this core is roughly moulded to the form of the figure and then covered with wax, the thickness of which is regulated by the nature of the subject, and the wax carefully modelled so as to show every minute detail. The model is carefully coated with a paste formed of three parts of plaster of Paris and 1 part of fine brick dust mixed with a solution of alum and sal ammoniac. It is now suspended by a wire in a box, which is then filled with the same mixture, until the model is embedded, and a wooden peg is placed to indicate where the channel (or get) can be most conveniently made. This done, the peg and wires are withdrawn, the holes left by the wires serving as air-holes during the casting. The mould is gently dried, and the heat then raised nearly to a red heat so as to melt the wax, some of which is recovered through the air-holes, while the remainder is lost. The molten metal is poured into the space vacated by the wax, the metal allowed to cool, and the mould placed in a vessel of water for a time. The mould is then carefully broken away, the casting removed, and the core scooped out, thus producing a perfect hollow casting.

A **Solid Casting** may be produced by the same method, the core being omitted. The model is composed wholly of wax moulded, the wax model is melted out and replaced by molten metal. In this case there is no need for false cores, flasks, or manipulation of the undercut parts.

Casting generally forms a separate branch of the goldsmith's art, as it can only be successfully performed by skilled operators in constant practice, with a ready command of the best materials and mechanical appliances for carrying out the process.

Casting in Cuttle-fish is especially suitable for single small articles, as a ring or a charm, as it can be done much more quickly than with the sand mould, and at the same time a smaller quantity of gold is needed. A good sized cuttle-fish should be selected, sawn into two parts, and the soft parts rubbed or filed perfectly flat ; three small wooden pegs inserted on the one side forms the peg-side of the mould ; and when the two sides are firmly pressed together the eye-side is obtained. When it is found that the two surfaces come in perfect contact the article is placed in the position for casting, the two sides pressed firmly together with the article between them, and a perfect impression obtained.

The pattern is then carefully removed, a channel made for the molten metal, and the parts of the mould tied together with iron binding wire. A cavity is then made in a piece of charcoal sufficiently large to hold the metal, the quantity of which may be, say, 3 or 6 dwts. The charcoal is tied to the cuttle-fish with the cavity close to the mouth of the mould. The metal is then fused by the direct impact of a blowpipe gas flame, and when quite liquid is gently tilted into the mould. The mould is then taken apart and the perfect casting obtained.

Casting in Bathbrick is a quick and reliable method for special forms used in the goldsmith's art. The process is similar to the preceding one, bathbrick being used instead of cuttle-fish. The special advantages are that the cuttle-fish mould can only be used once, whereas the bathbrick mould may be used two or three times, and that the cavity may be cut or carved with a tool, thereby dispensing with the model.

CHAPTER XXII.

FLUXES, &c.

Oxygen Excluders.—In melting alloys containing metals readily acted upon by oxygen, it is necessary to exclude the air as much as possible to prevent the formation of oxides. This is a matter of much importance, as the oxidation of a portion of the base metal in the alloy means the removal of a definite quantity of that metal, with consequent enrichment of the alloy. For example, the correct weight of gold, silver and copper required to make a quantity of 9-carat alloy may be put into the pot, but if some of the copper is oxidised the result may assay 9·2-carat. This is clearly a loss to the master if he sells the articles made from the alloy as 9-carat. To prevent this waste, some covering material to exclude the air from the pot during the melting is necessary. Charcoal in fine or coarse powder is a very suitable material for this purpose, as it takes up oxygen very readily, and thus prevents the gas from attacking the metal. Only sufficient to cover the molten metal should be used, as too much charcoal prevents the successful pouring of the metal, and tends to produce imperfect ingots.

In melting processes it is sometimes necessary to add substances to the melting charge to remove impurities from the materials under treatment. These compounds are known under the general name of **Fluxes**. The kind of flux to be used in a given case depends upon the nature of the impurities to be removed. A description of the common fluxes, with the chemical principles upon which their efficacy depends, is given below.

FLUXES.

Borax.—The chemical composition of this compound is denoted by the formula $Na_2B_4O_7$. It contains an excess of the acid forming oxide of boron, and on that account it most readily unites with metallic oxides, and forms with them a readily fusible glass or slag which separates completely from the molten metal. It may be used as a covering to prevent oxidation of a molten metal, or to dissolve any oxide which may be formed during the melting. It also slags off sulphides and arsenides.

Borax acts as a cover in the process of hard soldering, and also dissolves any oxide which may be formed during the heating, thus keeping the parts of the article to be united clean and ready to alloy perfectly with the solder when the proper temperature has been reached. The crystallised salt contains nearly half its weight of water of crystallisation, which is completely driven off by heat, and causes the intumescence or swelling up which is so characteristic of the crystallised salt. Vitrified or calcined borax should be used in operations in which the intumescence is a disadvantage.

Potassium Nitrate.—This salt is also called saltpetre, and its composition is denoted by the formula KNO_3. It contains nearly half its weight of oxygen, most of which is readily given up to bodies which combine with that element. It thus acts as a very powerful oxidising agent, and is added to a melting charge when oxidisable impurities have to be removed. Saltpetre, after oxidation, leaves a residue of potassium oxide (potash) which acts as a basic flux (see *Sodium Carbonate*). Sodium nitrate, or Chili saltpetre, is just as effective as the potassium salt, and, as it is cheaper, should be used when considerable quantities are required.

Potassium Chlorate, $KClO_3$.—This compound is a very powerful oxidising agent, as it readily parts with the whole of its oxygen. In some cases it may be used with or without potassium nitrate, but for most purposes the latter salt is sufficient.

Potassium Cyanide, KCN.—This compound fuses below a red heat, and has a powerful affinity for oxygen and sulphur. It reduces most metallic oxides and sulphides with liberation of the contained metals. A small quantity is useful in clearing the surface of molten metal just before pouring, especially if the surface has been exposed and oxidisation has taken place. It acts by reducing the oxide and returning the reduced metal to the alloy. Potassium cyanide should not be used in a melting charge if the object is to remove foreign metals by oxidation.

Sodium Carbonate, Na_2CO_3.—The principal function of this compound as a flux is to furnish the basic oxide, soda, which combines readily with infusible silica, SiO_2, and forms a fusible silicate or slag. It melts at a moderate temperature and dissolves many metallic oxides, thus acting as a flux to these bodies ; but it is not so effectual in this respect as borax. At high temperatures it may also act as an oxidising agent to iron, zinc, tin, &c. Sodium carbonate readily reduces silver chloride to the metallic state when fused with it. A mixture of 3 parts of sodium carbonate and 4 parts of potassium carbonate fuses at a lower temperature than either salt alone ; it is very useful when rapid fusion at a moderate temperature is required.

Ammonium Chloride (Sal Ammoniac), NH_4Cl.—This compound does not liquefy on heating, but passes directly into the gaseous state. At a moderately high temperature the vapour is a mixture of ammonia and hydrochloric acid gases, the latter of which acts upon some metals with formation of chlorides; if these are volatile they pass off as vapour. Sal ammoniac owes its purifying property to this action, and is sometimes used in the purification of gold.

Sodium Chloride (Common Salt), $NaCl$.—This compound is commonly used to act as a cover, and to prevent the too violent ebullition of the contents of a crucible. It melts at a red heat and is somewhat volatile at that temperature. It forms fusible and volatile compounds with antimony and arsenic, and is serviceable in removing these bodies during refining. Common salt is one of the ingredients in the process of wet colouring.

Mercuric Chloride (Bichloride of Mercury or Corrosive Sublimate), $HgCl_2$.—This body is a very useful refining agent. It acts by converting metals into chlorides, and may be used for removing deleterious metals from gold in the process of "toughening."

Potassium Tartrate (Cream of Tartar), $KH_5C_4O_6$.—This is a very useful compound, as it contains a considerable quantity of carbon, which acts as a reducing agent; it also furnishes a residue of potash, which acts as a powerful flux upon siliceous matters. The impure variety known as **argol** is good enough for most purposes.

Silica, SiO_2.—This compound is found most abundantly in nature in the free state as silica sand, quartz, rock crystal, &c.; and in combination with metallic oxides as silicates in rocks, stones, clays, &c., used for building and road making. Siliceous matter is brought into the shop on the boots of workmen, and thus forms a part of the ordinary "shop dirt." As this matter is usually **acid** in character and infusible at ordinary furnace temperatures, a **basic** flux is required in refining the "dirt." Silica is sometimes used as a flux for basic impurities when a high temperature is to be used in the melting operations. The hard white variety known as "silver sand" is the best for this purpose.

Oxides of Lead.—There are two well-known oxides of lead : the yellow oxide, massicot or litharge, PbO ; and the red oxide, red lead, Pb_3O_4. Either compound may be used for ordinary purposes. Lead oxide acts as a flux to siliceous matter, but is not often used for that purpose. When heated with carbonaceous matter it is reduced to the metallic state ; the lead thus liberated readily dissolves gold and silver. Advantage is taken of this, in "sweep" refining, to separate the precious metals from the slag formed in the melting down.

Glass.—Powdered glass may be used as a flux in some melting operations. It is a complex silicate, which melts at a moderate temperature, and may be used for fluxing basic oxides of an earthy character. It acts in a similar manner to borax, and is much cheaper; but a higher temperature is required in its use. Common bottle glass or window glass is best, and may be readily pounded to a fine powder in an iron mortar.

Carbon.—Well-made charcoal is a very useful substance for melting operations. A coarse powder is the most serviceable as a cover for molten metal. It should be used sparingly—that is, in quantities just sufficient to cover the surface, as an excess renders the operation of pouring more difficult than it need be. Carbon acts as a powerful reducing agent upon many oxides, and reduces them to the metallic state.

CHAPTER XXIII.

RECOVERY OF THE PRECIOUS METALS FROM THE WASTE PRODUCTS.

THE most costly metals in common use by goldsmiths are gold, platinum, and silver; and as these are liable to waste during many of the operations they have to undergo, the strictest economy and the most systematic care are necessary in order to prevent serious loss. In the case of a manufacturing goldsmith employing twenty workmen, there may be as much as £200 worth of precious metals lying about the premises in the shop-sweep, the waste from polishing, colour water, wash-hand water, &c. It is highly important, therefore, that he should be fully acquainted with the best methods of recovering these metals from the waste.

Recovery of Waste Gold.—Only those methods will be noticed which have most successfully stood the test of practical experience. The "shop-sweep" consists of the sweepings of the floors where gold dust has any chance of accumulating, the pounded melting pots, the refuse from the furnace, and the sediments from the wash-hand water tubs.

Every manufacturing goldsmith has his own particular method, which is more or less perfect; but the methods given below can be recommended with safety, as they are the results of many years' practical experience.

From the Shop Floors.—The shop floors should be swept each day, and the refuse be sorted the following day by the workman whose special duty is to pick out small pieces of gold or other metals there may be in it. The sweep is then passed through a fine sieve into a bin similar to that shown in Fig. 135.

The bin is placed in a recess or at one end of the shop. It consists of two wooden uprights, A, A, having grooves, in which the three front boards, B, B, B, fit loosely; the sides are fixed firmly to the upright and secured to the wall; the top is formed by the easily removable boards, C, C, the centre one being removed during the process of sifting; the inside of the bin is coated with gas-tar varnish in order to prevent any of the sweep sticking to the surface. When the sweep is ready to prepare for trial, the top and front boards are removed, thus forming a free space for the operation. The sorter should set aside as

much of the organic matter as possible. This should be burnt
from time to time as it accumulates, and the ash or residue first
pounded in a large cast-iron mortar, and then passed through
the sieve. All the sweep should be made to pass through a fine
sieve by burning and pounding the larger bits until they are
sufficiently small. If this method is carried out systematically
the refuse will be kept down.

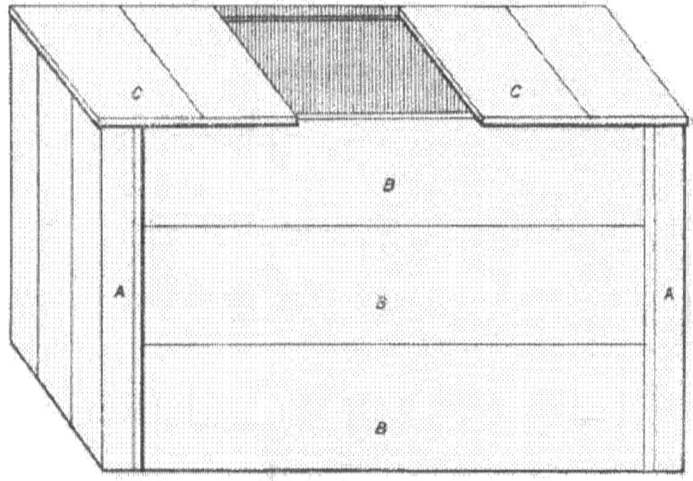

Fig. 135.—Bin for preserving the Shop-sweep in.

From Waste Water.—Waste water consists of that which has
been used for washing the work after certain processes, and also
that in which the hands have been washed; the latter is a very
important item. In the manufacturing of goldsmiths' work,
washing the hands should form part of the workman's daily
routine before leaving the premises, as much gold dust may
adhere to the hands, especially in warm weather. Waste water
is dealt with in filter tubs, arranged as shown in Fig. 136.

A strong frame or stage, A (Fig. 136), is erected in a lower
shop or in the yard; on this four tubs are placed in the order
B, C, D, E, as shown, B and C being equal in size; a bar of wood
is fixed across the top of B, and into this is inserted the screw
which holds in position an iron rod, the lower end of which has
also screwed on it a bung, F, fitting the hole in the centre of the
bottom. The tap, G', is fixed within 18 inches of the top, and
the bent overflow pipe, H, within 9 inches. The waste water
from the works passes through the pipe I into the tub B where
it settles down during the night; next day it is drawn off into
the tub C where it is again allowed to settle; afterwards it is

gently filtered through the tub E filled with rough sawdust;
the bottom of this tub has holes pierced in it in order to allow
the filtered water to pass into the lower tub D and then through
the exit pipe G into the drain; this water should be perfectly
clear.

The residue of colour water is filtered through a small wooden
bucket filled with alternate layers of sawdust and filter paper;
it rests upon two strips of wood placed across the top of

Fig. 136.—Filter Tubs.

tub C. Used tea leaves should be allowed to enter the
tub |B as they serve the double purpose of acting as a precipi-
tator and of keeping the gold dust down in the bottom of the
tub; protosulphate of iron (green copperas) dissolved in hot
water is occasionally poured into the tub B for the purpose of
precipitation.

The sawdust in the tub E should be changed at least once
each month; the mud-like matter contained in the old sawdust is

dried or burnt and then passed through the sieve into the bin.
Just prior to preparing the sweep for trials, the tub E is taken
out of the tub D and the bung F partly loosened so as to
allow the contents of tub B draining during the night. In the
morning the tub D is emptied and the water passed through the
filter tub E which may be placed near the drain ; tub D is then
replaced under the tub B, the bung of B taken out entirely, the
whole of the contents removed, and the inside cleaned out, for
which purpose it may be necessary to pull it partly down from
the stage ; it is then replaced as before, ready for use. The tub
C is then similarly emptied, cleaned, and replaced. At least
once each year the tubs and iron rod should be coated with gas-
tar varnish in order to preserve them.

The sediment from all the tubs is then placed conveniently
for draining off as much of the moisture as possible, dried, burnt,
and then sifted. As the sweep should not be too dry, some of
the residue water from the tub C should be added to the dry
dust until it has the consistency of moist soil. The sweep from
every source having been placed in the bin, a thorough mixing
is effected by passing it through a coarse riddle and throw-
ing it out of the bin, the front and top being removed for the
purpose, which will mix it up a little ; then passing it through a
fine sieve into the bin again, pulverising all the coarse parts by
burning, pounding, and sifting ; and, finally, well mixing the
whole with a shovel.

From the Polishings.—As polishings have a high percentage
of the precious metal, they should be treated separately and not
be mixed with the shop sweep. "Polishings" consist of the
materials used in connection with polishing, such as waste
pumice-stone, rotten-stone, rouge, &c. ; worn-out threads : cotton-
waste used for cleaning the laps and absorbing the polishing
refuse from the lathe ; worn-out brushes, emery, and sandpaper,
all of which contain gold or silver. These materials are collected
in trays specially provided for their reception.

This refuse is burnt in an iron pan and allowed to cool, then
passed through an extra fine sieve, and preserved in a box. The
coarse parts are pulverised until all the refuse has passed through
the sieve.

If the polishings are known to be worth more than five
shillings per ounce it is better and cheaper to refine them by the
method described under *Refining Polishings;* if less, they should
be subjected to trial and sold to the refiners.

Recovery of Gold and Silver from the Colour Water.—
As articles which have been coloured lose from 12 grains to 1
dwt. per ounce of their weight, according to the surface of the
articles, great care should be taken of the colour water, which
contains both gold and alloy. The gold and silver are separated
by precipitating the colour water in the jars mentioned when

describing the colouring processes, with a hot solution of proto-sulphate of iron (green copperas), stirring well and allowing the precipitate to settle ; the water is then passed through a filter paper placed in the earthenware funnel resting in one of the jars ; as the water accumulates in the jar it must be poured off through the sawdust in the bucket placed over the filter tub, as described, and as the precipitate accumulates it is removed, frequently cleaned, and preserved for drying. The sawdust and the filter papers are then burned in an iron pan, and the precipitate obtained from them added to that taken directly from the jars.

If rich enough, this should be refined by the method recommended for polishings ; if not, it should be mixed with the polishings and competitive offers invited from the refiners.

The Method of Receiving Trials of Sweep and Polishings.—When the sweep and polishings have been prepared two or three refiners are invited to take trials of them. The general rule is for each competitor to take two pounds weight of sweep and two ounces of polishings ; if the latter is rich, they agree to pay for one ounce, whether they purchase or not. If the refiners are not satisfied with the mixing, they throw the sweep out of the bin, mixing it while doing so, and then they throw it back again ; in some cases they take a portion trial each time the operation is performed, and as it may be repeated on an average eight or more times a thorough mixing is ensured. The polishings are also submitted to a careful turnover with a trowel, but, as the bulk is much smaller and much richer in value, the process is performed with more care and the material weighed with more accuracy. After the trials have been assayed by each refiner, each separate lot is sold to the one making the highest offer.

Cupellation.—The common base metals, lead, copper, tin, antimony, &c., are readily oxidised when heated in air ; the chemical compounds formed are called **oxides**. Most of these compounds either resist ordinary means of fusion, or are fused with difficulty. Very few are fusible at moderate temperatures, and the most important of these is lead oxide, which, at a red heat, fuses to a clear liquid. Moreover, this liquid is capable of dissolving the more infusible oxides, but in different degrees. Thus copper oxide is dissolved by 1 part of lead oxide, zinc oxide by 8 parts, and tin oxide by 12 parts respectively. Silver, gold, and platinum are not oxidised when heated in air, nor has molten lead oxide any action upon them.

The process of cupellation is based upon the above principles. When gold or silver is melted with lead an alloy of the two metals is formed ; if this alloy is melted, and kept at a red heat in air, the lead oxidises, but the other metal does not. If means are adopted for removing the oxide of lead as it forms, the other metal is finally obtained in the pure state. The removal of the

lead oxide is most readily effected by **bone ash,** which has the important property of freely absorbing molten lead oxide. The bone ash when slightly moistened with water to cause the particles to adhere together, is readily formed into small shallow vessels called **cupels** (Fig. 137). These cupels when dried by standing in a warm place for some time are ready for use.

Fig. 137.—Cupel.

Cupellation on the small scale is carried on in these vessels heated in a gas muffle, similar to the one shown in Fig. 129, p. 164. The process may be illustrated in the following manner :—Place a cupel in a muffle at a bright red heat, and leave it to get hot. Weigh accurately about 10 grains of fine gold or silver, and wrap the metal in five or six times its own weight of thin sheet lead. Place the packet on the hot cupel without removing it from the muffle. This is easily done by means of a pair of long tongs. If the action is watched, it will be noticed that small globules of an oily-looking liquid form on the surface of the molten metal, run towards the sides, and finally disappear in the bone ash. These are globules of molten oxide of lead. Dense fumes of oxide of lead (which is somewhat volatile) escape from the surface of the cupel, and from the oxidising metal. The metal gradually diminishes in quantity ; finally the dull-looking surface, after a display of iridescent colours, suddenly brightens, and the operation is finished.

If a piece of copper is put on a hot cupel, it gradually oxidises, but the solid oxide remains on the cupel. If, however, lead and copper are introduced together, the lead melts and forms a liquid alloy with the copper, and this oxidises freely at a bright red heat. The molten oxide of lead dissolves the oxide of copper as it is formed, and carries it into the cupel. By trial it is found that 16 parts of lead are required to carry 1 part of copper into the cupel. If a smaller quantity of lead is used a flat button of solid copper, coated with oxide, is left on the absorbing surface after the whole of the lead has disappeared.

It will be readily seen from the above that if an alloy of gold and copper is cupelled with a sufficient quantity of lead, the whole of the copper will be removed, and a button of fine gold obtained. Similarly, an alloy of gold, silver, and copper will leave a button of gold-silver alloy when cupelled.

Other base metals, such as tin and antimony, are much more difficult to remove if present in quantity, as a much larger proportion of lead is required. Traces of these metals, however, are removed in the ordinary process of cupellation.

A very impure alloy may be subjected to the preliminary process of **scorification.** The metal is wrapped in from ten to

13

fifteen times its weight of lead, and the packet put on a hot fire-clay dish called a **scorifier** placed in a hot muffle. The alloy melts and rapid oxidation takes place. The lead oxide formed, in part combines with silica from the clay and forms a basic silicate. The oxides of the base metals, which oxidise more rapidly than the lead in proportion to their relative quantities, dissolve in the liquid scoria. The result of this is that the lead alloy becomes purer as the scorification proceeds. When the metal has been reduced to about one half its original bulk, the molten mass is poured from the dish into a button mould and allowed to cool. When the glassy mass of scoria is broken away, a button of lead is obtained which contains the gold with much smaller quantities of the base metals than in the original alloy. This may now be cupelled in the ordinary way, and the fine gold obtained. If silver is present, the button is alloyed with the proper proportion, and again cupelled to obtain the parting alloy.

CHAPTER XXIV.

REFINING LEMEL, AND ASSAYING LEMEL BARS.

Lemel.—The term lemel is applied to the gold dust produced in the manufacture of goldsmiths' work by the processes of filing, cutting, turning, &c. The gold which has been entrusted to the care of the workman has to be fully accounted for; *e.g.*, a workman may have had 20 ounces of gold weighed out to him; the finished articles made from this may weigh 12 ounces, the scrap or cuttings 6 ounces—thus leaving 2 ounces as the weight of the lemel. As this lemel contains impurities, such as organic matter, iron filings from the files, bits of binding wire, &c., the workman must remove these before weighing the lemel. First of all he separates the scrap from the lemel by passing it through a sieve, then burns the lemel in an iron pan to remove the organic matter, and withdraws the iron particles by means of a magnet. The removal of these particles is very important, because if twenty workmen each leave 6 grains only of iron filings, this would cause much mischief in the lemel bar when melted. In order to guard against this, the refiner should always subject it to a further purification. Many methods of collecting lemel are in use, but the following are considered to be the best, if carefully carried out and judiciously applied.

Collecting Lemel—*Method No. 1.*—Take the following ingredients :—

Lemel, ...	20 ounces.
Potassium carbonate, ...	3 „
Sodium chloride (common salt), . .	2 „

First remove every particle of iron with the magnet, then well mix the salts with the lemel, and place the preparation in a skittle pot (Fig. 5), which has been previously examined and warmed. The crucible should not be quite filled with the mixture, because, if too full, the mixture is liable to overflow and to cause much loss. The mixture should not reach higher than within 1 inch of the top. The crucible should, therefore, either be of the proper size, or, if too small, a portion of the mixture should be reserved for addition after the first lot in the crucible has subsided.

The crucible is then placed in a hot furnace for about half an hour, carefully watched, and a little more salt added if the

mixture boils up too high. When fused, a very small lump of
potassium nitrate (saltpetre) is carefully added from time to
time for the purpose of refining the lemel more thoroughly.
The crucible is then carefully withdrawn, placed on the floor to
cool, and the button of lemel obtained by breaking up the
crucible with a hammer. The slag which is quite free from
metal may be pounded and put with the sweep. This button of
gold alloy is placed in a plumbago crucible with either a little
borax or charcoal, as flux, melted and poured into an ingot-
mould. This ingot may be worked up again, after an assay has
been taken of it, by reducing it to the quality required.

Method No. 2.—This is the most perfect and reliable method
known. Take the following ingredients :—

Ordinary lemel, ...	20 ounces.
E. Day's universal flux,* . . .	6 ,,

All iron is carefully removed with the magnet. Then the
flux is mixed well with the lemel, and placed in a clay crucible
(Fig. 4, p. 52), the soundness of which has been carefully
examined. The crucible is first gently warmed (in order to
prevent subsequent cracking) and then placed in a hot furnace
for about half an hour, when the mixture is quite fused; it is
occasionally stirred with a red-hot iron rod, a little potassium
nitrate and also a little borax being carefully and cautiously
added in order to thoroughly refine the mass. When the
mixture has properly melted, the crucible is carefully withdrawn, placed upon the floor to cool, and the button of gold
alloy obtained in the way described under *Method No. 1.* This
button may be worked up again after it has been melted and
cast into an ingot-mould, and an assay taken of it. There is no
advantage in reworking ordinary lemel bars over again, because,
if only a small particle of platinum or iridium should find its
way into the bar unnoticed, gold articles made therefrom may
be spoiled, thus causing much trouble; it is much better, particularly for goldsmiths, to sell it to the refiners as a parting
assay bar, and to purchase new gold with the money.

If, however, the lemel has been kept strictly free from anything of the kind, it may be melted and worked over again with
very little risk, especially if reduced to a lower quality and used
for wire.

In melting rough lemel into bars a larger quantity of
universal flux is needed. The mixture is placed in the fire (for
about an hour) until the whole is in a liquid state, carefully
withdrawn, and poured into an open ingot-mould. It is then
remelted (after the slag has been broken away) with a little
ammonium chloride and charcoal, and poured into an ordinary
ingot-mould; this also may be sold as a rough lemel bar.

---

* E. Day, Refiner and Bullion Dealer, Birmingham.

Collecting Gold and Silver from the Colour Water—
Method No. 1.—The precipitate from the colour water is washed
with hot water in order to remove every trace of acid, dried, burned
to a powder on an iron pan, pounded, and passed through a fine
sieve. It is then well mixed with its own bulk of "universal
flux," placed in a skittle pot, and heated in a hot furnace for
about one hour, during which time the process must be carefully
watched ; if the mixture is slow in fusing, the addition of a little
powdered glass will greatly assist the action of the flux. When
quite liquid, the mixture is well stirred with a red-hot iron rod.
The crucible is then carefully withdrawn, placed aside to cool,
and the button of alloy then obtained in the way already
described.

Method No. 2.—The sediment is prepared as in *Method No. 1.*
The ingredients taken are—

Sediment, ...	10 ounces.	
Potassium carbonate, . . .	5	,,
Sodium chloride (common salt), . .	2	,,
Pounded glass, ...	1	,,

These are reduced to a fine powder, well mixed together,
placed in the crucible, and heated in a hot furnace for about one
hour; a little chloride of ammonia (sal ammoniac) is occasionally
added in order to assist the fusion, and also a little sandiver,
which increases the power of the flux to draw off iron and other
impurities, so as to leave the gold alloy quite clear at the bottom
of the crucible ; the latter is then broken, and the button
removed.

Assay of Lemel Bar.—The process of melting lemel to
obtain the scrap in the form of a bar has already been described.
The bar so obtained is usually sold to the refiners, who offer a
price for it depending upon the result of an assay. The price
depends not only upon the actual amount of gold present, but
also upon the nature of the impurities. It is therefore to the
manufacturer's advantage to keep the lemel as clean as possible
and comparatively free from iron, which is a common impurity
derived from the tools. Unless the lemel has been carefully
melted, the composition of the bar will vary in different parts ;
hence, to protect himself against offering too high a price, the
refiner takes his assay quantities from different parts of the bar.
If three lots of 5 grains each have been taken, they are wrapped
separately in sixteen times their weight of lead, and cupelled
as described on p. 193. If the buttons have practically the
same weight, the bar is considered uniform. The buttons are
again cupelled with two and a half times their weight of pure
silver to obtain the parting buttons. These are then parted, and
the fine gold weighed. The comparison of the weights is a
further check upon the homogeneity of the bar.

CHAPTER XXV.

GILDING AND ELECTRO-DEPOSITION.*

THE electro-deposition of one metal upon another has now become of great importance in the manufacture of a great variety of articles. The metals selected for deposition have special properties which render them valuable for the purposes to which they are put. Thus gold and silver, and sometimes copper, are used for ornamental work on account of their lustre, colour, &c. ; while the principal value of nickel lies in the fact that it forms a dense, hard coating capable of resisting wear, and has a fairly good lustre when polished.

The Voltaic Battery.—When common zinc is put into dilute sulphuric acid the metal rapidly dissolves and hydrogen gas is given off freely, escaping from the liquid in bubbles. If pure zinc is used no action takes place, and the metal remains un-dissolved for any length of time. Common zinc, carefully cleaned by immersion in moderately strong sulphuric acid and then coated over with mercury (amalgamated zinc), acts in the same way as pure zinc ; commercial copper is also unattacked by dilute sulphuric acid. If, then, a strip of amalgamated zinc and a strip of copper are placed side by side, but not in contact, in a vessel containing dilute sulphuric acid no action is observed ; if, however, the metals are made to touch each other, or are joined together by a metal wire, an action is at once set up and bubbles of hydrogen gas collect on the copper plate. But examination of the solution after the action has gone on for some time shows that it is the zinc which dissolves in the acid and not the copper as might be inferred from the position of the bubbles of gas. Also, it is found that the connecting-wire undergoes an important physical change and becomes possessed of new properties. It attracts iron filings, deflects a magnetic needle, and gets hot. If the wire is cut the action ceases at once and the wire loses its new properties ; but if the ends are dipped into water containing an acid or a metallic salt in solution, a chemical decomposition is at once set up and the action between the zinc and the acid recommences. This acquisition of power on the part of the wire is said to be due to a current of electricity passing through it,

* A detailed description of the application of electrolysis to plating and decomposition will be found in McMillan's *Electro-Metallurgy.*

and as long as the current is running the wire retains its new properties.

The arrangement described in the last paragraph is a simple form of voltaic cell, and the essential parts are shown in Fig. 138. A is a vessel containing dilute sulphuric acid; Cu is the copper plate; Zn, the amalgamated zinc plate; B, a copper wire connecting the two plates. Directly the plates are connected the zinc commences to dissolve in the acid to form zinc sulphate, and hydrogen is liberated. The gas does not, however, collect on the zinc plate, but, after a series of secondary actions, is deposited upon the copper plate, from which the greater part escapes in bubbles. As the zinc dissolves **energy is** liberated. If zinc dissolves in acid under ordinary conditions practically the whole of the energy is liberated in the form of heat; but if the dissolution takes place under the conditions shown in Fig. 138 a large proportion of it is in the form of electrical energy. The source of this energy is clearly the zinc dissolving in the acid, and it is liberated on the surface of the plate. This action may be compared to that in an ordinary fire; the source of the energy in this case is the burning coal, and its seat the grate in which the action is taking place. Coincident with the liberation of electrical energy a propelling force is set up which drives a current of electricity through the liquid to the copper plate, and through the wire connection to the zinc again, thus com-

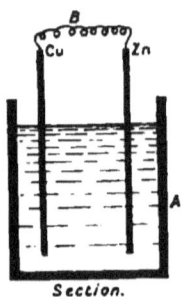

Section.

Fig. 138.—Voltaic Cell.

pleting a circle or **circuit**. This force is usually denoted by E.M.F. and is called **electromotive force**. As long as the circuit is intact and chemical action is going on at the surface of the zinc plate, the current will flow and carry with it the electrical energy.

Conductors.—All metals are conductors of electricity—that is, they allow the current to pass through them—but, at the same time, they all offer more or less **resistance** to its passage. They differ among themselves considerably in this respect. Copper is one of the best conductors and is commonly used. Its conducting power is seven times that of iron. The iron is said to offer more resistance to the passage of the current. The effect of this resistance is to convert some of the electrical energy into heat energy, and the conductor gets hot. But the resistance of a given wire depends not only upon the material of which it is made, but also upon its cross-section. The thinner the wire, the greater the resistance it offers and the hotter it becomes by the passage of a given current. Thus, a very thin wire of any metal may be easily raised to a red heat, or even melted.

Copper conductors are most largely used for general electrical purposes, and to prevent leakage they are covered with some non-conducting material or insulator. They are then said to be insulated.

Double Liquid Cells.—In a simple cell, such as that just described, the current falls off in strength very rapidly, and long before the zinc and acid are exhausted. This is largely due to a film of hydrogen gas forming on the copper plate. The gas is a very bad conductor, and greatly retards the passage of the current from the acid to the copper. It also, in conjunction with the zinc, reduces the effective E.M.F. of the combination, and thus further weakens the current. Double liquid cells are constructed so as to prevent the deposition of hydrogen; hence they are free from this source of weakness.

Bunsen's Cell.—This is one of the best and most largely used of the many different forms of voltaic cell; its parts are shown in Fig. 139. A is a glazed earthenware vessel containing dilute

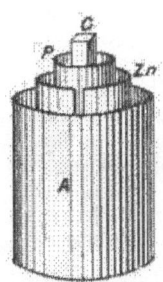

Fig. 139.—Bunsen Cell.

sulphuric acid (1 part acid to 9 parts water); Zn, a hollow cylinder of amalgamated zinc; P, an unglazed earthenware cell containing strong nitric acid and a rectangular block of gas carbon, C, which replaces the copper as the latter is dissolved by the nitric acid. The sulphuric acid solution on the outside of the porous pot, B, and the nitric acid inside soak into the walls and meet, so that a continuous mass of conducting liquid joins the zinc and carbon plates. As soon as the zinc and carbon are connected a current is set up in the wire, and continues for several hours without appreciable falling off. The function of the nitric acid is to oxidise the hydrogen to water and thus prevent its deposition on the carbon plate and the consequent polarisation, as it is called.

Daniell's Cell.—If the carbon is replaced by a strip of copper, and the nitric acid by a strong solution of copper sulphate, a constant cell is obtained. The hydrogen liberates copper from the copper sulphate, taking its place to form sulphuric acid, and the copper is deposited upon the copper plate. This offers no resistance to the current, and the polarisation is thus prevented. The E.M.F. of the Daniell cell is considerably less than that of the Bunsen cell, and the resistance in the cell is also greater; therefore the current it supplies is not so strong, but it will continue for a much longer time. For moderate currents, the Daniell is a very satisfactory cell; for strong currents, the Bunsen is to be preferred.

Dynamos and Accumulators.—For extensive operations a **Dynamo**, specially constructed for plating purposes, is now extensively used. Motive power, supplied either by a gas or steam engine, is necessary to work one of these machines. A description of the construction of a dynamo is beyond the limits of this work, but it may be mentioned that it is supplied with terminals which correspond to the poles of a battery, and when the machine is in motion it supplies the current and the necessary E.M.F. to carry on any kind of electro-deposition. Secondary batteries, called **accumulators**, are often used in conjunction with the dynamo. They are made up of a number of cells, each containing dilute sulphuric acid and specially prepared lead plates. When the terminals of the dynamo are connected with the poles of the accumulator battery, and a current is sent through it, the energy of the current is stored up in one of the plates. After properly charging, such a battery may be used for electrical work of any kind. When the terminals are connected the current runs out in the opposite direction to that in which it entered, and the battery gradually discharges itself. The name **storage** battery is often applied to this arrangement, as it may be charged when the dynamo is not wanted for other purposes, and discharged at any time when it is not convenient to run the dynamo.

Measurement of the Current.—As already stated, the current carries with it a store of electrical energy which is capable of doing work of various kinds, and the quantity of work done depends upon the quantity of available energy. It must then be a great advantage to be able to measure the current at command, and to know exactly what it can do. The E.M.F. of a particular kind of cell is fairly constant within certain limits, and depends upon the character of the plates, and also on the strength and character of the liquids in which they are immersed. It is independent of the size of the plates, or the quantity of the liquids in the cell. The E.M.F. of a battery depends upon the way in which the separate cells are linked together. Thus, in a Bunsen battery, if alternate zincs and carbons are linked together, and the free zinc and free carbon at the ends are used as terminals, the total E.M.F. is equal to the E.M.F. of one cell multiplied by the number of cells. This is called arranging the cells **in series**, and a considerable driving power is thus obtained. But if all the zincs are linked together in one group, and all the carbons in another, the E.M.F. is the same as for one cell, and the arrangement has the same effect as one large cell having plates of the same total area. This is called arranging the cells **in parallel**. A combination of the two methods is sometimes useful.

Electromotive force is measured in **volts**; and the apparatus used for measuring it is called a **voltmeter**.

Current quantity depends upon the E.M.F. and the total resistance in the circuit. It is directly proportional to the former and inversely proportional to the latter, and is summed up by the statement $C = \dfrac{E}{R}$, which is called **Ohm's Law** from the name of its discoverer. E is the E.M.F., and is measured in **volts**; R is the total resistance in and out of the battery, and is measured in **ohms**; C is the current quantity, and is measured in **amperes**.

For the intelligent electro-deposition of metals, two things must be measured, viz., the **potential difference** between the vat terminal and the **current quantity**; the first is measured by means of the voltmeter, the second by the ammeter. The E.M.F. of a battery or dynamo is measured by the difference of potential between the terminals or poles; when the poles are joined by a conductor, the difference of potential between any two points in it is less than that between the poles. The difference between the same two points can also be varied by putting in, or taking out, resistance as required.

Electro-Deposition of Metals.—The decomposition of copper sulphate by the current may be taken as a simple case of electro-deposition. Dissolve some blue vitriol in water and add a little sulphuric acid to it. Transfer the solution to a glass vessel, and immerse in it two strips of platinum foil attached by copper wires to the poles of a Bunsen cell. Bubbles of gas collect on, and escape from, the platinum plate connected with the carbon pole of the cell, and copper is deposited on the other plate. If the action were allowed to go on long enough, the whole of the copper would be deposited on the plate in the metallic state, and the solution would become quite colourless. The copper sulphate would be completely decomposed, and an equivalent quantity of sulphuric acid formed. This is expressed by the equation—

$$CuSO_4 + H_2O = Cu + H_2SO_4 + O.$$

If the platinum plate connected with the carbon pole (called the **anode**) is replaced by a copper plate of the same size, copper dissolves from it into the solution at the same rate as it is deposited upon the platinum plate connected with the zinc pole (called the **cathode**) and the solution will remain of the same strength. The introduction of an anode of the metal to be deposited forms the basis of modern methods of depositing metals for practical purposes. If an ammeter is put into the circuit, it is observed that the current from the same battery increases when the platinum plate is replaced by the copper anode, and that the metal deposits faster. This is due to the fact that the decomposition of the sulphate is compensated for by the formation of an equal quantity of the same salt, so that the energy of the current is only required for transferring the copper from one plate to the other. Exactly similar reactions take place when any metallic solution is decomposed by the current.

Electro-Deposition of Gold.—This process is more commonly called **electro-gilding**, and is a comparatively easy one when the proper working conditions are obtained. There are but few soluble compounds of gold, and the one most suitable for gilding is gold cyanide dissolved in a solution of potassium cyanide.

Preparation of the Solution—(1) *By the Ordinary Solution Method.*—Put ¼ ounce of fine gold into a porcelain evaporating basin : add a little pure hydrochloric acid, and then about one-third the quantity of pure nitric acid. Place the basin on a saucepan containing water (a water bath), and heat to the boiling point over a gas burner. Continue the boiling, and add more acid, if necessary, until the gold is completely dissolved. Evaporate the red solution until a moist crystalline mass is obtained ; moisten this thoroughly with water, and evaporate again ; repeat this once. By this means the whole of the free acid will be driven off and gold chloride obtained. Dissolve this in ½ pint of water, and transfer the solution to a glass vessel ; add strong ammonia to the solution, a little at a time, stirring with a glass rod between each addition, until no further precipitate is obtained and the liquid smells slightly of ammonia. Filter the solution through a filter paper fitted into a glass filter funnel ; transfer the whole of the precipitate to the filter, and wash it well with water ; collect the filtrate, and set it aside for a day or two, when a further slight deposit will take place. Dissolve 1½ ounces of 100 per cent. potassium cyanide in a pint of water ; push a hole through the bottom of the filter with a glass rod, and then wash off the whole of the precipitate from the filter into a glass vessel with the cyanide solution. The quantity of cyanide used should dissolve the whole of the gold precipitate and form a clear solution. Next dissolve ¾ ounce of cyanide in a pint of water, and again thoroughly wash the filter, allowing the solution to mix with the other. The filter paper will now be free from gold, and (after squeezing it, to remove adhering liquid) may be thrown away. The solution now measures 1 quart, and contains gold in the proportion of 1 ounce to the gallon of solution. Weaker and stronger solutions are also used, but the above gives excellent results. If a larger or smaller bulk of solution is required the materials must be taken in proportion.

The gold compound formed by the ammonia is called **fulminating gold**, and must not be dried, as it is explosive in the dry state. The second quantity of cyanide is added in order to furnish free cyanide, without which the solution does not work well.

(2) *By the Battery Method.*—Make a good cyanide solution containing from ¼ to 1 lb. of cyanide to the gallon, according to the quantity of gold to be introduced. Put this in the depositing

vat, and immerse in it a new porous pot filled with the cyanide
solution; raise the solution to a temperature of 150° F., and
keep it at that during the operation; connect a gold anode with
the carbon pole of the battery, and a copper cathode with the
zinc pole; suspend the gold plate in the bath and the copper
plate in the porous cell, and start the current. The gold will
gradually dissolve in the cyanide, and form the gilding solution.
The gold anode is weighed before being put in the bath, and
then removed, washed, dried, and weighed at intervals to determine the quantity dissolved. When the proper quantity has
been dissolved the current is stopped, and the solution is ready
for working. Solutions containing from ¼ to 1 ounce of gold per
gallon are mostly used.

The Process of Gilding.—The deposition of gold is best
effected from the hot solution. The most satisfactory way of
heating it is to use two vessels, one inside the other; the outer
one is partly filled with water, and the inner one contains the
gilding solution. An enamelled iron pan is most suitable for
the depositing bath. Any vessel which will hold the bath, and
in which water can be heated, will serve for the outer one. The
vessels are supported on an iron stand of suitable height, and a
gas burner on the Bunsen principle is placed underneath. A
thermometer is placed in the solution to register the temperature,
which should be about 150° F. (65° C.). By carefully regulating
the gas supply the proper temperature can be maintained for any
length of time. Two copper or brass rods, with binding screws
attached, are fixed across the bath, and are used for suspending
the gold anode and the work to be gilt. For small work, which
has only to receive a light deposit, the articles are connected
directly with one wire, and the anode with the other. They are
then dipped in and out of the bath until the proper thickness of
deposit has been obtained. The current may be supplied by a
dynamo giving a potential difference of 4 volts, or by a battery
of two or three Bunsen cells arranged in series. If a battery is
used, and is to be worked continuously for some time, large
cells—say, ½ gallon size—are required, as the duration of a
constant current depends upon the amount of liquid in the cells.
For occasional use a smaller cell—say, pint size—is sufficient.
The zinc plates should be well amalgamated, for with imperfect
plates the action in the cell continues whether the current is in
use or not; this causes a considerable waste of zinc and acid,
and necessitates more frequent charging of the battery. A
convenient strength for the sulphuric acid solution is 1 part of
strong acid to 9 parts water. In mixing, the acid must be
poured in a thin stream into the water, *and not the water into
the acid.* The mixture should be made in an earthenware jug,
and allowed to cool before adding it to the cell. Strong aquafortis is required. Fig. 140 shows a typical arrangement of the

necessary apparatus; but it must not be inferred that it is necessary to have the exact forms described.

The E.M.F. of the Bunsen cell is given as 1·96 volts, but this varies somewhat with the concentration of the acid, &c. Therefore, three cells linked in series will give 1·96 × 3 = 5·88 volts approximately, or two cells, 1·96 × 2 = 3·92 volts.

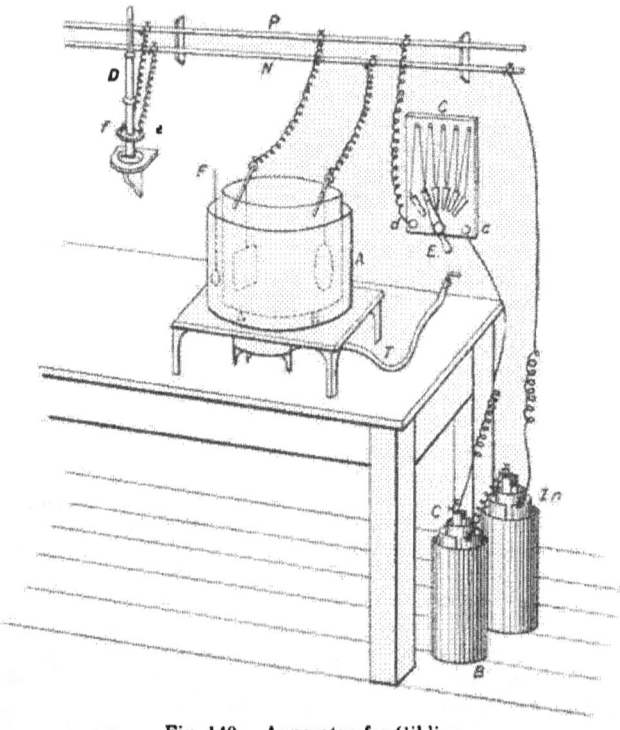

Fig. 140.—Apparatus for Gilding.

The potential difference at the leads, P, N, can be easily regulated by the introduction of resistance into the circuit. This is done by means of the resistance board, C. The resistance part of this consists essentially of a long piece of German silver wire which has a resistance about thirteen times greater than that of copper. Part of it is 18 and part 22 gauge. The binding screw c is connected with the lever E, which is arranged to move over the series of metal pieces to which the wire is connected, as shown in the figure. The end of the last turn of wire on the left is connected with the binding screw, d. When the lever is on the metal piece nearest to c the whole of the wire is

in the circuit, but when it is on the piece nearest to d none of
the wire is included. So that by altering the position of the
lever, varying lengths of the wire can be included in the circuit,
and the resistance altered within the limits of the board. The
lower portion of the lever is of wood and serves as a handle ; the
upper portion is of brass and presses tightly upon the metal
pieces so as to insure a good metallic connection.

The potential difference between P and N is measured by a
voltmeter. The one shown at D is a simple form, improvements
in which were designed and patented by Mr. T. J. Baker,
Teacher of Electro-Metallurgy at the Birmingham Municipal
Technical School. The essential parts of it are a long thin
insulated copper wire coiled round the outside of a metal tube,
and a piece of soft iron wire supported in a liquid in the tube
by means of a float. To the float is attached a vertical index,
which moves over a vertical scale fitted in a glass tube at the
top of the instrument. The free ends of the wire coil are
connected with binding screws, e, f. When these binding screws
are connected by wires with the leads, and a current is passing,
the position of the end of the index on the scale indicates the
potential difference in volts. The principle of the instrument is
very simple ; when the current divides at the leads, the small
fraction which passes through the coil of the voltmeter causes
the iron wire to be drawn down into the coil and the index to
move over the scale. The stronger the current which passes,
the greater will be the pull, and the higher the reading of the
instrument.

To obtain a uniform coherent deposit of gold, it is most essential that the articles to be coated with the precious metal should
be quite free from grease and oxide. If this is not carefully
attended to, a patchy, loosely coherent coat liable to strip will
be obtained Therefore the proper cleansing of the work before
deposition is by no means the least important part of the process.
As polished work is most often subjected to the process of
gilding, a brief description of its treatment may be given as
follows :—The article is first dipped into a hot potash bath, and
then thoroughly brushed with a suitable potash brush. The
potash solution may contain ¼ lb. of crude caustic potash to
1 gallon of water, and is best heated in an iron vessel. After
treatment with potash, which effectually removes grease, the
article is well swilled with water. It is then immersed in a
cyanide bath (cyanide dip) and moved about in it to remove any
oxide which may have been formed in the potash ; ¼ lb. of
potassium cyanide to 1 gallon of water makes a suitable dip.
It is then thoroughly swilled in clean water, and is ready for
transfer to the gilding bath.

The article is then suspended in the bath from the cathode
rod by a piece of soft copper wire ; 24 gauge wire is very suitable

for small work. In wiring the work, care must be taken that the wires shall leave no wire marks on prominent parts of the articles. The wiring is best done before cleansing, so as to avoid handling the work just before it goes into the bath. If the bath is at the proper temperature (about 150° F.), which is indicated by a thermometer placed in the solution, the current is started and regulated by the resistance board until a satisfactory deposit is obtained; the voltmeter is then read, and the pressure which gives the most satisfactory deposit noted. This pressure is then used for the same class of work. The work is raised from the bath from time to time to see that the deposition is proceeding satisfactorily. If only a thin coating is required, the time of immersion is short; but if a substantial one, a longer time is required. To determine the exact quantity of gold put upon an article, it is prepared for the bath as described, then dried in hot boxwood sawdust, and accurately weighed. It is now swilled again in water, immersed in the bath and the deposit made. It is then swilled, dried as before and reweighed. The increase in weight gives the amount of gold deposited. But careful regulation of the current and experience enables a skilful operator to work within close limits without the necessity of weighing, especially when thin deposits are required.

For gilding the inside of a hollow vessel, such as a presentation cup, the simplest plan is to connect the vessel with the zinc pole of the battery, fill it with the gilding solution, and immerse the gold anode in it, when the current will pass and the deposit of gold be effected. Any projecting portions may be coated by wrapping the anode in a piece of flannel and, after dipping it in the solution, applying it to the part to be coated. This arrangement is called the " mop."

The condition of the bath may be judged from the appearance of the gold anode. If it shows a clean dull yellow surface, the bath is working satisfactorily; if it is bright and crystalline in appearance, too much free cyanide is present and the metal is dissolving off the anode too rapidly; but if it has a dull dirty appearance, too little free cyanide is present. The first disorder may be remedied by the addition of small quantities of solid gold fulminate, which will dissolve in the free cyanide and thus remove it; the second, by the addition of more cyanide solution.

Colour of the Deposit.—The deeper shades of colour are obtained by working with the higher potential differences, as described above. By introducing more resistance, and thus reducing the pressure, lighter shades of yellow may be obtained but only through a moderate range. The pressure may vary from $\frac{1}{2}$ to 4 volts according to the class of work under treatment, and the colour desired.

To obtain a deposit of red gold, a complex bath containing

copper in addition to the gold is required. The anode should be either an alloy of gold and copper of the required colour, or a strip of good copper suspended by the side of the fine gold anode. The best way to make up the bath is to put in the ordinary gilding solution, and then add a solution of copper cyanide a little at a time, making trial deposits after each addition, until the required colour is obtained.

To obtain a deposit of **green gold** the bath must contain silver cyanide in addition to the gold. This may be added in the form of silver plating solution, and the bath tested by trial deposits as before. A gold-silver anode may be used, or a strip of silver suspended by the side of the gold anode.

When the work comes from the gilding bath it has the **dead** appearance characteristic of electro-deposited metals, and the coating is uniform and closely adherent. It is swilled in water, scratch-brushed, dried out in sawdust, and polished or burnished as desired.

The wires used for **slinging** the work in the bath become coated with gold, and when done with are put aside for the recovery of the gold.

The Process of Striking.—All the common metals, except iron and platinum, are attacked, and in part dissolved, when suspended in a bath containing free cyanide. The result of this is that the gilding solution becomes impure from the presence of other metals in it. The action of the free cyanide on the immersed article only lasts for a short time. For when the work has received a deposit of gold on its surface it is protected from further action ; or, at any rate, such action takes place much more slowly. On this account it is often the custom when a large number of articles are being treated, to first put on a thin coat of gold in an old solution, and finish the deposition in a newer solution. The first process is called **striking**, and prolongs the "life" of the new solution. Two baths are required.

Recovery of Gold from the Old Solution.—It must be carefully borne in mind that it is impossible to exhaust a gilding solution by using a gold anode. Old solutions, when they become too impure to be worked satisfactorily, are evaporated to dryness. The residue thus obtained contains the whole of the gold. The metal may be recovered by mixing the residue with red lead and charcoal, and melting it down in a crucible. The lead is reduced from the oxide and takes up the gold. On pouring, the mass of lead obtained contains the gold, which may be separated by the process of cupellation described under *assaying*. The simpler plan is to mix the residue with others containing gold, and sell it to the refiners.

Cyanide Copper Solution.—A solution of convenient strength is one containing 1 oz. of metal to the gallon. Dissolve 1 oz. of good copper sulphate crystals in one pint of water in a large beaker, and heat the solution to boiling. Add to this, dry sodium carbonate in powder, a little at a time, with stirring as long as a precipitate is obtained. Allow the precipitate of basic copper carbonate to subside, and wash it by decantation. Then add strong ammonia solution, a little at a time with stirring, until the whole of the precipitate is dissolved, and a deep blue solution is obtained. Then add potassium cyanide solution, and stir until the colour disappears; and make up the solution to 1 quart with water. This solution may be used to add to the bath for the production of red gold. Crystallised copper sulphate contains about a quarter its weight of metallic copper.

Cyanide Silver Solution.—A solution of convenient strength is one containing 2 ounces of silver to the gallon. Dissolve ½ ounce of fine silver in dilute nitric acid (1 part of acid and 1 part of water) and evaporate to dryness on a water bath ; add water and repeat the evaporation in order to get rid of free acid ; dissolve in water and transfer to a stoppered bottle. 1½ ounces of silver nitrate, which may now be bought for almost the price of the metal it contains, can also be used in place of the metallic silver, and the trouble of dissolving in acid be thus avoided. Make up the solution in the bottle to about 1 quart by addition of water, and add a solution of potassium cyanide (2 lbs. of cyanide to the gallon) gradually, with vigorous shaking, until the whole of the silver is precipitated as cyanide. Care must be taken not to add too much cyanide or some of the silver cyanide will be dissolved. Allow the precipitate to subside ; pour off the clear solution ; add water and shake again. After subsidence pour off the clear wash water. Repeat the washing two or three times. Now add cyanide solution to the washed precipitate, with shaking, until it is completely redissolved. Note the volume of cyanide solution used to redissolve the precipitate and add from ¼ to ⅓ the volume, according to the purity of the cyanide, of the same cyanide solution to furnish free cyanide to the bath. Make up the solution to 1 quart with water. This may now be used to mix with the gold bath for the production of green gold.

GILDING WITHOUT THE CURRENT.

Owing to differences in the chemical properties of metals it is possible to deposit one metal upon another by simply immersing the metal to be coated in a properly prepared solution of the metal it is desired to deposit. A very simple example of this is found in the deposition of copper upon iron. If a little copper sulphate is dissolved in water and a few drops of sulphuric acid are added, a piece of clean iron immersed therein will immediately be covered with a deposit of copper. The metal is, however, only loosely adherent. The explanation of the action is that the

14

iron, being chemically stronger than the copper, is able to replace
it in the sulphate solution. Iron sulphate is formed and an
equivalent quantity of copper is deposited upon the remaining
iron. The change is expressed by the equation—

$$CuSO_4 + Fe = FeSO_4 + Cu.$$

The action would go on until the whole of the iron had been
dissolved, or the whole of the copper deposited from the solution.
With some solutions, however, when a thin, firmly adherent
coat has been deposited the metal underneath is protected and
further action ceases. It is only when this is the case that the
process is of practical utility.

Water Gilding.—The process known as **water gilding** is based
upon the above property. A solution for depositing gold may
be made as follows :—6½ dwts. of fine gold are dissolved in nitro-
hydrochloric acid, as already described, and the pure gold
chloride obtained. This is dissolved in water and the solution
made up to 1 quart; 1 lb. of hydrogen potassium sulphate
(bisulphate of potash) is then added and the mixture boiled for
two hours. At the end of this time it has changed from yellow
to green and is ready for the gilding process. The articles to be
gilt are thoroughly cleansed, and, if of copper or brass, simply
immersed in the solution for half a minute. If German silver is
subjected to the process a piece of sheet zinc must be placed in
contact with the article during immersion. The article is then
taken out and well swilled in water, when it is found to have
received a fairly coherent, but thin, coating of gold.

Mercury Gilding.—This is a process which is now almost
obsolete. It is, however, interesting, as it was most extensively
used before the introduction of electro-deposition. The process
is based on the facts that mercury readily forms an amalgam
with gold, and, when the amalgam is strongly heated, is driven
off in the form of vapour, leaving the gold behind. The amalgam
is made by heating fine gold, or a gold alloy, to a low red heat in
a crucible and then adding eight times its weight of mercury.
The mass is kept hot, and stirred with an iron rod until the
gold is dissolved. The amalgam is then poured into a shallow
dish containing water, and worked with the fingers to expel the
excess of mercury. The pasty mass thus obtained is squeezed
in wash leather to remove a further proportion of the fluid
mercury, and is then ready for use. The expelled mercury
contains gold, and is used to prepare a fresh quantity of
amalgam.

The amalgam is placed on a flat stone, and the work to be
gilt, after being thoroughly cleansed and dried, is carefully
coated over with it. This is effected by means of a brass wire
brush, which is first dipped into a solution of nitrate of mercury
(made by dissolving mercury in moderately strong nitric acid

and diluting the solution with twenty times its volume of water), then rubbed over the amalgam, and, finally, over the work. The operation is continued until a satisfactory coating is obtained.

The article, after swilling in water, is held over a charcoal fire, and tapped gently to keep the amalgam uniformly distributed over the surface. When sufficiently heated it is allowed to cool, and is then scratch-brushed. It is again heated to expel the last traces of mercury. If any parts do not appear to be properly coated they are touched up with the amalgam before heating the second time. The article is now ready to be burnished or coloured by the wet or dry colouring process, as desired.

It is very difficult to avoid inhaling the mercury vapour during the process, and, on that account, it is a very unhealthy one.

CHAPTER XXVI.

HALL-MARKING GOLD AND SILVER PLATE.

Hall-Marking.—An idea of the regulations generally enforced in the British Isles may be gathered from those relating to the three principal cities of England in which Hall-marking is carried on. A complete treatment of the subject would fill a volume. Some of the following facts are gathered from Mr. William Redman's excellent work on Hall-marks:—"The public are greatly indebted to the Goldsmiths' Company for the effectual protection rendered by their vigilance against the frauds which prevail in this enlightened age. For more than 700 years ago it was found necessary by the honest workers in the precious metal to form themselves into a company or guild, to protect their craft against fraudulent workers, by allowing their goods to be publicly or officially examined and marked accordingly. But it was not till the year 1327 that the Company was incorporated by charter, and established on a firm basis."*

It is a well-known fact that from that time until now the Goldsmiths' Company have rendered good and valuable service to their country, and more especially to their craft, in many ways. From the time the Company was incorporated until the year 1822 the leopard's head crowned had been used as the government mark for 22-carat gold, as also for silver ·925; although on the 25th March, 1697, a new standard of silver was adopted, called Britannia, this being ·959 instead of ·925. This quality of silver not proving durable, the old standard of silver ·925 (same as now) was again legalised on June 1st, 1720. The marks then were the leopard's head crowned for the Hall-mark, and the lion *passant* for the standard mark.

Duty-Mark.—This mark was the Sovereign's head, which denotes the payment of duty; it was in force from December 1st, 1784, to April 30th, 1890.

In the year 1798, 18-carat gold was introduced, with the figure 18 and a crown for the standard mark. The next change that took place was in the year 1822, when the crown was taken from the head of the leopard; therefore the present

---

* For the purpose of reference, the author advises his readers to obtain William Redman's *Complete List of Hall-marks, and Date Letters, on Gold and Silver Plate and Jewellery.*

LONDON.

22 CARAT GOLD.

18 CARAT GOLD.

15 CARAT GOLD.

12 CARAT GOLD.

9 CARAT GOLD.

STANDARD SILVER.

Fig. 141.

BIRMINGHAM.

22 CARAT GOLD.

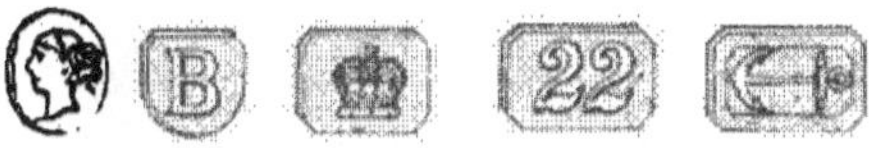

18 CARAT GOLD.

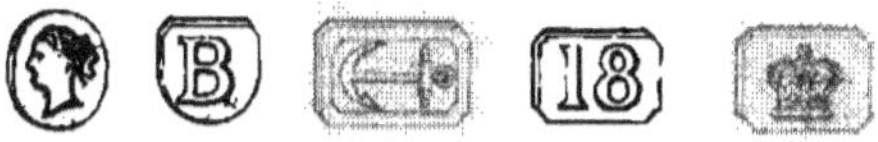

15 CARAT GOLD.

12 CARAT GOLD.

9 CARAT GOLD.

STANDARD SILVER

 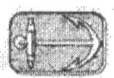 

Fig. 142.

CHESTER.

22 CARAT GOLD.

18 CARAT GOLD.

15 CARAT GOLD.

12 CARAT GOLD.

9 CARAT GOLD.

STANDARD SILVER

Fig. 143.

Hall-mark at London is a leopard's head without a crown. And in the year 1854, 15-, 12-, and 9-carat gold was authorised to be stamped at each Hall in the United Kingdom. In England the standard mark for 15-carat gold is 15˙.625; that for 12-carat gold, 12˙.5; and that for 9-carat gold, 9˙.375.

The Birmingham Assay Office was established in the year 1773; the Hall-mark is an anchor, and the standard marks, for both gold and silver, are the same as those used at London.

The new premises erected in Newhall Street are the largest and the most complete of all the seven offices. It has been stated that there are more goods assayed and stamped at this office than at all the provincial towns put together. In each department the work is carried on most systematically by a well-trained staff, while the guardians and wardens of the office spare no expense or trouble in vigilantly putting down fraud and in protecting the honour of the craft.

Assay for Hall-marking.—The processes of cupellation and parting on the small scale are adopted for the assay of gold alloys at assay offices for the purpose of Hall-marking. The following is a brief description of the complete process as carried on at assay offices in general.

The goods to be Hall-marked are accurately weighed and sent to the assay office with a statement of their weight, and the standard with which they are to be marked. On arriving at the office they are reweighed, and the checked weight entered in a book in conjunction with a number which is used for subsequent identification. The same number is given to the bearer on a printed form on which the checked weight is also stated. This form has to be signed by the sender when the goods are reclaimed. Before a manufacturer can have goods Hall-marked at an assay office he must have his initial punch registered at the office he wishes to use.

After the goods have been weighed they are passed on to an assayer who, after carefully examining them, cuts or scrapes portions of the metal from various parts of the articles until he has obtained about 5 grains of the alloy. This is usually so done as to cause as little inconvenience as possible to the manufacturer after the return of the goods. 5 grains form one assay quantity, and when a considerable bulk of metal is involved several such quantities are taken. Each assay is placed on a separate paper which bears the number of the work it belongs to, and also the number of assay quantities taken. This paper is called the **docket.**

The dockets are next sent to the weighing room and 5 grains carefully weighed from each on an accurate assay balance. To each quantity of alloy is added fine silver to the extent of two and a half times the weight of fine gold judged to be present in the alloy from its supposed standard. The alloy and the silver are now wrapped in pure lead known as **assay lead**. This is part of a thin strip of lead foil weighing sixteen times the weight of the alloy in the gold to be assayed. Thus, if 12-carat gold is the subject of the process $2\frac{1}{2} \times 16 = 40$ grains of lead are required. The docket is then folded up and placed on a wooden tray, and the assay packet with the remaining piece of lead is then placed upon it. The tray will usually hold 50 assays in 10 horizontal rows of 5 in a row. These include 2 check assays, each of which contains a weight of fine gold equal to that supposed to be present in the 5 grains of alloy to be assayed. These are assigned positions on the tray according to the discretion of the assayer. The group of assays thus formed is called a **fire**, and is next transferred to a metal tray provided with receptacles and arranged in exactly the same way as on the wooden tray.

The next process is the cupellation, by which the copper in the alloy is oxidised and carried into the cupel by the lead oxide, and the alloy of gold and silver prepared for the parting. The muffle intended to receive the assays contains the same number of cupels heated to bright redness. The pieces of lead are rapidly transferred from the tray to the cupel and are followed by the assay packets, which are arranged in the muffle in exactly the same order as on the tray. The door of the muffle is then closed and the temperature regulated, if necessary, so that the operation may proceed regularly. When the assays are worked off they are removed from the muffle by a specially constructed shovel and allowed to cool. The beads of metal are then removed from the cupels and placed in the receptacles of the metal tray in the proper order. Each button is then carefully examined and any adhering bone ash removed by tapping or brushing with a hard tooth brush. They are then hammered and drawn out into a narrow tongue under the rolls. The rolling hardens the metal, and it requires annealing during the process. This is readily effected by passing the strip slowly through a Bunsen flame. The strips are then coiled into **cornets** and are ready for parting.

The cornets are now transferred to platinum thimbles fitting into receptacles of a platinum basket. The whole is then placed in a vessel containing boiling nitric acid. After a few minutes the basket is removed and placed in a second quantity of hot acid ; this is repeated ; the whole of the silver has then dissolved out and a residue of fine gold is left. They are then thoroughly washed with distilled water to completely remove all traces of acid and silver nitrate. The cornets, which now present a spongy, blackish appearance, are dried and heated to redness in the platinum capsules to **brighten** them and render them fit for handling. They are now returned to their respective dockets on the wooden tray, and returned to the balance room for weighing. There they are weighed with the check assays and the carat of the original alloy determined. Should the assay prove unsatisfactory a second one is made upon a fresh portion of the alloy ; if this also is unsatisfactory a third, and special, test is made. If the result still gives a carat below that marked on the docket the articles are hammered out of shape and returned to the manufacturer with a report of their failure to come up to standard.

Since only small weights of metal are involved in the process considerable skill is required to obtain uniform results, and only experienced assayers are allowed to perform those parts of the operation which are vital to its success.

Trial Plates.—The check assays mentioned above are sometimes called trial plates, and the gold used in them is of special fineness. The reason for their use is that gold itself is slightly volatile at the muffle temperature, and a little absorption into the cupel also takes place. Also, a little copper may be retained after cupellation, and a little silver after parting. From these causes the "check" gold may weigh slightly lighter or heavier after it has undergone the operation. If lighter, the loss is added to the weight of the other gold buttons, and, if heavier, the increase is deducted from them. It is thus evident that care must be taken to work the "checks" under exactly the same conditions as the assays they are to check, or accuracy will not be obtained.

In connection with this it is well to bear in mind that ordinary fine gold is rarely more than 996 fine, and is often less. This may account for a particular alloy being slightly below the required standard.

LIST OF GOLD AND SILVER WARES REQUIRED BY LAW TO BE ASSAYED AND MARKED.

Enquiries having been made at this Office as to what Gold and Silver Wares are *required* by law to be Assayed and Marked, and also as to what Gold and Silver Wares are subject to Duty, the Assay Master informs the Members of the Trade in Birmingham, that *all* Gold and Silver Wares are required to be Assayed, Marked, and Duty paid on them, *except* the undermentioned Wares, which are especially exempted : --

Gold.	*Silver.*
Jewellers' Work, wherein any Jewels or other Stones are set.	Chains.
Rings (*Wedding Rings* excepted).	Necklace Beads.
Collets, for Rings or other Jewels.	Lockets and Bracelets.
Chains.	
Necklace Beads.	Filagree Work.
Lockets and Brooches.	Shirt Buckles or Brooches.
Buttons, Hollow or Raised.	
Sleeve Buttons.	Stamped Medals.
Thimbles.	Spouts to China, Stone, or Earthenware Teapots.
Coral Sockets and Bells.	
Ferrules.	
Pipe Lighters.	Tippings, Swages, or Mounts not weighing ten pennyweights each, *except Necks and Collars for Castors, Cruets, or Glasses, and appertaining to any sort of Stands or Frames.*
Cranes for Bottles.	
Very Small Book Clasps.	
Stock or Garter Clasps, Jointed.	
Very Small Nutmeg Graters.	

Gold.

Rims of Snuff Boxes, whereof Tops or Bottoms are made of Shells or Stone.

Sliding Pencils.
Toothpick Cases.
Tweezer Cases.
Pencil Cases.
Needle Cases.
Filagree Work.

Tippings or Swages on Stone, or Ivory Cases, Mounts, Screws, or Stoppers to Stone or Glass Bottles, or Phials.

Small or Slight Ornaments, put to Amber or other Eggs or Urns.

Wrought Seals, or Seals with Cornelian or other Stones set therein.

Watch Rings.
Watch Keys.
Watch Hooks.
Ear Rings.
Necklaces.
Eye Glasses.
Spectacles.
Shirt Pins.
Shirt Studs.
Bracelets.
Head Ornaments.
Waist Buckles.

Any Gold or Silver Vessel, or Manufacture of Gold or Silver, so richly Engraved, Carved, or Chased, or set with Jewels or other Stones as not to admit of an Assay being taken of, or a mark to be struck thereon, without Damaging, prejudicing, or defacing the same.

Things which, by reason of their smallness or thinness, are not capable of receiving the Marks, and not weighing ten pennyweights each.

Silver.

Silver Wares not weighing five pennyweights each, *except the following articles :—Neck Collars and Tops for Castors, Cruets, or Glasses, appertaining to any sort of Studs or Frames.*

Bottle Tickets.

Shoe Clasps.

Patch Boxes.

Salt Spoons.

Salt Shovels.

Salt Ladles.

Tea Spoons.

Tea Strainers.

Caddy Ladles.

Buckles (Shirt Buckles or Brooches before mentioned excepted).

———

NOTE.—All these Wares printed in italics are excepted out of the exemption, and are liable to be Assayed and Marked.

All Gold and Silver Wares liable to be Assayed and Marked are chargeable with Duty (Watch Cases only excepted).

Gold and Silver Wares not required to be Assayed and Marked may, nevertheless, be Assayed and Marked, and are not thereby liable to the duty.

WILLIAM WESTWOOD,

June, 1885.   ASSAY MASTER AT BIRMINGHAM.

Table of Offences.—To prevent any person falling into error through being unacquainted with the offences punishable by law, the following table issued by the Assay Office authorities, Birmingham, may prove useful to those interested in Hall-marking :—

TABLE OF OFFENCES UNDER THE STATUTES RELATING TO GOLD AND SILVER WARES.

Manufacturing, without first entering at Assay Office the residence and place of business, and Mark of the Manufacturer.

Not sending to Assay Office, with every parcel of Wares, a note stating date, name, and abode of maker, number of each species, and weight of parcel.

Marking any Ware with any other Mark than that registered at Assay Office.

Introducing iron or base metal into Ware.

Fraudulently erasing, obliterating, or defacing any Assay Mark or maker's Mark.

Altering the character of any Ware which has been assayed and marked or making any addition to it, without first taking it to the Assay Office, in order either to be assayed and marked as a new Ware, or for the sanction of the Office.

Dealer selling or having in his possession any Ware which shall be so altered or added to.

Selling or exchanging, or making or causing to be made, any Ware (not exempted) less than Standard.

Selling or exchanging Ware before it is marked.

Forging or counterfeiting any Instrument used at Assay Office.

Marking Wares with a Forged Instrument.

Counterfeiting Assay Marks.

Transposing Marks from one Ware to any other.

Having possession, without lawful excuse, [of] any Forged Instrument, or of any Ware marked with a Forged Instrument.

Cutting from any Ware an Assay Mark, with intent to place it on some other Ware.

Using, with intent to defraud, any Instrument of the Office.

Dealer selling or having possession of any Ware with Counterfeit Mark.

HENRY WESTWOOD, Assay Master.
J. BARHAM CARSLAKE, Law Clerk.

Birmingham, <i>Nov., 1896.</i>

Assay Office Report.—The Birmingham Assay Master's Reports for the years ending 30th June, 1896, 1895, and 1894 are thus summarised for the purpose of comparison.

	1894.	1895.	1896.
Dominical letter used, .	T	U	V
Gold Wares assayed and marked,	223,759 ozs.	239,472 ozs.	283,423 ozs.
Gold Wares assayed and broken up,	1,986 ,,	2,550 ,,	1,938 ..
Silver Wares assayed and marked,	1,401,449 ,,	1,796,056 ,.	2,117,622 ,,
Number of Gold and Silver Wares entered for assaying,	6,764,496	8,127,234	9,877,972
Number of assays made,	189,312	216,930	253,219

CHAPTER XXVII.

MISCELLANEOUS USEFUL INFORMATION.

Gold is first mentioned in the Bible, Genesis chap. ii. 11, and the word appears in the Sacred Scriptures more than three hundred times.

Silver is first mentioned in Genesis chap. xxiii. 15.

Gold articles are first mentioned in Genesis chap. xxiv. 22.

Jewels are first mentioned in the same chapter, v. 53; the date is supposed to be 1857 B.C.

Gold was discovered in California 1847 A.D.; Australia, 1851 A.D.; New Zealand and Nova Scotia, 1862 A.D.; South Africa (Transvaal), 1868 A.D.; Canada (Klondyke), 1896.

Test for Gold.—Gold may be distinguished from base metals by testing it with nitric acid. The old method of estimating the quality of gold by means of the test needles upon a touchstone is still in use by many. The process is to obtain pieces of wire of known standard qualities, and to rub them upon the stone; alongside these a similar mark is made with the unknown metals, then over the whole surface is placed nitric acid, which will destroy the small particles of alloy, leaving the pure gold upon the stone; by comparison the qualities may be estimated.

Special Acid Test (by the Author)—The ordinary nitric acid test only distinguishes gold which is below 9-carat qualities; but the following mixture will differentiate gold having a standard below 18-carat, and is therefore useful when the workman has got the various qualities mixed up in his box. For instance, nitric acid has no effect on 15- or 18-carat gold; but with this mixture the 15-carat gold will assume a dark or nearly black colour, while the 18-carat gold will be unaltered, and 9-carat gold will become green like brass under the influence of the acid; each quality of gold below 18-carat will show dark colour according to its standard.

The mixture is kept in a stoppered glass test bottle, and consists of

Nitric acid, ...	4 fluid ounces.
Water, ...	3 ,,
Hydrochloric acid (muriatic), . .	½ ,,

The testing is effected by moistening the stopper with the acid and applying it to a polished surface; the result is evident in the course of a few seconds. If there is a doubt whether the article is plated or well gilt, the surface is scraped or filed, and the acid again applied.

Soldering is a term applied to the process of uniting two or more parts together, or the fixing of ornamental decoration upon plain surfaces by solder. (Latin, *solidus*, solid.)

Gold Solder is the trade term for gold alloyed with an extra quantity of silver, whereby it is reduced a little below the standard of the gold to be soldered; the fusing point is also lowered, so that when heated by the gas the solder melts (or "runs," which is the trade term) much sooner than the gold. Therefore it is absolutely necessary to have a special solder for each quality of gold, while in the case of articles which have to pass through the process of colouring great care is required to have the solder good, otherwise the parts soldered will most certainly show.

The best method to adopt for making a suitable solder for any quality of gold over 12-carat is to add 5 grains of fine silver to each dwt. of the same gold as that to be soldered. For instance, if 15-carat gold solder is required, 5 grains of fine silver are added to every dwt. of 15-carat gold scrap, which is in the proportion of 4 dwts. 4 grains for 1 ounce of 15-carat gold scrap.

For fine filigree work an easy solder is generally used, and in this case 7 grains of fine silver are added for each dwt. of scrap gold.

Common Names of Chemical Substances.—The following table will be useful to workmen, who, as a general rule, are familiar with the common names only of the substances mentioned:—

Common Names.	Chemical Names.
Aqua-fortis.	Nitric acid.
Aqua-regia.	Nitro-hydrochloric acid.
Blue vitriol.	Copper sulphate (crystallised).
Cream of tartar.	Potassium bitartrate.
Calomel.	Mercurous chloride.
Chalk.	Calcium carbonate.
Salt of tartar.	Potassium carbonate.
Caustic potassa.	Potassium hydrate.
Chloroform.	Formyl chloride.
Common salt.	Sodium chloride.
Copperas or green vitriol.	Iron sulphate (crystallised).
Corrosive sublimate.	Mercuric chloride.
Dry alum.	Aluminium potassium sulphate.
Ethiops mineral.	Black mercury sulphide.
Galena.	Lead sulphide.
Glauber's salt.	Sodium sulphate (crystallised).
Iron pyrites.	Iron bisulphide.
Jewellers' putty.	Tin oxide.
Lime.	Calcium oxide.
Lunar caustic.	Silver nitrate.

Common Names.	Chemical Names.
Oil of vitriol.	Sulphuric acid.
Potash.	Potassium hydrate.
Red lead.	Lead oxide.
Rust of iron.	Iron oxide.
Sal ammoniac.	Ammonium chloride.
Soda.	Sodium hydrate.
Spirits of salt.	Hydrochloric or muriatic acid.
Saltpetre.	Potassium nitrate.
Spirits of hartshorn.	Ammonia.
Stucco, plaster of Paris.	Calcium sulphate.
Verdigris.	Basic acetate of copper.
Vermilion.	Mercury sulphide.
White precipitate.	Ammoniated mercury.
White vitriol.	Zinc sulphate (crystallised).

Metals have three important qualities or properties. The following list shows the relative position of those generally used by the goldsmith :—

Malleability.	Ductility.	Tenacity.
Gold.	Gold.	Wrought iron.
Silver.	Silver.	,, copper.
Copper.	Platinum.	Platinum.
Tin.	Wrought iron.	Silver.
Platinum.	Copper.	Gold.
Lead.	Zinc.	Yellow brass.
Zinc.	Tin.	Zinc.
Wrought iron.	Lead.	Tin.
Nickel.	Nickel.	Lead.

Costly Jewels and Precious Stones.—There are about seventy famous stones noted for their costliness and their history, some of which have been identified with famous intrigues. The crown jewels of all countries are also of high interest. The crown jewels of England, including the famous diamond known as the " Koh-i-noor," are of immense value, and are on view at the Tower of London. The crown jewels of France were at one time of great value, but they are now scattered, and only a few are to be seen at the Louvre in Paris. Russia has a most superb collection, including the Orloff diamond which was a lover's gift to Catherine of Russia. The Austrian crown jewels are very numerous, one of the most remarkable and highly-prized being the famous Australian yellow diamond. This stone has been in possession of the House of Austria since the time of Maria-Theresa. There is a diamond presenting a delicate green colour in the Green Vaults of Dresden. The Sultan also has a large and varied assortment of costly jewels, but by far the most costly collection of all is that of the Shah of Persia, whose jewels are said to range in value from £40 to £50,000 sterling each. Spain has still a fine collection, although it is said that Isabella sold many fine specimens. It has also been stated that there are several families whose investments in precious stones exceed half a million pounds sterling.

Americans have latterly been large buyers of jewels. Thus they have acquired several Mazarins from the French crown jewels, one of which was valued at nearly 500,000 dollars, and quite recently a stone worth 320,000 dollars.

In New York there is a pair of ear-rings worth 75,000 dollars, and a pearl necklace estimated at 100,000 dollars, while a few American ladies have collections which even Royalty might covet. As yet, however, the largest diamonds have not found their way to America.

DESCRIPTION OF SOME OF THE LARGEST DIAMONDS IN THE WORLD.

The following short descriptive list will be useful to the student for the purpose of comparison :—

The Koh-i-Noor.—It formerly belonged to the treasury of Delhi, and in the year 1526 came into the possession of the Sultan Baber. Its original weight was 793 carats, but this was reduced to 186 carats by an unskilled lapidary. It has changed hands several times under very singular circumstances, and, finally, in 1850 was presented to Her Majesty Queen Victoria.

It was shown in the Exhibition of 1851, and was afterwards examined by some of the best scientific men of the day as to the possibility of improving its shape and brilliancy. After much consideration it was entrusted to an expert at Amsterdam (Mr. Coster), who, at a comparatively small sacrifice of material, skilfully converted it into a brilliant matchless for its purity and fire. Its weight is now 106 carats, and it forms part of the crown jewels of England. Its estimated value is £140,000.

The Orloff Diamond.—This diamond forms a jewel in the sceptre of the Czars of Russia. Little is known as to its earliest history beyond the fact that it was formerly the property of Catherine of Russia, who is believed to have received it as a lover's gift. It weighs 193 carats. Its estimated value is £100,000.

The Nizam.—We are informed by Barbat that the King of Golconda has in his possession a magnificent stone in the rough state. It is known by the name of "Nizam." It weighs 340 carats. Its estimated value is £200,000.

The Great Mogul is a remarkable rose-cut diamond supposed to have been part of the rough Koh-i-Noor. It was probably stolen either at the sack of Delhi, or at the death of Radio Shah. It weighs 280 carats. Its estimated value is £420,000.

The Regent or Pitt Diamond.—This diamond forms part of the French crown jewels, and may be seen amongst the jewels in the Louvre in Paris. We are informed that in the year 1717 it was the property of the Duke of Orleans, then Regent of France, he having purchased it from Pitt, the Governor of Fort St. George, in that year. This diamond formerly weighed 410 carats; but after cutting, which occupied two years and cost £3500, it was reduced in weight to $136\frac{7}{8}$ carats. Its estimated value is £480,000.

The Star of the South.—This brilliant was found by a negro in the year 1853 at Bogagem in the province of Minas Geraes. In its rough state it weighed $254\frac{1}{2}$ carats, but after cutting it weighed only 125 carats. It is of an oval form, and has a considerable amount of fire in it; although not perfectly white, it is one of the finest large diamonds extant. It was cut by and was formerly the property of Mr. Coster of Amsterdam, but is now in the possession of one of the rajahs of India. It was sold, inclusive of the mounting, for £80,000.

The Great Sancy.—This diamond has a most remarkable history. It was found on the body of the Duke of Burgundy, and was afterwards, in the year 1479, bought by the King of Portugal. In 1489 he sold it to Nicholas de Barly, Baron de Sancy, from whom it derived its name. A very singular incident occurred to it. Sancy sent it to the king as a present by his servant, who, being attacked by robbers, swallowed the diamond, and after his death the stone was found in his body. This remarkable stone was once the property of the good Queen Bess. It is stated that it has been lately sold to some one in India. It weighs $53\frac{1}{2}$ carats. Its estimated value is £30,000.

The Florentine Brilliant is a rather thick stone of a yellowish colour. It is covered with facets, and resembles a rose diamond, but has only a point front and back. This stone, like others, met with many adventures, and finally came into the possession of Pope Julius II., who gave it to the Emperor of Austria. It weighs $139\frac{1}{2}$ carats. Its value is not known.

The Mattam Diamond.—This diamond belongs to the Rajah of Mattam, in Borneo. It is of a pear-shaped form, and indented at the thick end. It was found about the year 1760. A very large sum of money has been offered for this stone but refused. It weighs 367 carats. Its estimated value is £269,378.

The Piggot Diamond is a fine oval stone weighing $82\frac{1}{4}$ carats. It is said to have been sold in the last century for £30,000 ; it was subsequently bought by Rundell & Bridge for £6000, and afterwards sold to the Pasha of Egypt for £30,000. It is not known who the present possessor is.

The Nassak Diamond is a triangular stone with rounded facets. It was originally taken by the Marquis of Hastings at the conquest of the Deccan, and was in the possession of the

15

late Marquis of Westminster. It is said that this stone was worn by him on the hilt of his sword at the Drawing Room on the Queen's Birthday, immediately succeeding her accession to the British Throne. Its original weight was $89\frac{3}{4}$ carats, but after being cut by order of the Marquis its weight is $78\frac{2}{3}$ carats. Its estimated value is £30,000.

The English Dresden.—This large diamond belongs to the Gaikwar of Baroda. Its weight in the rough state was $119\frac{1}{2}$ carats, but by cutting it has been reduced to $76\frac{1}{2}$ carats. Its estimated value is £40,000.

The Cumberland Diamond.—This stone was purchased by the City of London and was presented to the Duke of Cumberland after the Battle of Culloden ; but, some time ago, it was restored to the Crown of Hanover by Her Majesty Queen Victoria. It weighs 32 carats. Its estimated value is £10,000.

The Eugénie Brilliant.—This perfect brilliant was purchased by the Emperor Napoleon III. It is of an oval shape, rather blunt at one end, but very beautifully cut. It became the property of the Empress Eugénie who sold it to the Gaikwar of Baroda. It weighs 51 carats. Its estimated value is £15,000.

The Mountain of Splendour.—This beautiful diamond is supposed to be one of the precious gems in the Persian Regalia. Its weight is 135 carats. Its estimated value is £145,800.

The Holland.—This stone is conical in shape, and forms one of the crown jewels of the Netherlands. Its weight is 36 carats. Its estimated value is £10,368.

The Porter Rhodes.—This diamond was found in the Kimberley Mine, South Africa, in the year 1880. It is the property of Mr. Porter Rhodes. Its original weight was 150 carats. It has lately been cut. Its estimated value is £200,000.

The Austrian Yellow.—It has been recorded that this beautiful stone has belonged to the House of Austria since the time of Maria-Theresa. Its weight is $139\frac{1}{2}$ carats. Its value is estimated at £50,000.

The Moon of Mountain.—This fine stone was purchased by Prince Orloff, and is now set in the imperial sceptre of Russia. Its weight is 120 carats. Its estimated value is 450,000 roubles.

There are several other well-known large diamonds ; but their value has not been estimated. A brief mention of these will be made in order to make this list more complete.

The Hope Diamond.—This stone is a most brilliant sapphire-blue colour, oval in form, and well proportioned. It is unique, as it is considered to be the finest blue diamond in existence. Its weight is $44\frac{1}{2}$ carats.

The Pasha of Egypt.—This stone is of an octagonal form, and of very good quality ; it is what is termed "brilliant-cut." Ibrahim Pasha is said to be its present possessor. Its weight is 40 carats.

The **Regent of Portugal** forms one of the Portuguese crown jewels. It was found by a negro, who received his freedom and a yearly pension of £50 as a reward. Its weight is 215 carats.

The **Jagersfontein** was found at the Cape in 1881. Its weight is 209¼ carats.

The **Stewart** was found in South Africa in 1872. Its weight is 288¾ carats.

The **Excelsior.**—This stone is the latest addition to the list of large diamonds, and is considered to be the largest diamond in the world. Fig. 144 is a full-size illustration drawn from a

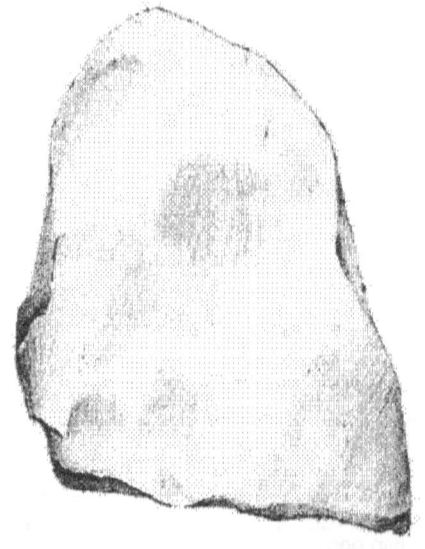

Fig. 144.—The " Excelsior," the largest diamond in the world.

model taken by my friend, Mr. Walter Lowe, a Birmingham man, by whom it was sent to the author together with the following authentic account :—

"I am sending you a model of the Jagersfontein 'Excelsior,' which was found on June 30th, 1893. This stone is a splendid diamond weighing 971 carats. It is a blue-white colour with only one small black spot. I was in Cape Colony at the time ; it was found by a kaffir, who put his foot upon it until a favourable opportunity presented itself, then he picked it up and ran to the manager, who gave 'him £150, a horse, saddle and bridle, and also his freedom.

"When it became known that a monster diamond had been found, the men in the mine became so excited that they shouted and threw up their hats with joy. As several wanted to possess a model of this wonderful diamond, I was entrusted with it for a time for that purpose. Having taken as many as necessary, and knowing how interested you are in such things, I thought you also would like to possess one. They say it is worth one million pounds."

The following announcement appeared in the *Birmingham Daily Mail*, Dec. 13, 1893 :—

THE LARGEST DIAMOND IN THE WORLD.

"The 'Excelsior,' the largest diamond in the world, is now deposited in one of the safes of the Bank of England. It was found in June last in the mines of Jagersfontein, Cape Colony, by Captain Edward Jorgansen, the inspector of the mine. In his opinion, corroborated by that of the director, Mr. Gifford, the 'Excelsior' is a stone of the purest water, and is worth about a million sterling. Exceptional precautions were taken to have it conveyed from the mine to the coast. A squadron of the 16th Lancers guarded the carriage to Cape Town, from which it was brought to London in the gunboat 'Antelope.' It is fully 3 inches in height, and nearly 3 inches in breadth, weighing 971 carats or about 7 ounces troy. The colour of the Jagersfontein diamond is white with a very slight bluish tint, and its lustre is matchless. At the centre is a very small black spot, which experts consider will be easily removed in the cutting. According to M. X. West, the British Government have offered half a million pounds sterling for this diamond to the proprietors, Messrs. Breitmeyer & Bernheimer, but the offer has been refused. It is also said that the directors of the Chicago Exhibition were willing to insure the diamond for three-quarters of a million, in order to show the eighth wonder of the world. The German Emperor is reported to be the probable purchaser of the 'Excelsior.'"

LARGE NUGGETS OF GOLD.

Gold is generally found in comparatively small quantities at a time, but occasionally the gold digger has the good fortune to find a large nugget. The following interesting list of Australian nuggets is based on a collection of models formed by one of the author's friends, who was a mining expert.

Name.	Weight.			Value.
	Lbs.	Ozs.	Dwts.	Sold for
The Daisy Hill, ...	8	1	0	£398
,, Webbville Bunninyong, . .	12	0	0	576
,, Union Jack Bunninyong,. .	23	5	0	1,124
,, Sir Dominic Daly, . . .	26	0	0	1,248
., Ballarat No. 1, . . .	30	0	0	1,440
,, Ballarat No. 2, . . .	30	11	2	1,458
., Bakery Hill, No. 1, . .	40	0	0	1,920
,, Nil Desperandum, . . .	45	0	0	2,160
., Bakery Hill, No. 2, . .	47	7	0	2,284
., Daulton Flat, . . .	52	1	0	2,500
,, Kohinoor, ...	69	0	0	3,312
., Bendigo, ...	81	0	0	3,888
.. Canadian Gully, . . .	84	3	15	4,032
,, Ballarat No. 3, . . .	93	1	11	4,584
.. Ballarat No. 4, . . .	98	10	12	4,746
., Welcome, ...	184	9	14	8,871
,, Welcome Stranger, . . .	191	0	0	9,168
,, Hillend, ...	620	0	0	30,000 (Nearly).

This world celebrated nugget was found by two men named Byers and Holtermann (Germans) on May 10th, 1872, at a depth of 250 feet. It is 4 feet 9 inches high, and 2 feet 2 inches broad. These two men worked for some time backed by the storekeeper, but losing all faith in the mine the latter stopped their credit. However, they still worked hard, living on the charity of their countrymen, until at last this surprise crowned their efforts, the finding of the nugget being witnessed by thousands in the mining camp.

Valuable Pearls.—It has been stated upon good authority that the Duchess of Cumberland, who is the youngest sister of the Princess of Wales, possesses the finest pearls in Europe, the set being valued at £200,000.

Egyptian Scarabæi.—The magnificent necklace worn by Mrs. Langtry as " Cleopatra " is composed of many ancient Egyptian scarabæi, some 2000 years old. One of the finger rings contains an amethyst scarab from the tomb of a princess of the house of Hathor, B.C. 1500.

THE CARAT.

The carat is not a fixed or real weight for gold, the term being used to denote the *quality* only. The following table shows the standards of quality and their equivalents, which are generally in 1000ths, the latter being the mode of expression generally used.

$\frac{41\frac{3}{5}}{1000}$	equal	1 carat.	$\frac{625}{1000}$	equal	15 carats.
$\frac{125}{1000}$	,,	3 carats.	$\frac{750}{1000}$	,,	18 ,,
$\frac{250}{1000}$	,,	6 ,,	$\frac{833\frac{1}{3}}{1000}$	,,	20 ,,
$\frac{375}{1000}$	,,	9 ,,	$\frac{916\frac{3}{3}}{1000}$	,,	22 ,,
$\frac{416\frac{3}{5}}{1000}$	,,	10 ,,	$\frac{958\frac{1}{4}}{1000}$	,,	23 ,,
$\frac{500}{1000}$	,,	12 ,,	$\frac{1000}{1000}$	,,	24 ,,
$\frac{538\frac{1}{4}}{1000}$	,,	14 ,,			

CARAT EQUIVALENTS OF DECIMALS.

1 Carat	=	·0416	9 Carats	=	·3750	17 Carats	=	·7083
2 Carats	=	·0833	10 ,,	=	·4166	18 ,,	=	·7500
3 ,,	=	·1250	11 ,,	=	·4583	19 ,,	=	·7916
4 ,,	=	·1660	12 ,,	=	·5000	20 ,,	=	·8333
5 ,,	=	·2083	13 ,,	=	·5416	21 ,,	=	·8750
6 ,,	=	·2500	14 ,,	=	·5833	22 ,,	=	·9166
7 ,,	=	·2916	15 ,,	=	·6250	23 ,,	=	·9583
8 ,,	=	·3333	16 ,,	=	·6666	24 ,,	=	1·0000

But the carat is used as a real *weight* for the purpose of weighing diamonds and other precious stones. 1 carat = 3·166 grains, or 151½ carats = 1 English ounce Troy.

How to Make Modelling Wax.—A special preparation by the author. Take the following ingredients :—

Best bees'-wax,	.	1 lb.	Venetian red,	.	½ lb.
Burgundy pitch,	.	¼ ,,	Common whiting,	.	¼ ,,

The whiting must be well dried, ground, and sifted through a fine sieve. Melt the wax and pitch in an iron pot ; as soon as it commences to boil add the colour and the whiting, and stir them well together ; then add about half a tallow candle, and when the whole has been well mixed pour the mixture into an earthenware vessel coated with fine whiting. To make the wax work finer to the tool, it is better to boil it two or three times, and before quite cold it should be well manipulated. Should the weather be cold and the wax too hard, the addition of a little more tallow will render it workable.

How to Make Cement for Engravers and Setters.—Take the following ingredients :—

Burgundy pitch,	.	2 lbs.	Bees'-wax, . .	1½ lbs.
Resin,	. . .	1½ ,,	Plaster of Paris, .	1 lb.

Melt the ingredients in an iron pot and keep carefully stirring until a thorough mixture has been effected ; then pour the mixture either into a vessel of cold water or upon an iron pan coated with plaster of Paris or whiting.

Chasers generally use pitch for *repoussé* work.

Some setters prefer shellac to cement.

Pickle is a term given to a solution of acid diluted with water, and used for the purpose of removing the coating of oxide from gold alloys, produced by the process of annealing; also for removing the borax from articles after the process of soldering. As there are three different kinds of pickle used in the manufacture of goldsmith's work, the methods of using each will be described.

Aquafortis Pickle is composed of 1 part aquafortis and 6 parts water. The solution is generally kept in an earthenware jowl, similar to Fig. 116, and when required to be used, a small quantity of it is made hot in a copper "boil-pan," placed over a fire, or over a Bunsen gas-jet ; the article is immersed in it, and allowed to remain for a short time ; then the pickle is poured off into the jowl, and the article well rinsed in water and then dried in box sawdust. If the articles are hollow, they should be boiled out in water after being boiled in pickle, for the purpose of completely removing the acid.

Sulphuric Acid Pickle is composed of 1 part sulphuric acid and 6 parts water. This solution is generally kept in a vessel made of lead. The pickle is made hot by placing the vessel over a gas-jet. When required to be used, the articles are placed in a perforated earthenware vessel called a "basket," and immersed in the solution ; after remaining in it for a short time, the articles are withdrawn, rinsed in water, &c.

Hydrochloric Acid Pickle is composed of 1 part hydrochloric acid and 8 parts hot water, and is used for immersing articles just prior to the process of wet-colouring, for the purpose of removing grease or other organic matter from the surface.

APPENDIX.

TECHNOLOGICAL EXAMINATIONS IN GOLDSMITHS' WORK, AND MANUFACTURE OF PERSONAL ORNAMENTS.

THE CITY AND GUILDS OF LONDON INSTITUTE TECHNOLOGICAL EXAMINATIONS.

Technological Examinations.—The progress of the Technological Examinations conducted under the auspices of the City and Guilds of London Institute received a great impulse from the passing of the Technical Institution Act, 1889, and especially in consequence of the large funds placed at the disposal of County and Borough Councils by the Local Taxation (Customs and Excise) Act of 1890, whereby £743,000 per annum became available for the advancement of technical education throughout England and Wales.

Technological examinations were first established in the year 1879, but the progress made from that date until the year 1881, although comparatively slow, was sure and reliable.

The following statistics will indicate the progress made since the year 1881* :—" The advance of students in attendance upon technological classes was from 2,500 in 1881 to 12,022 in 1890, the advance since that date is 13,202 to 26,609. The number of classes registered has risen from 262 in 1885 and 483 in 1890 to 519 in 1891, and 1,120 in 1896. In 1879 the papers examined were 202, in 1890 6,667, in 1891 7,416, and in 1896 10,874. These figures mark the progress made, and indicate the increasing importance of these examinations, especially since the Acts before mentioned came into force.

" By reviewing this extraordinary progress made in the direction of technical training, great credit must be given to the Trade Guilds of London, aided by the able advice, knowledge, and administrative power of Sir Philip Magnus, the Director of Technological Examinations, for the stimulus and financial support they have given in aid of technological instruction since the establishment of these examinations in 1879."

For we find in the year 1896 arrangements were made for sixty-six different subjects for examinations under the auspices of the above Institute, which must prove beneficial and stimulating to the trades generally.

It was not until 1892 that the goldsmiths and jewellers of this country could submit themselves for examination in connection with the City and Guilds of London Institute.

* The above facts are gathered from a paper read by Mr. J. H. Reynolds, Director of the Municipal Technical School, Manchester, at the annual meeting of the Association of Technical Institutions, held in the Clothworkers' Hall, London, in January, 1897.—*Education, Secondary and Technical*, March 6, 1897.

In 1891 the Birmingham Jewellers' and Silversmiths' Association, acting under the advice of Sir Philip Magnus, prepared and submitted to the City and Guilds of London Institute a syllabus of subjects for examination in goldsmiths' work and the manufacture of personal ornaments, which was in due course accepted by the Institute, and has since been included in their programme of technological examinations.

The work of preparing the syllabus was delegated to the Technical School Sub-Committee, to whom the hon. secretary, Mr. J. W. Tonks, gave valuable aid. The City and Guilds of London Institute showed their appreciation of the assistance rendered to them by the Association, by appointing Mr. Charles Green to be the examiner under their new syllabus of goldsmiths' work, who faithfully performed the duties of that important office for four years, when, through the pressure of Council and other duties, he reluctantly resigned his post, and Mr. J. W. Tonks was appointed his successor.

TECHNOLOGICAL INSTRUCTION.*

The City and Guilds of London Institute for the advancement of technical education is prepared, under certain conditions, to register classes for instruction in technology and manual training, to inspect and report on the working of such classes, and to afford facilities for carrying out an examination in any of the subjects enumerated in clauses 11 and 17, provided a Local Committee undertakes to superintend the classes, and to carry out the examination according to the rules laid down.

The examination in the subject of goldsmiths' work and manufacture of personal ornaments is in two grades—**I. Ordinary ; II. Honours.**

Candidates who pass in either the ordinary or honours grade will be arranged in two classes, a first and a second class, and certificates (first and second class) will be awarded to successful candidates in each grade.

Candidates who obtain a second-class certificate in either grade may be re-examined in any subsequent year for a first-class certificate in the same grade, but should they fail to obtain sufficient marks to entitle them to a first-class certificate, a second-class certificate will not be awarded to them. Candidates who have obtained a prize in either grade, or a first-class certificate in the ordinary grade, will not be re-examined in the same grade.

Prizes, consisting of silver and bronze medals, will be given in each grade, provided the merits of the candidates justify the examiner in recommending them ; and money prizes are also offered on like conditions by the Goldsmiths' Company.

SYLLABUS.

(44) Goldsmiths' Work and Manufacture of Personal Ornaments.

ORDINARY GRADE.

1. *Written Examination.* -The written examination will include questions founded on such subjects as the following :—

1. The variety of trades into which the manufacture of personal ornaments is divided, including outworkers.
2. Modes of commencing wrought work ; of the means of construction of different ornaments, and of separate or convertible pieces.
3. The tools necessary in the various branches of manufacture.

* *The Programme of Technological Examinations.*

4. Engraving; its various kinds, and their artistic treatment; tools and methods employed.

5. *Repoussé* work, chasing, and embossing; how and where applicable. Chasing of cast figures and surface treatment generally; principal tools used.

6. Wire and grain decoration; when, where, and how it should be applied.

7. Enamelling; difference between *champ-levé*, *cloisonné*, and enamel painting, with some account of their principles and practice; tools and materials used.

8. Finish of goldsmiths' work and personal ornaments in various branches.

II. *Practical Examination.*—Candidates will be required to show skill in not more than *two* of the following operations:—

1. Shaping and turning up a given geometric form as a basis for decoration.

2. Setting out a given engraved pattern.

3. Tracing and beating up the general effect of a given design in embossing or *repoussé*.

4. Cutting out and enamelling a given design on a prepared plate in two or more colours.

The practical examination will be held in the School Workshop, or in some other shop which may be placed at the disposal of the Institute. The materials will be supplied by the Institute.

HONOURS GRADE.

(The first Examination was in May, 1893.)

Candidates for Honours must have passed in a previous year in the Ordinary Grade.

I. *Written Examination.*—The examination will consist of advanced questions in the subjects of the written examinations for the ordinary grade, and will also include the following additional subjects:—

1. Alloys of gold suitable for different classes of work in all qualities with respective solders.

2. The means of production of stamped work; its advantages and application.

3. The use of models, and processes of casting small pieces.

4. Precious stones, pearls, and other materials used in personal ornaments.

5. The various styles and modes of setting.

II. *Practical Examination.*—Candidates will be required to show further skill in any of the operations included in the test for the ordinary grade, and they will also be required to execute in suitable material, during the year preceding the examination, an original piece of work. It may be

1. A specimen of mounted work.
2. A specimen of engraved work.
3. A specimen of chased, engraved, or *repoussé* work.
4. A specimen of enamelled work.

The same must be forwarded to London (carriage paid) a week prior to the date of the written examination. The specimens of work must be accompanied by a working drawing by the candidate himself, and must not exceed 6 inches in any dimension. A certificate, signed by the employer of the candidate, or by the teacher, and a member of the school committee, stating that the work has been executed by the candidate himself, without assistance, must be forwarded with the specimen. The work should show the candidate's skill in the branch of manufacture of personal ornaments in which he is chiefly engaged.

The fee for both parts of the examination in either grade is *two shillings*.

Full Technological Certificate.—A provisional certificate will be granted on results of the above examination. For the full technological certificate the candidate in the ordinary grade will be required to have passed the Elementary Examination of the Science and Art Department in geometrical as well as in freehand or model drawing, and for the full certificate in the honours grade to have also passed in the elementary stage, at least, in the Science and Arts Departments Examination in metallurgy. (Sections I. and III.)

Technological Examination Papers.—The following question papers set for students in former years will show the kind of knowledge and the degree of skill required by the candidates entering for the technological examinations held under the auspices of the City and Guilds of London Institute :—

(44) Goldsmiths' Work and Manufacture of Personal Ornaments.

(*Written Examination.*)

ORDINARY GRADE.

1. Classify, according to their respective branches or departments, the workmen employed in a large jewellery manufactory where various kinds of personal ornaments are produced. (30 marks.)

2. Give the processes in making a bracelet three-eighths of an inch wide (lined or not) up to the point of receiving its ornamentation. (30.)

3. Describe the mechanism of the back of a diamond star which may be used as a hair-pin, brooch, or pendant. (30.)

4. Explain the meaning of "flush joint," "mitre joint," "reversible joint." (20.)

5. Describe briefly the following tools and their uses :—Treblet, rimer, drillstock, belchering pliers, scorpers, saw frame. (20.)

6. Name five varieties of ornamental engraving, and describe how different effects are obtained in any three of these varieties. (30.)

7. What do you understand by *repoussé* work, and in what does it differ from chasing ? (25.)

8. Explain carefully what is meant by the "repairing" of cast figures. (20.)

9. Describe the kinds of surfaces to which wire decoration should be applied. (20.)

10. How would you proceed to make wire decoration, and on what parts of any ornaments should it be arranged (*a*) in bands, (*b*) in separate design ? (30.)

11. Give some account of the processes of "*champ-levé*" and "*cloisonné*" enamelling, and describe the different effects produced. (30.)

12. What is the best style of "cut out" for transparent enamels ? (20.)

13. Name and describe not more than six different styles of finish for goldsmiths' work. (30.)

14. Describe fully the process of dry colouring ; also wet colouring. (20.)

15. Explain methods of making ornaments from flat gold edged, in leaf, scroll, or other forms, and give sketches. (30.)

16. How would you apply wire decoration (*a*) to an oval brooch 1 inch in length, (*b*) to a bracelet ½ inch wide? (30.)

17. How would you make an ordinary bracelet snap? (20.)

18. Describe the processes in making a coronet (or claw) half-hoop ring up to the point of setting. (20.)

19. What do you understand by "knurling," "tapping," "saw piercing"? Explain processes and effects. (30.)

20. Describe the following tools and explain their uses: —Bow-saw frame, sparrow-hawk, knife file, draw plate, gapper, and side pliers. (25.)

21. What styles of engravings are best suited to goldsmiths' work ? Give three examples, and show by sketch their application. (30.)

22. Is there any important difference between embossing and chasing in (*a*) the methods of working, (*b*) the general character of the tools employed? If so, describe same. (20.)

23. Detail the treatment which a cast nude figure (say, a cherub or cupid) should undergo at the chaser's hands to fit it for a position upon a casket lid or any work of art. (20.)

24. Explain how you would prepare surfaces for opaque, and how for transparent, enamel in *champ-levé* style. (20.)

25. Give an account of the preparation for, and processes of, firing a piece of *cloisonné* work where many colours are employed. (25.)

26. Explain the best kind of preparation for finishing gold work of 18 carat quality in the following styles :—(a) Wet colour, (b) dry colour, (c) tinting (or pale gilding). (20.)

27. Give the names of five of the most important branch trades in connection with the manufacture of jewellery. (20.)

28. Describe the making of a heart-shaped domed pendant set with a trefoil of precious stones. (15.) How would you mount a diamond weighing half a carat, to be worn alternately as a ring, pin, or stud, in coronet or claw setting? (15.)

29. Name ten of the principal tools used by goldsmiths—one only of a kind. (10.) Describe the following :—*Nippers, mallet, rice, bracelet-irons, and clams.* (15.)

30. What kind of preparation of surface is best on gold or silver prior to engraving? (10.) Describe scroll work (various), nugget work and ornamental gothic, and give sketches. (20.) Describe an engraver's tools and method of working. (10.)

31. Explain the process of embossing, and describe its effects. (10.) Name three styles of chasing in general use. (10.) What kind of ground work is best for the relief of intersected ornament (strap work)? (10.) Give sketches of (a) *chaser's hammer*, (b) *matting, planishing, and curve punches.* (10.)

32. Describe the various kinds of plain wire and cord decoration interspersed with raised ornaments. Give sketches. (20.)

33. Describe the cutting out and filling up of a band ring ⅜ inch wide with "In memory of" in gold letters and ground of black enamel. (10.) Describe the same, but with letters enamelled and gold ground. (10.) Is the depth of the cutting out an important matter as regards the safety of the enamel? (10.) Should the depth of the cutting be regulated by the spread of the enamel from margin to margin, whether wide or narrow? (10.)

34. What is the best kind of finish for (a) a handsomely-chased article ; (5.) (b) a fine scroll engraved ditto ; (5.) (c) a quite plain or partly plain ditto? (5.)

35. Name five important branches of the jewellery trade, exclusive of chasing, engraving, and enamelling. (15.) What five different kinds of workmen are employed in a goldsmiths' establishment (omitting outworkers)? (15.)

36. How would you prepare and put together the parts of a brooch to form the design of a true lovers' knot in thin gold edged, waved, or ribbon style? (25.)

37. How would you mount an arrangement of brilliants as a claw-set cluster-pin, the centre stone raised, with screw fittings, to convert into stud or other ornament? (25.)

38. Name the five tools which, in your opinion, are the most useful to a goldsmith. (10.) Explain what is meant by charging, annealing, pickling (or boiling out). (10.) Give the best method of cleansing work after pickling. (10.)

39. What styles of engraving are mostly employed as decoration on goldsmiths' work? Give sketches. (20.) What do you suggest as most suitable to (a) a half-round (or belcher) bangle bracelet, (b) a gothic cross, (c) a sovereign purse finished bright (or tinted)? (20.) Give sketches of three different kinds of " gravers " ready for use. (15.)

40. What is *Repoussé?* In what respects is it superior to die or stamped work? In what does it differ from chasing, and why is it more artistic in operation and in effects? (25.)

41. Why is it necessary to "repair castings" in gold and silver, and particularly plain surfaces? (20.) Give sketches of six punches used in small articles—for scroll, planishing, matting, grain, cup, and chisel work. (20.)

42. What do you understand by wire and grain decoration? Give sketches of how you would apply it on a fichu brooch ⅜ inch wide, with plain edges or with circular centre and ends. (30.)

43. Explain the processes necessary to reproduce a pansy from nature on a concave surface in enamel painting. (20.)

44. Give the best method of polishing and finishing a double snake bracelet, one snake in gold and one in platinum, so as to produce the best effect in contrast. (20.)

45. Give three branches of the jewellery trade required to complete the making of a wrought brooch, set with gems. Also state three branches of the trade necessary to produce a stamped gold brooch without stones.

46. How would you commence to make a bracelet composed of several open bands, with a knife edge to the front of each; and how would you arrange an ornament in centre, so that it could be taken off and worn as a pendant for the neck?

47. How would you arrange to fix a watch in a flexible bracelet so that it could be taken out at pleasure, without injury, and worn separately, being easily replaced afterwards by the wearer herself. Explain by a sketch, if possible.

48. Name the tools you would probably require to make a badge composed of fifteen separate pieces, with a border of wrought scrolls.

49. State the positions on an ornament where you would engrave "strap work" with lined ground. Describe the qualities most requisite in an engraved inscription. What class of engraving would you consider proper upon a bishop's ring?

50. Explain the difference between *champ-levé* enamel and *cloisonné*. Describe the process of preparing the ground for enamel painting.

51. State how you would produce a brooch in *champ-leré* enamel, with bright red berries and translucent green leaves against a dead brown enamel background.

52. What is the difference between a chased surface and a *repoussé* design? Illustrate your answer by rough sketches.

53. Describe the process of chasing a cast figure of a Cupid in a boat; and name the tools necessary to complete it.

54. Explain how you would prepare the surface of a necklet 18 carat quality gold; and how you would finish it so that one portion would be bright, with other portions of the pattern in dull gold.

55. How many different workers would be required to turn a gold "spinning" into a finished bracelet "coloured gold?" Name the "branches" required to begin and finish a wrought diamond ring.

56. How would you commence a brooch in flowing scrolls? How would you make Etruscan dome or "bee-hive" work? Describe the manufacture of a convertible pin and stud, from start to finish, to be set with pearl and diamonds, and explain method for securing same in wear.

57. Name the principal tools used in making a coach-horn brooch. What are sparrow-hawks? Describe the tools or implements required for making and finishing a knife-edge bracelet band.

58. What is the difference between "engraving" and "cutting out"? Describe two kinds of scroll engraving, and explain how they differ. How do you produce flat engraved forms on an even surface, with a lower background of lines or dots? Name the tools used in this work.

59. If you had to represent a bunch of grapes upon a circular plate half

an inch in diameter, how should you do this—by chasing or by *repoussé* work? Explain why you choose the mode you prefer.

60. How would you proceed with the rough casting of a mouse in order to finish it perfectly, and to indicate the coat of the animal? State the tools required to finish a cast dragon-fly, the wings being separate.

61. What kind of surface is most suitable for wire and cord decoration (commonly called filigree work)? Explain (by sketch, if practicable) where "bosses," "bee-hives," and bolder lines of ornament would be most effective upon an oval brooch 1¼ inches in length.

62. What are enamels? Describe the process of "firing." Explain how the pattern is prepared by the *champ-levé* process. Name the class of personal ornaments to which the *cloisonné* system of enamelling had best be applied. What is done with an enamel painting after the last touches of colour have been fired?

63. How would you finish a gentleman's 18-carat gold locket, intended to be worn with a bright gold chain? Describe the best method of completing a 9-carat quality gold brooch so that it may resemble a coloured gold article of high quality.

64. State how many branches of the trade would be engaged in making (a) a gold albert chain; (b) a pair of gold sleeve links. *

65. Explain how you would begin to manufacture lockets; how you would joint a bracelet; and how you would provide a spring to a gold match-box.

66. Describe the tools required in forming a gold beetle, a diamond-set fox-head pin, and a brooch in hollow-twisted tube.

67. Show, by sketches if possible, three different styles in which you could engrave an inscription on a garter.

68. Which is the most effective way of displaying by engraving a design of flowers and fruit on a plain surface? Explain the difference between "shading" and "cutting-out" tools.

69. How would you best show an animal head on the centre of a brooch —by *repoussé*, or by chased work? State your reasons for the plan you choose. Should a hollow band bracelet be chased or embossed?

70. If a cast model of a snake amid grass were to be chased, how should you treat the snake so as to contrast with the grass?

71. Should you have to construct an enamelled centre brooch, which would be preferable—an engraved border, or one with wire decoration? Give reasons for the course you prefer.

72. What kind of enamelling is it in which the figure subject rises above the level of the enamelled ground? What class of enamels is that in which the Japanese excel? How do you execute *champ-levé* enamelling?

73. How would you finish 9-carat quality gold bright tube work? What is 18-carat gold dry colouring? How do you obtain the dead surface in finishing 15-carat gold articles?

• Questions Nos. 64 to 73 are those set at the examination in May, 1898.

HONOURS GRADE.

Candidates for Honours must have passed in a previous year in the Ordinary Grade.

The examination will consist of advanced questions in the subjects of the written examination for the ordinary grade, and will also include some of the following additional questions :-

1. Give a good working alloy for each of the five Government standards, viz.:—9, 12, 15, 18, and 22 carats (with special regard to ductility and colour), and name a suitable solder for each. (30.)

2. Give the alloys to make a bracelet of three strands; one strand to be of yellow, one of red, and one of green gold, with a view to the best contrasts and high finish, all of one quality. (30.)

3. Give the best alloy for effective use with platinum in bright finished work 18 carats. (20)

4. On what kinds or parts of goldsmiths' work can dies be used with advantage? Give examples (20.)

5. Describe the processes in making a carved half-hoop bracelet, diamond set, with settings and concaves of platinum. Describe also the best means of polishing the same. (30.)

6. Explain how you would make a mould of sand enclosing the model of a bird in flight for effective casting; the model not to exceed 2 inches from point to point. (30.)

7. Describe fully the manner of flush or gipsy setting; also of Roman setting in shield shapes. (20.)

8. Give some account of (1) heraldic engraving, style and treatment; also of (2) engraved strap work, with ground of lower level; and (3) the most suitable patterns for showing under transparent enamel. (30.)

9. What do you understand by light and shade, massing and colour in *repoussé* work, and on what forms are they respectively most effectively adopted. (30.)

10. Explain the processes required in the production of an enamel painting (any subject) from the preparation of the plate to completion. (30.)

11. Name three kinds of rubies in (more or less) general use with jewellers, and give their leading characteristics. (30.)

12. Show by sketches the forms of a rose diamond, a brilliant and a briolet, and give some account of their facets. (30.)

13. Describe how you would finish a silver set diamond collet necklace. (20.)

14. Give an alloy in 16 carats suitable for wire work—*e.g.*, *Chains, seals, rings*, &c. (10.) Give an alloy in same quality for "setting" gold. (10.) Give an alloy in same quality for casting in sand, with special view (in all cases) to soundness, ductility, and colour. (10.) Give suitable solders for each of the above alloys. (5)

15. Under what circumstances is the production of ornaments from dies advantageous and preferable to such as are wrought or hand-made? (15.)

16. Describe an ordinary casting mould, 15 by 10-inch frame, boards, screws, &c. (10.) Show how you would make up the said mould to cast six figures 1½ inches long from wax models at one pouring of the metal. (15.)

17. Give sketches of an opal about 2 carats weight, of oval shape and proportions, best adapted to the display of fine qualities. (10.) Describe the qualities of a fine opal. (5.) Describe also the following :—Tourmaline, topaz, turquoise, and state where they are found, and the usual style of cutting each of them. (15.) What is meant by *diamond boart, Baroky pearl, silky ruby?* (15.)

18. Describe the processes in drilling and setting a heart-shaped locket pendant in grain (paré) settings, with a brilliant star in centre and filled up all over with half pearls; state how you get security, and clear and form your grains, so as to show as little gold as possible. (30.)

19. Explain carefully the object of *repoussé* work. (10.) What form should it take, and what should its effects resemble? (10.)

20. Give the section of the proper depth for a Maltese cross in transparent red on a disc as large as a threepenny piece, before filling in. (10.) Is enamel more secure from flaw (or flying) in the *cloisonné* cells than it is in the *champ-leré* bed? And if so, why? (10.) What is meant by soft enamel, and why—under what circumstances—is it sometimes used? (10.)

21. Give one or more alloys calculated to bring out the finest effects in transparent enamels. (20.) Give the quality and component parts of a gold mixture best adapted to fine filigree work. (20.) Give the most suitable solder for same, and say in what form it should be used. (20.)

22. Explain the mechanism of a diamond head ornament (tiara), convertible into a necklet or a pair of bracelets, or into both necklet and bracelets. Give sketches. (30.)

23. Give some account of the making of a model of a horse in full gallop. Also of a nigger's head and neck, to be cast hollow, and say if they should be cast each in one piece or in sections, and describe processes. (30.)

24. Give the colours of the following stones and the usual styles of cutting them :—Peridot, jargoon, star sapphire. (30.) Show the difference between the "cut" of an emerald and a sapphire. (20.) What is the particular quality of the Alexandrite? (20.)

25. Describe brilliant collet setting in silver cut down. (20.) Give process of Roman setting, old style. (20.)

26. Explain difference in treatment between heraldic surface engraving and the same subject die sunk for sealing. (30.)

27. Explain the difference in treatment required to produce on a band or keeper ring a trail of forget-me-nots in natural colours in *champ-leré* and in *cloisonné* style. (30.)

28. Describe as fully as you can the various modes of decoration by means of which the Etruscans obtained such richness of effect on gold surfaces.

29. Explain the ancient and recently revived mode of enamelling in translucent colours on embossed and engraved surfaces.

30. (a) Give the relative proportions for alloy most adapted to yield the bright red gold in use on the Continent, and which contrasts so strongly with silver or platinum. (b) State also the proportions most suitable for gold intended to be "dry-coloured." (c) Describe the composition of the best solders for these two kinds of gold respectively.

31. Explain (by drawings also, if possible) the tools and appliances requisite to produce from a flat sheet of metal a hollow bead or oval with pierced band decoration across it.

32. Describe the process of "reversing" a model for a gold figure, 3 inches high, so that the amount of gold required for casting it may be reduced.

33. State the difference between the true chrysoberyl and the common or European cat's-eye. Describe the characteristics of the true turquoise; give instances of the modes by which it is imitated; and explain how fraud may be detected.

34. How would you set an opal? What stones consort best with turquoise? Should you set an emerald and a sapphire in the same piece or close together? If not, why? Describe Roman setting.

35. Give the best alloys for (a) 9-carat quality gold chains for bright finish : (b) 12-carat gold brooches, dead finished; and (c) 18-carat gold, bright finished, flexible bracelets.

16

36. Describe (by drawings if possible) the process by which hollow curb chain is manufactured.

37. Explain the mode of casting known as "*cire perdu*," by which every detail of the original model may be reproduced.

38. How would you produce rich translucent colours in red, blue, and green enamels, on common metal surfaces?

39. What is the best way to prevent thin silver enamelled surfaces from "puckering" or "rising" when fired?

40. What is the "girdle" of a brilliant? What is cutting "*en cabochon*"? What do you mean by "*dichroic*" as applied to precious stones?

41. Explain the differences in colour and in test qualities between the green garnet, the green tourmaline, and the peridot.

42. Describe "coronet" setting, "square" setting, "star" setting, "collet" setting, "hammered" setting, and "claw" setting, explaining (by sketches also, if possible) wherein the differences consist.

*43. Give an alloy for 9-carat quality gold suitable for *repoussé* work on an article after spinning or hammering into shape. Also state proportions for gold solder suitable for 15-carat quality gold work to be dead frosted. How do you prepare 18-carat quality green gold?

44. Describe the mode of manufacture of a diamond pendant suitable to convert, and to wear also as a brooch or hair ornament.

45. Specify, and show also by sketches, the various classes of wire, bead, and grain decoration on plain gold surfaces, as practised by the ancient Etruscans, and revived in modern days by Castellani.

46. Give details of the dies and tools required to produce a stamped link for flexible bracelet.

47. What are the processes employed in Limoges enamelling? How do you produce designs in opaque colours on translucent enamel surfaces?

48. Explain fully the best modes of casting and finishing a gold head and bust of Minerva. State different modes of casting and repairing various parts of cast patterns.

49. Show the culet, facets, and table of a precious stone. Describe the distinctive qualities of Alexandrite, chrysoberyl, labradorite.

50. Give the scientific reasons for the colours and distinctive qualities of the opal. Explain the difference between spinel, Siam, and Burmah rubies.

51. Where and why do you use platinum for one class of setting? How do you provide against stones falling out when set in the surface of a light bracelet band liable to spring in opening and closing? How are diamonds and pearls, close together or pavé set, secured from getting loose and being lost.

* Questions 43 to 51 are those set in the examination of May, 1898.

INDEX.

BELL AND BAIN, LIMITED, PRINTERS, GLASGOW.

A SELECTION FROM

CHARLES GRIFFIN & CO.'S PUBLICATIONS

OF

SCIENTIFIC AND TECHNICAL WORKS.

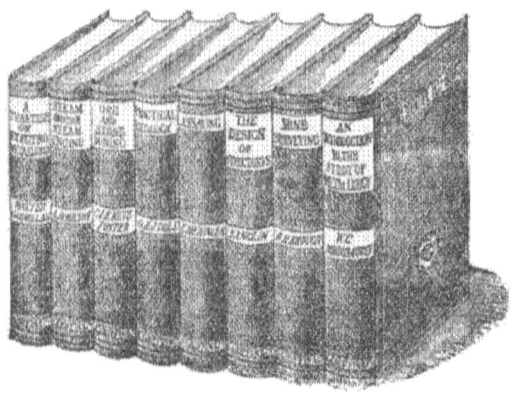

MESSRS. CHARLES GRIFFIN & COMPANY'S PUBLICATIONS may be obtained through any Bookseller in the United Kingdom, or will be sent Post-free on receipt of a remittance to cover published price. To prevent delay, Orders should be accompanied by a Cheque or Postal Order crossed "UNION OF LONDON AND SMITH'S BANK, Chancery Lane Branch."

. *For INDEX, see next page.*

☞ COMPLETE TECHNICAL, MEDICAL, and GENERAL CATALOGUES forwarded Post-free on Application.

LONDON:
EXETER STREET, STRAND.

1/8/05.
D.T. 64.

Griffin's Standard Publications

For Engineers, Electricians, Architects, Builders, Naval Constructors, and Surveyors.

THIRD EDITION, *Revised, with an Additional Chapter on Foundations.*
Numerous Diagrams, Examples, and Tables.   Large 8vo.   Cloth.   16s.

THE DESIGN OF STRUCTURES:

A Practical Treatise on the Building of Bridges, Roofs, &c.

BY S. ANGLIN, C.E.,

Master of Engineering, Royal University of Ireland, late Whitworth Scholar, &c.

"We can unhesitatingly recommend this work not only to the Student, as the BEST TEXT-BOOK on the subject, but also to the professional engineer as an EXCEEDINGLY VALUABLE book of reference."—*Mechanical World.*

THIRD EDITION, *Thoroughly Revised.   Royal 8vo.   With numerous*
Illustrations and 13 Lithographic Plates.   Handsome Cloth.   Price 30s.

A PRACTICAL TREATISE ON
BRIDGE-CONSTRUCTION:

Being a Text-Book on the Construction of Bridges in Iron and Steel.

FOR THE USE OF STUDENTS, DRAUGHTSMEN, AND ENGINEERS.

BY T. CLAXTON FIDLER, M. INST. C.E.,

Prof. of Engineering, University College, Dundee.

"The new edition of Mr. Fidler's work will again occupy the same CON-SPICUOUS POSITION among professional text-books and treatises as has been accorded to its predecessors.   SOUND, SIMPLE, AND FULL."—*The Engineer.*

In Medium 8vo.   Handsome Cloth.   Pp. i-xv + 248, with over
100 Illustrations.   Price 10s. 6d. net.

CONSTRUCTIONAL STEELWORK:

Being Notes on the Practical Aspect and the Principles of Design, together with an Account of the Present Methods and Tools of Manufacture.

BY A. W. FARNSWORTH,

Associate Member of the Institute of Mechanical Engineers.

"Will be found of value to all Architects and Engineers engaged in steelwork construc-tion."—*Building News.*

In Large 8vo. Handsome Cloth, Gilt, Uniform with *Stability of Ships* and *Steel Ships* (p. 38). With 34 Folding Plates and 468 Illustrations in the Text. 30s. net.

The Principles and Practice of
DOCK ENGINEERING.

By BRYSSON CUNNINGHAM, B.E., Assoc.M.Inst.C.E.,

Of the Engineers' Department, Mersey Docks and Harbour Board.

GENERAL CONTENTS.

Historical and Discursive.—Dock Design.—Constructive Appliances.—Materials.—Dock and Quay Walls.—Entrance Passages and Locks.—Jetties, Wharves, and Piers.—Dock Gates and Caissons.—Transit Sheds and Warehouses. — Dock Bridges. — Graving and Repairing Docks. — Working Equipment of Docks.—INDEX.

"We have never seen a more profusely-illustrated treatise. It is a most important standard work, and should be in the hands of all dock and harbour engineers."—*Steamship.*
"Will be of the greatest service to the expert as a book of reference."—*Engineer.*

FOURTH EDITION. In Two Parts, Published Separately.

A TEXT-BOOK OF
Engineering Drawing and Design.

VOL. I.—PRACTICAL GEOMETRY, PLANE, AND SOLID. 4s. 6d.
VOL. II.—MACHINE AND ENGINE DRAWING AND DESIGN. 4s. 6d.

BY

SIDNEY H. WELLS, WH.Sc., A.M.I.C.E., A.M.I.MECH.E.,

Principal of the Battersea Polytechnic Institute, &c.

With many Illustrations, specially prepared for the Work, and numerous Examples, for the Use of Students in Technical Schools and Colleges.

"A CAPITAL TEXT-BOOK, arranged on an EXCELLENT SYSTEM, calculated to give an intelligent grasp of the subject, and not the mere faculty of mechanical copying. . . . Mr. Wells shows how to make COMPLETE WORKING-DRAWINGS, discussing fully each step in the design."—*Electrical Review*

In Large Crown 8vo. Handsome Cloth. With 201 Illustrations. 6s. net.

AN INTRODUCTION TO
THE DESIGN OF BEAMS,
GIRDERS, AND COLUMNS
IN MACHINES AND STRUCTURES.

With Examples in Graphic Statics.

By WILLIAM H. ATHERTON, M.Sc., M.I.Mech.E.

"There should be a strong demand for this concise treatise."—*Page's Weekly.*

LONDON: CHARLES GRIFFIN & CO., LIMITED, EXETER STREET, STRAND.

SECOND EDITION, Revised.   With numerous Plates reduced from
Working Drawings and 280 Illustrations in the Text.   21s.

A MANUAL OF
LOCOMOTIVE ENGINEERING:

A Practical Text-Book for the Use of Engine Builders, Designers and Draughtsmen, Railway Engineers, and Students.

BY

WILLIAM FRANK PETTIGREW, M.INST.C.E.

With a Section on American and Continental Engines.

BY ALBERT F. RAVENSHEAR, B.Sc.,
Of His Majesty's Patent Office.

Contents. — Historical Introduction, 1763-1863. — Modern Locomotives: Simple. —
Modern Locomotives: Compound. - Primary Consideration in Locomotive Design. —
Cylinders, Steam Chests, and Stuffing Boxes.—Pistons, Piston Rods, Crossheads, and
Slide Bars.—Connecting and Coupling Rods.—Wheels and Axles, Axle Boxes, Hornblocks,
and Bearing Springs.—Balancing.— Valve Gear.—Slide Valves and Valve Gear Details.—
Framing, Bogies and Axle Trucks, Radial Axle Boxes.—Boilers.—Smokebox, Blast Pipe,
Firebox Fittings.—Boiler Mountings.—Tenders.   Railway Brakes.— Lubrication.—Con-
sumption of Fuel, Evaporation and Engine Efficiency.—American Locomotives.—Con-
tinental Locomotives.—Repairs, Running, Inspection, and Renewals.—Three Appendices.
—Index.

"Likely to remain for many years the STANDARD WORK for those wishing to learn
Design."—*Engineer.*
"A most interesting and valuable addition to the bibliography of the Locomotive."—
Railway Official Gazette.
"We recommend the book as THOROUGHLY PRACTICAL in its character, and MERITING A
PLACE IN ANY COLLECTION of . . . works on Locomotive Engineering."—*Railway News.*
"The work CONTAINS ALL THAT CAN BE LEARNT from a book upon such a subject. It
will at once rank as THE STANDARD WORK UPON THIS IMPORTANT SUBJECT."—*Railway Magazine.*

In Large 8vo.   Handsome Cloth.   With Plates and Illustrations.   16s.

LIGHT RAILWAYS
AT HOME AND ABROAD.

BY WILLIAM HENRY COLE, M.INST.C.E.,
Late Deputy-Manager, North-Western Railway, India.

Contents.—Discussion of the Term "Light Railways."—English Railways,
Rates, and Farmers. — Light Railways in Belgium, France, Italy, other
European Countries, America and the Colonies, India, Ireland.—Road Trans-
port as an alternative.—The Light Railways Act, 1896.—The Question of
Gauge.—Construction and Working.—Locomotives and Rolling-Stock.—Light
Railways in England, Scotland, and Wales.—Appendices and Index.

"Mr. W. H. Cole has brought together . . . a LARGE AMOUNT of VALUABLE INFORMA-
TION . . . hitherto practically inaccessible to the ordinary reader."—*Times.*
"Will remain for some time yet a STANDARD WORK in everything relating to Light
Railways."—*Engineer.*
"The author has extended practical experience that makes the book lucid and useful.
It is EXCEEDINGLY well done."—*Engineering.*
"The whole subject is EXHAUSTIVELY and PRACTICALLY considered.   The work can be
cordially recommended as INDISPENSABLE to those whose duty it is to become acquainted
with one of the prime necessities of the immediate future."—*Railway Official Gazette.*
"THERE COULD BE NO BETTER BOOK of first reference on its subject.   All classes of
Engineers will welcome its appearance."—*Scotsman.*

LONDON : CHARLES GRIFFIN & CO., LIMITED, EXETER STREET, STRAND.

SHORTLY. SECOND EDITION. Large 8vo, Handsome Cloth. With
Illustrations, Tables, &c.

Lubrication & Lubricants:

A TREATISE ON THE

THEORY AND PRACTICE OF LUBRICATION

AND ON THE

NATURE, PROPERTIES, AND TESTING OF LUBRICANTS.

BY LEONARD ARCHBUTT, F.I.C., F.C.S.,

Chemist to the Midland Railway Company,

AND

R. MOUNTFORD DEELEY, M.I.Mech.E., F.G.S.,

Chief Locomotive Superintendent, Midland Railway Company.

CONTENTS.—I. Friction of Solids.—II. Liquid Friction or Viscosity, and Plastic
Friction.—III. Superficial Tension.—IV. The Theory of Lubrication.—V. Lubricants,
their Sources, Preparation, and Properties.—VI. Physical Properties and Methods of
Examination of Lubricants.—VII. Chemical Properties and Methods of Examination
of Lubricants.—VIII. The Systematic Testing of Lubricants by Physical and Chemical
Methods.—IX. The Mechanical Testing of Lubricants.—X. The Design and Lubrication
of Bearings.—XI. The Lubrication of Machinery.—INDEX.

"Destined to become a CLASSIC on the subject."—*Industries and Iron.*
"Contains practically ALL THAT IS KNOWN on the subject. Deserves the careful
attention of all Engineers."—*Railway Official Guide.*

FOURTH EDITION. *Very fully Illustrated.* Cloth, 4s. 6d.

STEAM - BOILERS:

THEIR DEFECTS, MANAGEMENT, AND CONSTRUCTION.

BY R. D. MUNRO,

Chief Engineer of the Scottish Boiler Insurance and Engine Inspection Company.

GENERAL CONTENTS.—I. EXPLOSIONS caused (1) by Overheating of Plates—(2) By
Defective and Overloaded Safety Valves—(3) By Corrosion, Internal or External—(4) By
Defective Design and Construction (Unsupported Flue Tubes ; Unstrengthened Manholes ;
Defective Staying ; Strength of Rivetted Joints ; Factor of Safety)—II. CONSTRUCTION OF
VERTICAL BOILERS : Shells—Crown Plates and Uptake Tubes—Man-Holes, Mud-Holes,
and Fire-Holes — Fireboxes — Mountings — Management — Cleaning — Table of Bursting
Pressures of Steel Boilers—Table of Rivetted Joints—Specifications and Drawings of
Lancashire Boiler for Working Pressures (a) 80 lbs. ; (b) 200 lbs. per square inch respectively.

"A valuable companion for workmen and engineers engaged about Steam Boilers, ought
to be carefully studied, and ALWAYS AT HAND."—*Coll. Guardian.*
"The book is VERY USEFUL, especially to steam users, artisans, and young Engineers."—
Engineer.

BY THE SAME AUTHOR.

KITCHEN BOILER EXPLOSIONS: Why

they Occur, and How to Prevent their Occurrence. A Practical Handbook based on Actual Experiment. With Diagram and Coloured Plate.
Price 3s.

LONDON: CHARLES GRIFFIN & CO., LIMITED, EXETER STREET, STRAND.

In Crown 8vo, Handsome Cloth. With Numerous Illustrations. 5s. net.

EMERY GRINDING MACHINERY.

A Text-Book of Workshop Practice in General Tool Grinding, and the Design, Construction, and Application of the Machines Employed.

BY

R. B. HODGSON, A.M.Inst.Mech.E.,

Author of "Machines and Tools Employed in the Working of Sheet Metals."

INTRODUCTION.—Tool Grinding.—Emery Wheels.—Mounting Emery Wheels. —Emery Rings and Cylinders. — Conditions to Ensure Efficient Working.— Leading Types of Machines.—Concave and Convex Grinding.—Cup and Cone Machines. — Multiple Grinding. — "Guest" Universal and Cutter Grinding Machines.—Ward Universal Cutter Grinder.—Press.—Tool Grinding.—Lathe Centre Grinder.—Polishing.—INDEX.

Deals practically with every phase of his subject."—*Ironmonger*

" Eminently practical . . . cannot fail to attract the notice of the users of this class of machinery, and to meet with careful perusal."—*Chem. Trade Journal.*

SIXTH EDITION. Folio, strongly half-bound, 21s.

TRAVERSE TABLES:

Computed to Four Places of Decimals for every Minute of Angle up to 100 of Distance.

For the use of Surveyors and Engineers.

BY

RICHARD LLOYD GURDEN,

Authorised Surveyor for the Governments of New South Wales and Victoria.

*** *Published with the Concurrence of the Surveyors-General for New South Wales and Victoria.*

"Those who have experience in exact SURVEY-WORK will best know how to appreciate the enormous amount of labour represented by this valuable book. The computations enable the user to ascertain the sines and cosines for a distance of twelve miles to within half an inch, and this BY REFERENCE TO BUT ONE TABLE, in place of the usual Fifteen minute computations required. This alone is evidence of the assistance which the Tables ensure to every user, and as every Surveyor in active practice has felt the want of such assistance FEW KNOWING OF THEIR PUBLICATION WILL REMAIN WITHOUT THEM." —*Engineer.*

LONDON: CHARLES GRIFFIN & CO., LIMITED, EXETER STREET, STRAND.

WORKS BY
ANDREW JAMIESON, M.INST.C.E., M.I.E.E., F.R.S.E.,

Formerly Professor of Electrical Engineering, The Glasgow and West of Scotland Technical College.

PROFESSOR JAMIESON'S ADVANCED TEXT-BOOKS.

In Large Crown 8vo.   Fully Illustrated.

STEAM AND STEAM-ENGINES, INCLUDING TURBINES

AND BOILERS.   For the Use of Students preparing for Competitive Examinations.   With over 700 pp., over 350 Illustrations, 10 Folding Plates, and very numerous Examination Papers.   FOURTEENTH EDITION. Revised throughout.   10s. 6d.

"Professor Jamieson fascinates the reader by his CLEARNESS OF CONCEPTION AND SIMPLICITY OF EXPRESSION.   His treatment recalls the lecturing of Faraday."—*Athenæum.*
"The BEST BOOK yet published for the use of Students."—*Engineer.*

MAGNETISM AND ELECTRICITY.   For Advanced and

"Honours" Students.   By Prof. Jamieson, assisted by David Robertson, B.Sc., Professor of Electrical Engineering in the Merchant Venturers' Technical College, Bristol.   [*Shortly.*

APPLIED MECHANICS & MECHANICAL ENGINEERING.

Vol. I.—Comprising Part I., with 540 pages, 300 Illustrations, and 540 Examination Questions : The Principle of Work and its applications; Part II.: Friction ; Gearing, &c.   FIFTH EDITION.   8s. 6d.
"FULLY MAINTAINS the reputation of the Author."—*Pract. Engineer.*
Vol. II.—Comprising Parts III. to VI., with 608 pages, 371 Illustrations, and copious Examination Questions : Motion and Energy; Graphic Statics; Strength of Materials ; Hydraulics and Hydraulic Machinery.   FOURTH EDITION.   12s. 6d.
"WELL AND LUCIDLY WRITTEN."—*The Engineer.*
. *Each of the above volumes is complete in itself, and sold separately.*

PROFESSOR JAMIESON'S INTRODUCTORY MANUALS

Crown 8vo.   With Illustrations and Examination Papers.

STEAM AND THE STEAM-ENGINE (Elementary

Manual of).   For First-Year Students.   TENTH EDITION, Revised.   3/6.
"Should be in the hands of EVERY engineering apprentice."—*Practical Engineer.*

MAGNETISM AND ELECTRICITY (Elementary Manual

of).   For First-Year Students.   SIXTH EDITION.   3/6.
"A CAPITAL TEXT-BOOK . . . The diagrams are an important feature."—*Schoolmaster.*
"A THOROUGHLY TRUSTWORTHY Text-book.   PRACTICAL and clear."—*Nature.*

APPLIED MECHANICS (Elementary Manual of).

Specially arranged for First-Year Students.   SIXTH EDITION, Revised and Greatly Enlarged.   3/6.
"The work has VERY HIGH QUALITIES, which may be condensed into the one word 'CLEAR.'"—*Science and Art.*

IN PREPARATION.   300 *pages.   Crown 8vo.   Profusely Illustrated.*

MODERN ELECTRIC TRAMWAY TRACTION :

A Text-Book of Present-Day Practice.
For the Use of Electrical Engineering Students and those interested in Electric Transmission of Power.

BY PROF. ANDREW JAMIESON.

A POCKET-BOOK of ELECTRICAL RULES and TABLES.

For the Use of Electricians and Engineers.   By JOHN MUNRO, C.E., and Prof. JAMIESON.   Pocket Size.   Leather, 8s. 6d.   SEVENTEENTH EDITION.   [See p. 48.

WORKS BY

W. J. MACQUORN RANKINE, LL.D., F.R.S.,

Late Regius Professor of Civil Engineering in the University of Glasgow.

THOROUGHLY REVISED BY

W. J. MILLAR, C.E.,

Late Secretary to the Institute of Engineers and Shipbuilders in Scotland.

A MANUAL OF APPLIED MECHANICS:

Comprising the Principles of Statics and Cinematics, and Theory of
Structures, Mechanism, and Machines. With Numerous Diagrams.
Crown 8vo, cloth. SEVENTEENTH EDITION. 12s. 6d.

A MANUAL OF CIVIL ENGINEERING:

Comprising Engineering Surveys, Earthwork, Foundations, Masonry, Car-
pentry, Metal Work, Roads, Railways, Canals, Rivers, Waterworks,
Harbours, &c. With Numerous Tables and Illustrations. Crown 8vo.
cloth. TWENTY-SECOND EDITION. 16s.

A MANUAL OF MACHINERY AND MILLWORK:

Comprising the Geometry, Motions, Work, Strength, Construction, and
Objects of Machines, &c. Illustrated with nearly 300 Woodcuts,
Crown 8vo, cloth. SEVENTH EDITION. 12s. 6d.

A MANUAL OF THE STEAM-ENGINE AND OTHER PRIME MOVERS:

With a Section on GAS, OIL, and AIR ENGINES, by BRYAN DONKIN,
M.Inst.C.E. With Folding Plates and Numerous Illustrations.
Crown 8vo, cloth. FIFTEENTH EDITION. 12s. 6d.

LONDON: CHARLES GRIFFIN & CO., LIMITED, EXETER STREET, STRAND.

PROF. RANKINE'S WORKS—(*Continued*).

USEFUL RULES AND TABLES:

For Architects, Builders, Engineers, Founders, Mechanics, Shipbuilders, Surveyors, &c. With APPENDIX for the use of ELECTRICAL ENGINEERS. By Professor JAMIESON, F.R.S.E. SEVENTH EDITION. 10s. 6d.

A MECHANICAL TEXT-BOOK:

A Practical and Simple Introduction to the Study of Mechanics. By Professor RANKINE and E. F. BAMBER, C.E. With Numerous Illustrations. Crown 8vo, cloth. FIFTH EDITION. 9s.

*⁎⁎ The "*MECHANICAL TEXT-BOOK*" was designed by Professor* RANKINE *as an* INTRODUCTION *to the above Series of Manuals.*

MISCELLANEOUS SCIENTIFIC PAPERS.

Royal 8vo. Cloth, 31s. 6d.

Part I. Papers relating to Temperature, Elasticity, and Expansion of Vapours, Liquids, and Solids. Part II. Papers on Energy and its Transformations. Part III. Papers on Wave-Forms, Propulsion of Vessels, &c.

With Memoir by Professor TAIT, M.A. Edited by W. J. MILLAR, C.E. With fine Portrait on Steel, Plates, and Diagrams.

"No more enduring Memorial of Professor Rankine could be devised than the publication of these papers in an accessible form. . . . The Collection is most valuable on account of the nature of his discoveries, and the beauty and completeness of his analysis. . . . The Volume exceeds in importance any work in the same department published in our time."—*Architect.*

SHELTON-BEY (W. Vincent, Foreman to the Imperial Ottoman Gun Factories, Constantinople):

THE MECHANIC'S GUIDE: A Hand-Book for Engineers and Artizans. With Copious Tables and Valuable Recipes for Practical Use. Illustrated. *Second Edition.* Crown 8vo. Cloth, 7/6.

LONDON: CHARLES GRIFFIN & CO., LIMITED, EXETER STREET, STRAND.

THIRD EDITION, *Thoroughly Revised and Enlarged. With 60 Plates and Numerous Illustrations. Handsome Cloth. 34s.*

HYDRAULIC POWER

AND

HYDRAULIC MACHINERY.

BY

HENRY ROBINSON, M. INST. C.E., F.G.S.,

FELLOW OF KING'S COLLEGE, LONDON; PROF. EMERITUS OF CIVIL ENGINEERING, KING'S COLLEGE, ETC., ETC.

CONTENTS—Discharge through Orifices.—Flow of Water through Pipes.—Accumulators. —Presses and Lifts.—Hoists.—Rams.—Hydraulic Engines.—Pumping Engines.—Capstans. —Traversers.—Jacks.—Weighing Machines.—Riveters and Shop Tools.—Punching, Shearing, and Flanging Machines.—Cranes.—Coal Discharging Machines.—Drills and Cutters.—Pile Drivers, Excavators, &c.—Hydraulic Machinery applied to Bridges, Dock Gates, Wheels and Turbines.—Shields. — Various Systems and Power Installations — Meters, &c.—INDEX.

"The standard work on the application of water power."—*Cassier's Magazine.*

JUST OUT. Second Edition, Greatly Enlarged. With Frontispiece, several Plates, and over 250 Illustrations. 21s. net.

THE PRINCIPLES AND CONSTRUCTION OF

PUMPING MACHINERY

(STEAM AND WATER PRESSURE).

With Practical Illustrations of ENGINES and PUMPS applied to MINING, TOWN WATER SUPPLY, DRAINAGE of Lands, &c., also Economy and Efficiency Trials of Pumping Machinery.

BY HENRY DAVEY,

Member of the Institution of Civil Engineers, Member of the Institution of Mechanical Engineers, F.G.S., &c.

CONTENTS—Early History of Pumping Engines—Steam Pumping Engines— Pumps and Pump Valves—General Principles of Non-Rotative Pumping Engines—The Cornish Engine, Simple and Compound—Types of Mining Engines—Pit Work—Shaft Sinking—Hydraulic Transmission of Power in Mines—Valve Gears of Pumping Engines—Water Pressure Pumping Engines —Water Works Engines—Pumping Engine Economy and Trials of Pumping Machinery — Centrifugal and other Low-Lift Pumps — Hydraulic Rams, Pumping Mains, &c.—INDEX.

"By the 'one English Engineer who probably knows more about Pumping Machinery than ANY OTHER.' . . . A VOLUME RECORDING THE RESULTS OF LONG EXPERIENCE AND STUDY."—*The Engineer.*

"Undoubtedly THE BEST AND MOST PRACTICAL TREATISE on Pumping Machinery THAT HAS YET BEEN PUBLISHED."—*Mining Journal.*

LONDON: CHARLES GRIFFIN & CO., LIMITED, EXETER STREET, STRAND

Royal 8vo. Handsome Cloth. With numerous Illustrations and Tables. 25s.

THE STABILITY OF SHIPS.

BY

SIR EDWARD J. REED, K.C.B., F.R.S., M.P.,

KNIGHT OF THE IMPERIAL ORDERS OF ST. STANISLAUS OF RUSSIA; FRANCIS JOSEPH OF
AUSTRIA; MEDJIDIE OF TURKEY; AND RISING SUN OF JAPAN; VICE-
PRESIDENT OF THE INSTITUTION OF NAVAL ARCHITECTS.

In order to render the work complete for the purposes of the Shipbuilder, whether at
home or abroad, the Methods of Calculation introduced by Mr. F. K. BARNES, Mr. GRAY,
M. REECH, M. DAYMARD, and Mr. BENJAMIN, are all given separately, illustrated by
Tables and worked-out examples. The book contains more than 200 Diagrams, and is
illustrated by a large number of actual cases, derived from ships of all descriptions.

" Sir EDWARD REED'S 'STABILITY OF SHIPS' is INVALUABLE. The NAVAL ARCHITECT
will find brought together and ready to his hand, a mass of information which he would otherwise have to seek in an almost endless variety of publications, and some of which he would
possibly not be able to obtain at all elsewhere."—*Steamship.*

THE DESIGN AND CONSTRUCTION OF SHIPS. By JOHN
HARVARD BILES, M.INST.N.A., Professor of Naval Architecture in the
University of Glasgow. [*In Preparation.*

THIRD EDITION.   Illustrated with Plates, Numerous Diagrams, and
Figures in the Text.   18s. net.

STEEL SHIPS:
THEIR CONSTRUCTION AND MAINTENANCE.

*A Manual for Shipbuilders, Ship Superintendents, Students,
and Marine Engineers.*

By THOMAS WALTON, NAVAL ARCHITECT,

AUTHOR OF "KNOW YOUR OWN SHIP."

CONTENTS.—I. Manufacture of Cast Iron, Wrought Iron, and Steel.—Composition of Iron and Steel, Quality, Strength, Tests, &c. II. Classification of
Steel Ships. III. Considerations in making choice of Type of Vessel.—Framing
of Ships. IV. Strains experienced by Ships.—Methods of Computing and
Comparing Strengths of Ships. V. Construction of Ships.—Alternative Modes
of Construction.—Types of Vessels.—Turret, Self Trimming, and Trunk
Steamers, &c.—Rivets and Rivetting, Workmanship. VI. Pumping Arrangements. VII. Maintenance.—Prevention of Deterioration in the Hulls of
Ships.—Cement, Paint, &c.—INDEX.

" So thorough and well written is every chapter in the book that it is difficult to select
any of them as being worthy of exceptional praise. Altogether, the work is excellent, and
will prove of great value to those for whom it is intended."—*The Engineer.*

" Mr. Walton has written for the profession of which he is an ornament. His work
will be read and appreciated, no doubt, by every M.I.N.A., and with great benefit by the
majority of them."—*Journal of Commerce.*

UNIFORM WITH THE ABOVE.

THE PRINCIPLES AND PRACTICE OF

DOCK ENGINEERING.

By BRYSSON CUNNINGHAM, B.E., M.INST.C.E.

See p. 27.

LONDON: CHARLES GRIFFIN & CO., LIMITED, EXETER STREET, STRAND.

GRIFFIN'S NAUTICAL SERIES.

EDITED BY EDW. BLACKMORE,
Master Mariner, First Class Trinity House Certificate, Assoc. Inst. N.A.;
AND WRITTEN, MAINLY, by SAILORS for SAILORS.

"THIS ADMIRABLE SERIES."—*Fairplay.*   "A VERY USEFUL SERIES."—*Nature.*
"The volumes of MESSRS. GRIFFIN'S NAUTICAL SERIES may well and profitably be
read by ALL interested in our NATIONAL MARITIME PROGRESS."—*Marine Engineer.*
"EVERY SHIP should have the WHOLE SERIES as a REFERENCE LIBRARY. HAND-
SOMELY BOUND, CLEARLY PRINTED and ILLUSTRATED."—*Liverpool Journ. of Commerce.*

The British Mercantile Marine: An Historical Sketch of its Rise
and Development. By the EDITOR, CAPT. BLACKMORE. 3s. 6d.
"Captain Blackmore's SPLENDID BOOK . . . contains paragraphs on every point
of interest to the Merchant Marine. The 242 pages of this book are THE MOST VALU-
ABLE to the sea captain that have EVER been COMPILED."—*Merchant Service Review.*

Elementary Seamanship. By D. WILSON-BARKER, Master Mariner,
F.R.S.E., F.R.G.S. With numerous Plates, two in Colours, and Frontispiece.
FOURTH EDITION, Thoroughly Revised. With additional Illustrations. 6s.
"This ADMIRABLE MANUAL, by CAPT. WILSON BARKER, of the 'Worcester,' seems
to us PERFECTLY DESIGNED."—*Athenæum.*

Know Your Own Ship: A Simple Explanation of the Stability, Con-
struction, Tonnage, and Freeboard of Ships. By THOS. WALTON, Naval Architect.
With numerous Illustrations and additional Chapters on Buoyancy, Trim, and
Calculations. EIGHTH EDITION. 7s. 6d.
"MR. WALTON'S book will be found VERY USEFUL."—*The Engineer.*

Navigation: Theoretical and Practical. By D. WILSON-BARKER
and WILLIAM ALLINGHAM. SECOND EDITION, Revised. 3s. 6d.
"PRECISELY the kind of work required for the New Certificates of competency.
Candidates will find it INVALUABLE."—*Dundee Advertiser.*

Marine Meteorology: For Officers of the Merchant Navy. By
WILLIAM ALLINGHAM, First Class Honours, Navigation, Science and Art Department.
With Illustrations, Maps, and Diagrams, and *facsimile* reproduction of log page.
7s. 6d.
"Quite the BEST PUBLICATION on this subject."—*Shipping Gazette.*

Latitude and Longitude: How to find them. By W. J. MILLAR,
C.E. SECOND EDITION, Revised. 2s.
"Cannot but prove an acquisition to those studying Navigation."—*Marine Engineer.*

Practical Mechanics: Applied to the requirements of the Sailor.
By THOS. MACKENZIE, Master Mariner, F.R.A.S. SECOND EDITION, Revised. 3s. 6d.
"WELL WORTH the money . . . EXCEEDINGLY HELPFUL."—*Shipping World.*

Trigonometry: For the Young Sailor, &c. By RICH. C. BUCK, of the
Thames Nautical Training College, H.M.S. "Worcester." SECOND EDITION, Revised.
Price 3s. 6d.
"This EMINENTLY PRACTICAL and reliable volume."—*Schoolmaster.*

Practical Algebra. By RICH. C. BUCK. Companion Volume to the
above, for Sailors and others. Price 3s. 6d.
"It is JUST THE BOOK for the young sailor mindful of progress. —*Nautical Magazine.*

The Legal Duties of Shipmasters. By BENEDICT WM. GINSBURG,
M.A., LL.D., of the Inner Temple and Northern Circuit: Barrister-at-Law. SECOND
EDITION, Thoroughly Revised and Enlarged. Price 4s. 6d.
"INVALUABLE to masters. . . . We can fully recommend it."—*Shipping Gazette.*

A Medical and Surgical Help for Shipmasters. Including First
Aid at Sea. By WM. JOHNSON SMITH, F.R.C.S., Principal Medical Officer, Seamen's
Hospital, Greenwich. THIRD EDITION, Thoroughly Revised. 6s.
"SOUND, JUDICIOUS, REALLY HELPFUL."—*The Lancet.*

LONDON: CHARLES GRIFFIN & CO., LIMITED, EXETER STREET, STRAND.

GRIFFIN'S NAUTICAL SERIES.

Introductory Volume.   Price 3s. 6d.

THE
British Mercantile Marine.

By EDWARD BLACKMORE,

MASTER MARINER; ASSOCIATE OF THE INSTITUTION OF NAVAL ARCHITECTS;
MEMBER OF THE INSTITUTION OF ENGINEERS AND SHIPBUILDERS
IN SCOTLAND; EDITOR OF GRIFFIN'S "NAUTICAL SERIES."

GENERAL CONTENTS.—HISTORICAL: From Early Times to 1486—Progress under Henry VIII.—To Death of Mary—During Elizabeth's Reign—Up to the Reign of William III.—The 18th and 19th Centuries—Institution of Examinations—Rise and Progress of Steam Propulsion—Development of Free Trade—Shipping Legislation, 1862 to 1875—"Locksley Hall" Case—Shipmasters' Societies—Loading of Ships—Shipping Legislation, 1884 to 1894—Statistics of Shipping. THE PERSONNEL: Shipowners—Officers—Mariners—Duties and Present Position. EDUCATION: A Seaman's Education; what it should be—Present Means of Education—Hints. DISCIPLINE AND DUTY—Postscript—The Serious Decrease in the Number of British Seamen, a Matter demanding the Attention of the Nation.

"INTERESTING and INSTRUCTIVE . . . may be read WITH PROFIT and ENJOYMENT."—*Glasgow Herald.*
"EVERY BRANCH of the subject is dealt with in a way which shows that the writer 'knows the ropes' familiarly."—*Scotsman.*
"This ADMIRABLE book . . . TEEMS with useful information—Should be in the hands of every Sailor."—*Western Morning News.*

FOURTH EDITION, *Thoroughly Revised.   With Additional Illustrations.   Price 6s.*

A MANUAL OF
ELEMENTARY SEAMANSHIP.

BY
D. WILSON-BARKER, MASTER MARINER; F.R.S.E., F.R.G.S., &c., &c.
YOUNGER BROTHER OF THE TRINITY HOUSE.

With Frontispiece, Numerous Plates (Two in Colours), and Illustrations in the Text.

GENERAL CONTENTS.—The Building of a Ship; Parts of Hull, Masts, &c.—Ropes, Knots, Splicing, &c. — Gear, Lead and Log, &c. — Rigging, Anchors — Sailmaking — The Sails, &c — Handling of Boats under Sail—Signals and Signalling—Rule of the Road—Keeping and Relieving Watch—Points of Etiquette—Glossary of Sea Terms and Phrases—Index.

* The volume contains the NEW RULES OF THE ROAD.

"This ADMIRABLE MANUAL, by CAPT. WILSON-BARKER of the 'Worcester,' seems to us PERFECTLY DESIGNED, and holds its place excellently in 'GRIFFIN'S NAUTICAL SERIES.' . . . . Although intended for those who are to become Officers of the Merchant Navy, it will be found useful by ALL YACHTSMEN."—*Athenæum.*

* For complete List of GRIFFIN'S NAUTICAL SERIES, see p. 39.

LONDON: CHARLES GRIFFIN & CO., LIMITED, EXETER STREET, STRAND.

GRIFFIN'S NAUTICAL SERIES.

SECOND EDITION, *Revised and Illustrated. Price 3s. 6d.*

NAVIGATION:
PRACTICAL AND THEORETICAL.

By DAVID WILSON-BARKER, R.N.R., F.R.S.E., &c., &c.,

AND

WILLIAM ALLINGHAM,
FIRST-CLASS HONOURS, NAVIGATION, SCIENCE AND ART DEPARTMENT.

With Numerous Illustrations and Examination Questions.

GENERAL CONTENTS.—Definitions—Latitude and Longitude—Instruments of Navigation—Correction of Courses—Plane Sailing—Traverse Sailing—Day's Work — Parallel Sailing — Middle Latitude Sailing — Mercator's Chart—Mercator Sailing—Current Sailing—Position by Bearings—Great Circle Sailing—The Tides—Questions—Appendix: Compass Error—Numerous Useful Hints. &c.—Index.

"PRECISELY the kind of work required for the New Certificates of competency in grades from Second Mate to extra Master. . . . Candidates will find it INVALUABLE."—*Dundee Advertiser.*

"A CAPITAL LITTLE BOOK . . . specially adapted to the New Examinations. The Authors are CAPT. WILSON-BARKER (Captain-Superintendent of the Nautical College, H.M.S. 'Worcester,' who has had great experience in the highest problems of Navigation), and MR. ALLINGHAM, a well-known writer on the Science of Navigation and Nautical Astronomy." —*Shipping World.*

Handsome Cloth. Fully Illustrated. Price 7s. 6d.

MARINE METEOROLOGY,
FOR OFFICERS OF THE MERCHANT NAVY.

By WILLIAM ALLINGHAM,
Joint Author of "Navigation, Theoretical and Practical."

With numerous Plates, Maps, Diagrams, and Illustrations, and a facsimile Reproduction of a Page from an actual Meteorological Log-Book.

SUMMARY OF CONTENTS.

INTRODUCTORY.—Instruments Used at Sea for Meteorological Purposes.—Meteorological Log-Books.—Atmospheric Pressure.—Air Temperatures.—Sea Temperatures.—Winds.—Wind Force Scales.—History of the Law of Storms.—Hurricanes, Seasons, and Storm Tracks.—Solution of the Cyclone Problem.—Ocean Currents.—Icebergs.—Synchronous Charts.—Dew, Mists, Fogs, and Haze.—Clouds.—Rain, Snow, and Hail.—Mirage, Rainbows, Coronas, Halos, and Meteors.—Lightning, Corposants, and Auroras.—QUESTIONS.—APPENDIX.—INDEX.

'Quite the BEST publication, AND certainly the MOST INTERESTING, on this subject ever presented to Nautical men."—*Shipping Gazette.*

** For Complete List of GRIFFIN'S NAUTICAL SERIES, see p. 39.

LONDON: CHARLES GRIFFIN & CO., LIMITED, EXETER STREET, STRAND.

GRIFFIN'S NAUTICAL SERIES.

SECOND EDITION, REVISED.   With Numerous Illustrations.   Price 3s. 6d.

Practical Mechanics:
Applied to the Requirements of the Sailor.
BY THOS. MACKENZIE,
Master Mariner, F.R.A.S.

GENERAL CONTENTS.—Resolution and Composition of Forces—Work done by Machines and Living Agents—The Mechanical Powers: The Lever; Derricks as Bent Levers—The Wheel and Axle: Windlass; Ship's Capstan; Crab Winch—Tackles: the "Old Man"—The Inclined Plane; the Screw—The Centre of Gravity of a Ship and Cargo — Relative Strength of Rope : Steel Wire, Manilla, Hemp, Coir—Derricks and Shears- Calculation of the Cross-breaking Strain of Fir Spar—Centre of Effort of Sails—Hydrostatics : the Diving-bell; Stability of Floating Bodies; the Ship's Pump, &c.

"THIS EXCELLENT BOOK . . . contains a LARGE AMOUNT of information."—*Nature.*

"WELL WORTH the money . . . will be found EXCEEDINGLY HELPFUL."—*Shipping World.*

"NO SHIPS' OFFICERS' BOOKCASE will henceforth be complete without CAPTAIN MACKENZIE'S 'PRACTICAL MECHANICS.' Notwithstanding my many years' experience at sea, it has told me *how much more there is to acquire.*"—(Letter to the Publishers from a Master Mariner).

"I must express my thanks to you for the labour and care you have taken in 'PRACTICAL MECHANICS.' . . . IT IS A LIFE'S EXPERIENCE. . . . What an amount we frequently see wasted by rigging purchases without reason and accidents to spars, &c., &c.! 'PRACTICAL MECHANICS' WOULD SAVE ALL THIS."—(Letter to the Author from another Master Mariner).

WORKS BY RICHARD C. BUCK,
of the Thames Nautical Training College, H.M.S. 'Worcester.'

A Manual of Trigonometry:
With Diagrams, Examples, and Exercises.   Price 3s. 6d.
SECOND EDITION, Revised and Corrected.

. Mr. Buck's Text-Book has been SPECIALLY PREPARED with a view to the New Examinations of the Board of Trade, in which Trigonometry is an obligatory subject.

"This EMINENTLY PRACTICAL and RELIABLE VOLUME."—*Schoolmaster.*

A Manual of Algebra.
Designed to meet the Requirements of Sailors and others.   Price 3s. 6d.

. These elementary works on ALGEBRA and TRIGONOMETRY are written specially for those who will have little opportunity of consulting a Teacher. They are books for "SELF-HELP." All but the simplest explanations have, therefore, been avoided, and ANSWERS to the Exercises are given. Any person may readily, by careful study, become master of their contents, and thus lay the foundation for a further mathematical course, if desired. It is hoped that to the younger Officers of our Mercantile Marine they will be found decidedly serviceable. The Examples and Exercises are taken from the Examination Papers set for the Cadets of the "Worcester."

"Clearly arranged, and well got up. . A first-rate Elementary Algebra. —*Nautical Magazine.*

. For complete List of GRIFFIN'S NAUTICAL SERIES. see p. 39.

LONDON: CHARLES GRIFFIN & CO., LIMITED, EXETER STREET, STRAND.

GRIFFIN'S NAUTICAL SERIES.

SECOND EDITION, Thoroughly Revised and Extended. In Crown 8vo.
Handsome Cloth. Price 4s. 6d.

THE LEGAL DUTIES OF SHIPMASTERS.

BY

BENEDICT WM. GINSBURG, M.A., LL.D. (CANTAB.),

Of the Inner Temple and Northern Circuit; Barrister-at-Law.

General Contents.—The Qualification for the Position of Shipmaster—The Contract with the Shipowner—The Master's Duty in respect of the Crew: Engagement; Apprentices; Discipline; Provisions, Accommodation, and Medical Comforts; Payment of Wages and Discharge—The Master's Duty in respect of the Passengers—The Master's Financial Responsibilities—The Master's Duty in respect of the Cargo—The Master's Duty in Case of Casualty—The Master's Duty to certain Public Authorities—The Master's Duty in relation to Pilots, Signals, Flags, and Light Dues—The Master's Duty upon Arrival at the Port of Discharge—Appendices relative to certain Legal Matters: Board of Trade Certificates, Dietary Scales, Stowage of Grain Cargoes, Load Line Regulations, Life-saving Appliances, Carriage of Cattle at Sea, &c., &c.—Copious Index.

" No intelligent Master should fail to add this to his list of necessary books. A few lines of it may SAVE A LAWYER'S FEE, BESIDES ENDLESS WORRY."—*Liverpool Journal of Commerce.*
" SENSIBLE, plainly written, in CLEAR and NON-TECHNICAL LANGUAGE, and will be found of MUCH SERVICE by the Shipmaster."—*British Trade Review.*

SECOND EDITION, Revised. With Diagrams. Price 2s.

Latitude and Longitude:
How to Find them.

BY W. J. MILLAR, C.E.,

Late Secretary to the Inst. of Engineers and Shipbuilders in Scotland.

" CONCISELY and CLEARLY WRITTEN . . . cannot but prove an acquisition to those studying Navigation."—*Marine Engineer.*
" Young Seamen will find it HANDY and USEFUL, SIMPLE and CLEAR."—*The Engineer.*

FIRST AID AT SEA.

THIRD EDITION, Revised. With Coloured Plates and Numerous Illustrations, and comprising the latest Regulations Respecting the Carriage of Medical Stores on Board Ship. Price 6s.

A MEDICAL AND SURGICAL HELP
FOR SHIPMASTERS AND OFFICERS
IN THE MERCHANT NAVY.

BY

WM. JOHNSON SMITH, F.R.C.S.,

Principal Medical Officer, Seamen's Hospital, Greenwich.

. The attention of all interested in our Merchant Navy is requested to this exceedingly useful and valuable work. It is needless to say that it is the outcome of many years PRACTICAL EXPERIENCE amongst Seamen.
" SOUND, JUDICIOUS, REALLY HELPFUL."—*The Lancet.*

. For Complete List of GRIFFIN'S NAUTICAL SERIES, see p. 39.

LONDON: CHARLES GRIFFIN & CO., LIMITED, EXETER STREET, STRAND.

GRIFFIN'S NAUTICAL SERIES.

EIGHTH EDITION. *Revised, with Chapters on Trim, Buoyancy, and Calcula-tions. Numerous Illustrations. Handsome Cloth, Crown 8vo. Price 7s. 6d.*

KNOW YOUR OWN SHIP.

By THOMAS WALTON, NAVAL ARCHITECT.

Specially arranged to suit the requirements of Ships' Officers, Shipowners, Superintendents, Draughtsmen, Engineers, and Others.

This work explains, in a simple manner, such important subjects as :—Displacement. —Deadweight.— Tonnage.— Freeboard.— Moments.— Buoyancy.— Strain.— Structure.— Stability.—Rolling.—Ballasting.—Loading.—Shifting Cargoes.—Admission of Water.— Sail Area.—&c.

"The little book will be found EXCEEDINGLY HANDY by most officers and officials connected with shipping. . . . Mr. Walton's work will obtain LASTING SUCCESS, because of its unique fitness for those for whom it has been written."—*Shipping World.*

BY THE SAME AUTHOR.

Steel Ships: Their Construction and Maintenance.

(See page 38.)

FIFTEENTH EDITION, *Thoroughly Revised, Greatly Enlarged, and Reset Throughout. Large 8vo, Cloth. pp. i-xxiv + 708. With 280 Illustra-tions, reduced from Working Drawings, and 8 Plates. 21s. net.*

A MANUAL OF
MARINE ENGINEERING:

COMPRISING THE DESIGNING, CONSTRUCTION, AND WORKING OF MARINE MACHINERY.

By A. E. SEATON, M.I.C.E., M.I.Mech.E., M.I.N.A.

GENERAL CONTENTS. — PART I.—Principles of Marine Propulsion. PART II.—Principles of Steam Engineering. PART III.—Details of Marine Engines : Design and Calculations for Cylinders, Pistons, Valves, Expansion Valves, &c. PART IV.—Propellers. PART V.—Boilers. PART IV.—Miscellaneous.

"The Student, Draughtsman, and Engineer will find this work the MOST VALUABLE HANDBOOK of Reference on the Marine Engine now in existence."—*Marine Engineer.*

EIGHTH EDITION, Thoroughly Revised. Pocket-Size, Leather. 8s. 6d.

A POCKET-BOOK OF

MARINE ENGINEERING RULES AND TABLES,

FOR THE USE OF

Marine Engineers, Naval Architects, Designers, Draughtsmen, Superintendents and Others.

By A. E. SEATON, M.I.C.E., M.I.Mech.E., M.I.N.A.,
AND
H. M. ROUNTHWAITE, M.I.Mech.E., M.I.N.A.

"ADMIRABLY FULFILS its purpose."—*Marine Engineer.*

SECOND EDITION. In Large 8vo. Handsome Cloth.

CHEMISTRY FOR ENGINEERS.

BY

BERTRAM BLOUNT, AND A. G. BLOXAM,

F.I.C., F.C.S., A.I.C.E.,
Consulting Chemist to the Crown Agents for
the Colonies.

F.I.C., F.C.S.,
Consulting Chemist, Head of the Chemistry
Department, Goldsmiths' Inst.,
New Cross.

GENERAL CONTENTS.—Introduction—Chemistry of the Chief Materials of Construction—Sources of Energy—Chemistry of Steam-raising—Chemistry of Lubrication and Lubricants—Metallurgical Processes used in the Winning and Manufacture of Metals.

"The authors have SUCCEEDED beyond all expectation, and have produced a work which should give FRESH POWER to the Engineer and Manufacturer."—*The Times.*

"PRACTICAL THROUGHOUT . . . an ADMIRABLE TEXT-BOOK, useful not only to Students, but to ENGINEERS and MANAGERS OF WORKS in PREVENTING WASTE and IMPROVING PROCESSES."—*Scotsman.*

For Companion Volume by the same Authors, see "CHEMISTRY FOR MANUFACTURERS," p. 71.

Pocket Size, Leather Limp, with Gilt Edges and Rounded Corners, printed on Special Thin Paper, with Illustrations, pp. i-xii + 834. Price 18s. net.

(THE NEW "NYSTROM")

THE MECHANICAL ENGINEER'S REFERENCE BOOK

A Handbook of Tables, Formulas and Methods for Engineers, Students and Draughtsmen.

By HENRY HARRISON SUPLEE, B.Sc., M.E.

Tables, Formulas, and Reference Data for Mechanical Engineers, comprising machine design and information relating to the drawing office and the designing department; intended as a successor to the well-known Pocket-Book written many years ago by the late JOHN W. NYSTROM.—*Publishers' Note.*

WORKS BY WALTER R. BROWNE, M.A., M.INST.C.E.,

Late Fellow of Trinity College, Cambridge.

THE STUDENT'S MECHANICS:
An Introduction to the Study of Force and Motion.

With Diagrams. Crown 8vo. Cloth, 4s. 6d.

" Clear in style and practical in method, 'THE STUDENT'S MECHANICS' is cordially to be recommended from all points of view."—*Athenæum.*

FOUNDATIONS OF MECHANICS.

Papers reprinted from the *Engineer.* In Crown 8vo, 1s.

Demy 8vo, with Numerous Illustrations, 9s.

FUEL AND WATER:
A Manual for Users of Steam and Water.

BY PROF. FRANZ SCHWACKHÖFER OF VIENNA, AND
WALTER R. BROWNE, M.A., C.E.

GENERAL CONTENTS.—Heat and Combustion—Fuel, Varieties of—Firing Arrangements: Furnace, Flues, Chimney—The Boiler, Choice of—Varieties—Feed-water Heaters—Steam Pipes—Water: Composition, Purification—Prevention of Scale, &c., &c.

"The Section on Heat is one of the best and most lucid ever written."—*Engineer.*
"Cannot fail to be valuable to thousands using steam power."—*Railway Engineer.*

LONDON: CHARLES GRIFFIN & CO., LIMITED, EXETER STREET, STRAND.

GRIFFIN'S LOCAL GOVERNMENT HANDBOOKS.

WORKS SUITABLE FOR MUNICIPAL AND COUNTY ENGINEERS, ANALYSTS, AND OTHERS.

See also Davies' *Hygiene*, p. 99, and MacLeod's *Calculations*, p. 110.

Gas Manufacture (The Chemistry of). A Handbook on the Production, Purification, and Testing of Illuminating Gas, and the Assay of Bye-Products. By W. J. A. BUTTERFIELD, M.A., F.I.C., F.C.S. With Illustrations. THIRD EDITION, Revised. Vol. I., 7s. 6d. net. Vol. II., *in preparation*.   [See page 77

Water Supply: A Practical Treatise on the Selection of Sources and the Distribution of Water. By REGINALD E. MIDDLETON, M.Inst.C.E., M.Inst.Mech.E., F.S.I. With Four Plates and Numerous Diagrams. Crown 8vo. 8s. 6d. net.
[See page 77.

Central Electrical Stations: Their Design, Organisation, and Management. By C. H. WORDINGHAM, A.K.C., M.I.C.E. SECOND EDITION. 24s. net. [See p. 48.

Sewage Disposal Works: A Guide to the Construction of Works for the Prevention of the Pollution by Sewage of Rivers and Estuaries. By W. SANTO CRIMP, M.Inst.C.E., F.G.S. SECOND EDITION, Revised and Enlarged. Large 8vo, Handsome Cloth. With 37 Plates. Price 30s.   [See page 76.

Trades' Waste: Its Treatment and Utilisation, with Special Reference to the Prevention of Rivers' Pollution. By W. NAYLOR, F.C.S., A.M.Inst.C.E. With Numerous Plates, Diagrams, and Illustrations. 21s. net.   [See page 76.

Calcareous Cements: Their Nature, Preparation, and Uses. With some Remarks upon Cement Testing. By GILBERT REDGRAVE, Assoc.Inst.C.E., and CHAS. SPACKMAN, F.C.S. With Illustrations, Analytical Data, and Appendices on Costs, &c. 15s. net.   [See page 76.

Road Making and Maintenance: A Practical Treatise for Engineers, Surveyors, and others. With an Historical Sketch of Ancient and Modern Practice. By THOMAS AITKEN, Assoc.M.Inst.C.E., M. Assoc. Municipal and County Engrs.; M. San. Inst. With numerous Plates, Diagrams, and Illustrations. 21s.
[See page 79

Light Railways at Home and Abroad. By WILLIAM HENRY COLE, M.Inst.C.E., late Deputy Manager, North-Western Railway, India. Large 8vo, Handsome Cloth, Plates and Illustrations. 16s.   [See page 30.

Practical Sanitation: A Handbook for Sanitary Inspectors and others Interested in Sanitation. By GEO. REID, M.D., D.P.H., Medical Officer, Staffordshire County Council. With Appendix on Sanitary Law, by Herbert Manley, M.A., M.B., D.P.H. TWELFTH EDITION, Thoroughly Revised. 6s.   [See page 78.

Sanitary Engineering: A Practical Manual of Town Drainage and Sewage and Refuse Disposal. By FRANCIS WOOD, A.M.Inst.C.E., F.G.S., Borough Surveyor, Fulham. Fully Illustrated. 8s. 6d. net.   [See page 78.

Dairy Chemistry: A Practical Handbook for Dairy Managers, Chemists, and Analysts. By H. DROOP RICHMOND, F.C.S., Chemist to the Aylesbury Dairy Company. With Tables, Illustrations, &c. Handsome Cloth, 16s.   [See page 73.

Milk: Its Production and Uses. With Chapters on Dairy Farming, The Diseases of Cattle, and on the Hygiene and Control of Supplies. By EDWARD F. WILLOUGHBY, M.D. (Lond.), D.P.H. (Lond. and Camb.), Inspector of Farms and General Scientific Adviser to Welford & Sons, Ltd. 6s. net.   [See page 73.

Flesh Foods: With Methods for their Chemical, Microscopical, and Bacteriological Examination. A Handbook for Medical Men, Inspectors, Analysts, and others. By C. AINSWORTH MITCHELL, B.A., F.I.C., Mem. Council Soc. of Public Analysts. With numerous Illustrations and a coloured Plate. 10s. 6d. [See page 74.

Foods: Their Composition and Analysis. By A. WYNTER BLYTH, M.R.C.S., F.C.S., Public Analyst for the County of Devon, and M. W BLYTH, B.A., B.Sc. With Tables, Folding Plate, and Frontispiece. FIFTH EDITION, Thoroughly Revised. 21s.   [See page 72.
"AN ADMIRABLE DIGEST of the most recent state of knowledge."—*Chemical News.*

LONDON: CHARLES GRIFFIN & CO., LIMITED, EXETER STREET, STRAND.

ELECTRICAL ENGINEERING.

SECOND EDITION, *Revised. In Large 8vo. Handsome Cloth. Profusely Illustrated with Plates, Diagrams, and Figures. 24s. net.*

CENTRAL ELECTRICAL STATIONS:

Their Design, Organisation, and Management.

BY CHAS. H. WORDINGHAM, A.K.C., M.INST.C.E., M.INST.MECH.E.,
Late Memb. of Council Inst. E. E., and Electrical Engineer to the City of Manchester :
Electrical Engineer-in-Chief to the Admiralty.

ABRIDGED CONTENTS.

Introductory.—Central Station Work as a Profession.—An an Investment.—The Establishment of a Central Station —Systems of Supply.—Site.—Architecture.—Plant.—Boilers —Systems of Draught and Waste Heat Economy.—Coal Handling, Weighing, and Storing —The Transmission of Steam. — Generators.—Condensing Appliances.—Switching Gear, Instruments, and Connections.—Distributing Mains.—Insulation, Resistance, and Cost.—Distributing Networks.—Service Mains and Feeders.—Testing Mains.—Meters and Appliances —Standardising and Testing Laboratory —Secondary Batteries.—Street Lighting. — Cost. — General Organisation — Mains Department. — Installation Department. — Standardising Department.— Drawing Office —Clerical Department.—The Consumer.—Routine and Main Laying.—INDEX.

"One of the MOST VALUABLE CONTRIBUTIONS to Central Station literature we have had for some time."—*Electricity.*

In Large 8vo. Handsome Cloth. Profusely Illustrated. 12s. 6d. net.

ELECTRICITY CONTROL.

A. Treatise on Electric Switchgear and Systems of Electric Transmission.

BY LEONARD ANDREWS,
Associate Member of the Institution of Civil Engineers, Member of the Institution of
Electrical Engineers, &c

General Principles of Switchgear Design.—Constructional Details.—Circuit Breakers or Arc Interrupting Devices.—Automatically Operated Circuit-Breakers.—Alternating Reverse Current Devices. — Arrangement of 'Bus Bars, and Apparatus for Parallel Running. — General Arrangement of Controlling Apparatus for High Tension Systems. — General Arrangement of Controlling Apparatus for Low Tension Systems.—Examples of Complete Installations.—Long Distance Transmission Schemes.

"Not often does the specialist have presented to him so satisfactory a book as this. . . . We recommend it without hesitation to Central Station Engineers, and, in fact, to anyone interested in the subject."—*Power.*

SEVENTEENTH EDITION, Thoroughly Revised and Enlarged. 8s. 6d.

A POCKET-BOOK

OF

ELECTRICAL RULES & TABLES

FOR THE USE OF ELECTRICIANS AND ENGINEERS.

BY JOHN MUNRO, C.E., & PROF. JAMIESON, M.INST.C.E., F.R.S.E.
With Numerous Diagrams. Pocket Size. Leather, 8s. 6d.

GENERAL CONTENTS.

Units of Measurement. — Measures. — Testing. — Conductors. — Dielectrics. — Submarine Cables.—Telegraphy.—Electro-Chemistry.—Electro-Metallurgy.—Batteries.—Dynamos and Motors.—Transformers.—Electric Lighting.—Miscellaneous.—Logarithms.—Appendices.

"WONDERFULLY PERFECT. . . . Worthy of the highest commendation we can give it."—*Electrician.*
"The STERLING VALUE of Messrs. MUNRO and JAMIESON'S POCKET-BOOK."—*Electrical Review.*

LONDON : CHARLES GRIFFIN & CO., LIMITED, EXETER STREET, STRAND.

AT PRESS. In Handsome Cloth. Profusely Illustrated.

WIRELESS TELEGRAPHY.

BY

DR. GUSTAVE EICHHORN.

CONTENTS.—Oscillations.—Closed Oscillation Systems.—Open Oscillation Systems.—Coupled Systems.—The Coupling Compensating the Aerial Wire.— The Receiver.—Comparative Measurement in the Sender.—Theoretical Results and Calculations in respect of Sender and Receiver.—Closely-Coupled Sender and Receiver.—Loose-Coupled Sender and Receiver.—Principal Formulæ.— The Ondameter.—Working a Wireless Telegraph Station.—Modern Apparatus and Methods of Working.—Conclusion.—Bibliography.—INDEX.

IN ACTIVE PREPARATION. Large 8vo, Handsome Cloth. Fully Illustrated.

ELECTRICITY METERS.

BY

HENRY G. SOLOMON.

CONTENTS. — Introductory. — General Principles of Continuous-Current Meters.—Continuous-Current Quantity Meters.—Continuous-Energy Motor Meters —Different Types.—Special Purposes, *i.e.*, Battery Meters. Switchboard Meters. Tramcar Meters.—General Principles of Single- and Polyphase Induction Meters.- Single-phase Induction Meters.—Polyphase Meters.— Tariff Systems.—Prepayment Meters —Tariff and Hour Meters.—Some Mechanical Features in Meter Design.—Testing Meters.—INDEX.

ELECTRICAL PRACTICE IN COLLIERIES.

BY D. BURNS, M.E., M.INST.M.E.

(See page 58.)

GRIFFIN'S ELECTRICAL PRICE-BOOK.

EDITED BY H. J. DOWSING.

(See page 31.)

MODERN ELECTRIC TRAMWAY TRACTION.

BY PROFESSOR ANDREW JAMIESON.

(See page 34.)

LONDON: CHARLES GRIFFIN & CO., LIMITED, EXETER STREET, STRAND.

By PROFESSORS J. H. POYNTING & J. J. THOMSON.

In Five Volumes.   Large 8vo.   Sold Separately.

A TEXT-BOOK OF PHYSICS.

BY

J. H. POYNTING,

SC.D., F.R.S.,

Late Fellow of Trinity College, Cambridge;
Professor of Physics, Birmingham
University.

AND

J. J. THOMSON,

M.A., F.R.S.,

Fellow of Trinity College, Cambridge; Prof
of Experimental Physics in the University
of Cambridge.

INTRODUCTORY VOLUME, fully Illustrated.   THIRD EDITION,
Revised.   Shortly.

PROPERTIES OF MATTER.

CONTENTS. — Gravitation. — The Acceleration of Gravity. — Elasticity. — Stresses and
Strains. — Torsion. — Bending of Rods. — Spiral Springs — Collision. — Compressibility of
Liquids. — Pressures and Volumes of Gases. Thermal Effects Accompanying Strain. —
Capillarity. — Surface Tension. — Laplace's Theory of Capillarity. — Diffusion of Liquids —
Diffusion of Gases. — Viscosity of Liquids. — INDEX.

" Students of physics cannot fail to derive benefit from the book." — *Knowledge.*
" We regard this book as quite indispensable not merely to teachers but to physicists o ever
grade above the lowest." — *University Correspondent.*

VOLUME II.   THIRD EDITION.   Fully Illustrated.   Price 8s. 6d.

SOUND.

CONTENTS. — The Nature of Sound and its chief Characteristics. — The Velocity of Sound
in Air and other Media. — Reflection and Refraction of Sound. — Frequency and Pitch of
Notes. — Resonance and Forced Oscillations. — Analysis of Vibrations. — The Transverse
Vibrations of Stretched Strings or Wires — Pipes and other Air Cavities. — Rods. — Plates.
— Membranes. — Vibrations maintained by Heat. — Sensitive Flames and Jets. — Musical
Sand. — The Superposition of Waves.   INDEX.

" The work . . . . . may be recommended to anyone desirous of possessing an EASY,
UP-TO-DATE STANDARD TREATISE on Acoustics." — *Literature.*
" Very clearly written. . . . . The names of the authors are a guarantee of the
SCIENTIFIC ACCURACY and UP-TO-DATE CHARACTER of the work." — *Educational Times.*

JUST OUT.   VOLUME III.   Fully Illustrated.   Price 15s.

HEAT.

CONTENTS. — Temperature. — Expansion of Solids — Liquids. — Gases. — Circulation
and Convection. — Quantity of Heat; Specific Heat. — Conductivity. — Forms of Energy;
Conservation; Mechanical Equivalent of Heat. — The Kinetic Theory — Change of State;
Liquid Vapour. — Critical Points — Solids and Liquids. — Atmospheric Conditions. —
Radiation. — Theory of Exchanges. — Radiation and Temperature. — Thermodynamics. —
Isothermal and Adiabatic Changes. — Thermodynamics of Changes of State, and Solu-
tions. — Thermodynamics of Radiation. — INDEX.

Remaining Volumes in Preparation—

LIGHT; MAGNETISM AND ELECTRICITY.

THE MEAN DENSITY OF THE EARTH : An Essay to which the
Adams Prize was adjudged in 1893 in the University of Cambridge.   By J. H.
POYNTING, Sc.D., F.R.S., Late Fellow of Trinity College, Cambridge; Professor of
Physics, Birmingham University.   In Large 8vo, with Bibliography, Illustrations in
the Text, and Seven Lithographed Plates.   12s. 6d.

" An account of this subject cannot fail to be of GREAT and GENERAL INTEREST to the scientific
mind.   Especially is this the case when the account is given by one who has contributed so
considerably as has Prof. Poynting to our present state of knowledge with respect to a very
difficult subject. . . .   Remarkably has Newton's estimate been verified by Prof. Poynting." —
Athenæum.

Griffin's Geological, Prospecting, Mining, and Metallurgical Publications.

LONDON: CHARLES GRIFFIN & CO., LIMITED, EXETER STREET, STRAND.

Demy 8vo, Handsome cloth, 18s.

Physical Geology and Palæontology,

ON THE BASIS OF PHILLIPS.

BY

HARRY GOVIER SEELEY, F.R.S.,

PROFESSOR OF GEOGRAPHY IN KING'S COLLEGE, LONDON.

With Frontispiece in Chromo-Lithography, and Illustrations.

"It is impossible to praise too highly the research which PROFESSOR SEELEY'S 'PHYSICAL GEOLOGY' evidences. IT IS FAR MORE THAN A TEXT-BOOK—it is a DIRECTORY to the Student in prosecuting his researches."—*Presidential Address to the Geological Society,* 1885, *by Rev. Prof. Bonney, D.Sc., LL.D., F.R.S.*

"PROFESSOR SEELEY maintains in his 'PHYSICAL GEOLOGY' the high reputation he already deservedly bears as a Teacher." — *Dr. Henry Woodward, F.R.S., in the "Geological Magazine."*

"PROFESSOR SEELEY'S work includes one of the most satisfactory Treatises on Lithology in the English language."—*American Journal of Engineering.*

Demy 8vo, Handsome cloth, 34s.

Stratigraphical Geology & Palæontology,

ON THE BASIS OF PHILLIPS.

BY

ROBERT ETHERIDGE, F.R.S.,

OF THE NATURAL HIST. DEPARTMENT, BRITISH MUSEUM, LATE PALÆONTOLOGIST TO THE GEOLOGICAL SURVEY OF GREAT BRITAIN, PAST PRESIDENT OF THE GEOLOGICAL SOCIETY, ETC.

With Map, Numerous Tables, and Thirty-six Plates.

"No such compendium of geological knowledge has ever been brought together before."—*Westminster Review.*

"If PROF. SEELEY'S volume was remarkable for its originality and the breadth of its views, Mr. ETHERIDGE fully justifies the assertion made in his preface that his book differs in construction and detail from any known manual. . . . Must take HIGH RANK AMONG WORKS OF REFERENCE."—*Athenæum.*

OPEN-AIR STUDIES IN GEOLOGY:

An Introduction to Geology Out-of-doors.

By PROFESSOR GRENVILLE COLE, M.R.I.A., F.G.S.

For details, see Griffin's Introductory Science Series, p. 85.

LONDON: CHARLES GRIFFIN & CO., LIMITED, EXETER STREET, STRAND.

Crown 8vo. Handsome Cloth. 2s. 6d.

RESEARCHES ON THE PAST AND PRESENT HISTORY

OF

THE EARTH'S ATMOSPHERE.

Including the latest Discoveries and their Practical Applications.

By DR. THOMAS LAMB PHIPSON.

PART I.—THE EARTH'S ATMOSPHERE IN REMOTE GEOLOGICAL PERIODS.
PART II.—THE ATMOSPHERE OF OUR PRESENT PERIOD.
APPENDICES; INDEX.

*** Dr. Phipson's work presents, amidst much which is of interest to the Scientist and the General Reader alike, a short *résumé* of his discovery of the origin of Atmospheric Oxygen, the existence of which he attributes wholly to the action of Solar Radiation upon vegetable life. The book will be found replete with much that is new, curious, and interesting, both in connection with Weather Lore, and with Scientific Meteorology.—*Publisher's Note.*

"The book should prove of interest to general readers, as well as to meteorologists and other students of science."—*Nature.*

By GRENVILLE A. J. COLE, M.R.I.A., F.G.S.,
Professor of Geology in the Royal College of Science for Ireland, and Examiner in the University of London.

See also the two following pages (54, 55), and page 85.

AIDS IN
PRACTICAL GEOLOGY:
WITH A SECTION ON PALÆONTOLOGY.

By PROFESSOR GRENVILLE COLE, M.R.I.A., F.G.S.

FOURTH EDITION, Thoroughly Revised. With Frontispiece and Illustrations. Cloth, 10s. 6d.

GENERAL CONTENTS.—
PART   I.—SAMPLING OF THE EARTH'S CRUST.
PART II.—EXAMINATION OF MINERALS.
PART III.—EXAMINATION OF ROCKS.
PART IV.—EXAMINATION OF FOSSILS.

"Prof. Cole treats of the examination of minerals and rocks in a way that has never been attempted before . . . DESERVING OF THE HIGHEST PRAISE. Here indeed are 'Aids' INNUMERABLE and INVALUABLE. All the directions are given with the utmost clearness and precision."—*Athenæum.*

"That the work deserves its title, that it is full of 'AIDS,' and in the highest degree 'PRACTICAL,' will be the verdict of all who use it."—*Nature.*

"This EXCELLENT MANUAL . . . will be A VERY GREAT HELP. . . . The section on the Examination of Fossils is probably the BEST of its kind yet published. . . . FULL of well-digested information from the newest sources and from personal research."—*Annals of Nat. History.*

LONDON: CHARLES GRIFFIN & CO., LIMITED, EXETER STREET, STRAND

GRIFFIN'S "NEW LAND" SERIES.

*Practical Hand-Books for the Use of Prospectors, Explorers,
Settlers, Colonists, and all Interested in the opening
up and Development of New Lands.*

EDITED BY GRENVILLE A. J. COLE, M.R.I.A., F.G.S.,
Professor of Geology in the Royal College of Science for Ireland, and Examiner in
the University of London.

In Crown 8vo. Handsome Cloth. 5s.

With Numerous Maps Specially Drawn and Executed for this Work.

NEW LANDS:

THEIR RESOURCES AND PROSPECTIVE ADVANTAGES.

By HUGH ROBERT MILL, D.Sc., LL.D., F.R.S.E.,

INTRODUCTORY.—The Development of New Lands.—The Dominion of
Canada.—Canada, Eastern Provinces.—Canada, Western Provinces and
Territories.—Newfoundland.—The United States.—Latin America, Mexico.—
Latin America, Temperate Brazil and Chili.—Latin America, Argentina.—
The Falkland Islands.—Victoria.—New South Wales.—Queensland.—South
Australia.—Tasmania.—Western Australia.—New Zealand.—The Resources
of South Africa.—Southern Rhodesia.—INDEX.

"PAINSTAKING . . . COMPLETE . . . of great PRACTICAL ASSISTANCE."—*The Field.*

"A want admirably supplied. . . . Has the advantage of being written by a professed Geographer."—*Geographical Journal.*

IN PREPARATION.

BUILDING CONSTRUCTION IN WOOD, STONE, AND
CONCRETE. By JAMES LYON, M.A., Professor of Engineering in the Royal College of Science for Ireland;
sometime Superintendent of the Engineering Department in
the University of Cambridge; and J. TAYLOR, A.R.C.S.I.

*** Other Volumes, dealing with subjects of PRIMARY
IMPORTANCE in the EXAMINATION and UTILISATION of Lands
which have not as yet been fully developed, are in preparation.

LONDON : CHARLES GRIFFIN & CO., LIMITED, EXETER STREET, STRAND.

GRIFFIN'S "NEW LAND" SERIES.

THIRD EDITION, *Revised.*   *With Illustrations.*   *Handsome Cloth, 5s.*

PROSPECTING FOR MINERALS.

A Practical Handbook for Prospectors, Explorers, Settlers, and all interested in the Opening up and Development of New Lands.

BY

S. HERBERT COX, Assoc. R.S.M., M. Inst. M.M., F.G.S., &c.

GENERAL CONTENTS.—Introduction and Hints on Geology—The Determination of Minerals: Use of the Blow-pipe, &c.—Rock-forming Minerals and Non-Metallic Minerals of Commercial Value: Rock Salt, Borax, Marbles, Lithographic Stone, Quartz and Opal, &c., &c.—Precious Stones and Gems—Stratified Deposits: Coal and Ores—Mineral Veins and Lodes—Irregular Deposits—Dynamics of Lodes: Faults, &c.—Alluvial Deposits—Noble Metals: Gold, Platinum, Silver, &c.—Lead—Mercury—Copper—Tin—Zinc—Iron—Nickel, &c.—Sulphur, Antimony, Arsenic, &c.—Combustible Minerals—Petroleum—General Hints on Prospecting—Glossary—Index.

"This ADMIRABLE LITTLE WORK . . . written with SCIENTIFIC ACCURACY in a CLEAR and LUCID style. . . . An IMPORTANT ADDITION to technical literature . . . will be of value not only to the Student, but to the experienced Prospector. . . . If the succeeding volumes of the NEW LAND SERIES are equal in merit to the First, we must congratulate the Publishers on successfully filling up a gap in existing literature —*Mining Journal.*

"This EXCELLENT HANDBOOK will prove a perfect *Vade-mecum* to those engaged in the practical work of Mining and Metallurgy."—*Times of Africa.*

With many Engravings and Photographs. Handsome Cloth, 4s. 6d.

FOOD SUPPLY.

By ROBERT BRUCE,
Agricultural Superintendent to the Royal Dublin Society.

With Appendix on Preserved Foods by C. A. MITCHELL, B.A., F.I.C.

GENERAL CONTENTS.—Climate and Soil—Drainage and Rotation of Crops—Seeds and Crops—Vegetables and Fruits—Cattle and Cattle-Breeding—Sheep and Sheep Rearing—Pigs—Poultry—Horses—The Dairy —The Farmer's Implements—The Settler's Home.

"BRISTLES WITH INFORMATION."—*Farmers' Gazette.*

"The work is one which will appeal to those intending to become farmers at home or in the Colonies, and who desire to obtain a general idea of the true principles of farming in ALL ITS BRANCHES."—*Journal of the Royal Colonial Inst.*

"A most READABLE and VALUABLE book, and merits an EXTENSIVE SALE."—*Scottish Farmer.*

"Will prove of service in ANY PART OF THE WORLD."—*Nature.*

LONDON: CHARLES GRIFFIN & CO., LIMITED, EXETER STREET, STRAND.

SIXTH EDITION. With Frontispiece and 716 Illustrations. Price 34s.

ORE & STONE MINING.

By Sir C. LE NEVE FOSTER, D.Sc., F.R.S.,
LATE PROFESSOR OF MINING, ROYAL COLLEGE OF SCIENCE.

REVISED, AND BROUGHT UP-TO-DATE

By BENNETT H. BROUGH, F.G.S., Assoc.R.S.M.

GENERAL CONTENTS.

INTRODUCTION. Mode of Occurrence of Minerals.—Prospecting.—Boring. —Breaking Ground.—Supporting Excavations.—Exploitation.—Haulage or Transport.—Hoisting or Winding.—Drainage.—Ventilation.—Lighting.— Descent and Ascent.—Dressing—Principles of Employment of Mining Labour. —Legislation affecting Mines and Quarries.—Condition of the Miner.— Accidents.—Index.

"Dr. Foster's book was expected to be EPOCH-MAKING, and it fully justifies such expectation. . . . A MOST ADMIRABLE account of the mode of occurrence of practically ALL KNOWN MINERALS. Probably stands UNRIVALLED for completeness."—*The Mining Journal.*
"This EPOCH-MAKING work . . . appeals to MEN OF EXPERIENCE no less than to students."—*Berg- und Hüttenmännische Zeitung.*
"This SPLENDID WORK."—*Oesterr. Ztschrft. für Berg- und Hüttenwesen.*

In Crown 8vo. Handsome Cloth. With nearly 300 Illustrations, many of them being full page reproductions of views of great interest. Price 7s. 6d. net.

THE ELEMENTS OF MINING AND QUARRYING.

An Introductory Text-Book for Mining Students.

By Sir C. LE NEVE FOSTER, D.Sc., F.R.S.,
Professor of Mining at the Royal College of Science, London, with which is Incorporated the Royal School of Mines; lately one of H.M. Inspectors of Mines.

GENERAL CONTENTS. — INTRODUCTION. — Occurrence of Minerals. — Prospecting.—Boring.—Breaking Ground.—Supporting Excavations.—Exploitation.—Haulage or Transport.—Hoisting or Winding.—Drainage.—Ventilation. —Lighting.—Descent and Ascent.—Dressing, &c.—INDEX.

"A remarkably clear survey of the whole field of mining operations."—*Engineer.*
"Rarely does it fall to the lot of a reviewer to have to accord such unqualified praise as this book deserves. . . . The profession generally have every reason to be grateful to Sir C. Le Neve Foster for having enriched educational literature with so admirable an elementary Text-book."—*Mining Journal.*

FIFTH EDITION, *Revised and Greatly Enlarged.   With 4 Plates and 670 Illustrations.   Price* 24s. *net.*

A TEXT-BOOK OF COAL-MINING:

FOR THE USE OF COLLIERY MANAGERS AND OTHERS ENGAGED IN COAL-MINING.

By HERBERT WILLIAM HUGHES, F.G.S.,
Assoc. Royal School of Mines, General Manager of Sandwell Park Colliery.

GENERAL CONTENTS.

Geology.—Search for Coal.—Breaking Ground.—Sinking.—Preliminary Operations. — Methods of Working. — Haulage. — Winding. — Pumping.— Ventilation.—Lighting.—Works at Surface.—Preparation of Coal for Market. —INDEX.

"Quite THE BEST BOOK of its kind . . . as PRACTICAL in aim as a book can be . The illustrations are EXCELLENT."—*Athenæum.*
"We cordially recommend the work."—*Colliery Guardian.*
"Will soon come to be regarded as the STANDARD WORK of its kind."—*Birmingham Daily Gazette.*

Eleventh Edition, Revised. With Numerous Diagrams.
Cloth, 7s. 6d.

A TREATISE ON MINE-SURVEYING:

*For the use of Managers of Mines and Collieries, Students
at the Royal School of Mines, &c.*

By BENNETT H. BROUGH, F.G.S., Assoc.R.S.M.,

Formerly Instructor of Mine-Surveying, Royal School of Mines.

" Its CLEARNESS of STYLE, LUCIDITY of DESCRIPTION, and FULNESS of DETAIL have long ago won
for it a place unique in the literature of this branch of mining engineering, and the present edition fully
maintains the high standard of its predecessors. To the student, and to the mining engineer alike, ITS
VALUE is inestimable. The illustrations are excellent."—*The Mining Journal.*

In Large Crown 8vo. Fully Illustrated. 6s. net.

THE INVESTIGATION OF MINE AIR:

*An Account by Several Authors of the Nature, Significance, and Practical
Methods of Measurement of the Impurities met with in the
Air of Collieries and Metalliferous Mines.*

EDITED BY

Sir CLEMENT LE NEVE FOSTER, D.Sc., F.R.S.,
And J. S. HALDANE, M.D., F.R.S.

" We know of nothing essential that has been omitted. The book is liberally supplied
with illustrations of apparatus."—*Colliery Guardian.*

At Press. In Crown 8vo, Handsome Cloth. Latest Addition to
GRIFFIN'S MINING SERIES.

MINING LAW.

By CHARLES J. ALFORD.

Contents.—The Principles of Mining Law.—The Mining Law of Great
Britain.—British India.—Ceylon.—Burma.—The Malay Peninsula.—British
North Borneo.— Egypt. — Cyprus. — The Dominion of Canada. — British
Guiana.— The Gold Coast Colony and Ashanti.—Cape of Good Hope.—
Natal. — Orange River Colony. — Transvaal Colony. — Rhodesia. — The
Commonwealth of Australia.—New Zealand, &c.—Index.

In Large 8vo. Third Edition. *Price 10s. 6d.*

Mine Accounts and Mining Book-Keeping.

For Students, Managers, Secretaries, and others.

With Examples taken from Actual Practice of Leading Companies.

By JAMES GUNSON LAWN, A.R.S.M., A.M.Inst.C.E., F.G.S.,

Professor of Mining at the South African School of Mines.

Edited by Sir C. LE NEVE FOSTER, D.Sc., F.R.S.

" It seems IMPOSSIBLE to suggest how Mr. LAWN'S book could be made more COMPLETE or
more VALUABLE, careful, and exhaustive."—*Accountants' Magazine.*

THE MINING ENGINEERS' REPORT BOOK AND DIRECTORS'

AND SHAREHOLDERS' GUIDE TO MINING REPORTS. By
Edwin R. Field, M.Inst.M.M. With Notes on the Valuation of
Mining Property and Tabulating Reports, Useful Tables, &c., and
provided with detachable blank pages for MS. Notes. Pocket Size,
Strongly Bound in Leather. 3s. 6d.

" An ADMIRABLY compiled book which Mining Engineers and Managers will find
EXTREMELY USEFUL."—*Mining Journal.*

In Medium 8vo. With Numerous Plates, Maps, and Illustrations.
21s. net.

CYANIDING GOLD & SILVER ORES.

A Practical Treatise on the Cyanide Process; its Application, Methods of Working, Design and Construction of Plant, and Costs.

By H. FORBES JULIAN,

Mining and Metallurgical Engineer: Specialist in Gold : Late Technical Adviser of the Deutsche Gold und Silber Scheide Anstalt, Frankfort-on-Maine.

And EDGAR SMART, A.M.I.C.E.,

Civil and Metallurgical Engineer.

"A handsome volume of 400 pages which will be a valuable book of reference for all associated with the process."—*Mining Journal.*
"The authors are to be congratulated upon the production of what should prove to be a standard work."—*Page's Magazine.*

In Large Crown 8vo. With Plates and Illustrations. Handsome Cloth.
7s. 6d.

THE CYANIDE PROCESS OF GOLD EXTRACTION.

A Text-Book for the Use of Metallurgists and Students at Schools of Mines, &c.

By JAMES PARK, F.G.S., M.Inst.M.M.,

Professor of Mining and Director of the Otago University School of Mines; late Director Thames School of Mines, and Geological Surveyor and Mining Geologist to the Government of New Zealand.

THIRD ENGLISH EDITION. Thoroughly Revised and Greatly Enlarged. With additional details concerning the Siemens-Halske and other recent processes.

"Deserves to be ranked as amongst the BEST OF EXISTING TREATISES."—*Mining Journal.*

THIRD EDITION, Revised. *With Plates and Illustrations. Cloth, 3s. 6d.*

GETTING GOLD:

A GOLD-MINING HANDBOOK FOR PRACTICAL MEN.

By J. C. F. JOHNSON, F.G.S., A.I.M.E.,

Life Member Australasian Mine-Managers' Association.

GENERAL CONTENTS.—Introductory : Prospecting (Alluvial and General)— Lode or Reef Prospecting—Geneaiology of Gold—Auriferous Lodes—Drifts— Gold Extraction—Lixiviation—Calcination—Motor Power and its Transmission —Company Formation — Mining Appliances and Methods — Australasian Mining Regulations.

"PRACTICAL from beginning to end . . . deals thoroughly with the Prospecting, Sinking, Crushing, and Extraction of gold."—*Brit. Australasian.*

In Crown 8vo. Illustrated, Fancy Cloth Boards. 4s. 6d.

GOLD SEEKING IN SOUTH AFRICA:

A Handbook of Hints for Intending Explorers, Prospectors, and Settlers.

By THEO KASSNER,

Mine Manager, Author of the Geological Sketch Map of the De Kaap Gold Fields.

With a Chapter on the Agricultural Prospects of South Africa.

"As fascinating as anything ever penned by Jules Verne."—*African Commerce.*

Large 8vo.   Handsome Cloth.   With Illustrations.
12s. 6d. net.

METALLURGICAL ANALYSIS & ASSAYING:
A THREE YEARS' COURSE
FOR STUDENTS OF SCHOOLS OF MINES.

By W. A. MACLEOD, B.A., B.Sc., A.O.S.M. (N.Z.),

Formerly Assist.-Director, Thames School of Mines (N.Z.), and Lecturer in Chemistry, University
of Tasmania ; Director of Queensland Government School of Mines, Charters Towers ;

And CHAS. WALKER, F.C.S.,

Formerly Assist.-Demonstrator in Chemistry, Sydney University ; Lecturer in Chemistry
and Metallurgy, Charters Towers School of Mines

PART I.—Qualitative Analysis and Preparation and Properties of Gases.
PART II.—Qualitative and Quantitative Analysis.   PART III.—Assaying,
Technical Analysis (Gas, Water, Fuels, Oils, &c.).

"The publication of this volume tends to prove that the teaching of metallurgical
analysis and assaying in Australia rests in competent hands."—*Nature.*

In Crown 8vo, Beautifully Illustrated with nearly 100
Microphotographs of Steel, &c.   7s. 6d. net.

MICROSCOPIC ANALYSIS OF METALS.

By FLORIS OSMOND & J. E. STEAD, F.R.S., F.I.C.

CONTENTS.—Metallography considered as a method of Assay.— Micro-
graphic Analysis of Carbon Steels.—Preparation of Specimens.—Polishing.
—Constituents of Steel ; Ferrite ; Cementite ; Pearlite ; Sorbite ; Martensite ;
Hardenite ; Troostite ; Austenite.—Identification of Constituents.—Detailed
Examination of Carbon Steels.—Conclusions, Theoretical and Practical.—
Apparatus employed.—APPENDIX.

"There has been no work previously published in English calculated to be so useful to
the student in metallographic research."—*Iron and Steel Trades' Journal.*

THIRD EDITION. With Folding Plates and Many Illustrations.   36s.

ELEMENTS OF
METALLURGY.
A PRACTICAL TREATISE ON THE ART OF EXTRACTING METALS
FROM THEIR ORES.

By J. ARTHUR PHILLIPS, M.INST.C.E., F.C.S., F.G.S., &c.

And H. BAUERMAN, V.P.G.S.

GENERAL CONTENTS. — Refractory Materials. — Fire-Clays. — Fuels, &c.—
Aluminium. — Copper. — Tin. — Antimony. — Arsenic. — Zinc. — Mercury.—
Bismuth. — Lead. — Iron. — Cobalt. — Nickel. — Silver. — Gold. — Platinum.

"Of the THIRD EDITION, we are still able to say that, as a Text-book of
Metallurgy, it is THE BEST with which we are acquainted."—*Engineer.*

"A work which is equally valuable to the Student as a Text-book, and to the
practical Smelter as a Standard Work of Reference. . . . The Illustrations
are admirable examples of Wood Engraving."—*Chemical News.*

AT PRESS. SECOND EDITION, *Revised Throughout and Enlarged.* *Re-set on Larger Page. With Valuable Bibliography, New Maps, Illustrations, &c.*

PETROLEUM AND ITS PRODUCTS.

A PRACTICAL TREATISE.

By SIR BOVERTON REDWOOD,

F.R.S.E., F.I.C., Assoc.R.C.S.,

Hon. Corr. Mem. of the Imperial Russian Technical Society ; Mem. of the American Chemical Society ; Adviser to the Home Office and to the Corporation of London under the Petroleum Acts, &c., &c.

With Plates (One Coloured) and Illustrations. Price 8s. 6d. net.

A HANDBOOK ON PETROLEUM.

FOR INSPECTORS UNDER THE PETROLEUM ACTS,

And for those engaged in the Storage, Transport, Distribution, and Industrial Use of Petroleum and its Products, and of Calcium Carbide. With suggestions on the Construction and Use of Mineral Oil Lamps.

By CAPTAIN J. H. THOMSON,

H.M. Chief Inspector of Explosives,

AND

SIR BOVERTON REDWOOD,

Author of "Petroleum and its Products."

CONTENTS.—I. Introductory.—II. Sources of Supply.—III. Production.—IV. Chemical Products, Shale Oil, and Coal Tar.—V. Flash Point and Fire Test.—VI. Testings.—VII. Existing Legislation relating to Petroleum.—VIII.—IX.—Precautions Necessary.—X. Petroleum Oil Lamps.—XI. Carbide of Calcium and Acetylene.—Appendices.—INDEX.

"A volume that will enrich the world's petroleum literature, and render a service to the British branch of the industry. . . . Reliable, indispensable, a brilliant contribution."— *Petroleum.*

OIL FUEL:

ITS SUPPLY, COMPOSITION, AND APPLICATION.

By SIDNEY H. NORTH.

(*See page 29*).

THE PETROLEUM LAMP: Its Choice and Use. A Guide to the Safe Employment of Mineral Oil in what is commonly termed the Paraffin Lamp. By CAPT. J. H. THOMSON and Dr. BOVERTON REDWOOD. Popular Edition, Illustrated. 1s. net.

"The book contains a great deal of interesting reading, much of which is thoroughly practical and useful. It is a work which will meet every purpose for which it has been written."— *Petroleum.*

LONDON: CHARLES GRIFFIN & CO., LIMITED, EXETER STREET, STRAND.

Griffin's Metallurgical Series.

STANDARD WORKS OF REFERENCE

FOR

Metallurgists, Mine-Owners, Assayers, Manufacturers, and all interested in the development of the Metallurgical Industries.

EDITED BY

Sir W. ROBERTS-AUSTEN, K.C.B., D.C.L., F.R.S.

In Large 8vo, Handsome Cloth.   With Illustrations.

INTRODUCTION to the STUDY of METALLURGY. By the EDITOR. FIFTH EDITION. 18s. (See p. 63.)

GOLD (The Metallurgy of). By THOS. KIRKE ROSE, D.Sc., Assoc. R.S.M., F.C.S., Chemist and Assayer of the Royal Mint. FOURTH EDITION. 21s. (See p. 63.)

LEAD AND SILVER (The Metallurgy of). By H. F. COLLINS, Assoc. R.S.M., M.Inst.M.M. Part I., Lead, 16s; Part II., Silver, 16s. (See p. 64.)

IRON (The Metallurgy of). By T. TURNER, A.R.S.M., F.I.C., F.C.S. SECOND EDITION, Revised. 16s. (See p. 65.)

STEEL (The Metallurgy of). By F. W. HARBORD, Assoc. R.S.M., F.I.C., with a Section on Mechanical Treatment by J. W. HALL, A.M.Inst.C.E. SECOND EDITION. 25s. net. (See p. 65.)

Will be Published at Short Intervals.

METALLURGICAL MACHINERY: the Application of Engineering to Metallurgical Problems. By HENRY CHARLES JENKINS, Wh.Sc., Assoc. R.S.M., Assoc. M.Inst.C.E., of the Royal College of Science.   (See p. 64).

ALLOYS. By the EDITOR.

*** Other Volumes in Preparation.

LONDON: CHARLES GRIFFIN & CO., LIMITED, EXETER STREET, STRAND.

FIFTH EDITION, thoroughly Revised and considerably Enlarged. Large 8vo, with numerous Illustrations and Micro-Photographic Plates of different varieties of Steel. 18s.

An Introduction to the Study of
METALLURGY.

BY

Sir W. ROBERTS-AUSTEN, K.C.B., D.C.L., F.R.S., A.R.S.M.,
Late Chemist and Assayer of the Royal Mint, and Professor of Metallurgy in the Royal College of Science.

GENERAL CONTENTS.—The Relation of Metallurgy to Chemistry.—Physical Properties of Metals.—Alloys. The Thermal Treatment of Metals.—Fuel and Thermal Measurements. —Materials and Products of Metallurgical Processes.—Furnaces.—Means of Supplying Air to Furnaces.—Thermo-Chemistry.—Typical Metallurgical Processes.—The Micro-Structure of Metals and Alloys.—Economic Considerations.

" No English text-book at all approaches this in the COMPLETENESS with which the most modern views on the subject are dealt with. Professor Austen's volume will be INVALUABLE, not only to the student, but also to those whose knowledge of the art is far advanced."—*Chemical News.*

FOURTH EDITION, Revised, Considerably Enlarged, and in part Re-written. With Frontispiece and numerous Illustrations. 21s.

THE METALLURGY OF GOLD.

BY

T. KIRKE ROSE, D.Sc.Lond., Assoc.R.S.M.,
Chemist and Assayer of the Royal Mint.

GENERAL CONTENTS.—The Properties of Gold and its Alloys.—Chemistry of Gold.— Mode of Occurrence and Distribution.—Placer Mining.—Shallow Deposits.—Deep Placer Mining. — Quartz Crushing in the Stamp Battery. — Amalgamation. — Other Forms of Crushing and Amalgamating.—Concentration.—Stamp Battery Practice.—Chlorination: The Preparation of Ore.—The Vat Process.—The Barrel Process.—Chlorination Practice in Particular Mills.—The Cyanide Process.—Chemistry of the Process.—Pyritic Smelting. —The Refining and Parting of Gold Bullion—The Assay of Gold Ores.—The Assay of Bullion—Economic Considerations.—Bibliography.

"A COMPREHENSIVE PRACTICAL TREATISE on this important subject."—*The Times.*
"The MOST COMPLETE description of the CHLORINATION PROCESS which has yet been published."—*Mining Journal.*
"Adapted for all who are interested in the Gold Mining Industry, being free from technicalities as far as possible, but is more particularly of value to those engaged in the Industry."—*Cape Times.*

LONDON: CHARLES GRIFFIN & CO., LIMITED, EXETER STREET, STRAND.

GRIFFIN'S METALLURGICAL SERIES.

JUST OUT. SECOND EDITION, Revised. With Numerous Illustrations.
Large 8vo. Handsome Cloth. 25s. net.

With Additional Chapter on The Electric Smelting of Steel.

THE METALLURGY OF STEEL.

BY F. W. HARBORD, ASSOC.R.S.M., F.I.C.,

Consulting Metallurgist and Analytical Chemist to the Indian Government,
Royal Indian Engineering College, Coopers Hill.

With 37 Plates, 280 Illustrations in the Text, and nearly 100 Micro-
Sections of Steel, and a Section on

THE MECHANICAL TREATMENT OF STEEL.

BY J. W. HALL, A.M.INST.C.E.

ABRIDGED CONTENTS.—The Plant, Machinery, Methods and Chemistry of the Bessemer
and of the Open Hearth Processes (Acid and Basic).—The Mechanical Treatment of Steel
comprising Mill Practice, Plant and Machinery.—The Influence of Metalloids, Heat
Treatment, Special Steels, Microstructure, Testing, and Specifications.

"A work which we venture to commend as an invaluable compendium of information upon
the metallurgy of steel."—*Iron and Coal Trades' Review.*

The *Engineer* says, at the conclusion of a review of this book :—"We cannot conclude without
earnestly recommending all who may be interested as makers or users of steel, which practically
means the whole of the engineering profession, to make themselves acquainted with it as speedily
as possible, and this may be the more easily done as the published price, considering the size
of the book, is extremely moderate."

SECOND EDITION, Revised. Price 16s.

THE METALLURGY OF IRON.

BY THOMAS TURNER, ASSOC.R.S.M., F.I.C.,

Professor of Metallurgy in the University of Birmingham.

IN LARGE 8VO, HANDSOME CLOTH, WITH NUMEROUS ILLUSTRATIONS
(MANY FROM PHOTOGRAPHS).

General Contents.—Early History of Iron.—Modern History of Iron.—The Age of Steel.
—Chief Iron Ores.—Preparation of Iron Ores.—The Blast Furnace.—The Air used in the
Blast Furnace.—Reactions of the Blast Furnace.—The Fuel used in the Blast Furnace.—
Slags and Fluxes of Iron Smelting.—Properties of Cast Iron.—Foundry Practice.—Wrought
Iron.—Indirect Production of Wrought Iron.—The Puddling Process.—Further Treatment
of Wrought Iron.—Corrosion of Iron and Steel.

"A MOST VALUABLE SUMMARY of knowledge relating to every method and stage
in the manufacture of cast and wrought iron . . . rich in chemical details. . . .
EXHAUSTIVE and THOROUGHLY UP-TO-DATE."—*Bulletin of the American Iron
and Steel Association.*

"This is A DELIGHTFUL BOOK, giving, as it does, reliable information on a subject
becoming every day more elaborate."—*Colliery Guardian.*

"A THOROUGHLY USEFUL BOOK, which brings the subject UP TO DATE. OF
GREAT VALUE to those engaged in the iron industry."—*Mining Journal.*

** For Professor Turner's *Lectures on Iron-Founding*, see page 68.

LONDON: CHARLES GRIFFIN & CO., LIMITED, EXETER STREET, STRAND.

SECOND EDITION, Revised, Enlarged, and in part Re-written.
With Additional Sections on MODERN THEORIES OF ELECTROLYSIS
Costs, &c. Price 10s. 6d.

A TREATISE ON
ELECTRO-METALLURGY:

Embracing the Application of Electrolysis to the Plating, Depositing,
Smelting, and Refining of various Metals, and to the Reproduction of Printing Surfaces and Art-Work, &c.

BY

WALTER G. M^cMILLAN, F.I.C., F.C.S.,

*Secretary to the Institution of Electrical Engineers; late Lecturer in Metallurgy
at Mason College, Birmingham.*

With numerous Illustrations. Large Crown 8vo. Cloth.

"This excellent treatise, . . . one of the BEST and MOST COMPLETE
manuals hitherto published on Electro-Metallurgy."—*Electrical Review.*

"This work will be a STANDARD."—*Jeweller.*

"Any metallurgical process which REDUCES the COST of production
must of necessity prove of great commercial importance. . . . We
recommend this manual to ALL who are interested in the PRACTICAL
APPLICATION of electrolytic processes."—*Nature.*

SECOND EDITION, Thoroughly Revised and Enlarged. In large 8vo.
With Numerous Illustrations and Three Folding-Plates. 21s. *net.*

ELECTRIC SMELTING & REFINING:

A Practical Manual of the Extraction and Treatment
of Metals by Electrical Methods.

Being the "ELEKTRO-METALLURGIE" of DR. W. BORCHERS.

Translated from the Latest German Edition by WALTER G. M^cMILLAN,
F.I.C., F.C.S.

CONTENTS.

PART I.—ALKALIES AND ALKALINE EARTH METALS: Magnesium,
Lithium, Beryllium, Sodium, Potassium, Calcium, Strontium, Barium,
the Carbides of the Alkaline Earth Metals.

PART II.—THE EARTH METALS: Aluminium, Cerium, Lanthanum,
Didymium.

PART III.—THE HEAVY METALS: Copper, Silver, Gold, Zinc and Cad-
mium, Mercury, Tin, Lead, Bismuth, Antimony, Chromium, Molybdenum,
Tungsten, Uranium, Manganese, Iron, Nickel, and Cobalt, the Platinum
Group.

"COMPREHENSIVE and AUTHORITATIVE . . . not only FULL of VALUABLE INFOR-
MATION, but gives evidence of a THOROUGH INSIGHT into the technical VALUE and
POSSIBILITIES of all the methods discussed."—*The Electrician.*

"Dr. BORCHERS' WELL-KNOWN WORK . . . must OF NECESSITY BE ACQUIRED by
every one interested in the subject. EXCELLENTLY put into English with additional
matter by Mr. M^cMILLAN."—*Nature.*

"Will be of GREAT SERVICE to the practical man and the Student."—*Electric Smelting.*

In Large 4to, Library Style.   Beautifully Illustrated with 20 Plates, many in Colours, and 94 Figures in the Text.   £2, 2s. net.

PRECIOUS STONES:

Their Properties, Occurrences, and Uses.

A Treatise for Dealers, Manufacturers, Jewellers, and for all Collectors and others interested in Gems.

By Dr. MAX BAUER,

Professor in the University of Marburg,

TRANSLATED BY L. J. SPENCER, M.A. (CANTAB.), F.G.S.

GENERAL CONTENTS.—General Properties of Gems: Their Natural Characters, Occurrence, Application, and Uses.—Detailed Description of Particular Gems: The Diamond, Rubies, Sapphires; Emeralds, Tourmalines, and Opals; Felspars, Amphiboles, Malachite.—Non-mineral Gems: Amber, &c.—Optical Features, Transparency, Translucency, Opacity, Refraction and Dispersion, &c.—APPENDIX: Pearls; Coral.

"The plates are remarkable for their beauty, delicacy, and truthfulness. A glance at them alone is a lesson on precious stones, whilst the perusal of the work itself should add a new interest to any casket of jewels or cabinet of gems, or even to a jewellers' window."—*Athenæum.*

"The work is one to be recommended to every jeweller."—*The Jewellers' Circular.*

In Large Crown 8vo.   With Numerous Illustrations.   8s. 6d.

The Art of the Goldsmith and Jeweller

A Manual on the Manipulation of Gold and the Manufacture of Personal Ornaments.

By THOS. B. WIGLEY,

Headmaster of the Jewellers and Silversmiths' Association Technical School, Birmingham.

ASSISTED BY

J. H. STANSBIE, B.Sc. (Lond.), F.I.C.,

Lecturer at the Birmingham Municipal Technical School.

GENERAL CONTENTS.—Introduction.—The Ancient Goldsmith's Art.—Metallurgy of Gold.—Prices, &c.—Alloys. Melting, Rolling, and Slitting Gold.—The workshop and Tools.—Wire Drawing.—Rings.—Chains and Insignia.—Antique Jewellery and its Revival.—Etruscan Work.—PRECIOUS STONES.—Cutting.—Polishing and Finishing.—Chasing, Embossing, and Repoussé Work.—Colouring and Finishing.—Enamelling.—Engraving.—Moulding and Casting Ornaments, &c.—Fluxes. &c.—Recovery of the Precious Metals.—Refining and Assaying.—Gilding and Electro Deposition.—Hall Marking.—Miscellaneous.—Appendix.

Extra Crown 8vo.   With 48 Illustrations.   3s. 6d. net.

LECTURES ON IRON-FOUNDING.

By THOMAS TURNER, M.Sc., A.R.S.M., F.I.C.,

Professor of Metallurgy in the University of Birmingham

CONTENTS.—Varieties of Iron and Steel.—Application of Cast Iron.—History.—Production.—Iron Ores.—Composition.—The Blast Furnace.—Materials.—Reactions.—Grading Pig Iron.—Carbon, Silicon, Sulphur, Phosphorus, Manganese, Aluminium, Arsenic, Copper, and Titanium.—The Foundry.—General Arrangement.—Re-melting Cast Iron.—The Cupola.—Fuel Used.—Changes due to Re-melting.—Moulds and Moulding.—Foundry Ladles.—Pouring and Pouring Temperature.—Common Troubles.—Influence of Shape and Size on Strength of Castings.—Tests.

"Ironfounders will find much information in the book."—*Iron Trade Circular* (Ryland's).

Griffin's Chemical and Technological Publications.

THIRD EDITION, Revised, Enlarged, and Re-issued.   Price 6s. net.

A SHORT MANUAL OF
INORGANIC CHEMISTRY.

BY

A. DUPRÉ, Ph.D., F.R.S.,

AND

WILSON HAKE, Ph.D., F.I.C., F.C.S.,
Of the Westminster Hospital Medical School.

"A well-written, clear and accurate Elementary Manual of Inorganic Chemistry. . . . We agree heartily with the system adopted by Drs. Dupré and Hake. WILL MAKE EXPERIMENTAL WORK TREBLY INTERESTING BECAUSE INTELLIGIBLE."—*Saturday Review.*

"There is no question that, given the PERFECT GROUNDING of the Student in his Science, the remainder comes afterwards to him in a manner much more simple and easily acquired. The work IS AN EXAMPLE OF THE ADVANTAGES OF THE SYSTEMATIC TREATMENT of a Science over the fragmentary style so generally followed. BY A LONG WAY THE BEST of the small Manuals for Students."—*Analyst.*

LABORATORY HANDBOOKS BY A. HUMBOLDT SEXTON,
Professor of Metallurgy in the Glasgow and West of Scotland Technical College.

OUTLINES OF QUANTITATIVE ANALYSIS.
FOR THE USE OF STUDENTS.

With Illustrations.   FOURTH EDITION.   Crown 8vo, Cloth, 3s.

"A COMPACT LABORATORY GUIDE for beginners was wanted, and the want has been WELL SUPPLIED. . . . A good and useful book."—*Lancet.*

OUTLINES OF QUALITATIVE ANALYSIS.
FOR THE USE OF STUDENTS.

With Illustrations. FOURTH EDITION, Revised. Crown 8vo, Cloth, 3s. 6d.

"The work of a thoroughly practical chemist."—*British Medical Journal.*
"Compiled with great care, and will supply a want."—*Journal of Education.*

ELEMENTARY METALLURGY:
Including the Author's Practical Laboratory Course.   With many Illustrations.   [See p. 66.

THIRD EDITION, Revised.   Crown 8vo.   Cloth, 6s.

"Just the kind of work for students commencing the study of metallurgy."—*Practical Engineer.*

LONDON : CHARLES GRIFFIN & CO., LIMITED, EXETER STREET, STRAND.

In Two Vols., Large 8vo, With Illustrations. Sold Separately.

CHEMISTRY FOR ENGINEERS AND MANUFACTURERS.

A PRACTICAL TEXT-BOOK.

BY

BERTRAM BLOUNT, F.I.C., & A. G. BLOXAM, F.I.C.

VOLUME I. Price 10s. 6d.

CHEMISTRY OF ENGINEERING, BUILDING, AND METALLURGY.

General Contents.—INTRODUCTION—Chemistry of the Chief Materials of Construction—Sources of Energy—Chemistry of Steam-raising—Chemistry of Lubrication and Lubricants—Metallurgical Processes used in the Winning and Manufacture of Metals.

VOLUME II. Price 16s.

JUST OUT. SECOND EDITION, Thoroughly Revised.

THE CHEMISTRY OF MANUFACTURING PROCESSES.

General Contents.—Sulphuric Acid Manufacture—Alkali, &c.—Destructive Distillation—Artificial Manure—Petroleum—Lime and Cement—Clay and Glass—Sugar and Starch—Brewing and Distilling—Oils, Resins, and Varnishes—Soap and Candles—Textiles and Bleaching—Colouring Matters, Dyeing, and Printing—Paper and Pasteboard—Pigments and Paints—Leather, Glue, and Size—Explosives and Matches—Minor Manufactures.

"Certainly a GOOD and USEFUL BOOK, constituting a PRACTICAL GUIDE for students by affording a clear conception of the numerous processes as a whole."—*Chemical Trade Journal.*

SECOND EDITION. In Large 8vo, Handsome Cloth. With 800 pages and 154 Illustrations. 25s. net.

OILS, FATS, BUTTERS, AND WAXES:

THEIR PREPARATION AND PROPERTIES, AND MANUFACTURE THEREFROM OF CANDLES, SOAPS, AND OTHER PRODUCTS.

BY C. R. ALDER WRIGHT, D.Sc., F.R.S.,

Late Lecturer on Chemistry, St. Mary's Hospital Medical School ; Examiner in "Soap" to the City and Guilds of London Institute.

Thoroughly Revised, Enlarged, and in Part Rewritten

BY C. AINSWORTH MITCHELL, M.A., F.I.C.

"Will be found ABSOLUTELY INDISPENSABLE."—*The Analyst.*
"Will rank as the STANDARD ENGLISH AUTHORITY on OILS and FATS for many years to come."—*Industries and Iron.*

LONDON : CHARLES GRIFFIN & CO., LIMITED, EXETER STREET, STRAND.

4

FIFTH EDITION, Thoroughly Revised, Greatly Enlarged and Re-written.
With additional Tables, Plates, and Illustrations.   21s.

FOODS:
THEIR COMPOSITION AND ANALYSIS.

BY A. WYNTER BLYTH, M.R.C.S., F.IC., F.C.S.,
Barrister-at-Law, Public Analyst for the County of Devon, and
Medical Officer of Health for St. Marylebone.

AND M. WYNTER BLYTH, B.A., B.Sc., F.C.S.

GENERAL CONTENTS. — History of Adulteration. — Legislation. —Apparatus.—"Ash."—Sugar. —Confectionery. — Honey. — Treacle. —Jams and Preserved Fruits.—Starches. — Wheaten-Flour. — Bread. — Oats. — Barley.—Rye.—Rice. — Maize. —Millet.—Potatoes.—Peas.—Lentils. — Beans.— **Milk**.—Cream. — Butter. —Oleo-Margarine.—Cheese.— Lard. — Tea. — Coffee. — Cocoa and Chocolate. — **Alcohol**. — Brandy. — Rum. — Whisky.—Gin.—Arrack.—Liqueurs.—Absinthe.—Yeast.—Beer.—Wine. — Vinegar. — Lemon and Lime Juice. — Mustard. — Pepper. — Sweet and Bitter Almonds.—Annatto.—Olive Oil.—**Water Analysis.**—**Appendix:** Adulteration Acts, &c.

" Simply INDISPENSABLE in the Analyst's laboratory."—*The Lancet.*
"A new edition of Mr. Wynter Blyth's Standard work, ENRICHED WITH ALL THE RECENT DISCOVERIES AND IMPROVEMENTS, will be accepted as a boon."—*Chemical News.*

THIRD EDITION.   In Large 8vo, Cloth, with Tables and Illustrations.
Price 21s.

POISONS:
THEIR EFFECTS AND DETECTION.

BY A. WYNTER BLYTH, M.R.C.S., F.I.C., F.C.S.,
Barrister-at-Law, Public Analyst for the County of Devon, and
Medical Officer of Health for St. Marylebone.

GENERAL CONTENTS.

I.—Historical Introduction. II.—Classification—Statistics—Connection between Toxic Action and Chemical Composition—Life Tests—General Method of Procedure—The Spectroscope—Examination of Blood and Blood Stains. III.—Poisonous Gases. IV.—Acids and Alkalies. V.—More or less Volatile Poisonous Substances. VI.—Alkaloids and Poisonous Vegetable Principles. VII.—Poisons derived from Living or Dead Animal Substances. VIII.—The Oxalic Acid Group. IX.—Inorganic Poisons. *Appendix:* Treatment, by Antidotes or otherwise, of Cases of Poisoning.

"Undoubtedly THE MOST COMPLETE WORK on Toxicology in our language."—*The Analyst (on the Third Edition).*
"As a PRACTICAL GUIDE, we know NO BETTER work."—*The Lancet (on the Third Edition).*

⁎ In the THIRD EDITION, Enlarged and partly Re-written, NEW ANALYTICAL METHODS have been introduced, and the CADAVERIC ALKALOIDS, or PTOMAINES, bodies playing so great a part in Food-poisoning and in the Manifestations of Disease, have received special attention.

LONDON: CHARLES GRIFFIN & CO., LIMITED, EXETER STREET, STRAND.

Crown 8vo, Handsome Cloth.   Fully Illustrated.   10s. 6d.

FLESH FOODS:

With Methods for their Chemical, Microscopical, and Bacteriological Examination.

A Practical Handbook for Medical Men, Analysts, Inspectors and others.

By C. AINSWORTH MITCHELL, B.A.(Oxon),

Fellow of the Institute of Chemistry; Member of Council, Society of Public Analysts.

With Numerous Tables, Illustrations, and a Coloured Plate.

CONTENTS.—Structure and Chemical Composition of Muscular Fibre.—of Connective Tissue, and Blood.—The Flesh of Different Animals.—The Examination of Flesh.—Methods of Examining Animal Fat.—The Preservation of Flesh.—Composition and Analysis of Sausages.—Proteids of Flesh.—Meat Extracts and Flesh Peptones.—The Cooking of Flesh.—Poisonous Flesh.—The Animal Parasites of Flesh.—The Bacteriological Examination of Flesh.—The Extraction and Separation of Ptomaines.—INDEX.

" A compilation which will be most useful for the class for whom it is intended."—*Athenæum.*
" A book which NO ONE whose duties involve considerations of food supply CAN AFFORD TO BE WITHOUT.'—*Municipal Journal.*

In Large 8vo. Handsome Cloth. With numerous Illustrations.
Each Volume Complete in Itself, and Sold Separately.

TECHNICAL MYCOLOGY:

THE UTILISATION OF MICRO-ORGANISMS IN THE ARTS AND MANUFACTURES.

A Practical Handbook on Fermentation and Fermentative Processes for the Use of Brewers and Distillers, Analysts, Technical and Agricultural Chemists, and all Interested in the Industries dependent on Fermentation.

By Dr. FRANZ LAFAR,

Professor of Fermentation-Physiology and Bacteriology in the Technical High School, Vienna.

With an Introduction by Dr. EMIL CHR. HANSEN, Principal of the Carlsberg Laboratory, Copenhagen.

TRANSLATED BY CHARLES T. C. SALTER.

Vol. I.—SCHIZOMYCETIC FERMENTATION. 15s.

Including the Theory of Fermentation, the Principles of Sterilization, and Pure Culture Processes.

Vol. II., Part I.—EUMYCETIC FERMENTATION. 7s. 6d.

The Morphology, Chemistry Physiology, and Fermentative Processes of the Eumycetes, Zygomycetes, and Saccharomycetes.

"The first work of the kind which can lay claim to completeness in the treatment of a fascinating subject. The plan is admirable, the classification simple, the style is good, and the tendency of the whole volume is to convey sure information to the reader."—*Lancet.*

*** The publishers trust that before long they will be able to present English readers with the whole of the second volume, arrangements having been concluded whereby, upon its appearance in Germany, the English translation will be at once put in hand. This is now being done with Part I., which will be issued shortly, and which will be followed by the two final parts.

LONDON : CHARLES GRIFFIN & CO., LIMITED, EXETER STREET, STRAND

In Crown 8vo, Handsome Cloth. Price 7s. 6d. net.

FERMENTS
AND THEIR ACTIONS.

A Text-book on the Chemistry and Physics of Fermentative Changes.

By CARL OPPENHEIMER, Ph.D., M.D.,
Of the Physiological Institute at Erlangen.

TRANSLATED FROM THE GERMAN BY

C. AINSWORTH MITCHELL, B.A., F.I.C., F.C.S.

ABRIDGED CONTENTS.—Introduction. — Definition.—Chemical Nature of Ferments.—Influence of External Factors.—Mode of Action.—Physiological Action.—Secretion.—Importance of Ferments to Vital Action.—Proteolytic Ferments.—Trypsin.—Bacteriolytic and Hæmolytic Ferments.—Vegetable Ferments.—Coagulating Ferments.—Saccharifying Ferments. — Diastases. — Polysaccharides. — Enzymes. — Ferments which decompose Glucosides.—Hydrolytic Ferments.—Lactic Acid Fermentation.—Alcoholic Fermentation.—Biology of Alcoholic Fermentation.—Oxydases.—Oxidising Fermentation.—Bibliography.—INDEX.

"Such a veritable *multum in parvo* has never yet appeared. The author has set himself the task of writing a work on Ferments that should embrace human erudition on the subject."—*Brewers' Journal.*

Crown 8vo. Handsome Cloth.

[Companion Volume to "FERMENTS," by the same Author.]

TOXINE AND ANTI-TOXINE.

By CARL OPPENHEIMER, Ph.D., M.D.,
Of the Physiological Institute at Erlangen.

TRANSLATED FROM THE GERMAN BY

C. AINSWORTH MITCHELL, M.A., F.I.C., F.C.S.

With Notes and Additions by the Author, since the publication of the German Edition.

Deals with the theory of Bacterial, Animal, and Vegetable Toxines, such as Tuberculin, Ricin, Cobra Poison, &c.

Bacteriologists, Medical Students, and Scientific Workers will find this book most valuable.

THIRD EDITION. In Handsome Cloth. Fully Illustrated.

PRINCIPLES AND PRACTICE OF BREWING.
FOR THE USE OF STUDENTS AND PRACTICAL MEN.

By WALTER J. SYKES.

REVISED BY ARTHUR R. LING, F.I.C., F.C.S.,
Editor of the Journal of the Institute of Brewing.

In Crown 8vo. Handsome Cloth.

A PRACTICAL LABORATORY HANDBOOK ON
THE BACTERIOLOGY OF BREWING.

By WALTER A. RILEY, F.C.S.

ABRIDGED CONTENTS. — Laboratory Handbook and Apparatus. — Sterilisation. — Nutritive Liquids. — Microscope, Reagents, &c. — Methods of Analysis. — Practical Methods, including the use of "Brettanomyces," Cider and Wine Fermentations—Determining Races of Yeasts, &c.—Practical Notes on Yeast.

LONDON: CHARLES GRIFFIN & CO., LIMITED, EXETER STREET, STRAND.

SECOND EDITION, REVISED AND ENLARGED.

With Tables, Illustrations in the Text, and 37 Lithographic Plates.   Medium 8vo.   Handsome Cloth.   30s.

SEWAGE DISPOSAL WORKS:

A Guide to the Construction of Works for the Prevention of the Pollution by Sewage of Rivers and Estuaries.

By W. SANTO CRIMP, M.INST.C.E., F.G.S.,

Late Assistant-Engineer, London County Council.

"Probably the MOST COMPLETE AND BEST TREATISE on the subject which has appeared in our language. . . Will prove of the greatest use to all who have the problem of Sewage Disposal to face."—*Edinburgh Medical Journal.*

Beautifully Illustrated, with Numerous Plates, Diagrams, and Figures in the Text. 21s. net.

TRADES' WASTE:

ITS TREATMENT AND UTILISATION.

A Handbook for Borough Engineers, Surveyors, Architects, and Analysts.

By W. NAYLOR, F.C.S., A.M.INST.C.E.,

Chief Inspector of Rivers, Ribble Joint Committee.

CONTENTS.—I. Introduction.—II. Chemical Engineering.—III.—Wool De-greasing and Grease Recovery.—IV. Textile Industries: Calico Bleaching and Dyeing.—V. Dyeing and Calico-Printing.—VI. Tanning and Fellmongery.—VII. Brewery and Distillery Waste.—VIII. Paper Mill Refuse.—IX. General Trades' Waste.—INDEX.

"There is probably no person in England to-day better fitted to deal rationally with such a subject."—*British Sanitarian.*
"The work is thoroughly practical, and will serve as a handbook in the future for those who have to encounter the problems discussed."—*Chemical Trade Journal.*

Now READY. In Handsome Cloth. With 59 Illustrations. 6s. net.

SMOKE ABATEMENT.

A Manual for the Use of Manufacturers, Inspectors, Medical Officers of Health, Engineers, and Others.

By WILLIAM NICHOLSON,

Chief Smoke Inspector to the Sheffield Corporation.

CONTENTS.— Introduction. — General Legislation against the Smoke Nuisance. — Local Legislation.—Foreign Laws.—Smoke Abatement.—Smoke from Boilers, Furnaces, and Kilns. — Private Dwelling-House Smoke.— Chimneys and their Construction. — Smoke Preventers and Fuel Savers. — Waste Gases from Metallurgical Furnaces. — Summary and Conclusions.—INDEX.

SECOND EDITION. In Medium 8vo. Thoroughly Revised and Re-Written.
15s. net.

CALCAREOUS CEMENTS:

THEIR NATURE, PREPARATION, AND USES.

With some Remarks upon Cement Testing.

By GILBERT R. REDGRAVE, ASSOC. INST. C.E.,

Assistant Secretary for Technology, Board of Education, South Kensington,

AND CHARLES SPACKMAN, F.C.S.

"INVALUABLE to the Student, Architect, and Engineer."—*Building News.*
"Will be useful to ALL interested in the MANUFACTURE, USE, and TESTING of Cements."—*Engineer.*

LONDON: CHARLES GRIFFIN & CO., LIMITED, EXETER STREET, STRAND.

With Four Folding Plates and Numerous Illustrations. Large 8vo.
8s. 6d. net.

WATER SUPPLY:

A Practical Treatise on the Selection of Sources and the Distribution of Water.

By REGINALD E. MIDDLETON, M.Inst.C.E., M.Inst.Mech.E., F.S.I.

ABRIDGED CONTENTS.—Introductory.—Requirements as to Quality.—Requirements as to Quantity.—Storage Reservoirs.—Purification.—Service Reservoirs.—The Flow of Water through Pipes. — Distributing Systems. — Pumping Machines. — Special Requirements.

"As a companion for the student, and a constant reference for the technical man, we anticipate it will take an important position on the bookshelf."—*Practical Engineer.*

THIRD EDITION, Revised. Fully Illustrated. In Two Volumes.

VOLUME I. Price 7s. 6d. net.
,, II.—READY SHORTLY.

THE CHEMISTRY OF
GAS MANUFACTURE:

A Hand-Book on the Production, Purification, and Testing of Illuminating Gas, and the Assay of the Bye-Products of Gas Manufacture.

By W. J. ATKINSON BUTTERFIELD, M.A., F.I.C., F.C.S.,
Formerly Head Chemist, Gas Works, Beckton, London, E.

"The BEST WORK of its kind which we have ever had the pleasure of reviewing."—*Journal of Gas Lighting.*

With Diagrams and Illustrations. 5s. net.

ACETYLENE:
THE PRINCIPLES OF ITS GENERATION AND USE.

By F. H. LEEDS, F.I.C., F.C.S.,
Member of the Society of Public Analysts and of the Acetylene Association;

AND W. J. ATKINSON BUTTERFIELD, M.A., F.I.C., F.C.S.
Consulting Chemist, Author of "The Chemistry of Gas Manufacture."

"Brimful of information."—*Chem. Trade Journal.*
"We can thoroughly recommend the book to the manufacturer as a reliable work of reference, to the user as supplying valuable hints on apparatus and methods procedure, and to the student as a safe and certain guide."—*Acetylene.*

Large 8vo. Handsome Cloth. Price 16s. net.

FIRE AND EXPLOSION RISKS:
A Handbook of the Detection, Investigation, and Prevention of Fires and Explosions.

By DR. VON SCHWARTZ.

Translated from the Revised German Edition
By C. T. C. SALTER.

ABRIDGED GENERAL CONTENTS.—Fires and Explosions of a General Character — Dangers arising from Sources of Light and Heat.—Dangerous Gases.—Risks Attending Special Industries. — Materials Employed. — Agricultural Products. — Fats, Oils, and Resins.—Mineral Oils and Tar.—Alcohol, &c.—Metals, Oxides, Acids, &c.—Lightning Ignition Appliances, Fireworks.

"The work affords a wealth of information on the chemistry of fire and kindred topics."—*Fire and Water.*
"A complete and useful survey of a subject of wide interest and vital importance."—*Oil and Colourman's Journal.*

LONDON: CHARLES GRIFFIN & CO., LIMITED, EXETER STREET, STRAND.

TWELFTH EDITION, Revised and Enlarged.   Price 6s.

PRACTICAL SANITATION:

A HAND-BOOK FOR SANITARY INSPECTORS AND OTHERS INTERESTED IN SANITATION.

By GEORGE REID, M.D., D.P.H.,

Fellow, Mem. Council, and Examiner, Sanitary Institute of Great Britain, and Medical Officer to the Staffordshire County Council.

With an Appendix on Sanitary Law.

By HERBERT MANLEY, M.A., M.B., D.P.H.,

Medical Officer of Health for the County Borough of West Bromwich.

GENERAL CONTENTS.—Introduction—Water Supply: Drinking Water, Pollution of Water—Ventilation and Warming — Principles of Sewage Removal — Details of Drainage ; Refuse Removal and Disposal—Sanitary and Insanitary Work and Appliances—Details of Plumbers' Work—House Construction — Infection and Disinfection — Food, Inspection of ; Characteristics of Good Meat ; Meat, Milk, Fish, &c., unfit for Human Food—Appendix : Sanitary Law ; Model Bye-Laws, &c.

"Dr. Reid's very useful Manual . . . ABOUNDS IN PRACTICAL DETAIL."
—*British Medical Journal.*

"A VERY USEFUL HANDBOOK, with a very useful Appendix. We recommend it not only to SANITARY INSPECTORS, but to HOUSEHOLDERS and ALL interested in Sanitary matters."—*Sanitary Record.*

COMPANION VOLUME TO REID'S SANITATION.

In Crown 8vo. Handsome Cloth. Profusely Illustrated.   8s. 6d. net.

Sanitary Engineering:

A Practical Manual of Town Drainage and Sewage and Refuse Disposal.

For Sanitary Authorities, Engineers, Inspectors, Architects, Contractors, and Students.

BY

FRANCIS WOOD, A.M.Inst.C.E., F.G.S.,

Borough Engineer and Surveyor, Fulham ; late Borough Engineer, Bacup, Lancs.

GENERAL CONTENTS.

Introduction.—Hydraulics.—Velocity of Water in Pipes.—Earth Pressures and Retaining Walls.—Powers.—House Drainage. - Land Drainage.—Sewers.—Separate System.—Sewage Pumping.—Sewer Ventilation.—Drainage Areas.—Sewers, Manholes, &c.—Trade Refuse.—Sewage Disposal Works.--BACTERIOLYSIS.—Sludge Disposal.—Construction and Cleansing of Sewers.—Refuse Disposal.—Chimneys and Foundations.

"The volume bristles with information which will be greedily read by those in need of assistance. The book is one that ought to be on the bookshelves of EVERY PRACTICAL ENGINEER."—*Sanitary Journal.*

"A VERITABLE POCKET COMPENDIUM of Sanitary Engineering. . . . A work which may, in many respects, be considered as COMPLETE . . COMMENDABLY CAUTIOUS . . . INTERESTING . . . SUGGESTIVE."—*Public Health Engineer.*

LONDON : CHARLES GRIFFIN & CO., LIMITED, EXETER STREET, STRAND.

In Large 8vo. Handsome Cloth. With 4 Plates and Several Illustrations. 16s. net.

THE CHEMISTRY OF INDIA RUBBER.

A Treatise on the Nature of India Rubber, its Chemical and Physical Examination, and the Determination and Valuation of India Rubber Substitutes.

Including the Outlines of a Theory on Vulcanisation.

By CARL OTTO WEBER, Ph.D.

"Replete with scientific and also with technical interest. . . . The section on physical properties is a complete *résumé* of every thing known on the subject."—*India-rubber Journal.*

JUST OUT. In Large Crown 8vo. **Fully Illustrated.**

GLUE, GELATINE,

AND THEIR ALLIED PRODUCTS,

A Practical Handbook for the Manufacturer, Agriculturist, and Student of **Technology.**

By THOMAS LAMBERT,
Analytical and Technical Chemist.

CONTENTS.—Historical.—GLUE.—GELATINE.—Size and Isinglass.—Treatment of Effluents produced in Glue and Gelatine Making.—Liquid and other Glues, Cements, &c.—Uses of Glue and Gelatine.—Residual Products.—Analysis of Raw and Finished Products.—APPENDIX.—INDEX.

In Large Crown 8vo, Handsome Cloth. Fully Illustrated.

PAPER TECHNOLOGY:

AN ELEMENTARY MANUAL ON THE MANUFACTURE, PHYSICAL QUALITIES, AND CHEMICAL CONSTITUENTS OF PAPER AND OF PAPERMAKING FIBRES.

With Selected Tables for Stationers, Publishers, and Others.

By R. W. SINDALL, F.C.S.

CONTENTS.—Introduction.—Technical Difficulties relating to Paper.—The Manufacture of Rag Paper, Hand-made, Machine-made : Esparto Papers ; Chemical Wood Pulp ; Mechanical Wood Pulp ; Wood Pulp Papers ; Art Papers ; Hemp, Jute, and other Papers.—The Physical Qualities of Paper : Weight, Thickness, Strength, Elasticity, &c.—The Chemical Constituents of Paper : Clay, Pearl Hardening, Gelatine, Casein, Rosin, Alum, Starch, Pigments, Aniline Dyes, &c.—Chemical Analysis of Paper.—Microscopical Analysis.—Conditions Affecting Quality.—"C.B.S. Units."—Vegetable Fibres used in Papermaking.—Chemical and Physical Characteristics of Fibres.—Cellulose.—Statistics relating to Paper.—Tables.—Bibliography.—INDEX.

In Large 8vo. Handsome Cloth. With Plates and Illustrations. 7s. 6d. net.

THE MANUFACTURE OF INK.

A Handbook of the Production and Properties of Printing, Writing, and Copying Inks.

By C. A. MITCHELL, M.A., F.I.C., AND T. C. HEPWORTH.

GENERAL CONTENTS.—**Historical.**—Inks and their Manufacture.—**Writing Inks.**—Carbon and Carbonaceous Inks.—Tannin Materials for Ink.—Nature of Inks.—Manufacture of Iron Gall Ink.—Logwood, Vanadium, and Aniline Black Inks.—Coloured Inks.—Examination of Writing Inks. — **Printing Inks.** — Early Methods of Manufacture.—Manufacture of Varnish Inks.—Preparation and Incorporation of the Pigment.—Coloured Printing Inks.—Copying Inks. **Marking Inks.**—Natural Vegetable Inks.—Safety Inks and Papers. — Sympathetic Inks. — Ink Powders and Tablets. — Appendices. — Patent Specifications, &c.

"Thoroughly well arranged . . and of a genuinely practical order."—*British Printer.*

LONDON : CHARLES GRIFFIN & CO., LIMITED, EXETER STREET, STRAND.

THE TEXTILE INDUSTRIES.

SECOND EDITION, *Thoroughly Revised Throughout. In Two Large Volumes. Handsome Cloth.*

A MANUAL OF DYEING:

FOR THE USE OF PRACTICAL DYERS, MANUFACTURERS, STUDENTS, AND ALL INTERESTED IN THE ART OF DYEING.

BY

E. KNECHT, Ph.D., F.I.C.,

Head of the Chemistry and Dyeing Department of the Technical School, Manchester; Editor of "The Journal of the Society of Dyers and Colourists;"

CHR. RAWSON, F.I.C., F.C.S.,

Late Head of the Chemistry and Dyeing Department of the Technical College, Bradford ; Member Council of the Society of Dyers and Colourists;

And RICHARD LOEWENTHAL, Ph.D.

GENERAL CONTENTS.—Chemical Technology of the Textile Fabrics—Water—Washing and Bleaching — Acids, Alkalies, Mordants — Natural Colouring Matters—Artificial Organic Colouring Matters—Mineral Colours—Machinery used in Dyeing—Tinctorial Properties of Colouring Matters—Analysis and Valuation of Materials used in Dyeing, &c., &c.

" This authoritative and exhaustive work . . . the MOST COMPLETE we have yet seen on the subject."—*Textile Manufacturer.*

JUST OUT. In Large 8vo, Handsome Cloth. Pp. i-xv + 405. 16s. net.

THE SYNTHETIC DYESTUFFS,

AND

THE INTERMEDIATE PRODUCTS FROM WHICH THEY ARE DERIVED.

BY JOHN CANNELL CAIN, D.Sc. (MANCHESTER AND TÜBINGEN), Technical Chemist,

AND JOCELYN FIELD THORPE, PH.D. (HEIDELBERG), Lecturer on Colouring Matters in the Victoria University of Manchester.

Part I. Theoretical. Part II. Practical. Part III. Analytical.

Companion Volume to Knecht & Rawson's "Dyeing." In Large 8vo. Handsome Cloth, Library Style. 16s. net.

A DICTIONARY OF

DYES, MORDANTS, & OTHER COMPOUNDS

USED IN DYEING AND CALICO PRINTING.

With Formulæ, Properties, and Applications of the various substances described, and concise directions for their Commercial Valuation, and for the Detection of Adulterants.

BY CHRISTOPHER RAWSON, F.I.C., F.C.S.,

Consulting Chemist to the Behar Indigo Planters' Association ; Co-Author of "A Manual of Dyeing;"

WALTER M. GARDNER, F.C.S.,

Head of the Department of Chemistry and Dyeing, Bradford Municipal Technical College; Editor of the "Journ. Soc. Dyers and Colourists;"

AND W. F. LAYCOCK, Ph.D., F.C.S.,

Analytical and Consulting Chemist.

"Turn to the book as one may on any subject, or any substance in connection with the trade, and a reference is sure to be found   The authors have apparently left nothing out."—*Textile Mercury.*

LONDON CHARLES GRIFFIN & CO., LIMITED, EXETER STREET, STRAND.

Large 8vo. Profusely Illustrated with Plates and Figures in the Text.
16s. net.

THE SPINNING AND TWISTING OF LONG VEGETABLE FIBRES
(FLAX, HEMP, JUTE, TOW, & RAMIE).

A Practical Manual of the most Modern Methods as applied to the Hackling, Carding, Preparing, Spinning, and Twisting of the Long Vegetable Fibres of Commerce.

By HERBERT R. CARTER, Belfast and Lille.

GENERAL CONTENTS.—Long Vegetable Fibres of Commerce.—Rise and Growth of the Spinning Industry.—Raw Fibre Markets.—Purchasing Raw Material.—Storing and Preliminary Operations.—Hackling.—Sorting.—Preparing.—Tow Carding and Mixing.—Tow Combing.—Gill Spinning.—The Roving Frame.—Dry and Demi-sec Spinning.—Wet Spinning.—Spinning Waste.—Yarn Reeling.—Manufacture of Threads, Twines, and Cords.—Rope Making.—The Mechanical Department.—Modern Mill Construction.—Steam and Water Power.—Power Transmission.

"Meets the requirements of the Mill Manager or Advanced Student in a manner perhaps more than satisfactory. . . . We must highly commend the work as representing up-to-date practice."—*Nature.*

In Large 8vo, Handsome Cloth, with Numerous Illustrations. 9s. net.

TEXTILE FIBRES OF COMMERCE.
A HANDBOOK OF
The Occurrence, Distribution, Preparation, and Industrial Uses of the Animal, Vegetable, and Mineral Products used in Spinning and Weaving.

By WILLIAM I. HANNAN,
Lecturer on Botany at the Ashton Municipal Technical School, Lecturer on Cotton Spinning at the Chorley Science and Art School, &c.

With Numerous Photo Engravings from Nature.

"USEFUL INFORMATION. . . . ADMIRABLE ILLUSTRATIONS. . . . The information is not easily attainable, and in its present convenient form will be valuable."—*Textile Recorder.*

In Large 8vo, with Illustrations and Printed Patterns. Price 21s.

TEXTILE PRINTING:
A PRACTICAL MANUAL.
Including the Processes Used in the Printing of
COTTON, WOOLLEN, SILK, and HALF-SILK FABRICS.

By C. F. SEYMOUR ROTHWELL, F.C.S.,
Mem. Soc. of Chemical Industries; late Lecturer at the Municipal Technical School, Manchester.

GENERAL CONTENTS. — Introduction. — The Machinery Used in Textile Printing.—Thickeners and Mordants.—The Printing of Cotton Goods.—The Steam Style.—Colours Produced Directly on the Fibre.—Dyed Styles.—Padding Style.—Resist and Discharge Styles.—The Printing of Compound Colourings, &c.—The Printing of Woollen Goods.—The Printing of Silk Goods.—Practical Recipes for Printing.—Useful Tables.—Patterns.

"BY FAR THE BEST and MOST PRACTICAL BOOK ON TEXTILE PRINTING which has yet been brought out, and will long remain the standard work on the subject. It is essentially practical in character."—*Textile Mercury.*

"THE MOST PRACTICAL MANUAL of TEXTILE PRINTING which has yet appeared. We have no hesitation in recommending it."—*The Textile Manufacturer.*

LONDON: CHARLES GRIFFIN & CO., LIMITED, EXETER STREET, STRAND.

Large 8vo.   Handsome Cloth.   12s. 6d.

BLEACHING & CALICO-PRINTING.

A Short Manual for Students and Practical Men.

By GEORGE DUERR,

Director of the Bleaching, Dyeing, and Printing Department at the Accrington and Bacup
Technical Schools; Chemist and Colourist at the Irwell Print Works.

ASSISTED BY WILLIAM TURNBULL
(of Turnbull & Stockdale, Limited).

With Illustrations and upwards of One Hundred Dyed and Printed Patterns
designed specially to show various Stages of the Processes described.

GENERAL CONTENTS.—COTTON, Composition of; BLEACHING, New
Processes; PRINTING, Hand-Block; Flat-Press Work; Machine Printing—
MORDANTS—STYLES OF CALICO-PRINTING: The Dyed or Madder Style, Resist
Padded Style, Discharge and Extract Style, Chromed or Raised Colours,
Insoluble Colours, &c.— Thickeners — Natural Organic Colouring Matters
—Tannin Matters— Oils, Soaps, Solvents —Organic Acids—Salts—Mineral
Colours—Coal Tar Colours—Dyeing—Water, Softening of—Theory of Colours
—Weights and Measures, &c.

"When a READY WAY out of a difficulty is wanted, it   IN BOOKS LIKE THIS that it is found."—
Textile Recorder.
"Mr. DUERR'S WORK will be found MOST USEFUL. . . .   The information given is of GREAT
VALUE. ,   The Recipes are THOROUGHLY PRACTICAL."—*Textile Manufacturer.*

SECOND EDITION.   Revised and Enlarged.   With Numerous
Illustrations.   4s. 6d.

GARMENT
DYEING AND CLEANING.

A Practical Book for Practical Men.

By GEORGE H. HURST, F.C.S.,
Member of the Society of Chemical Industry.

GENERAL CONTENTS.—Technology of the Textile Fibres—Garment Cleaning
—Dyeing of Textile Fabrics—Bleaching—Finishing of Dyed and Cleaned Fabrics—
Scouring and Dyeing of Skin Rugs and Mats—Cleaning and Dyeing of Feathers—
Glove Cleaning and Dyeing—Straw Bleaching and Dyeing—Glossary of Drugs
and Chemicals—Useful Tables.

" An UP-TO-DATE hand book has long been wanted, and Mr. Hurst has done nothing
more complete than this. An important work, the more so that several of the branches of
the craft here treated upon are almost entirely without English Manuals for the guidance
of workers. The price brings it within the reach of all."—*Dyer and Calico-Printer.*
" Mr. Hurst's work DECIDEDLY FILLS A WANT   . . ought to be in the hands of
EVERY GARMENT DYER and cleaner in the Kingdom"—*Textile Mercury.*

LONDON: CHARLES GRIFFIN & CO., LIMITED, EXETER STREET, STRAND.

"Boys could not have a more alluring introduction to scientific pursuits than these charming-looking volumes."—Letter to the Publishers from the Head-master of one of our great Public Schools.

Handsome Cloth, 7s. 6d. Gilt, for Presentation, 8s. 6d.

OPEN-AIR STUDIES IN BOTANY:

SKETCHES OF BRITISH WILD FLOWERS IN THEIR HOMES.

By R. LLOYD PRAEGER, B.A., M.R.I.A.

Illustrated by Drawings from Nature by S. Rosamond Praeger, and Photographs by R. Welch.

GENERAL CONTENTS.—A Daisy-Starred Pasture—Under the Hawthorns —By the River—Along the Shingle—A Fragrant Hedgerow—A Connemara Bog—Where the Samphire grows—A Flowery Meadow—Among the Corn (a Study in Weeds)—In the Home of the Alpines—A City Rubbish-Heap— Glossary.

"A FRESH AND STIMULATING book . . . should take a high place . . . The Illustrations are drawn with much skill."—*The Times.*
"BEAUTIFULLY ILLUSTRATED. . . . One of the MOST ACCURATE as well as INTERESTING books of the kind we have seen."—*Athenæum.*
"Redolent with the scent of woodland and meadow."—*The Standard.*

With 12 Full-Page Illustrations from Photographs. Cloth.
Second Edition, Revised. 8s. 6d.

OPEN-AIR STUDIES IN GEOLOGY:

An Introduction to Geology Out-of-doors.

By GRENVILLE A. J. COLE, F.G.S., M.R.I.A.,

Professor of Geology in the Royal College of Science for Ireland, and Examiner in the University of London.

GENERAL CONTENTS.—The Materials of the Earth—A Mountain Hollow —Down the Valley—Along the Shore—Across the Plains—Dead Volcanoes —A Granite Highland—The Annals of the Earth—The Surrey Hills—The Folds of the Mountains.

"The FASCINATING 'OPEN-AIR STUDIES' of PROF. COLE give the subject a GLOW OF ANIMATION . . . cannot fail to arouse keen interest in geology."—*Geological Magazine.*
"A CHARMING BOOK, beautifully illustrated."—*Athenæum.*

Beautifully Illustrated. With a Frontispiece in Colours, and Numerous Specially Drawn Plates by Charles Whymper. 7s. 6d.

OPEN-AIR STUDIES IN BIRD-LIFE:

SKETCHES OF BRITISH BIRDS IN THEIR HAUNTS.

By CHARLES DIXON.

The Spacious Air.—The Open Fields and Downs.—In the Hedgerows.—On Open Heath and Moor.—On the Mountains.—Amongst the Evergreens.— Copse and Woodland.—By Stream and Pool.—The Sandy Wastes and Mud-flats.—Sea-laved Rocks.—Birds of the Cities.—INDEX.
"Enriched with excellent illustrations. A welcome addition to all libraries."—*West-minster Review.*

LONDON: CHARLES GRIFFIN & CO., LIMITED. EXETER STREET, STRAND.

Twenty-second Annual Issue.   Handsome cloth, 7s. 6d.

(To Subscribers, 6s.).

THE OFFICIAL YEAR-BOOK

OF THE

SCIENTIFIC AND LEARNED SOCIETIES OF GREAT BRITAIN AND IRELAND.

COMPILED FROM OFFICIAL SOURCES.

Comprising (together with other Official Information) LISTS of the PAPERS read during the Session 1904-1905 before all the LEADING SOCIETIES throughout the Kingdom engaged in the following Departments of Research:—

§ 1. Science Generally: *i.e.*, Societies occupying themselves with several Branches of Science, or with Science and Literature jointly.
§ 2. Mathematics and Physics.
§ 3. Chemistry and Photography.
§ 4. Geology, Geography, and Mineralogy.
§ 5. Biology, including Microscopy and Anthropology.

§ 6. Economic Science and Statistics.
§ 7. Mechanical Science, Engineering, and Architecture.
§ 8. Naval and Military Science.
§ 9. Agriculture and Horticulture.
§ 10. Law.
§ 11. Literature.
§ 12. Psychology.
§ 13. Archæology.

§ 14. MEDICINE.

" FILLS A VERY REAL WANT."—*Engineering.*

" INDISPENSABLE to any one who may wish to keep himself abreast of the scientific work of the day."—*Edinburgh Medical Journal.*

" The YEAR-BOOK OF SOCIETIES is a Record which ought to be of the greatest use for the progress of Science."—*Lord Playfair, F.R.S., K.C.B., M.P., Past-President of the British Association.*

" It goes almost without saying that a Handbook of this subject will be in time one of the most generally useful works for the library or the desk."—*The Times.*

" British Societies are now well represented in the 'Year-Book of the Scientific and Learned Societies of Great Britain and Ireland.'"—(Art. " Societies " in New Edition of " Encyclopædia Britannica," vol. xxii.)

Copies of the FIRST ISSUE, giving an Account of the History, Organization, and Conditions of Membership of the various Societies, and forming the groundwork of the Series, may still be had, price 7/6.   *Also Copies of the Issues following.*

The YEAR-BOOK OF SOCIETIES forms a complete INDEX TO THE SCIENTIFIC WORK of the sessional year in the various Departments.   It is used as a HANDBOOK in all our great SCIENTIFIC CENTRES, MUSEUMS, and LIBRARIES throughout the Kingdom, and has become an INDISPENSABLE BOOK OF REFERENCE to every one engaged in Scientific Work.

READY IN OCTOBER EACH YEAR.

LONDON: CHARLES GRIFFIN & CO., LIMITED, EXETER STREET, STRAND.